Praise for *A Hundred Pieces of Me* and Lucy Dillon

'A **warm, heart-breakingly brilliant** novel that will make you re-evaluate your ideas of love and life along with the main character, Gina. Tissues essential.' Ali Harris

'A **hugely uplifting** reading experience . . . It makes one think nostalgically back, optimistically forwards, but most of all of the moment that one's in. And I can think of few lovelier "me" moments than the joy of being curled up with a **truly magical** novel like this one. I'll be recommending it very far and wide.' Fiona Walker

'I finished *A Hundred Pieces of Me* and I was in bits! Such a brilliant book. **So satisfying and clever and deeply moving.** I'll be passing it on to all my friends.' Sophie Kinsella

'A lovely "one more chapter before bed" story, full of beautifully drawn characters that truly affected me. **Simply wonderful**.' Milly Johnson

'A **gorgeous** story – perfect for an indulgent and **absorbing** treat.' Lulu Taylor

'This vibrant and uplifting novel has not only entertained me hugely, but **made me change the way I look at life**.' Katie Fforde

'A **modern fairy-tale** for grown ups' *Sun* on *The Secret of Happy Ever After*

'**Witty**, heart-warming and a **very real** tale of loss and redemption' *Stylist* on *Walking Back to Happiness*

'Heart-warming, **fun** and **romantic**.' *Closer* on *Lost Dogs and Lonely Hearts*

'A **charming, heartwarming, entertaining** read for all would-be dancefloor divas' *Glamour* on *The Ballroom Class*

Also by Lucy Dillon

The Ballroom Class
Lost Dogs and Lonely Hearts
Walking Back to Happiness
The Secret of Happy Ever After

www.lucydillon.com
www.facebook.com/LucyDillonBooks
twitter.com/lucy_dillon
#100piecesofme

Lucy Dillon

a
hundred
pieces
of
me

HODDER

First published in Great Britain in 2014 by Hodder & Stoughton
An Hachette UK Company

14

Copyright © Lucy Dillon 2014

The right of Lucy Dillon to be identified as the Author of the
Work has been asserted by her in accordance with the Copyright,
Designs and Patents Act 1988.

A CIP catalogue record for this title is available from the British Library.

Paperback ISBN 978 1 444 72707 4
Ebook ISBN 978 1 444 72708 1

Printed and bound by CPI Group (UK) Ltd, Croydon, CR0 4YY

Hodder & Stoughton policy is to use papers that are natural,
renewable and recyclable products and made from wood grown in
sustainable forests. The logging and manufacturing processes are expected
to conform to the environmental regulations of the country of origin.

Hodder & Stoughton Ltd
338 Euston Road
London NW1 3BH

www.hodder.co.uk

For Patricia Routledge,
always an inspiration, more now than ever

Prologue

Longhampton, June 2008

Gina wraps her new scarf tightly around her wrist, like a bandage. It's a scarlet cashmere one that she bought on the way home from work two days ago, the colour of lipstick and poisoned apples and danger. For something that cost so much, it took no time to buy: she was cold, she'd always wanted a beautiful big cashmere scarf, and the usual sensible voice of caution, reminding her of the gas bill or the council tax, had gone, and in the silence Gina could hear her own voice asking aloud, *Why not?*

'Why not?' always makes Gina feel queasy. She isn't a 'why not?' sort of person. But this whole week has felt like careering downhill on a sledge, swerving and dodging as shock after shock has rushed at her. The price tag on the scarf didn't even register.

The bright colour is still taking her by surprise. Gina doesn't normally like red – her house and her wardrobe are calming shades of sea blue and slate grey – but something in the bold scarlet feels right. It looks alive against her pale skin, somehow Spanish against her wavy dark hair, her brown eyes. This red is bold and definite, grabbing attention, fixing her against the greyness of the town.

Gina's extravagant scarf is the only giveaway of the reason she and Stuart are sitting here. The red slash lurking at the corner of her eye whispers that now is the time to indulge herself. Now might be the last chance to do it.

She glances at Stuart again, to see if he's noticed the scarf. He hasn't. He's frowning over some notes he made for today's consultation: he sat up until 2 a.m. in bed with his laptop while she was pretending to sleep, the greenish light reflecting the planes of his handsome face, his forehead lined with concentration.

Stuart's absorbing everything. There's a lot of information to absorb, on the Internet, from the hospital, from the friends of friends. Words and terms are floating around her but nothing will settle in her brain. They melt away like snowflakes as soon as they touch her.

The door behind them opens and Mr Khan hurries in, fresh from some other crisis, full of apologies for keeping them waiting. Stuart stiffens in his seat. Gina remembers the suspended moment in school exams when the invigilator coughed and told them to turn over their papers. Weeks and months hanging in the air, the desperate scrabble to go back, one more week's revision, but it's too late. It's already over. Half panic, half relief.

Now.

'Hello, Georgina ... Gina?' he says, with an easy smile. 'Lovely, yes, Gina, and this is your ...?'

'Fiancé, Stuart Horsfield, hello,' says Stuart, and Gina

still thinks it sounds strange, but everything that's happening to her seems to be happening to someone else. She grips his hand. It's strong and comforting.

While Mr Khan flips through her notes Gina makes herself look around the room so she won't try to read the scrawled words in front of him. Maybe that's why doctors make their handwriting so bad, she thinks, so it can't be read upside-down from the other side of the desk.

She notes everything deliberately. There's a window, looking onto the car park, white gloss paint, a calendar and a candy-pink cyclamen (very hard to kill off). There's a mirror on the wall by the door, simple, unframed, too far from the desk to be intended for the doctor.

A cool shiver of fear runs over Gina's skin. It's for the patients. So they can adjust their faces, wipe away their mascara smears before they go back to the silent waiting area outside. Stuart's fingers tighten around hers.

Mr Khan clicks the lid back on his chunky silver fountain pen, pushing it in with his palm and letting a sigh escape from his downturned lips. He doesn't smile. And that's when Gina knows. She struggles to stay in the moment. Part of her is flying above it, her consciousness shooting backwards, out of her head, detaching her. Is this really happening to me? she wonders. How can I tell?

A bleak longing to go back sweeps through her, and she has to force herself to concentrate on the now.

Now.

Now.

'So, Georgina,' he says, 'I'm afraid I have some bad news.'

Chapter One

ITEM: a gold blown-glass Christmas-tree decoration
in the shape of an angel playing a trumpet

Longhampton, December 2013

Gina stands back and breathes in the sharp dark-green
scent of the Douglas fir, and thinks, Yes, *this* is why I
bought this house. For Christmas.

It's an extravagantly tall, old-fashioned tree and it fills
what she'd earmarked from their very first viewing as a
specific Christmas-tree space in the black-and-white-tiled
entrance hall of 2 Dryden Road. The springy branches are
ready to be hung with glass baubles, topped with a star, the
special iron tree-stand hidden by a pile of presents underneath. The final Victorian touch to a lovingly renovated
Victorian family home.

Gina smiles at it, pleased. It's taken a long time, renovating the house themselves, after work, at weekends. The
mental picture of this tree, of this moment, has kept her
going through the endless months of sanding, plastering,
builders turning the electricity off without warning, washing
in a bucket: the backdrop to her own slow crawl back to

normality. It's been one tiny goal at a time – a finished room, a complete lap of the park – and now, finally, it's here: Christmas in Dryden Road.

As she reaches for the first bauble, a memory skims the back of her mind, moving too fast for her to place it: she's filled with a sudden glow of contentment, a deep-red sort of Christmassy anticipation that wraps round her like a sudden soft blanket of joy. It's more like *déjà vu* than a memory: the satisfying sensation of something clicking into place.

What is it? The smell of pine and cinnamon sticks? The slithery rustle of tinsel? The cosiness of the central heating ticking into life as the afternoon shadows start to fall? Gina probes in the shapeless depths of her early memories but can't find the exact moment. She doesn't have a lot of child-hood memories, and the precious few she does have are blurred by over-examination, and she's never sure whether she's remembering actual facts, or something her mother's told her happened. But this happy feeling is familiar.

It's probably dressing the tree, she thinks, turning back to the box of ornaments in their tissue nest. It's a tradition: first Saturday in December, tree goes up. Decorating it was always something she and her mum, Janet, did, just the two of them, listening to a Christmas compilation tape and sharing a tin of Roses, Gina handing the baubles to Janet, Janet fixing them in the same spots every year. They lived in lots of houses while Gina was growing up, but the tree routine was always the same.

Gina has a box of baubles, including some old favourites handed on by her mum, and she's adopted Janet's ritual of buying a new one every Christmas. She picks up the decoration she bought for this year: it's a golden angel, playing a trumpet. Next year, she thinks, suddenly light inside with hope, will be better. It's a long time since Gina's felt simply content; the uncomplicated pleasure is so unfamiliar that she's horrified by how long it's been.

A few snowflakes blow past the window and Gina hopes it's not snowing in the New Forest where Stuart's office is on a Christmas jolly. Instead of their usual all-you-can-eat bonanza in the local Chinese restaurant, the whole sales department of Midlands Logistics has been treated to some sort of karting event, followed by a murder mystery dinner.

Stuart will almost certainly be leading one of the teams. He cycles; he plays cricket; he's still captaining his football team at thirty-six, with his modest but determined attitude. The other football WAGs, most of whom have not-so-secret crushes on Stu, joke that he's the Longhampton David Beckham. Without the tattoos. Obviously. Stuart's not a fan of tattoos.

She hangs another silver bauble, then stops: it'd be nice to share this with Stu, she thinks. He shouldered the back-breaking part of the renovation when she wasn't up to it; it's only fair that they should share the fun stuff. Decorating the tree is something they should do together, a new tradition they can start of their own.

Gina puts the lid on the box so the cats can't get into it, and goes through to the sitting room where she's been ordering presents on her laptop. There aren't that many shopping days left, and she's barely started their family list. She turns up Phil Spector's Christmas album to an indulgently loud level, but has only got as far as Stuart's aunts when her credit card's declined.

She checks again. Declined.

Gina frowns at it. It's their joint card, the one that's supposed to be for household bills. Stuart must have bought something big, probably for his bike – she'd paid off the balance last month in full, ready for Christmas. The website says the cut-off date for presents to Australia is Monday; if Auntie Pam in Sydney wants her usual tin of shortbread, it's got to be sent today.

Gina chews her lip, then dials Stuart's mobile. Her card's already at the limit with her car's MOT and insurance, and Pam's *his* auntie. After two rings it goes to voicemail, which doesn't surprise her – if he's karting, his mobile will be sensibly stowed in his locker – so she calls his workmate Paul, who picks up after a couple of rings.

'Hello, Paul, it's Gina,' she says, wandering around the sitting room, drawing the heavy curtains, clicking on the lamps. 'Sorry to bother you – hope I'm not interrupting any murdering!'

'Hey, Gina.' Paul sounds as if he's somewhere noisy: she can hear 'Merry Christmas Everyone' by Slade in the background.

'I'm trying to get hold of Stu. When he finishes what he's doing, can you ask him to give me a ring?'

'Stuart?'

'Um, yes. Are you supposed to refer to him as Hercule Poirot or something?'

'Sorry?'

Gina pauses in front of the mirror over the fireplace and stares at her reflection in the age-spotted glass; as usual, after a trip to the hairdresser, she doesn't look like herself.

Her short black hair is smooth, swooping across her long face in a sophisticated fringe that will last four more hours before frizzing. The haircut is part of her resolution to make more effort this year. More effort with her business, with Stuart, with . . . everything.

'Gina? Sorry, I'm not with Stuart.'

'He's not with you?'

'Not unless he's stupid enough to be in Cribbs Causeway shopping!' Paul pauses, then laughs. 'Oh, bollocks, I've probably blown his big surprise, haven't I? He'll be out getting your present from somewhere. What'll it be this year? A kayak?'

'Yes, that's probably it.' Gina tries to laugh. She can't. Her face feels heavy, her cheeks suddenly doughy. 'Ha! Sorry to bother you, Paul. Have a good weekend!'

She hangs up and, half-heartedly, tries on Paul's explanation, but it doesn't fit.

Stuart packed a weekend bag; he ironed his own shirts. He told her several times – once too many, come to think of it – that it was a karting weekend, then a murder mystery dinner, and they'd be busy from Friday morning through to Sunday afternoon but not to worry if she couldn't get hold of him because the hotel was in a forest with no reception 'which is best for team-building'.

Too much detail. Stuart's even an over-efficient liar.

Gina sinks onto the sofa, still gripping her phone, and Loki, the less disdainful of their two cats, shoots away from her.

She has to force the two concepts to mesh. Stuart: lying. Reliable, upright Stuart, who got the decorations down from the attic for her before he left, who emptied the bins and changed the cat litter.

All practical things, she realises. Thoughtful, but house-mate-y. That's what they are, after five years of marriage, housemates. Her last birthday present had been a sander, for the upstairs floorboards.

The weird thing is, Gina doesn't feel devastated, just sad. It's only confirmed something she realises now that she already knew. Has known for months, but not wanted to acknowledge. She's been buying how-to-fix-your-relation-ship books and hiding them in the airing cupboard; Stuart's just been more practical, as usual.

She gazes at her half-dressed tree out in the hall. It's making a cookie-cutter Christmas-tree shape against the pale blue staircase behind, and underneath the dull ache that's filling her chest like gravel, Gina feels a faint flutter of that elusive happiness.

Something pushes her towards the tree, to finish decorat-ing the branches. There's at least half a day before he gets back when this house is going to be perfect. It deserves it.

Gina levers herself off the sofa and sleepwalks into the hall, to her box of decorations and memories. While the Ronettes sing in the background, she carries on slipping glass baubles onto the knotty pine branches, breathing in the rosemary-scented resin and letting the dark heart of the tree fill her senses until there's no room for any thoughts about the future or the past.

Outside, beyond the glossy holly wreath and the brass knocker on the freshly painted front door, it snows.

Now, Longhampton

It was no coincidence, thought Gina, gazing around her empty new flat, that Heaven was commonly assumed to be a big white room with absolutely nothing in it. Something about this clean, peaceful space made her feel calmer than she had in weeks.

She stepped towards the big picture window with its panoramic view over the brown and grey rooftops beyond the high street, and experienced a strange elation like sparkling mineral water rinsing through her veins. She hadn't expected to feel quite so positive about the first day of her new life, single, in a new place. The last few weeks had been hard, and Gina's bones ached with invisible bruises, but now underneath there was a first-day-of-school excitement.

Fresh paint. Empty rooms. Smooth walls, ready to be filled, like a brand-new notebook.

Some of it was adrenalin at having sold the house and rented this new flat in just a fortnight. Some of it was relief to be away from the atmosphere that had hung over Dryden Road after Stuart's bombshell, which, like an actual bombshell, had left a sort of miserable crater where Christmas was supposed to have been. Even though he'd moved out almost as soon as he'd admitted where he'd really been that weekend (Paris), his presence had lingered in every stray sock and framed holiday photo, of which there were many. Almost overnight, Gina felt as if she'd woken up in the house of a happily married couple of strangers.

She knew that was her own fault, which only made it worse. She'd deliberately set out to make Dryden Road into a sort of scrapbook of her and Stuart's life together: it was feathered with tiny mementoes of parties and anniversaries, and quirky collections in frames. Gina never met a shelf she couldn't fill, which was why it came as a bit of surprise to feel so instantly at home in the cloud-like emptiness of this modern flat, above the optician's, next to the deli.

212a High Street was the exact opposite of the house she'd just left in the desirable poets' streets area of Longhampton, the neglected Victorian terrace that she and Stuart had coaxed from damp shabbiness to what Gina's house magazines liked to call a 'forever home'. Gina was a conservation officer for the council; putting back the dado rails and moulded ceiling roses was a labour of love. 2 Dryden Road's final gift to them for their split nails and silent hours' sanding was a quick sale: it wasn't their forever home but several other families wanted it to be.

If Dryden Road was a busy Victorian scrapbook collage, 212a High Street was a blank page. It was an open-plan conversion, painted throughout in soft vanilla eggshell with brand new carpets and wooden floors, resolutely featureless. No fireplaces, no skirting, no picture rails, just plain walls and big double-glazed windows that turned the town's skyline into a living picture across one wall of the sitting room. It reminded Gina of a gallery, full of light and air, a place that invited you to pause and think. The moment she'd walked in with the estate agent, her eyes gritty from another sleepless night, a sense of stillness had come over her, and she'd handed over the rental deposit the same afternoon.

That had been a week ago, the last week in January.

Bright sunshine was warming the flat despite the chill outside, and Gina turned slowly on her heel, assessing the available space, and stopped at the long wall next to the window. It demanded one really fabulous piece of art, something beautiful that she could sit, gaze at and get lost in. She didn't have the right painting or print yet, but she'd formed a middle-of-the-night plan to get rid of everything she didn't need or love from the old house, and buy one amazing . . . thing.

Everything from the old house.

Her stomach rippled with nerves at the unknown months ahead. The nerves tended to ambush her, creeping up when she wasn't concentrating to dive-bomb her good mood like seagulls. Once the novelty of her new place wore off, Gina knew it was going to be tough, dating again at thirty-three, unravelling her life from Stuart's, and having to make new friends to replace the ones he would be taking with him. Gina had only one real mate, Naomi, whom she'd known since school; the rest of their social circle had been Stuart's football and cricket friends.

But this flat would help her start again, she told herself. Everything she loved would be on show, all the time, instead of hidden in cupboards. And she could decide what she brought into it. There wasn't room for much, so she'd have to be selective. From now on; everything that came into this flat had to make her happy or be useful, or ideally both.

One of the self-help books Naomi had pressed into her hands had been about a man who'd got rid of all his possessions, except a hundred vital things. He'd felt freed by it, apparently. Gina wondered if she could do that. It did seem wrong to spoil the serene minimalism with clutter. And the discipline would be good for her. What hundred things did she actually need?

Could you get rid of that much stuff and keep anything of yourself? Or was that the whole point? You could focus on being you, instead of relying on your things to explain who you were.

The thought made Gina cold and light-headed, but not necessarily scared.

Her mobile buzzed in her pocket. It was the removal men, coming with the boxes from Dryden Road. She hadn't been there for the packing. Naomi, in her role as cheerleader and supporter, had been firm about it. Well, bossy. In a nice way. 'You've been through enough, you're knackered, and they're the experts,' she'd insisted. 'Pay them to do it. I'll pay them to do it. If you put your back out packing you'll only have to fork out for massages later.'

Naomi had been right. She was usually right.

'Hello, Gina? It's Len Todd Removals, and we're about to leave your property. Just checking you're in to take delivery of the boxes that aren't going to storage.'

Some of the bigger items, like Gina's huge velvet Liberty sofa and her inlaid arts-and-crafts wardrobe, had gone straight to the Big Yellow on the outskirts of town, to wait until she could bring herself to sell them, or find a flat big enough to house them. The rest – the drawers, the cupboards, the shelves – was all on its way to her.

Gina checked her watch. Two o'clock. They'd arrived at

her old house before eight, but even so ... A whole life bubble-wrapped in under a day. 'You're not finished already?'

'All in the van. You had a fair bit of stuff, though, love, I'll give you that.'

'I know.' She winced. 'Sorry. I should have had a clear-out.'

Gina had assumed Stuart would take more than he did. Instead, he'd swept through in one morning while she was at work, packed a few small items and stuck Post-it notes on large articles (like the new bed, which he'd suddenly remembered he'd paid for) and left a note saying she could have the rest – he didn't want to make life difficult.

At first Gina had been hurt by how little of their combined life Stuart wanted, and then it turned out that he didn't need a lot because his new life already had a toaster. And a duvet. And other personal touches. Within two days of his big revelation, Naomi – whose husband Jason played football with Stuart – had ferreted out the fact that he had moved in with his Other Woman, the woman he'd taken to Paris. Bryony Crawford, a friend from his cycling club, who lived in the Old Water Mill development. As soon as Naomi told her that, Gina knew exactly what kind of person Bryony would be. Storage wouldn't be a priority. Stainless-steel-surface cleaners would.

Gina pushed the thought away, as it started to unfurl into further, more troubling mental images. Everything coming into this flat, she reminded herself, had to be positive. Including thoughts. And she was *glad* none of her beautiful

15

possessions would be ending up in the Old Water Mill, even if it meant paying for them to be in storage for a bit.

'Are you there, love?' Len Todd sounded concerned.

'Yes,' she said. 'I'll expect you in – what? Half an hour?'

'Great.' The removal man paused. 'You'd better clear some room.'

Len Todd, and his Removals, arrived at half past two, bumping the first of the cardboard boxes up the side stairs to Gina's first-floor flat.

'If you could put it in the spare room,' she said, opening the door to the small second bedroom, so far bedless. 'The plan's to fill that with boxes, with a few in the sitting room, if necessary, to keep as much of the flat as clear as possible.'

'No problem.'

He parked the box in a corner, and stepped aside to make way for a full-size wardrobe case, being lugged in by a second man. And then a third, with a fourth and fifth already dropping something heavy on the stairs outside with a muffled swearword.

Gina flattened herself against the hallway wall. Suddenly the calm white flat wasn't feeling quite so spacious, with this stream of sturdy men hauling in boxes nearly as big as she was. A dark cloud passed over her bright mood and she braced herself against it. There were a lot of hurdles to get over in the next few days: solicitors, unpacking, name changes. She needed this positive forward motion to lift her over them.

As a box marked 'Kitchen' went past, Gina had a

sudden flash of her warm-hearted house, the amiable third person in her marriage to Stuart, being cut up and broken down, packed into boxes and brought into this new place in chunks. All this stuff had made perfect sense in those rooms; it was why she hadn't even tried to have a sort-out before she left. How could she have thrown anything away? Now, though, her old home was separated into individual bits, like a jigsaw she could never put back together in the same way.

It was the same with all the pieces of her life so far – they wouldn't fit back together to make the same shape ever again. So which bits should she keep?

The removal man seemed to sense her panic. Gina guessed they'd seen enough marital divisions of property to know a break-up when they packed one. 'Why don't you take yourself over the road for a cup of tea while we get on with this?' said Len Todd, with a friendly nod. 'I'll give you a ring when we're done. Don't suppose you've got a kettle, have you?'

'In the kitchen – there's coffee and milk and, er, you'll find mugs in the kitchen box.' Naomi had packed Gina an emergency basket with all the essentials. The comforting simplicity of the single mug, single bowl, single spoon in her sleek Scandinavian-style kitchen had made her think that perhaps her hundred-things life-plan might work. It was quite restful, the lack of choice.

'We won't be long.' He patted her arm. 'And don't you worry. It'll feel like home in no time.'

'Yes,' said Gina, with a bright smile she didn't feel.

★ ★ ★

For the next hour or so Gina sat in the delicatessen next to her flat and drank two coffees, watching the late-afternoon bustle of the high street, an unmade to-do list started in the notebook next to her phone on the table.

She ignored a call from her mother and, more guiltily, from Naomi. Both of them, Gina knew, wanted to be supportive on this day of big changes, but her instinct was to focus all her energy inwards, on herself. She tried to keep a vision in her head of her sunny, open flat and all its possibilities; what she was going to do with it; whether she should paint one wall a bright sunshine yellow to pin this positivity for days when she wasn't quite so energised.

Len Todd rang at twenty to four, just as the first heavy dots of rain began to speckle the pavement, and she hurried round.

He was waiting at the foot of the stairs that led up to her flat, looking, it had to be said, shattered. 'All done,' he said, and dropped the keys into her hand: her old keys, and the new ones. 'We got it all in in the end.'

Gina laughed, and tipped him, but it wasn't until she opened the front door that she understood properly what he'd meant.

The flat was completely crammed with cardboard boxes. Crammed, from floor to ceiling.

The movers had left a narrow corridor through the spare room so she could get inside, and they'd lined two walls of her bedroom with wardrobe crates. The sitting room was now two-thirds filled, the white walls lost behind brown ones. She had to turn sideways to get into the kitchen-diner. Her possessions loomed over her every way she looked.

Gina was stunned by the unexpected invasion. It felt crushing, claustrophobic. Before her shock could tip over into tears, she started pushing the boxes away from the big white wall, where her special painting was to go. She needed to be able to see that wall, even if every other one was blocked.

Her muscles ached as she dragged the heavy boxes around but she forced herself on. I've got to start sorting right now, she told herself, or I'll never be able to sit down.

Gina's previous vision of sitting in the empty flat, languidly considering one item at a time from a single box evaporated. She tipped four boxes of bedding into the corner of her bedroom, and wrote 'KEEP', 'SELL', 'GIVE AWAY', 'DUMP' on the empty cases in big letters, lining them up in the limited space in front of the sofa. Then she took a deep breath and pulled the brown tape off the nearest box.

Everything was bubble-wrapped and at first Gina couldn't work out what the first item was, but as she unrolled the plastic, she saw it was an antique blue glass vase. She had to think twice about where it had come from, then remembered that she'd bought it when she was at university.

I *loved* this, she thought, surprised. Where's it been?

A memory slipped into the forefront of her mind, of stopping outside the window of a junk shop in Oxford . . . fifteen years ago now? It had been drizzling, she'd been late for a lecture, but something about the curved shape had leaped out of the cluttered display, a suspended raindrop of bright cobalt blue in the middle of a load of tatty brass and china. Gina could picture it in her rooms at college, on the window overlooking a courtyard, but she struggled to remember where it had been in Dryden Road: in the landing alcove with some dried lavender in it. There, but invisible, just filling a space.

She sat back on her heels, feeling the weight of the glass. The vase had cost twenty-five pounds – a fortune in her student days – and had always been full of striped tulips from the market, left until they decayed in that pretentious student style, falling in tissue thinness onto the stone ledge of her windowsill. Kit had started it: he'd brought her flowers on his first visit, and she'd been unable to bring herself to throw them out. And after someone had said, 'Oh, you're the girl who always has flowers!' Gina had made a point of keeping the vase full because she wanted to be the Girl Who Always Had Flowers.

At least I don't do that any more, she thought, with a twinge of embarrassment at how much she'd wanted people to like her at university. She wasn't in touch with a single one of them now.

Gina started to put the vase into the GIVE AWAY box; over the years she'd collected lots of different vases, for lilies, hyacinths, roses. She didn't need one that reminded her of Kit, and of all the expectations she'd had at university of where her life would be by now. All her life, she realised, she'd been creating this paper trail of possessions, hoping that they'd keep her attached to her own memories, but now she'd found out they didn't. The last years meant nothing. They were gone. All the photo albums in the world wouldn't keep them real.

But as she held it, she stopped seeing those things and

instead saw a vase. A rather nice vase that made Gina think that, actually, she'd had a bit of an eye for quality even as a student. Its bold sculptural shape had got lost in Dryden Road's collage of colour and detail, but it was perfect for this flat. The white background reframed it: it was still a beautiful frozen raindrop of glass, bright cobalt blue, ready for flowers to fill it.

Gina edged around the boxes until she was in front of the big picture window, and placed the vase squarely in the centre of the windowsill, where the sun would shine through it as it had done at college, revealing the murky wet shapes of the flower stems, rigid below the papery petals.

She stood for a moment, trying to catch the slippery emotions swirling in her chest. Then a cloud moved outside and the last light of the day deepened the blue of the glass. As it glowed against the blank white sill, something twitched inside her, a memory nudging its way back to the surface. Not of an event but of a feeling, the same bittersweet fizz she'd felt when she'd unpacked her belongings in her university room, waiting for the happiest days of her life to roar around the corner, despite her secret worry that maybe she'd already had them, anticipation sharpened with a lick of fear. Was that a memory? Was it just the same feeling in a different place? Because her life was starting again now too?

Gina took a deep breath. She wasn't going to keep the vase because it reminded her of college or because a visitor might be impressed with her good taste. She was keeping it because she liked it. And when she looked at it, it made her happy. It caught the light, even on a grey day. It was beautiful.

She hadn't bought it for her student rooms. She'd bought it fifteen years ago – for this flat.

The blue glass vase glowed in the weak, wintry sunshine, and the white flat didn't look quite so white any more. Gina stood for a long minute, letting nothing into her head except the liquid swoop and the deep, jewel-like colour.

Then, with a more confident hand, she reached into the box for the next ball of bubble-wrap.

Chapter Two

ITEM: a brown leather satchel, with
GJB embossed on the front

Hartley, September 1991

Georgina is experiencing very mixed feelings about her new school satchel.

This morning, on the kitchen table, it had looked all right. Shiny and conker-brown, with brass buckles and a corrugated section inside for putting pens in. She could tell it was expensive – although Georgina wasn't fooled by that. It was a Trojan satchel. A satchel containing a whole stack of her mother's guilt about sending her to yet another new school although, nominally, it was a present from Terry.

Terry is her stepfather. Before he was her stepfather, he was the unmarried son of her grandmother's friend-from-church, Agnes, and then he was the lodger in her mother's spare room when they'd moved out of Gran's house, where they'd been living since Georgina's dad died. Now they're living in their own house, near Terry's new job, a few hundred miles away. Mum, Terry and Georgina, the new family. The satchel seems to have been Terry's idea.

'You don't get a second chance to make a first impression,' said Terry, when she inspected it over breakfast. He works in medical sales, and has meticulously ironed shirts that he presses himself, even though Georgina's mum irons like a demon. Tea towels, pants, even socks, if they have frills on them.

'Say thank you, Georgina,' Janet had prompted her, before she'd even had time to think about not saying it.

'Thank you, Terry,' Georgina had said obediently, and looked down at her new school shoes, so as not to catch whatever variety of look her mum and Terry were exchanging.

Her shoes are navy blue, with the Mary Jane strap that everyone had wanted at St Leonard's. Mum had finally given in after months of pleading, but the shoes – exactly the right shade of blue – aren't making Georgina as happy as she'd hoped.

Half an hour later, pretending to read safety notices outside the registration room, Georgina knows for definite that the shoes are wrong. The satchel is beyond wrong. The other first-years around her are wearing the exact same brown blazer and white shirt but her over-tidy newness is making her different – she can already pick out the kids with older brothers and sisters by their cool, worn-in, hand-me-down uniform and bags. And their confident manner, the way they're laughing and bumping against their mates, at ease with teasing and physical contact.

Georgina wishes she knew how to make friends. How come some people have that knack, she wonders. What do they say? How do they know the right people to home in on?

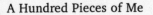

Think about Dad.

The three photographs of Captain Huw Pritchard that she still has flash into her mind: Dad in his Welsh Guards uniform, Dad in shorts on holiday, Dad with an SAS moustache in a rugby shirt, holding a pint of beer. He looks handsome in all of them, happy and sociable. The sort of man who doesn't even *think* about making friends, they just happen.

Georgina digs her nails into her palm. I can't just be like Mum, she thinks. Dad fitted in everywhere he was posted. I must have *some* friend-making genes. What would he have done?

She ignores the fact that she doesn't know what her dad would have done because she can barely remember him. A dark streak of unfocused longing sweeps through her and, as the bell goes, she dives forward, carried by the hope that she'll look like she knows someone if she barges in with the rest, but when she gets a seat, no one comes to sit next to her.

The teacher – Mrs Clarkson, flustered in a mohair jumper – arrives, and Georgina fiddles with her pencil case. She's sat too near the front. Again. The next class, she'll aim for the middle.

Did she hear the faint hiss of '. . . satchel'?

'Good morning, first-years,' Mrs Clarkson shouts over the racket. 'Are we all here? Let's make a start.'

As she gets the register out, the door's flung open and a small girl barrels in, wearing a blazer that's so big her fingers are hidden by the sleeves. Her tie is knotted low and thick, more like a cravat, and she's cradling her stack of books in one arm. No bag.

No bag, thinks Georgina, making a mental note.

'Sorry I'm late, miss,' the girl gasps. 'Missed . . . bus.'

'Oh, that bus,' says Mrs Clarkson, sarcastically. 'Never seems to stop for McIntyres. Which one are you?'

'Naomi, miss.' The girl grins. She has two dimples. Georgina notes Naomi's stubby plaits are the same colour as her satchel, a bright chestnut.

'Don't be late again, Naomi. Now sit down.' The teacher looks up and sees Georgina for the first time. She blinks. 'There. Next to . . .?'

'Georgina Bellamy, miss,' says Georgina, and someone definitely sniggers.

'Quiet!' snaps Mrs Clarkson, but it's too late. This time Georgina can hear 'satchel' *and* 'Georgina'.

Naomi slides into the seat; she smells strongly of Impulse. As the teacher starts dictating their timetable, Georgina's aware that Naomi doesn't have a pencil – silently, she passes her one of hers, her name stamped on it in gold (another gift from Terry).

They write down the unfamiliar new lessons – personal studies, RE, domestic science – then Georgina feels a nudge.

Naomi pushes a note at her. Her writing is round, with big circles over the *i*s, something Janet has specifically forbidden Georgina even to contemplate doing.

Is this your satchel?

Georgina shrugs, not wanting to rise to the teasing, but Naomi nudges her again, nodding under the desk.

What's the point in denying it? Everyone's seen it. And anyway, Georgina thinks, with a flicker of defiance, so what? She writes, *yes*, in her neat cursive.

Naomi shoots her a sympathetic glance, and in that second, even though Georgina is taller, bigger and probably older than Naomi, she feels herself being taken under a wing.

My brother's got a locker. You can dump it in there on way to next lesson if you want?

Georgina stares at her half-filled-in timetable, stunned at the way Naomi's read her mind. She'd happily ditch the satchel but in it there's something precious: an entry tag from Ascot racecourse, pale pink and gold-embossed. She doesn't remember her dad giving it to her, but apparently he did when he came back from the day's outing with her mum, their anniversary treat. Dad tied the tag to her chubby toddler wrist and she paraded around 'like a lady at the races'. It's her lucky charm.

Georgina's father died not long after the trip to Ascot. She doesn't have enough things like the tag. Things that prove the stories her mum tells her actually happened. Not that Mum tells her much. Captain Huw Pritchard was on a secret operation for the army when he was killed.

'He was very brave,' is about as much as Janet'll say before her lips go flat and her eyes glisten.

But the thought of ditching the satchel makes Georgina feel traitorous. She doesn't want to be rude to Terry. He's not awful, just a bit boring, and embarrassing with his old car. Her mum watches her like a hawk for signs of disrespect. Though if she has to take the satchel home bearing scars of a playground kickabout, won't that be worse?

Rebellion doesn't come easily to Georgina. If she can find a reason, though, that's different. Swiftly, while Mrs

Clarkson is explaining about lunch queues, she reaches under the desk, unbuckles the hard clasps and gets the tag out from its secret place. She slips it into the inside pocket of her blazer, zips it up safely. Then she writes, *thanks*, on the note.

Naomi grins at her, dimpling, and Georgina feels something change in the atmosphere around her. The class has moved on, is whispering about Mrs Clarkson's funny eye, not about her. She grins back at Naomi, feeling the happy warm tingle of being liked. It might be OK, this school.

Naomi flicks her gaze to the teacher, then crosses her eyes, and Georgina splutters in delighted surprise.

'Georgina! Naomi!' snaps Mrs Clarkson.

They spin forward and Georgina sees the wall chart by the board: uniforms of the British Army from 1707 to the present day. It's a sign. It makes her tingle again. Georgina is big on signs.

The next day Naomi arrived at Gina's new flat at half past nine for their regular Saturday-morning coffee date. It was a routine they'd got into when Jason and Stuart were at football practice together, and now carried on while Jason took two-year-old Willow to the out-of-town supermarket for some father-daughter bonding and illicit Haribo.

Naomi wasn't great at hiding her feelings at the best of times, but the horror on her face as she squeezed her way past the boxes stacked in the hallway was so blatant that Gina nearly laughed.

'Oh, my God, Gee,' said Naomi, struggling to unhook her jacket from where it had caught on a stray coat-hanger. 'Where did all this come from?'

'Where'd you think?' Gina moved a box of electrical leads away from the door so Naomi could get in. 'Dryden Road. It came yesterday. I've been up half the night unpacking.'

'Wouldn't it be easier to stick it all in storage? Sort it out bit by bit? Seriously, this would give me a panic attack.'

Naomi wasn't a collector like Gina. She and Jason lived in a new home on the edge of town, an exclusive development with views of the park and the cathedral. Their house was modern, and so tidy Naomi had a robot Hoover that could go round the whole downstairs without getting stuck on any clutter.

Gina wiped her forehead with the back of her hand. She'd already despatched three boxes that morning and dropped off some books and kitchen clutter at the charity shop. 'I can't afford more storage. You have no idea how much it costs to keep your sofa under a warm roof. It'd be cheaper to rent my possessions their own flat. Anyway, it would just stay there. This way I've got to sort through it. Sort or die.'

'You joke, but this is like something from one of those documentaries.' Naomi eyed the towering stack of boxes marked 'Crockery'. 'The ones where they have to dig people out from under their lifetime collection of used Christmas wrapping paper.'

'It's not as bad as that. Look, I've got a system,' said Gina. She gestured towards the sorting boxes by the window.

GIVE AWAY was stacked with paperbacks, vases and a bedside radio. SELL had a couple of limited-edition Emma Bridgewater plates that had once taken pride of place on her Welsh dresser. KEEP had only one thing: a 1940s brass desk-lamp Gina had found years ago in an antiques shop. In her head, when she'd bought it, it had formed the basis of a classic New York-themed study, but had always got lost in the clutter of her house. Here, against the white walls and empty shelves, it would be a proper feature.

'Wow. You're going to make some homeless kitties *very* happy.' Naomi got as near to the big window as she could, and peered down at the drizzly high street, already busy with weekend shoppers. 'I see you've got plenty of charity shops to choose from down there.'

'There are five,' said Gina. 'Local dog rescue, Breast Cancer Care, Oxfam, Marie Curie Nurses, and Hospice at Home. I've already taken four bags to the dogs' home. What?' she added, when Naomi turned back, her eyebrows raised. 'Don't look at me like that. I don't *have* to support the breast-cancer shop. The dogs are nearer. And they open earlier.'

'I don't mean that.' Naomi picked her way back to where Gina was standing. 'I mean, are you feeling up to sorting things out? On your own?'

'I'm fine,' said Gina, surprised. She'd thought she looked quite good: not having access to a bathroom's worth of cosmetics had pared her routine down to an almost Parisian minimalist chic. 'Really. It's my heart that's broken, nothing else. Why? Do I look like death warmed up?'

'You look shattered.' Naomi was always honest. Kind, but as honest as a lifelong friend – and someone who'd grown up with older brothers – could be. 'You've got that shiny-eyed look you used to get when you wanted to pretend you were feeling better than you were. Are you sure you're not pushing yourself too hard? This is *me*. It's OK to be honest.'

'I'm fine.' Gina didn't want sympathy from Naomi right now: it would unbalance her fearless mood to be reminded that she needed looking after. 'I look ropy because I've been up half the night chucking stuff into boxes.' She paused, then said, with a ferocity that was only just covered by her smile, 'I know what ill feels like. I'm not ill. I'm feeling a bit . . . raw, but not ill, OK?'

Naomi tried to look satisfied with that, but Gina noticed she folded her arms. 'Well, you know best, Gee. But you've got to tell me if things get too much. You don't have to live here in all this chaos. Come and stay with us until you've sorted the boxes out. Hey, do that! Willow would *love* to have her fairy godmother around. And we've got room . . .'

'That's kind but there's no need.' Gina waved wryly at the mess. 'I have to get this under control in one go, or it'll never get done. And it's therapeutic, working out what to throw away, what I don't need any more. What might benefit someone else. It's good.'

'Yeah, that's the bit I'm having trouble with. You, getting rid of things.' She pretended to feel Gina's forehead. 'You sure you're all right?'

'The more I chuck out, the better I feel.'

'Well, don't I feel bad,' said Naomi, with a wry sigh. 'I've just brought you one more bag to sort through. Some of it's to eat, though. I bet you're not eating enough.'

'I'm hardly wasting away,' Gina scoffed, then stopped as she remembered she hadn't actually eaten since . . . the previous morning? Over the past few days her appetite had come and gone with the unpredictable surges of energy that propelled her into mad activity, then dropped away, leaving her staring, amazed and exhausted, at the unfamiliar place she was in.

'Knew you wouldn't have. That's why I brought breakfast.' Naomi pointed at the bag. 'Don't want you keeling over. Where am I going to get another best mate at this late stage? Eh? Not to mention a reliable babysitter.'

Despite her cheery tone, Naomi's eyes were searching her face with a motherly concern that made Gina feel a bit tearful. She gestured towards the open-plan kitchen. 'Climb through and make us some tea, then. I unpacked the kitchen boxes last night. You won't believe how much stuff we had in that kitchen. Do you know how many mugs there were? Forty-five.'

'*Forty-five?*' Naomi gave it the full comic timing pause. 'Was that all?'

'I know. Two charity bags full. There were seven different "I heart" mugs. Made me look very fickle.'

'So how many did you keep?'

'Five?' Gina made it sound light but every keep-sell-chuck decision felt like a bigger statement to the universe about her future life. Keeping two champagne flutes was a hopeful message. She'd chucked the three-tier light-up punchbowl: end-of-season football parties were never going to happen again. Thank God. 'I thought five was a good number. Somewhere between simple living and I-still-believe-I'll-have-people-round-for-coffee.'

Naomi considered it, then nodded. 'I like that reasoning. Did you keep that glass cake stand? For birthday parties?'

'I did. Where there's cake, there's hope.'

'I agree. Now, where are your plates?'

The kitchen was brand new and very streamlined, with no visible handles or appliances. The granite work surface gleamed after Gina's cleaning fit in the small hours, and two of the kitchen boxes had been sorted and despatched. Only the bare essentials had made it onto the worktop: one balloon whisk, one spatula, one wooden spoon, one Microplane grater, one silver fish slice, all stored in a Victorian earthenware jar. Somehow the functionality of it, Gina thought, made her appear more like a serious cook than the cupboards full of unused pasta machines and juicers had.

The juicer was dumped in the box of appliances marked SELL by the door, along with a waffle-maker, a mini slow-cooker and a coffee-grinder among others. It had been an expensive wedding present, but Gina was happy to see the back of it. Just looking at it brought back the gritty, bitter taste of apple core: it reminded her of the endless 'healthy' juice drinks Stuart had made when she had been too sick to eat. He'd never cleaned it out, and the crusty plastic parts had lingered on the side of the sink for days. The moment Gina put the juicer in the box she'd felt lighter. Lighter, but slightly reckless, as though she'd just chucked out an instruction manual for something.

Naomi found the side plates in a cupboard; there were six, all plain white. 'Wow, this is a change from Dryden Road,' she said, stroking the smooth almond units, with their sleek handles. 'Very modern. What have you done with that lovely old hanging airer from the kitchen? Is it in storage?'

'I had to leave it. And the Welsh dresser. And the butcher's block. The buyers wanted the kitchen exactly as it was, so I got the estate agent to haggle them up.'

'You left the butcher's block?' Surprise broke through Naomi's politely encouraging expression. 'The one you dragged back from that holiday in *Yorkshire*?'

Gina shrugged. 'Where was I going to put it? Anyway, it's part of that kitchen, not this one. What? Why are you pulling that face?'

'Because you made such a fuss about . . . Are you getting enough sleep? Sorry, forget I said that. I guess it's just that . . .' Tact and concern struggled on Naomi's face. 'It's just that you put so much of yourself into that house,' she finished. 'You don't have to walk away from it all just because . . . well, you know.'

'It's someone else's house now,' said Gina, and she didn't mean the family who'd bought it.

Naomi almost said something, then changed her mind. She patted Gina's arm. 'Let's have a croissant. They're in the bag.'

Gina lifted the paper carrier-bag onto the counter top. Inside there was an expensive three-wick hyacinth-scented candle; a couple of glossy magazines; a tub of cookie-dough ice cream; a bottle of wine; and some still warm croissants. All old favourites. Nearly the same selection of treats Naomi had brought round after every hospital treatment, barring the wine. In the end, Gina had got wine in for Naomi to drink while she was sitting with her – one of them, at least, deserved to be excused the juicer.

'Ah, yes. I remember these. No self-help books?'

'Nope. I reckoned you were a bit past them now. And it sounds like your mum's sent you all the best ones already.'

'I don't know about the *best* ones . . . Did I tell you she accidentally gave me one of hers in her last consignment – *How to Cope with Your Child's Divorce*?'

'God, really?'

'Really.' Gina put the ice cream in the freezer for later. The chiller drawers were beautifully free of stray peas and old ice-cube trays. 'I'm very tempted to write "It's not always about you, Mum" across the first page and give it back to her. You'd think she was the one who'd been dumped, the way she's acting.'

Naomi laughed, but then looked remorseful. 'You won't, though, will you? I know Janet drives you mad, but she means well. And when you've lost two husbands before you're fifty . . .'

'". . . you know what it's like to be alone." Yeah, we've had that conversation. And no, of course I won't say anything.'

'Sorry. I don't mean to nag. I know it's easier to be patient with other people's mothers. But at least Janet's around, and not constantly swanning off to foreign parts with her new bloke like mine. ' Naomi put the kettle on. 'So – what's the latest with Stuart? Is he still texting you, or has he picked up the phone?'

'Still texting. It's better that way. It's not like we've got a lot to say to each other. Has Jason seen him since . . . since he moved out?'

'No. He wasn't at football this week. Jay won't tell me anything anyway. You know what blokes are like. What happens in the changing room stays in the changing room.' Naomi's lip curled eloquently. 'But he sends his love. He thinks Stuart's lost his mind. Says if there's anything we can do . . .'

'Thanks.' Gina pulled the horn off a croissant. 'But I'm hoping it's going to be straightforward. I mean, we've no kids to argue about, the house has been sold, he's got the cats. It's just a case of giving all the details to the solicitors and letting them get on with it. Rory – thanks for the recommendation, by the way, he's brilliant – says he can probably get things sorted out in about three months. Four months if people are away.'

'Good. I'm glad the practical stuff's in hand. But what about *you*? You're being so calm.' Naomi poured boiling water onto the tea bags and poked them impatiently. 'I'd be going after that cheating bastard with a pair of nail scissors. Seriously, you just have to say the word.' She pushed the mug over the counter with a fake-menacing smile that was only half joking. 'It doesn't have to be nail scissors. It could be Veet. Or laxatives.'

Gina cupped her scalding mug in her hands, and tried to work out how she did feel, right now. 'Most of the time I'm fine. Sometimes I'm . . . not. But it's mainly a relief. Things weren't right with me and Stuart. Maybe I should have been braver and ended it myself, instead of letting it fail.'

'You didn't *fail*. You two had a lot to deal with,' said Naomi at once. '*Way* more than most couples have to face in a lifetime.'

'But that's what's so awful.' She winced. 'Isn't going through bad times together supposed to make you stronger? I know that's what everyone's thinking – they got through that, how come they split up now?'

'No one's thinking that. If they're thinking anything, it's that Stuart's having an early on-set midlife crisis and you've kicked him out. How long were you together? Nine years? Ten?'

'Nearly nine. And married for five and a bit.' Gina winced. What was that feeling? Shame? Despair? Nostalgia? Marriages weren't meant to collapse so soon. Not round here. 'Do you need a steamer, by the way? For some reason, we got three for wedding presents. I'm going to put a notice up on the board at work. I'm having a purge. '

'Gina, you don't *have* to throw everything away.'

'I do. I want to.' She gestured at the boxes. 'Where would I put it anyway? This flat is a fresh start. All white and clean and *mine*. Whatever I choose to put in it has to say something about who I am now.'

'*Riiight.*' Naomi picked at her croissant and tried to look encouraging.

Gina carried on. It was the first time she'd explained her plan in words, and saying it aloud made it feel more definite. 'There's no room here for anything I don't really love or need, so I'm going to keep a hundred things that I can't live without. The rest has to go. And then I'll be able to appreciate the hundred things properly, instead of having drawers of stuff I never look at.'

'Whoa there!' Naomi put her croissant down. 'You're a hoarder, you've always been a hoarder. Is this the

37

interior-designer version of cutting all your hair off and having a dolphin tattooed on your bum?'

'I'm just being practical. I can't unpack my old house here. There's no room, and that house is gone. That person's gone. And I've been carting all this stuff around with me for years, so it's about time I had a sort-out.'

'But why a hundred? You know that's not a lot, right? You probably had a hundred *candlesticks* in your old house.'

'It's a nice round number. And it's not going to include essentials, like, you know, underwear. But I need *some* rules, otherwise where do I start? One thing I have decided, though,' Gina added. 'I'm going to sell a load of stuff and buy myself something really nice. A present for my new place.'

'That's a *great* idea.' Naomi nodded more enthusiastically. 'Let me know if you need a bit of help with that. I do a lot of eBaying.'

'Really?' Gina was surprised. Not just that Naomi had time to eBay, but that she wanted to. The Hewsons weren't short of money: Naomi had just gone back to work full-time as the all-seeing, all-knowing practice manager at the dental surgery, and Jason was a senior partner with an IT recruitment company.

'Yes, it's brilliant for keeping the clutter under control,' said Naomi, blithely. 'I do a cull of the house three or four times a year. Jason's golf stuff, clothes Willow's grown out of, books, Christmas presents – you'd be amazed what people will buy with the right description.' She wiggled her fingers. 'I quite enjoy doing the descriptions.'

Gina raised an eyebrow. 'And doesn't your inability to

call a spade a gardening management solution get in the way of a sale?'

'That's the weird thing! People appreciate a bit of honesty. I just haven't told Jay's mum what my seller name is. Otherwise she'd realise that all those china angels she keeps giving us aren't actually in the display cabinet she thinks they are.'

Naomi did her half-wink grin, and Gina thought how little she'd changed in the years they'd known each other. The hair had been a variety of colours and styles, and there were a few crows' feet round the sharp green eyes, but otherwise it was the same bossy, thoughtful, faintly anarchic Naomi she'd encountered on her first day at senior school. Gina felt a sudden clutch of relief that they'd met when they had. It could so easily have been someone else with a space next to them in the classroom. Someone else who had Naomi McIntyre as their best mate, dragging them out of so many gloomy days, instead of letting them wallow.

'I've got something for you, actually,' said Gina, and clambered her way back into the sitting room to find the shopping bag she'd filled earlier. 'Although after what you've just said I don't know if you deserve it.'

Naomi accepted the bag with a groan. 'Is this where you get your own back by re-gifting me all my own Christmas presents?'

'No! Have a look.' Gina sat back, anticipating the reaction with a glow of pleasure.

It took a moment, but when Naomi's shriek of joy came, Gina felt like Santa Claus.

'Oh, my God! *Gina!*' Naomi lifted out a precious stack of

old 1990s magazines, *Q*, *Melody Maker*, *New Woman*, her face bright with delight. 'Oh, my God, I can't believe you still have these! Are you really sure you don't want them?'

'I've got loads. I couldn't keep all of them, and I knew you'd appreciate a bit of nostalgia. Maybe you can put them in storage for Willow. Bit of her mum's past.' Gina wasn't joking. So much of her and Naomi's teenage years had been spent poring over magazines together, in breaks, in the common room, in Naomi's noisy kitchen at home. The music magazines in particular meant a lot to Gina: she'd never felt she belonged till she'd got into music, and suddenly the world outside had opened up. You didn't need to wonder which people to try to make friends with if they were already wearing your favourite band's tour T-shirt.

'Just don't eBay them, please,' she added. 'Not straight away, anyway.'

'Are you kidding?' Naomi was turning the pages reverentially. 'This is bringing back so many memories. Oh, no! Look at the old Rimmel adverts . . . You are *amazing*. And what's this?' She reached into the bag and pulled out a black T-shirt, printed with a band logo that was still stiff. Naomi looked up. 'Didn't you buy one like this at that gig we went to in Oxford? The one where you met Kit? It's not this one, is it?' She sniffed the old cotton. 'It smells like it's brand new.'

'It is.' Gina stared at the T-shirt. It had felt right to pass it on last night when she'd put it into the bag, but now, seeing it in Naomi's hands, she felt as if part of her past was slipping under the waters, vanishing as it left her home. She caught herself. This stuff had to go, and it was better that it went to someone who'd understand why she'd treasured it. 'I bought two, in case one shrank in the wash, or Mum found out where we'd been and I never got to go to a gig again. That's the spare.'

'But where's yours?'

'I think I gave it to Kit.'

Naomi looked up, and her eyes were sad. 'Oh, Gee. I can't take this, then.'

'No, I want you to.' Gina hadn't talked about Kit in a long time. Naomi was the only person she *could* talk to about him. 'Keep it for Willow. I couldn't wear it now – it's way too small for me. It'd just go back in a drawer, and I need to be ruthless.'

She glanced away. The logo had hooked up a memory that had been stuffed at the back of her mind, hidden away like the T-shirt: Kit sprawled across an unmade single bed, sleeping off a late night in his blue-checked boxers and her T-shirt, his long arms thrown over his head, pulling the T-shirt up his flat stomach with its gentle curves and hollows. Gina had told herself to remember how perfect he looked.

It felt like a very long time ago, and her heart contracted at the freshness of the T-shirt print in Naomi's hands.

'No, listen, I'll happily take the mags, but not this,' said Naomi, seeing the change in Gina's face. 'I want *you* to keep it and give it to Willow when she's old enough to appreciate what a cool godmother she's lucky enough to have.'

Gina forced a smile, but the image wouldn't go away. She wasn't in it. That morning had happened to *her*, she'd *been* there, but now, even with this T-shirt as evidence, it was as if she was remembering a film she'd seen ages ago. Those mornings with Kit had felt like the beginning of something, the first steps along a long road they'd look back over together, and yet it had stopped, and now it was as if it had never actually happened. It would be the same with Stuart. All those expectations and assumptions, months and years, experiences and memories . . . gone.

Her stomach flipped as if she'd got too close to a sharp drop.

'Where have the last few years gone, Naomi?' she blurted out. 'How are we suddenly this old?'

'We're not old, you daft cow,' said Naomi. 'We're just getting started. Life isn't meant to begin till forty, and that's years off.'

'But I feel old. I feel time's going so fast and I don't even know what I—'

'We're just getting started,' Naomi repeated, more firmly. She reached across and took her hand, her eyes locking on Gina's, full of concern and support and an unspoken understanding of all the things that made Gina feel suddenly exhausted whenever she forgot to concentrate on her fresh start. 'There's lots more time than you think. Promise.'

Gina managed a watery smile, and squeezed Naomi's hand.

She didn't need things to remind her of her past. Not when she had Naomi. Honest, sympathetic, practical Naomi.

When Naomi had left, Gina tidied up the cups and plates and, out of habit, went to put the beautiful scented candle in a cupboard somewhere, to keep for later. For best. For visitors.

She stopped, the box in her hand. She had no cupboards or visitors. She was the only person here, so why save the candle for someone else when it had been given to *her*?

Before she could think too hard about it, Gina slid the glass jar out of the box and put it on the windowsill, the only clear flat space in the flat. Then she lit it. After a moment or two, the pale blue scent of hyacinths began to fill the room: the spicy-crisp smell of the chilly winter months before spring broke through the greyness.

Chapter Three

ITEM: The Marras T-shirt, student union tour, 1996

Oxford, 1996

Georgina is having the best night of her life so far, and it's only just gone ten.

She glances from side to side before taking a covert swig from Naomi's dad's hip-flask, then realises that no one's going to tell her not to. No one's watching, and no one cares that she's two years under the legal drinking age; everyone around her is either drunk, or on something, or snogging someone, or all three. She fizzes inside with an exhilaration that has nothing to do with the vodka and everything to do with the music pounding through her, and takes another large gulp, which burns her throat, but she grimaces and swallows.

Naomi says vodka doesn't taste of anything but Georgina isn't so sure. Not that she's going to say anything. Mixed with the hormones and sweat in the air, compressed by the low, dark ceiling of this student-union function room, it tastes of liquid headache, but it's going to have to do, because even with Naomi's kohl eyeliner on, she still has a nervous suspicion that they look under-age and, anyway, they only have enough money for the bus back to Naomi's brother's student halls where they're crashing for the night.

So, technically, this *is* a university visit. It's just to the student union, not to the library, as she assured her mother and Terry.

And it's brilliant. Gina has the feeling she should be scared, but she's not. Or if she is, it's a good kind of scared.

'This's the most amazing night 'f my life,' Naomi slurs, grabbing her arm. Her eyes are shining with the intense joy that Georgina knows will turn into intense weeping in about thirty minutes, and this is just the support act. The Marras, whose album Gina has listened to about a million times, aren't even on for another hour. 'You were so right about us coming here!'

'Thanks!' Georgina yells back, pleased.

Something she wouldn't say, even to Naomi: when she's listening to music, Georgina imagines the interesting person she's going to be when she finally gets to university. Here. Two more years – six terms, five A levels – and she'll get the chance to be someone new. Georgina Bellamy had a brace, and prefect's tie. *Gina* Bellamy is a writer. An actress. She has a fringe, sexy boots and mystique.

Naomi giggles. 'Georgina, you're so . . .'

'Gina,' says Georgina, firmly. 'Gina.'

'What?' Naomi looks like she might be about to give her the bit of her mind that remains after half a hip-flask of vodka but at that moment the band launches into the one song the audience has heard of, a cover of 'Heroes': they're not stupid enough to end on one of their own.

Georgina and Naomi are shoved forward by the crush of sweating bodies.

Naomi squeals, somewhere in the distance, but Georgina closes her eyes and lets the music wash through her, the beat vibrating and booming outside and inside her body, like she's not even there. She feels weightless, lifted by the force of the crowd as the band powers through the verse. Then the key shifts, like a huge car changing gear, and the whole room tips over into the chorus, bouncing, yelling, pushing. Georgina's lips form the words, but the music is so loud she can't hear her own voice; she can sense, not hear, everyone else singing and it makes her feel tearful. A wave of pure drunken happiness drowns her as she smiles blindly into the darkness pulsing behind her eyelids, stinging with sweat and smeary mascara.

When she does open her eyes, her dry lips parted ready to sing the chorus, he's looking straight into her face. A boy (man?) with longish blond curly hair, like an angel's, and wide-set blue eyes that shine with the same dazed pleasure as hers. His black T-shirt's damp, his face is sheeny with sweat – everyone's is, so many bodies packed together – and she can smell the heat from his body. It's a sharp male smell, dangerous and exciting.

"'We could be heroes,'" Georgina sings, and it comes out towards him. He smiles and she blushes hotly. Hotter. But she's not embarrassed. Not even slightly. This is an entirely new feeling. Georgina is embarrassed at least five times a day: by her stepdad, her 'exemplary' grades, her neurotic mother's constant notes to the head, her shoes. She never has the right shoes.

They stare into each other's faces and Georgina has the weirdest feeling that she's known him from somewhere before. His face isn't new to her. She feels like she's arrived somewhere she's been heading for all her life. It's intensely comforting and freaky at the same time.

The crowd are squeezing them closer, and her heart is beating in her throat. They're still singing, but he's leaning closer and, without warning, as the guitar solo soars over their heads, he shouts, 'Kit!' right in her ear, and there's a sharp tug inside, as if a giant fish hook has landed in her chest. For a second Georgina wonders if she's *actually* hurt, and puts a hand up in surprise.

He grabs it, and cups it to his ear, trying to mime 'Tell me your name.' The skin of her arm goosebumps at the sensation of his fingers round her wrist. She shouts, 'Gina!'

Her voice is drowned, however, by a roar rumbling down from the front. Hard elbows jab in her back, and Gina turns to see a massive rugby-player surfing across the raised hands, upside-down and so close she can smell the beer on his breath, the acrid sweat on his T-shirt. His eyes lock on hers as he crashes nearer, his fist out-stretched like Superman. It's aiming straight for her head.

Gina panics, but she's trapped by the crush of bodies around her, arms pinned to her sides. All she can think as he hurtles towards her is, Mum. How'm I going to explain being in hospital to Mum?

She opens her mouth to scream as the boy – Kit – grabs her by the belt of her jeans and drags her away with surprising strength. Gina feels eighteen stones of solid prop forward brush past her shoulder and slam into the lads next to her. The whooping crowd bends away like a field of corn, pushing her into Kit's arms, but before Gina can register the sensation of his skin against hers, hot and intimate in the general crush, it moves back again, and she's shoved into a stranger's side, half-lifting her off her feet. By the time she gets her balance on the slippery floor, another surge has surrounded her in a thick forest of strangers. Black T-shirts and clammy backs and a communal body odour, dark under the aftershave and deodorant.

She looks but Kit's gone. Adrenalin – and disappointment and vodka – rakes her body so hard she wants to cry.

Gina's foot feels wet and she realises she's lost her slip-on pump. Naomi's nowhere to be seen, and she needs the loo. The spell's broken. Close to tears, she fights her way out of the audience to the back of the hall.

The few cool people hanging at the back ignore her. Gina stands there with ringing ears, one sock sodden with spilled beer. Then, just at the moment she most wants to go home, Kit appears out of the thicket of the audience, with a shoe in his hand. He doesn't see her at first, and Gina has the luxury of watching him looking for her, his blond hair hanging damply in his eyes. Then he spots her, and his anxious expression turns to a smile. Gina holds her breath as he approaches.

'Cinderella, I presume?' He offers her the shoe.

'Gina,' she says, taking it. It's not the one she lost, but she doesn't care. It's roughly the right size and her foot's soaking. Why let a small detail like that spoil the moment?

'Hang on.' Kit frowns as she tries to force her heel in. '*Is* that yours?'

'Near enough,' she says. They're both talking too loudly; she assumes his ears are buzzing like hers. 'Well, no. To be honest, it's not.' She smiles apologetically. 'And I'm not Cinderella.'

He laughs, and turns back to the crowd, only just thinning out as the band milk the applause. 'Look, it'll be in there somewhere, we can find it once this lot have finished.'

We. We can go and find it.

'Can you hop as far as the bar? If I help you?' Kit's blue eyes are dark when he looks at her, and Gina has the sudden thrilling sensation that he feels exactly the same way she does. As if she could climb right inside him, as if everything else in this crowded room is slightly blurry in comparison with his sharp outline.

She nods. He grabs her hand and Gina lets Kit lead her to the five-deep bar where the student serving waves at him and makes a 'Drink?' gesture. His hand is warm and damp and grips hers tightly, ostensibly so they don't become separated in the crowd, but there's no crowd where they're standing and he only lets go to collect the beers.

They take their drinks to a quieter corner and before Gina can even worry about what they're going to talk about, they're talking. About the band, about her lost shoe, about the bar, about their favourite music, about the amazing coincidence that Kit's mates with Naomi's brother, Shaun. His amused blue eyes never leave her face, and Gina feels as if she's been here before, as if they've known each other all their lives.

They have another beer, and discover they both love Nick Drake, and are left-handed, and always wanted a cat but were never allowed one. And the headliners arrive but Kit and Gina are still talking in the dark corner of the bar, the space between them slowly disappearing. She only hears The Marras in the distance, but that's fine. It's as if they're playing in a corner of her bedroom.

This is the best night of my life, she thinks, light-headed with a funny serene happiness that makes her feels as if she's floating like a helium balloon over the crowd of dancers. Nothing will ever feel better than this.

And it's not even midnight.

To get to her mother's home in Hartley, Gina had to drive past 7 Church Lane, the house Janet had coveted for as long as they'd lived in the area.

It was the handsomest house on a road of handsome houses – 1930s mock-Tudor detached, all clean black-and-white half-timbering, with flowerbeds edging a velvety lawn, and a cherry tree in exactly the right spot in the garden, poised like a flattering hat on a beautiful face. As if to mark it out as the best house in the row, a red postbox was set into the brick wall outside the sunburst wrought-iron gate, the GR monogram picked out in gold.

G for Gina, she used to think as a teenager, ever monitoring her surroundings for Signs. R for who? It had made her tingle with anticipation and a bit of dread, that her R was out there, but might not find her in boring Hartley.

Janet used to swivel in the passenger seat of Terry's brown Rover P6 as they drove past, but at the same time as her eyes were clearly drinking in 7 Church Lane's domestic perfection, she insisted she had no interest in being 'the sort of person who is that obsessed with their lawn – it takes a lot of work, keeping it up, a real burden'. As an adolescent, from her slumped position in the back seat (in case anyone from school saw her out in Terry's ancient car), Gina had secretly mouthed along in unison with her mother's observations. Even now Janet's voice was permanently connected with the geography of the drive back home – the apple tree that should be cut back, the conservatory that would be better with a sloping roof. Once or twice, Terry had caught Gina's eye in the rear-view mirror, the twinkle in his expression offering a gentle solidarity with Janet's self-delusion, and Gina had felt a funny mixture of guilt and relief that made her drop her gaze, even though part of her wanted to grin back. Maybe even roll her eyes.

It was unsettling to see that flash of a different man, not because there was anything remotely sinister about Terry and his sandy moustache and sensible shoes, but because it was too complicated to think of him as an actual person with a sense of humour. When he was boring-sales-rep Terry, he fitted into the tortuous equation of loyalty and resentment she'd worked out, a system of concessions and balances that allowed her to miss her real handsome, heroic dad, while also being not ungrateful to the man who'd stepped in to fill an unenviable gap. Acknowledging Terry's realness also meant contemplating the relationship he had with her mother, and – hard as it was to imagine her mother having any truck with the sort of unhygienic activity Gina read about in Naomi's eye-opening magazines – that made her want to die of squeamishness.

As an adult, driving down the road Terry's P6 must have covered thousands of times in their endless family round of school, work, 'runs out' and shopping, Gina wished she'd smiled back. Poor Terry was just trying to build some bridges, in his diplomatic way. She felt sorry for him, then even sorrier, because her mother *still* wished they'd cut the apple tree back outside the vicarage, and she understood a little more of what Terry had put up with all those years.

Today 7 Church Lane's borders were full of early daffodils, a cheerful splash of colour in the wintry sunshine. Gina paused outside the house to let another car past, and cast her critical housing planner's eye over the freshly whitewashed exterior. Though she loved old properties, 7 Church Lane didn't do much for her. There was so much twee period detail inside and out that you had to live by its rules, and she knew it was much darker and smaller inside than you'd think. One of those houses that's nicer to look at from outside, than to live in. Maybe that was why Mum wanted it, she thought, then batted the mean thought away as she set off again.

The twin tubs of daffodil bulbs that Gina and Stuart had given Janet for their last ever joint Christmas present had just started to come out by the front door, pale green fingers of leaf with tightly rolled buds reaching up through compost. They were all right, but obviously they weren't as good as the glorious golden trumpets showing off further up the road.

Gina rang the bell and stared at the shoots, a distant irritation tickling her. When those bulbs had been planted in some far-off John Lewis nursery last autumn, she'd still been married. And while she'd been juggling credit cards at 1 a.m., ordering extravagant Christmas flowers for their various families, Stuart had been covertly texting Bryony, arranging meet-ups in Birmingham. The bulbs of their divorce had been planted at the same time as the bloody daffodils. They'd even bloomed at the same time.

Stuart had never remembered birthdays or Christmases; Gina had always done it for both of their families, out of paranoia that she might miss someone's last one. And even though her mother knew full well Gina sent the stupid planter of daffodils, she'd still cooed with delight and told Stuart he was so clever to have chosen her favourites.

Daffodils weren't even her favourites. Janet's favourite, Gina knew for a fact, was the carnation, the world's dullest flower.

All these thoughts went through her mind at the speed of light, and she was still frowning at the tub when the door opened moments after she'd knocked, and Janet appeared on the doorstep, the sinews of her neck tight with concern.

Janet Bellamy was fifty-six and still attractive in a girlish way. She wore a lot of pink, and owned one pair of trousers, specifically for gardening. Gina had inherited her high, sharp cheekbones, but not her fine gold hair or her slight frame. When Janet was happy, she could easily pass for late forties; when she was anxious, which was more usual, she could look much older.

'I was worried about you!' she said, grabbing Gina's arm

before she'd even had time to open her mouth. 'You said you'd be here at two! I thought there might be a problem with the car!'

'No, it's fine.' Gina submitted to her mother's anxious peck. 'I just stopped to drop off some donations to the charity shop. You should say if you want any books, by the way. I'm getting rid of a lot now I don't have bookcases.'

Janet intensified her grip. 'You have got breakdown cover, haven't you? I meant to check.'

Last time it had been 'Do you know where your fuse box is? I worry that you could be trapped in a power cut,' as if getting divorced had left Stuart with sole custody of the marital brain, as well as the tools.

'Yes,' said Gina. 'Of course I have breakdown cover.'

'Well, make sure you do. You've got to think about these things now.'

'Now what?'

'Now you're . . .' Janet took a deep breath. 'Now you don't have anyone to fall back on. Come on in, I'll put the kettle on.'

Fall back on. For God's sake. Gina stared at her mother's retreating back. What century was this? 'Mum, I'm perfectly capable of looking after myself. You do realise Stuart couldn't tell a gearbox from an egg box?' She followed her mother down the hall, lined with watercolours of pale flowers. 'That's why he cycled everywhere. He was a terrible driver.'

Janet's kitchen was spotless and smelt of lemons. Every time Gina walked into it as an adult, she longed to call a conservation officer and get it listed as a perfect example of a late-1980s fitted kitchen, right down to the Eternal Beau tea service and complete collection of Delia Smith cookery books. She perched on a high stool at the breakfast bar, tucking her feet away awkwardly.

'That's not the point, Georgina.' Janet flicked on the kettle, and it boiled immediately. It had probably been on the boil since the dot of two o'clock. 'Stuart thought ahead when it came to problems, didn't he? He had everything covered when you were ill. I take my hat off to him – he was better than some of those doctors, the amount of research he did.'

Gina gritted her teeth. Janet idolised Stuart. He could have skinned rabbits for fun then nailed them to the front door, and Janet would still have said he was the best thing since sliced bread after his stellar performance as Supportive Husband 'when it mattered'.

'I know, Mum. He was . . . he is a nice guy.'

What Gina couldn't explain to her mother was that while she appreciated what Stuart had done – she truly did, he'd been amazing – in the end she wanted a husband who'd be wonderful when it *didn't* matter. To be thoughtful without warning, to produce red tulips just to cheer her up, to reduce her to laughter with a well-timed private joke. Stuart had never been like that. He fixed things, which always made Gina feel anxious and lacking. When there wasn't something to be Done – the house renovation, their next holiday, her illness – they'd slumped into an uneasy silence, with nothing to say.

It was ironic, as Gina had pointed out to Rory, her solicitor, that getting divorced should at least have handed them one final joint project to tackle. Something to talk about as they divided up the house.

Janet dropped three tea bags into the pot, poured water on them carefully, then turned and gave Gina a reproachful look. 'Decent men like Stuart . . . They're like hen's teeth. I should know.'

'*I* know,' said Gina. 'But to be honest, Mum, neither of us was happy. Not for a while.'

'Really? You two always seemed happy enough.' She snapped the lid back on the tea caddy a bit too hard. 'And, in any case, marriage isn't about being *happy* all the time. It's about knowing where you are with someone. And you knew where you were with Stuart.'

'Until he started cheating on me with a younger woman from his cycle club,' Gina pointed out.

'Georgina!'

Gina had no idea what sort of husband her father had been in the four years Janet had been married to him, but she often wondered if some aspect of his personality, rather than the manner of his sudden death, had had anything to do with her mother's obsession with straight-forward men who filed every bank statement and did exactly what you expected them to, every time, in every circumstance. It wasn't something she could ever imagine asking her. The few times she'd tried to start a conversation about her dad, as an adult rather than an inquisitive child, she'd been met with a wounded expression that had shut down her enquiries. Asking about her father, apparently, was an insult to the man 'who'd brought her up'. It was, Gina thought, a weird reversal of the way she'd always assumed that liking 'the man who'd brought her up' would be an insult to her father.

'Mum, I don't want to talk about Stuart,' she said. 'It's over. I need to focus on moving forward now. I've actually had quite a good weekend so far – all my things have been delivered to the new flat and I've been sorting stuff out. Naomi came round yesterday, she says hello . . .'

Gina ran out of words. Janet was arranging a packet of digestives on a plate, tiling them neatly in a circle. It made her feel like a visitor, even though she knew her mother had done exactly the same thing every night at five forty-five when Terry came in. The biscuits never came out until the tea was made; it stopped them going stale, apparently.

'Mum?' she prompted. 'I know it's sad, but getting divorced isn't the end of the world. I'm not old. I mean, I'm about the same age as you were when you met Terry.'

There was a sigh, then a long pause. The local radio station mumbled in the background, and Gina felt a lethargic Sunday-ish atmosphere fill the room. Something about this house at weekends always made her feel fourteen again, complete with the looming sense that she should be getting on with something. In this case, the paperwork she needed to complete for Rory, and for the bank, and all the other faceless individuals who needed to know her new situation.

'Mum?' It came out more tetchy than she'd meant it to.

'I heard what you said. I was trying to think of the right thing to say, so you won't jump down my throat,' said Janet, peevishly. 'I'm trying to help, Georgina. You can be very hard to help, you know. I lie awake worrying about you. Do you think you might be in shock? I know I'm struggling to make sense of it. You seem to be rushing into all this.'

'I'm just trying to be practical,' Gina insisted. 'It's not that I'm not upset, and I'm sorry you're upset too, but I've got to get on with things. Who knows what's round the corner?'

'Who knows indeed?' said Janet, darkly.

Gina felt her positive mood slowly draining away. It was so much easier to be optimistic in her new flat, even with all the boxes looming over her, than in Janet's house. It was so . . . airless. The caddies lined up alongside the kettle – tea, coffee, sugar – hadn't switched positions in twenty years. The only thing that changed was the calendar from the local dairy that hung on the pantry door. Each month featured tastefully backlit cows in different locations around the area.

Her leg twitched, and she had an urge to move before she said anything she didn't mean just to shock her mother out of that pursed expression. 'Do you want me to take the tray through?' she asked. 'I've got a few bits and pieces of yours next door.'

Janet sniffed, and permitted her to carry the tray into the front room. Gina put it down on the coffee table, next to the remote control and the television guide, folded back at the day's viewing, then opened her mouth to start a fresh conversation, about the bag of things she'd brought and her new flat. The big wall, and what she could put on it. Work. Anything but Stuart.

But by the set of her jaw Janet wasn't about to let the previous topic go so quickly: moving rooms had just given her time to change tack. 'Don't bite my head off, but I've been thinking. Maybe you two should go to counselling,' she said, perching on the edge of her seat, knees tight together in her camel skirt. 'I just wonder if you're not being a bit . . . hasty?'

'Hasty?' Gina repeated, then felt annoyed, as an answering doubt rose up in her. *Was she?*

Gina's reactions to Stuart's affair still surprised her. Pain, shame, regret, relief – it was like pulling a fruit machine handle, a different combination came up every time. Guilt was a regular middle-of-the-night visitor. Maybe she should have tried harder, been more grateful for a safe man who didn't drink, gamble or complain about nursing her through some unbelievably violent bouts of vomiting.

'Yes, hasty in throwing away a perfectly good marriage,' said Janet, encouraged by her silence. 'Stuart's been through a lot too, dealing with your illness. Maybe you need to get things out in the open.'

'I suggested counselling ages ago. Stuart didn't want to discuss our private life in front of a stranger, he said. And, anyway, he's *living* with his new girlfriend now, Mum. I'd say that's pretty final.' Anger tightened inside Gina's chest as she spoke the words. 'He's been seeing her for *months*,' she went on masochistically. 'They went to Dublin for her birthday when he'd told me he was on a weekend football tournament! Are you seriously saying I should ignore the fact that he'd been cheating on me for most of last year? I wasn't ill then.'

'Of course I'm disappointed in him.' Janet frowned, but only as if, Gina thought, Stuart had reversed into Gina's car, not left her for someone else. 'But life throws these things at you. It's not a fairy tale, marriage. You have to *work* through bad times. The trouble is you've always had unreasonably high expectations, ever since . . . Well, it's just a shame you didn't meet *Stuart* when you were at school.' She pressed her lips together meaningfully.

There was a pause, during which Gina realised her mother was somehow managing to blame Kit for her divorce. 'Are you talking about Kit?' she asked, more to make her say it than anything else.

'Well,' said Janet, 'things might have turned out very differently if you'd met Stuart first, that's all.'

Gina sat back in her chair, lost for words. Well, lost for appropriate words. It would have been a lie to say she never thought about Kit – vague shapes flickered across her consciousness at least once a day, more a shadow than an active memory – but unpacking her old house seemed to have shaken him out of the past, like a bird from a tree. Twice in two days, an actual figure, not a faint tang of regret.

Janet was watching her, and Gina thought she looked delighted at having found not only someone else to blame for Stuart and Gina's divorce, but also at being able to pin it on Kit, the cause of everything bad that had ever happened to her daughter.

'Mum,' said Gina, heavily, 'how on earth can Kit have had anything to do with my marriage ending?'

'Hasn't he?'

'No!' Gina didn't know what to say that wouldn't make her look guilty. 'This is entirely the fault of me and Stuart.

No, actually, it's not *anyone*'s fault. We should never have got married in the first place.'

'Oh, Georgina! How can you say that?'

'Because it's true.'

'I suppose it's my fault that—' Janet started, but Gina stopped her.

'No, Mum,' said Gina, shortly. 'It's no one's fault. Sometimes things just don't work out.'

They sat in stubborn silence until Gina got up to get the bag she'd left by the door. 'I don't want to fall out,' she said, in a more conciliatory tone. 'I've brought some things of yours that I found while I was going through my boxes. Look, here's your carving set, from last Easter. And some recipe books I borrowed, and your flan dish . . .' Gina stacked them on the coffee table, relieved to see them become part of her mother's house now. 'And those books about . . . you know.'

The pile of self-help books about Being On Your Own that Gina had found monumentally depressing. At least the self-help books Naomi had given her had been cheerful in a brutal sort of way. Practical shoves to get you back on the path to fulfilment whether you liked it or not. Janet seemed to have found a special sub-section of guides to maintaining your grief at a low simmer for the rest of your life. Gina didn't want to join her mother in the 'very supportive' circle of lone middle-aged women she'd joined, moving from book group to flower arranging, privately ranking each other in order of abandonment, from divorcees to widows.

'There's no need to give those back,' said Janet. 'Don't you think you should hang on to—?'

'No, thank you. I've read them.' Before she could protest, Gina put a large cut-crystal bowl on top, anchoring them to the table. 'And this is your trifle bowl, isn't it?'

'I don't think so,' said Janet. 'Mine's Dartington crystal.'

'I think it is. I borrowed it from you a while back.'

Janet peered at it, then sighed. 'It's your Auntie Gloria's.'

Auntie Gloria was actually Janet's Auntie Gloria, a matronly figure of whom Gina had only the vaguest memories. She had smelt of dry fruitcake, and had been a live-in nanny-housekeeper for a big family near St Albans.

'Do you remember the lovely trifles she used to make for tea in that? With Bird's Custard. Remember?' Janet added, seeing Gina's blank look. 'You used to love them. She put sprinkles on top for you. Red, white and blue.'

'Oh, yes,' Gina murmured, automatically. Auntie Gloria could have kept frogspawn in it for all she remembered. Janet's memories of her own childhood teas were more familiar, through repetition, than Gina's own.

After Gina's dad had been killed, Janet had left Leominster and its reminders of their old life, and moved back in with her parents in Kent for a while. Gina didn't have many memories of that time, beyond Janet wearing a particular blue dress for weeks on end, but she'd happily accepted second-hand memories of her early childhood there – picnics with aunties, and trips to see donkeys on a farm in Granddad's Ford Granada. It sounded nice. Neither grandparent was around to corroborate the various stories, but Gina had the few images from the photo album imprinted on her brain from regular intense inspection, and mostly they seemed happy.

Her mother had been on the other side of the camera, taking the photos while Gina gazed solemnly from under her dark fringe. She appeared later on, when Terry arrived on the scene with his top-of-the-range SLR camera and insisted on posing them in front of his car, which was always more in focus than they were. Janet and Gina both, it turned out, had automatic 'photo faces': a bright, slightly fixed smile that remained exactly the same in every photo, regardless of weather or setting.

Janet was holding the bowl, gazing into it as if she could see the past in its depths, family trifles and all. 'Gloria always had nice things,' she said. 'This was a wedding present, from that family she was with for years. From Liberty, she said it was. Lead crystal. They were very good to her. Mind, she was very good to them. Gave them twenty-two years of her life.'

Gina experienced a familiar tug of collector's acquisitiveness but she squashed it. She had to focus on the flat, and how there was room only for her in it. 'It's lovely, but the thing is, Mum, I've got no storage, really. I don't have room for trifle bowls.'

She didn't think it was worth trying to explain her hundred-things target to her mother. Janet didn't hold with anything that smacked of New Age philosophy or not having enough tablecloths.

'But it was Auntie Gloria's! She'd have wanted you to have it.' Janet offered it to her. 'Have it, to remember Gloria by. It's a lovely thing.'

Gina steeled herself. This was exactly the trait she was trying to overcome. 'Mum, I don't remember her. She died when I was *five*. And I'm not going to remember her by a glass bowl I never get out of the cupboard, am I? You should tell me about her instead. Then I can keep the memories in my head.'

'There's no need to be flippant, Georgina.' Janet's gaze returned to the heavy etched glass. 'Poor Gloria. She was a nice old dear. It's a shame you can't remember her – she made your christening cake. Cream, with pale yellow daisies.'

That was a detail Gina hadn't heard before; there were no photos of her christening cake in the sparse album. She felt pleased. 'Really? So do I take after her at all? Do you?'

'She was like you in some respects,' said Janet. 'She could hang wallpaper better than any decorator, and she was . . . romantic. Gloria would never admit it, but your granny always said she was in love with the father of that family she worked for, Dr Meredith. It was why she stayed so long. Best years of her life she spent there.'

'Really?' Gina leaned forward in her chair. Her mother rarely confided stuff like this. 'Did he love her?'

Janet shook her head. 'I don't think so. I mean, she was good-looking enough, had plenty of other offers but, no, Gloria was fussy. And by the time she decided he wasn't going to, well . . . By the time she left, it was too late for her to have a family of her own. And I think Gloria regretted that.' She gave Gina a meaningful look. 'It was all very well her getting flowers at Christmas from those four she brought up, but it's not the same as your own kiddies visiting you, is it?'

Gina groaned inwardly. She knew where the conversation would be heading now. 'Mum, please. Not today.'

'I'm just saying that I don't want you to end up missing out on a family of your own because—'

'Did I *say* I wanted a family? And, Mum, I'm only thirty-three.'

Janet ignored her. 'Then I'm sorry but you have to be practical. You know I'd be happy to help out if you wanted to have one of those check-ups. You know, so you've got an idea of where you stand.'

Gina's fingernails dug into her palms. Janet's yearning for grandchildren had started out as playful hints, but it had got much less playful since all her friends had started crying off coffee mornings to babysit their 'little ones'. 'That's very generous, but it's the last thing on my mind right now.'

'You could freeze your eggs!' Janet gabbled. 'Then you don't have to rush into anything. I read an article in the *Daily Mail* about it.'

Gina shoved her hands into her hair, then looked at her mother, sitting, back straight, in the same brown leather chair she'd sat in every night while Gina was at school. By the window, the better to see the quick crossword by. Terry had sat in the matching armchair opposite the television; the cushion Janet had finished stitching for his fiftieth birthday still plumped ready for his return.

Sunday afternoons in this house: cold ham and *Songs of Praise* and heavy silences. It rushed up at Gina so vividly she could smell it. Everything she'd longed to get away from as a teenager, and thought in some ways she had – yet here she was, even down to the same Sunday-afternoon paranoia that she hadn't wrung enough out of the weekend as Monday approached. And the time ticking inexorably past, metronomed by the carriage clock on the 1950s slate mantelpiece.

If only Terry were still around. There was absolutely no way Janet would have said something like that if he'd been sitting there, coughing in the discreet tension-breaking way he had. He'd oil the waters, as he had done so many times in Gina's childhood, so well, in fact, that she'd only noticed years later when she was old enough to appreciate how hard it was to defuse tension between two very similar women.

'Mum,' she said carefully, the effort clipping each word into a hard shape, 'I can't freeze my eggs because the chemotherapy might have damaged my ovaries. I can ask about tests when I go for my check-up later this year but I wouldn't hold your breath.'

'You don't know what medical advances they might make in the next few years,' said Janet, obstinately. 'Positive thinking, Georgina!'

Gina bit her tongue. Janet didn't know the full extent of her treatment, the scouring, brutal effect it had had on her body while it was killing off the invading cells. She didn't know, because she hadn't wanted to know. Hospitals made Janet hysterical – understandably – so Stuart had passed on edited updates, all calm and authoritative, almost as handsome as a doctor himself. Her mother's distress had made Gina feel even worse so she'd hidden away from it. Only Stuart and Naomi had been allowed to see her while she was at her greyest, her most exhausted.

The memory of that time dragged at her again, and Gina felt weary. She had work in the morning, and boxes to clear at home. She looked up, ready to tell her mother that she had to get away, but caught an expression of unguarded vulnerability in Janet's eyes that stopped the words in her throat. Her mother seemed lonely, and older, but at the same time defiant, like a child, not ready to back down.

Janet caught her looking and raised her chin. 'I never know what to say to you, Georgina,' she said, in a wobbly voice. 'It always seems to come out wrong.'

What's the correct response to that, thought Gina. Exhaustion tugged at her bones, and she wished she were back in her flat, sorting, progressing, winnowing her life.

But this was her mother, half of her reason for being alive in the first place, even if they still couldn't talk without crashing into conversational sandbanks.

'I just don't want you to end up lonely,' said Janet, and Gina heard the silent 'like me' beneath it.

She took a deep breath. Fresh start, she reminded herself. Including with Mum.

'I'm not going to end up lonely. I've told Naomi that if Willow plays her cards right she'll be inheriting my diamond earrings and shoe collection. If that doesn't keep her popping round in my old age, I don't know what will. Now, do you want some fresh tea ?' she said, even though the one she had wasn't cold.

'That'd be nice, love,' said Janet, and managed a smile.

Stuart texted Gina while she was waiting at the traffic lights outside Longhampton, the trifle bowl rewrapped in two copies of the *Longhampton Gazette* on the back seat.

The message flashed up on the phone:

Mountain bike repair kit? Not in bag. Pls check ur boxes. Also pls send loan details for accountant. S

Gina ground her teeth. That was basically what it came down to. Nine years of trust and laughter and tears and hopes. Reduced to admin.

She still hadn't got used to the bluntness of Stuart's messages, carefully stripped of anything that might read like a change of heart. And even though Gina knew something had shifted, the distant click of a door closing behind her, she still hadn't completely crushed the traitorous flicker in her heart that maybe the message would read, 'I screwed up. Please forgive me'. Just so she could ignore it, if she wanted.

But it was always just about stuff. Who had what. Where was this, who paid for that.

She stared out at the sky, now leaden with invisible rain. In about fifteen hours, she had to go back to her office and open her files on other people's homes, set her mind to absorbing the stress and paperwork for them. The last thing Gina needed, with her energy leaking away by the minute, was a reminder that the only thing her husband wanted from the remnants of their own dream home was a bicycle repair kit. Not the wedding photos, not their albums, not the thoughtful presents she'd chosen for him over the years. Not her.

Gina flipped the phone over and tried not to think about Auntie Gloria and her beautiful, unused trifle bowl.

Chapter Four

ITEM: the complete works of William Shakespeare –
complete with essay notes, margin notes and notes
passed between Naomi and me in English class

November 1996, Hartley High School

The sixth-form common room is emptying after break as Gina hovers by the pay-phone, and checks her watch again.

11.26 a.m.

She bounces on her toes. He'd said call at half eleven. Should she call early? Would that look too keen?

Yes, it would. Gina is desperate to hear Kit's voice but at the same time paralysed with shyness. This is the best moment, just before it's happened, and she's hoarding it like chocolate cake, too nice to eat.

She looks around for Naomi's copper hair in the crowd around the door, where books are dumped between lessons. She'd said she'd wait till Naomi got back, but Naomi's always late.

11.27 a.m.

Gina's ostensibly ringing to find out if Kit has got the

tickets for a gig at one of the student unions; it's an underground band they both thought only they'd heard of, booked before the band in question had had a surprise chart hit. It's going to make her late for the one class no one's ever late for, but now that's not remotely important, not compared with hearing Kit's voice.

Butterflies swarm around her stomach and, unable to stand it any longer, she lifts the receiver.

A hand claps on her shoulder. 'Who're you calling?'

Gina jumps, but it's only Naomi, smelling suspiciously strongly of mints and perfume. 'Who'd you think?'

'Oooh. What did he say?'

'I haven't called him yet.'

'What? Why not?'

'Because I was waiting for you. And . . .' Gina looks round: no one's listening. 'Because I'm nervous?'

'Psch.' Naomi looks scornful but excited. 'Get on with it!'

Gina glances at the big clock on the wall. 11.30 a.m. It's time. She piles her coins ready. She has so much change it's nearly falling off the ledge. The humiliation of running out mid-conversation is unthinkable. She hesitates. 'Do you think it looks better to wait until . . .?'

'No.' Naomi holds out her hand for the phone. 'Do you want me to ring?'

'No! I'm doing it! Is anyone looking at me?'

'Course not. I don't know why you can't just call Loverboy from home. Where you could, you know, *enjoy* talking to him.'

'Are you kidding? You know what Mum's like. She'd go mental.'

Naomi looks amused. 'What's she going to do when you get to university? Glue your knickers on and tie you to a big stretchy rope?'

'Probably. Look, it's still OK for us to stay with Shaun if Kit's managed to get the tickets, right? He's definitely going to let us stay in his room?' Gina's eyes widen. 'And you're definitely up for it?'

'Yeah. A weekend with my pain-in-the-arse brother so my best mate can get off with some blond surfer dude who looks like Kurt Cobain's public-school cousin, totally top of my list.' She looks wry. 'The things I do for you.'

'It's not like that, Nay.' Gina's normally good with words, but she can't explain this. She used to think that it-was-like-a-thunderbolt stuff was ridiculous – until she met Kit, and something clicked inside them both. They'd spent the whole weekend after the student union event just talking. Through the night, all next morning, till the second the train left. Tripping over words, shared thoughts, matching coincidences as if they might run out of time. '*Kit*'s not like that . . . We've got so much in common, he writes me actual letters. He makes me feel like there's something special about me . . .'

'Because there *is*, dumbo.'

'And he really wants to see me.' That's the bit Gina can't quite get her head around. That Kit wants to see her as much as she wants to see him, when he's got the whole of Oxford University to pick from. 'And I *soooo* want to see him.'

'I know. It's amazing. He's a god. But can you please get on with it?'

Gina's fingers tremble as she jabs the buttons. It rings at the other end. She gives Naomi a thumbs-up, and they bounce in silent, hysterical glee.

Then the ringing stops. 'Hello?'

Gina's heart swoops and plunges around her chest at the sound of Kit's soft, slightly posh voice. He's right there in her head, his voice already familiar. The common room vanishes around her as her world shrinks into the darkness of her ear.

'Hello,' she croaks. 'It's Gina.'

'Gina! Hello!'

Next to her, Naomi rolls her eyes but still leans in.

'Good news, I got four tickets,' he says. 'Are you still up for coming, then?'

'Um, yeah. That'd be cool.'

Naomi mouths, 'Cool,' and looks appalled, and Gina has to turn round to stop herself giggling.

'Fantastic. My treat, by the way,' he says, before she can ask how much the tickets were. 'It's going to cost you enough to get here.'

'That's not a problem.' Gina's dipping into her savings; she's claiming it's another college visit. She'd better get into Oxford after all this. Although Kit will be gone by then. Graduated, and straight into the adult world. He told her he's already been offered finance-sector jobs, but he really wants to go travelling before he settles into a career. Already Gina hates the idea of him so far away, out of her reach.

'How long can you stay?' he asks casually. 'I remember you said the other night that you'd never had a proper curry.

I'd love to take you to this great Nepalese place we go to a lot – if you've got time . . .'

Naomi taps her watch, and points to her copy of *Romeo and Juliet*, their A-level set text, then at the clock.

11.35 a.m. Suddenly the time seems meaningless.

'That'd be amazing,' says Gina. 'I'm not very good with spices, though. My mum thinks garlic's a gateway to all sorts of trouble.'

He laughs, a charming, inviting sound, right in her ear. The corners of her soul curl up, tingling with anticipation.

'We. Are. Going. To. Be. Late,' Naomi hisses. 'It's Psycho Marshall.'

Gina sighs and reaches forward with a finger to tap Naomi's set text. *Romeo and Juliet*. Then she points at herself and swoons.

'I'll say you're having lady troubles,' Naomi whispers, and leaves her to it.

Gina's project-management company, Stone Green, was based in a converted warehouse overlooking the Longhampton canal. She had the smallest office, just one large room full of her mood boards and two old maps of the area on the bare brick wall, but it had the best windows, stretching around two sides of the room.

On a good day she could sit and watch the tawny ducks with their strings of ducklings weave along the bank, battling stoically against the wind. On a less than good day she could gaze down at the iron-grey water and wonder how many shopping trolleys had passed under the bridge since the last barge had cruised through in 1934.

Whatever the weather, Gina liked staring out of the long window at the leisurely ripples of the water. When she had awkward phone calls to make to the planning department about her clients' projects, and five different tradesmen's diaries to mesh together, and frazzled homeowners to calm down, the canal put things in perspective: winter came and went, the ducks always returned. Something about the shapes picked out in the brickwork on the opposite bank made her feel better, too: there was no need for the ornamental work there, not on an industrial canal, but some Victorian architect had clearly thought it worth doing. When the flat grey water mirrored the pale diamonds, Gina found the energy to chase up the most tedious final details. One day they might matter too.

A month after she'd been made redundant by the council, Gina had taken a year's lease on the office and set up on her own as a freelance project manager for renovations like the one she'd organised on her own house. She'd dealt with enough confused applicants drowning in paperwork (usually the wrong paperwork) to know that there were people out there willing to pay someone else to handle planning applications, as well as hunt down double-booked plumbers and translate builder-ese into something understandable.

Her first job, via a recommendation from a colleague in the planning department, had been co-ordinating a barn conversion in Much Larton for a young family. The eco-barn had featured in a house-building magazine, and since then, a steady stream of work had come her way, mainly via the builders she'd used herself, none of whom particularly enjoyed dealing direct with inexperienced clients. The office had been Stuart's idea. When she'd signed the unit-rental contract, Gina had immediately felt a lurch of terror and pride that she hadn't had when she'd signed the wedding register or the mortgage agreement for her own house. This was hers. Her vision, her responsibility.

Downstairs, there was a communal kitchen area with a microwave, a kettle and a cupboard for mugs next to a noticeboard that occasionally had a handwritten note about items for sale. As the year wore on, Gina got to know the others in the units above and below: Sara the wedding planner, Josh and Tom, the web designers, David the tax accountant. They shared a nervy camaraderie, joking as the kettle boiled about the madness of setting up on their own in a recession. Sara was a brisk networker and chair of Longhampton Women In Business; she had organised a Christmas party at the pizza place nearby, and after a few glasses of wine, Gina had gazed at her random office-mates with real affection. They were all loners like her, escapees from bigger workplaces where they had never quite fitted in. But she drew the line at joining the pub quiz team Sara set up. After the constant hum of speculation about everyone and everything that had buzzed round the planning department, she liked the sense of being almost in an office but not quite.

If I were going back into Planning now, she thought, as she let herself into the foyer with her swipe card for the first time since she'd moved into her new flat, they'd be like lemmings peering over their cubicles trying to work out what was wrong that I'd had to have time off work. There'd be a sweepstake on how long I had to live by lunchtime.

Gina pushed open the door to the kitchen, thankful that she didn't have to run the gamut of what she'd called the Coffee Coven back at the council, particularly Sheila the office manager and her 'Are you okay, hon?' eagle eyes that never missed an absent engagement ring or blood-test plaster. Naomi had told her to ignore the murmurs in the kitchen when she'd first returned after her sick leave, but she couldn't: once you were labelled, that was it. You weren't you, you were the Thing That You'd Done. She was the Cancer Survivor. It could have been worse: her old colleague Roger was Mr Thai Bride, even though Ling, his wife, was actually from Wolverhampton.

She'd come in early this morning, but from the faint sound of Radio 1 in the unit above, the web designers had beaten her. Gina opened the crockery cupboard and lifted the jute bag full of mugs onto the counter. She hadn't told Naomi the whole truth about her mug purge: yes, she'd given a lot to the charity shops, but there had been some she couldn't bring herself to throw away. Fifteen, in total, sitting in mug limbo under the sink.

Gina didn't intentionally collect mugs, just as she didn't intentionally collect scarves, or wooden spoons, but there was something about them that she couldn't resist. They were like postcards, keeping a reminder of happy times in her everyday life: the 'I ♥ NY' mug from her first trip there with Naomi, the Oxford University mug, the Love and Kisses cup that had been her first Valentine's present from

Stuart. Echoes of her old life that were too personal to spot, unwanted, on the shelves in the Oxfam shop but too personal to keep in her new flat, reminding her of what she'd lost.

Gina lined them up in the crockery cupboard, and stood back. To her surprise, they already felt a bit less personal. They looked . . . random. She frowned. A bit ugly.

As she stared at their jarring colours and slogans, something slowly loosened its grip on her heart. Once David had made his newest client a coffee in the 'I ♥ NY' mug, she wouldn't own it any more. It wouldn't mean she and Naomi hadn't been there, that they hadn't clutched each other in fits of giggles at the gusts of hot air from the subway, and at the fire hydrants and yellow cabs, everything just like the movies. Gina remembered the giddiness of that long weekend with a sudden pang; there'd never be another trip like the ones she and Naomi had made in their carefree, careless twenties. That time had gone.

There was a commotion outside the kitchen window as a man and his dog jogged past on the towpath. The little white terrier set the ducks quacking on the canal, its joyful barks ricocheting off the red-brick walls.

Gina peered out to check her duck family were OK, and when she turned back to the cupboard, it was as if the mugs had always been there in the office. A collection of random office mugs. Familiar, friendly. Someone else's. She took a deep breath, and felt another piece of her past floating away. She wouldn't miss this one.

The faint lightness of a good mood crept around her, as she pinned her list of kitchen gadgets for sale (most of her wedding list) to the noticeboard, then went upstairs to start the first Monday of her new life.

The morning sun streamed in an uplifting lemony wash through the tall warehouse window on the landing, but there were only four letters and a lot of junk mail in the pigeonhole outside her door, which put a dampener on Gina's mood.

She was trying not to worry but January had been quiet. There'd been the usual burst of activity before Christmas, mainly wives calling her at the end of their tether, determined to get unfinished DIY projects tidied away before the family arrived, but apart from some conversations about a listed-building renovation in Rosehill that sounded problematic already, Gina didn't have much lined up. She hadn't had the energy to chase leads as she'd done in the autumn, when work was the only thing that blotted out the growing sense of impending doom that swamped her the second she put her key in the door at Dryden Road at the end of each day. So far Gina's diary for February contained only the pencilled dates of her meetings with her solicitor, and a project Naomi had commissioned before Christmas – a timber outhouse for their garden that would be half a playhouse for Willow and half a man-house for Jason, their joint birthday present in April. The file on that was already half as thick as a finished project, thanks to Naomi's very specific instructions.

Gina sorted through her in-tray, filed her receipts for the previous week, then turned to the paperwork she'd brought from home. There were some letters that were better dealt with here than in her new place. She had started to feel quite protective of her fresh white nest, and its growing clear spaces.

The envelope was franked with the name of the other big firm of solicitors in Longhampton, the one she wasn't using. Gina took a deep breath and opened it. It ran to several pages, three of which were checklists. Stuart, it seemed, had changed his mind about 'keeping things amicable' and was now going for the sort of forensic examination of their joint finances usually conducted by the meaner outposts of HM Revenue and Customs.

Gina blinked in dismay at the pages, unable to reconcile this man with the soppy new boyfriend who'd surprised her with the Love and Kisses mug. Thank God I don't have to look at that any more, she thought. Before the memory of the rose petals that had filled it swam into proper focus, the phone rang.

She grabbed it, relieved. 'Hello, Stone Green Project Management—'

'Good morning. Am I speaking to Gina Horsfield?' It was a woman's voice. She sounded pleasant but no nonsense, and Gina hoped this wasn't anything to do with her last tax return.

'Yes.' She shoved the letter under a catalogue from a stationery supplier so she wouldn't have to be reminded of Stuart's demands to see her pension provision, then something made her add, 'It's actually Gina Bellamy.'

'Oh, I'm sorry? I'm looking at your feature here online and it says Gina Horsfield.'

From that, Gina knew there were two possible online

features the caller could have been looking at. One was the interiors spread featuring an unusually tidy Dryden Road, showcasing her 'faithful but very personal renovation of a four-bedroom Victorian family home', Stuart in crisp chinos, her in a polka-dot pinny. The cats standing in for the 'family'. The other was the eco-barn. Gina sort of hoped they'd be discussing the barn. 'Yes, well, it was then. It's Bellamy now.' She made an 'argh' face at the window. That didn't sound right either. Gina Bellamy had plaits, or a student-union pint glass in her hand. But, then, she'd only been Gina Bellamy since she was eleven when Terry had formally adopted her. Maybe she should go right back to Gina Pritchard now. But who was Gina Pritchard? She barely knew who Huw Pritchard had been.

A sudden swaying sensation rushed through her, a feeling of being unattached to anything.

'Still Stone Green, though! How can I help you?' she asked quickly.

'I'm looking for a project manager to help me with a renovation in your area. My name's Amanda Rowntree, I've just been looking at your house in *25 Dream Homes*, and it's really lovely.' There was the sound of a mouse clicking. 'Definitely a dream home. And no hand-stitched bunting in sight, which is a plus.'

Gina's heart sank. It was Dryden Road. She made herself think positively about it: it *had* been a lovely place. 'Thank you. I'm not a big fan of bunting.'

'And I like the way you've brought out the period features but at the same time not made it look . . . cutesy. It actually looks like a real person lives there, not Miss Marple or Jane

Austen or someone.' More clicking. 'The kitchen's great. Is it Fired Earth?'

'No, it was made specially for us by a local carpenter.' Gina tried not to think about her soft-closing tulipwood cabinets, her butcher's block. 'I designed it myself with him. We worked out exactly how far I needed to reach from the oven to those handmade cooling racks for cakes and roasts. It's not that much more expensive to get things exactly as you want them, and details are what make it *your* house, in the end.'

'Perfect. That's just what I wanted to hear. I need someone with a good eye for detail because ours is going to be a big renovation, and I'm not going to be able to spend as much time as I want on site, unfortunately.'

'That's not a problem,' said Gina. 'I'm a bit of a detail freak. I named my company after my favourite paint shade in that house. The pantry?'

'Did you? Ah, I see the one you mean. Nice. Well, to be honest, the décor's the least of our problems at the moment.' Amanda was starting to sound a little more relaxed. 'We bought the property several months ago and, what with one thing or another, we've only just got the plans back from the architect and it looks like it's going to be more complicated than we initially thought.'

'It's listed?' Gina started flipping through the various local properties that fell under that heading. There were a handful of big houses, mostly in the leafy outskirts of Longhampton, but they didn't come on the market often. Ashington Hall? The Dower House?

'How did you know? Yes, it is. Grade Two.'

'Oh. Well, that will make things more complicated. The preservation element can get a bit tricky, but it's very rewarding in the end. Listed buildings are full of stories – you're not just buying a house, you're living in a little moment of history.'

'Have you had much experience with them?'

'Yes, I've project-managed several listed renovations for clients who felt they needed some extra support with the red tape. And actually, I used to work on the other side of the fence, as it were, in the council planning department.'

There was a long groan at the other end, which told Gina exactly where Amanda had got to already with her application: the Listed Building Consent form.

'No, don't panic! I've always felt quite strongly that houses are supposed to be lived in, whatever their age,' she went on. 'You can't create museums, you've got to work out ways of supporting them as living spaces. Old houses can be surprisingly robust. The fact that they're still standing says a lot.'

She meant it too. There'd been plenty of snippy inter-departmental emails between her boss, Ray, and the conservation officers, about which was more important: the building or the human beings living in it. Gina had always tried to find ways to keep everyone happy. Secretly, she'd been on the side of the houses, but not for the same reasons as the conservation purists. Houses without people in them felt lonely to her. Humans were the blood moving around their rooms, the air in their chimneys, the sound of laughter and conversation in their halls. What was the point of keeping them intact but lifeless?

Amanda Rowntree made a hmm noise. 'Well, this one doesn't seem that robust. It's going to need a lot of work, according to the architect.'

'They all say that. Have you engaged a builder yet?'

'No. No, my architect's in London but I thought it'd be a good idea to get local builders and a local project manager. You know the reliable tradesmen and you'd co-ordinate them so it's as efficient as possible. And it's nice to have that continuity within the house. Local craftsmen and materials and so on.'

'It is,' agreed Gina. They'd probably also be cheaper than a team of London trades. Amanda didn't sound like the kind of owner who'd have missed that advantage. She pulled out her day book and opened it to a fresh page, her mood lifting with the prospect of a decent project. This was karma, rewarding her mug sacrifice with some work. 'So tell me more about the house. What period is it?'

'It's a mish-mash. Some Georgian, some Victorian. Some maybe older. Seven bedrooms, not enough bathrooms, some nice outbuildings, which we're hoping to get planning permission to convert into a studio for my husband . . .'

'Recording studio?'

'No, he's a photographer.'

'Oh, really? How interesting.'

'Mm.' Amanda brushed over it before Gina could ask what kind of photography. Obviously it wasn't *that* interesting in the circles she moved in. 'Anyway, he'll be there most of the time to oversee the work, answer questions, and so on. I'm based in London but I'm abroad a lot, and my diary is really hectic for the rest of this year. Obviously I want to be as involved as I can be but . . .' Her voice trailed off as if this required no further explanation.

'Well, sometimes it's better to be off site while it's chaotic,' said Gina. 'You can keep in touch with Skype and FaceTime . . .'

'No, I mean it's more that I'm busy than not in the country,' said Amanda. 'I can't leave meetings to make decisions about electrical sockets. I need someone I can rely on to do that for me.'

Not the husband? Maybe he was the sort of arty photographer who didn't get involved in electrical sockets. Or maybe he was too busy as well. Gina pushed it to one side: it was a mistake to pre-judge clients. 'I think the best thing is for us to have a meeting at the property so I can get a sense of what you're aiming to achieve,' she said. 'You've had a look at my website, but I can send you some more details of other projects I've worked on, if you'd like to see what experience I've got with similar houses.'

'That would be great. I'm going to be back in Longhampton on . . .' more clicking, and a muffled hand-over-phone instruction to an assistant '. . . on Thursday morning to meet the conservation officer for some – what he calls – guidance.' There was a pause and when Amanda spoke again she sounded almost despairing. 'Just for my own information . . . Do they treat everyone as if you're about to bulldoze the house and build a car park over the top?'

'Generally, yes.' Gina could guess exactly which conservation officer Amanda had spoken to: Keith Hurst. Or 'Hurst Case Scenario', as he was known in the office, on account of his oft-repeated theory that a good conservation officer assumed the worst and worked backwards. 'But don't worry, I know how to handle them.'

'Really?'

'Really. Would you like me to arrange to have a builder come out too?' Gina woke up her laptop, checking to see when Lorcan Hennessey was back from his holiday. He was her first-choice builder: thorough, easy-going, and sympathetic to the quirks of old houses. 'I've got a couple of experienced foremen I've worked with on listed properties. They could give you some idea of costs, maybe put the conservation officer's mind at rest that you're not bringing in the bulldozers.'

'You're going to need more than that with this guy. When I told him I was based in London, he almost shut the conversation down then and there.'

'Oh dear.' Gina knew what that was about: Hartstone Hall out by Much Larton, bought by a London developer, green-lit by Keith, abandoned after six months, due to lack of cash. Fifteen years ago. It still rankled. 'But I can help you shape your application so it's as appealing as possible from their point of view. We can talk about it. No obligation, obviously.'

'Thanks. It's not as if we're planning to *ruin* the place. I just want to be able to *live* in it.'

'I know exactly what you mean. So whereabouts is the house?' Gina's mouse clicked on her favourite property website; she was normally obsessive about monitoring the local fantasy home market but she'd lost track of it a bit lately.

'I'll send you a link. It's called the Magistrate's House.'

Gina's hand stopped moving. Of course it would be the Magistrate's House. Her heart plunged inside her chest like a shot bird, falling blackly into the pit of her stomach. The elegantly proportioned double façade of the Magistrate's House rose in front of her mind's eye, three storeys, with long Georgian windows, red-streaked ivy winding around the central porthole window, the old brickwork now cleaned and repointed, the sashes replaced and the glass polished . . . 'I didn't know that was on the market,' she said.

'No? We found it through a private search agency. It might not have been advertised. Is it a house you know?'

'Um, yes.' Gina swallowed. First someone else had snaffled her husband from under her nose, now someone else had bagged her dream house. 'It's one of the nicest properties in the area. One of the oldest. I've always . . . always liked it. Congratulations. It's got the potential to be stunning.'

'Good.' Amanda seemed pleased. 'Well, I'll email over some contact details, and I'll look forward to meeting you on Thursday.'

'You too,' said Gina, but Amanda had hung up while she was still staring out at the canal, where two interloping seagulls were skimming greedily across the water. They seemed too big for the canal, too opaque and white. The ducks were nowhere to be seen.

A few minutes later, Amanda's email popped up on the corner of Gina's screen with directions and notes, but Gina didn't need a map reference – she knew exactly where the house was.

The Magistrate's House lay on the outskirts of a village

called Langley St Michael, and its location – opposite the old Norman church and surrounded by cider-apple orchards, untouched by modern estates or mobile phone masts – summed up its comfortable position in the social hierarchy of the area. Most of Langley St Michael was a designated conservation area; houses there were lovingly returned to their former lime-rendered glory, not improved with extensions. If anything, extensions were discreetly nipped off, like unsightly warts.

Gina knew the history of the Magistrate's House; she'd traced it at her council desk, while pretending to update her project files. It had been the family seat of the Warwicks, wealthy eighteenth-century wine merchants who'd first imported sherry and Madeira into the county, and exported the local cider. The house had been passed proudly from one red-nosed Sir Henry to another, until a persistent outbreak of daughters had disrupted the line in the middle of Queen Victoria's reign, and it had been sold to a Birmingham couple who'd made their substantial fortune in bicycle parts. They'd had no children to carry it through the strained post-war years, and during the Blitz, clutches of bewildered refugees from London had been packed into makeshift dorms where housemaids had once slept three to a bed. In the Fifties, a local doctor had rolled up his sleeves and taken on the now shabby house, and it had become the epicentre of cocktail parties and parish-council meetings, until his widow had sold it after his death in 1998. A developer had proposed converting it into a hotel but plans had (been) stalled, twice, and the Magistrate's House had slowly fallen into a state of magnificent decay.

Gina and Stuart had been out to see the house three times, once with the estate agent, once with her mother, who had loved the address but shuddered at the damp wine cellars ('Too dark, and that pond's dangerous for children') and once with their builder, Lorcan. Like Gina, Lorcan saw the possibilities in ramshackle buildings, and talked about them as if they were wayward old relatives who could be set right with a bit of attention.

'She's in a rough state now, but she's got great bones,' he'd said, patting a flaking window frame, and Gina, her heart already decorating the grand master bedroom in draped brocades, knew what he meant. It was a handsome house, even in its unloved, morning-after state. It just needed a family to wake it up, to transfuse it with life.

Stuart hadn't felt the same. Everything she had loved about the place rang alarm bells for him. The complicated roof. The decaying sash windows. The listed status. He wasn't wrong, which made it even worse. And the timing had been terrible: a few weeks later, she'd had her diagnosis, and Stuart's third reaction, after 'Shit' and 'Let's get married right now', had actually been, 'Thank God we didn't buy that money-pit in Langley.'

Gina stared, unseeing, at Amanda's email. Dryden Road had probably been the right house to buy. It had been straightforward, habitable, if gloomy, during the grinding months of Gina's chemotherapy, and then, when she had finally recovered enough to go back to work, renovating its square Victorian rooms had given her and Stuart enough conversation to fill the strange anti-climax that had followed her final sign-off at the hospital.

But when it was done, Gina thought, it was done. The house had been the helpful third person in their marriage, the one who'd kept them together, jollying them along with discussions about mixer taps and pendant lights when they'd had nothing else to say to each other. All the while the Magistrate's House had lingered in Gina's mind, the one that got away. The might-have-been house.

And now it was someone else's.

Chapter Five

ITEM: a green Victorian witch-ball on a long
brass chain, for hanging in a hallway to lure
and trap any lurking evil spirits

Langley St Michael, March 2010

Gina looks down at the witch-ball she's holding and sees
her own face reflected back at her, green, like Glinda
the good witch.

The witch-ball had been given to her by a nice old lady
she'd advised about re-roofing an old farm cottage out near
Rosehill. The hollyhocks and foxgloves in the garden had
reminded Gina of a gingerbread house and, she'd found
out over several cups of tea, the cottage had been in Mrs
Hubert's family since the land around it was all farmed,
something she could remember herself. She'd helped with
the harvest as a little girl.

'Apples and pears, right up to St Mary's Church on the
hill! And the dray horses grazing where that hospital is
now!' she'd said, as if she could still see their feathery hooves
out of the corner of her pale eye.

Ever since then, Gina has seen St Mary's Road into

Longhampton through a different filter. She likes the way houses capture their moment in history, imprinting crinolines and flat caps to the landscape while time and change wash around them, like the tide. Then, when they're fragile and at risk of being lost, Gina can save them *and* the tissue layer of the past over the present day, iron boot scrapers keeping the rasp of muddy button boots alive next to Internet cable covers.

But no sooner had Mrs Hubert got her roof finished than she'd had a fall, the children had appeared from Bristol to sweep her off to residential care and the house was sold. The skinny lass who'd picked pears in the perry orchards that lay underneath Meadows Shopping Mall was now sitting in the converted drawing room of the house once owned by Longhampton's jam magnates. Gina wonders whether Mrs Hubert can see the former residents floating in surprise through the new stud walls, indignant at the descendants of farmers and housemaids inhabiting their family home.

The witch-ball is from the cottage, of course. Long before the fall, before Mrs Hubert's house was cleared for auction, the old lady had hidden it in the back of Gina's car, and wouldn't listen when Gina tried to give it back. Accepting gifts was absolutely, totally against all council rules. She'd offered to buy it, anxious not to hurt her feelings, but Mrs Hubert had refused outright. 'It's terrible bad luck, dear!' she said. 'You can only give them away, look.' The hands had folded over hers. Bird-like, so translucent that the blue veins and the spreading coffee-brown liver spots merged, but strong. 'And none of us need go looking for more bad luck, do we?' she'd added, with a squeeze that made Gina wonder how much of her mind Mrs Hubert could read.

And so she'd guiltily driven home to Dryden Road with a genuine Victorian witch-ball in the boot. It was the most perfect witch-ball Gina had ever seen: about the size of a Galia melon, a rich festive green with a burnished brass loop at the top, like a giant Christmas tree bauble, so it could be hung by the door, ready to lure a malevolent spirit then trap it in the strands of filigree glass inside.

Gina looks at the witch-ball now, in her lap. She really wanted to hang it in the hallway, above the encaustic tiles she's been regrouting, but Stuart doesn't want it in the house; he thinks it's superstitious nonsense. After the experience Gina's had of dry facts, of single-minded chemical truths, she wants to make a bit more room in her world for superstition, but Stuart's adamant, and his flat refusal to see the beauty in it pinches out another guttering flame inside her.

Gina isn't sure why she's brought her witch-ball to the Magistrate's House. She isn't even sure why she's here now. She and Stuart looked at dozens of other properties before they bought Dryden Road, but this was the one place that filled her with its energy. Even now, Gina feels a connection with it, a need to know its forgotten stories. In the middle of the night, jarred out of sleep by thoughts that go round and round in circles, she'd had a strange, romantic picture of hanging the witch-ball in the abandoned doorway, leaving it for the lucky person who buys the crumbling house and turns it back into the family home that she can see hovering over the broken shell like a ghostly negative. The house needs protecting until it can attract a new family.

It could have been them. Gina loses herself in her favourite private fantasy of what might have been, imagining herself floating through the garden, now landscaped and not overgrown with weeds; she's rosy-cheeked and healthy, snipping dead heads off the fondant-coloured roses that form banks of drifting scent between the drive and the house.

She pictures herself in the cool, cream-tiled kitchen, making apple pies with deft, floury hands; Stuart in the book-lined study, transformed into an enthusiastic reader of Victorian fiction; both of them in the bedroom, in a brass-framed bed, passion licking and burning between them again like the first purple flames of the coal fire in the tiled hearth. It's idyllic but not impossible. They'd have grown with the house, she thinks, they'd have stretched up to match its convivial dining room and welcoming hall.

Gina rubs her eyes, suddenly tired. In the fantasy, she and the house are always sharper than Stuart, and obviously she never gets cancer. It's been nine months since her final appointment with Mr Khan. There are no signs of her original cancer, and the chances of it coming back, as long as she's on the daily Tamoxifen, are 'very low, in a woman your age'. Stuart had taken them all out for a celebration dinner; Jason and Naomi had bought champagne; Janet had cried with relief. Everyone had felt relief, apart from Gina.

Gina just felt, secretly, that a bigger balance had been squared. She was back to zero. Twenty-nine, and back to zero.

She looks down at the witch-ball, gleaming in her lap like a magical pea. It's a stupid idea to leave it here. It's a delicate thing, just old silvered glass – an easy target for a kid with an air rifle. As she moves, the light shifts on it, and Gina shivers at the thought of seeing another face behind her.

Gina had always thought a witch-ball was supposed to trap spirits but Mrs Hubert said it was to warn you of any witches creeping up on you. This is a fresh start but there are lots of things behind her. Like Mrs Hubert, Gina thinks it's better to be able to see them than to pretend they're not there.

It wasn't the best day to see the house. The local radio weather forecast was promising early rain that would make the damp feel damper and the halls seem darker, but as Gina turned down the short tree-lined drive, a burst of sunshine emerged from behind the clouds, and her heart fluttered at the sight of the red roof rising above the trees, the symmetrical chimney stacks at each end.

She parked her red Golf next to the array of cars already assembled along the gravel turn: a black Range Rover, a BMW estate, and the council's pool Astra. No sign of Lorcan's van yet.

Good, she thought, getting out. She'd deliberately arrived ten minutes early so that she had time to gather herself, put the old dreams firmly away, before she went in.

As she headed towards the terraced lawns at the side of the house, Gina's expert eye spotted signs of deterioration since she'd last been there. There were some tiles missing off the roof, and two of the crenellated chimney pots were visibly leaning. The mental calculator in her head started clicking: she was well over fifty thousand pounds before she'd even looked lower than the roofline.

Fixing damage was one thing, but Gina knew that even when you'd arrested decay, houses like these had expensive tastes. Agas that burned great quantities of oil, grounds that demanded weekly gardeners, and a heart that had to be stoked with atmosphere and activity, as well as furniture. You needed the social life, too. Weekending friends, their children and dogs; mellow, wine-warmed autumn dinners in the kitchen; village book groups in the drawing room; and ebullient New Year's Eves spilling into the candlelit garden. Those high ceilings would have echoed the silence of two people who barely spoke to each other down to them, reproach lingering, like dust, in every unused spare room.

Gina walked round the gravel path and stopped by a stone bench, positioned to give the best view of the house from one side, as well as a sweeping panorama of the terraced gardens from the other. She gazed at the beautiful lines of the front elevation, trying to flush any lingering traces of regret from her system before she met Amanda. She'd already warned Lorcan not to say anything about her own interest in the place; he'd understood.

This house would have ruined Stuart and me, Gina reminded herself, unable to stop searching for more signs of structural damage she didn't really want to find, the same way you'd half hope, half dread to see wrinkles on the face of a still-attractive ex.

The sun went behind a cloud, and Gina felt an unexpected loneliness, for Stuart and the happiness they'd once had. There had been happiness. He *had* carried her over the threshold of their first place together, joked about nurseries and trampolines ruining his lawn. She'd never get that time back: it was gone. Those chances had been blown. Gina let the sadness run through her for a moment rather than fight it: it dissipated faster that way.

From the outside, she thought, blinking tears away hard, it'll just look like I'm taking in the project. That's fine.

She heard a van door slam, and the sound of boots crunch on the gravel, but didn't turn because her eyelashes were wet. The steps came nearer, and Gina was aware of a solid male presence behind her, one that smelt of a light, lemony aftershave and clean clothes. It didn't say anything, which confirmed her suspicions about who it was.

'Morning, Lorcan,' she said. 'Just putting some old memories to bed. Don't say anything to Amanda, will you?'

'Course not. About what?' The voice wasn't Irish. It was southern English.

Gina spun round. The man standing behind her was wearing jeans and a Pixies T-shirt under a half-zipped fleece, with a builder's bag slung over one shoulder. She didn't recognise him, but Lorcan had said he might bring along a few 'trades' to advise on specialist work and, like Lorcan himself, most of his mates were of the old band T-shirt persuasion.

'Oh, er, nothing,' she said. 'I'm just . . . just . . .'

'Just looking. I know. It's a lovely old place.' He dumped the bag and took a step nearer, standing next to her with his arms folded, his head tilted to take in the view. 'You can almost see them wafting out of those french windows, spot of croquet on the front lawn, fancy hats and boaters . . .'

'Pimm's in hand, light music playing inside.' Gina paused. 'Weather permitting. You don't tend to picture the endless afternoons playing Scrabble while it's too wet to go out, do you?'

'Ha! Indeed you don't. But isn't that when you imagine the roaring log fire and eight-foot Douglas pine with teeny tiny candles? And urchins arriving for the annual mince pie and half a crown in the kitchens?'

Gina liked this game: she played it herself. 'Ah, yes. Chestnuts roasting on the hearth, and the ominous letters arriving from the Front? Brought in on a silver tray during a raucous cocktail party?' She mimed a gramophone needle screeching to a stop.

He tipped his head to one side, considering. 'Would that tray be carried by the faithful old retainer butler with the hunch? Or by the parlourmaid who is secretly in love with the youngest son now in a million pieces at the Front?'

Gina laughed, and glanced across at him. He was good-looking: dark hair, flecked with early silver streaks at the temples, and grey eyes framed with dark lashes and thick brows. He looked a bit like Lorcan, and Gina wondered if they were cousins. There were a lot of cousins in Lorcan's family, most of them builders of some description. Or roadies. Or both.

'Or am I thinking of *Downton Abbey*?' he added, with a pretend frown.

Gina smiled back. It made it so much easier to deal with contractors if they had a sense of humour.

'It's nicer than Downton Abbey,' she said. 'It's big, but it's manageable without butlers. It's going to be lovely.'

'You reckon?'

'It needs a lot doing to it, sure,' she said, 'but I hope they're not going to use that as an excuse to start hacking it about.'

'How do you mean?'

'Oh, you know, some architects claim it's impossible to repair, so they might as well knock things down and put in glass extensions and sunken rooms and that sort of thing. Not that they'll get permission,' she added, in case the architect had been getting ideas and promising the builders extra work.

'No?' He seemed interested.

'It's on a list of significant local buildings so the council will have strong opinions about anything that damages the historic fabric. Hopefully I can find a way around it so everyone's happy, but to be honest, I'll be advising them to renovate sensitively. Don't want to dislodge the ghosts of any bereaved parlourmaids. Or disgruntled butlers.'

He raised an eyebrow. 'You're the project manager. Of course. Sorry, for a minute there I thought you might be from the council.'

'Nope. What gave it away?'

'The sense of humour?'

'Ha,' said Gina. 'Busted. Well, *hopefully* I'm the project manager. I'm just here for a preliminary meeting to discuss the job.'

'It sounds as if you already know quite a lot about this house.'

Something in the man's voice made Gina look at him properly, instead of the house. He was shading his eyes with his hand, and suddenly a penny dropped.

The hands were smooth, not coarse and nicked like a builder's. He was dressed like a builder, but there was a chunky submariner's watch on one tanned wrist and his fleece didn't have the usual company logo on it. Or much brick dust. Historic buildings tended to attract the more artisan specialists – gentleman lime plasterers, cabinetmakers who only worked on Duchy estates – but even so . . .

'Sorry, I don't think we've met before,' said Gina. 'Are you with Lorcan?'

He smiled, and pushed the hair out of his eyes, squinting into the light. 'I didn't realise I carried a bag of tools so convincingly. No, I'm Nick. You're going to be helping me not to ruin this house. Well, I hope you are, anyway. Nick Rowntree. Hello.'

Gina felt the blood drain from her face. How long had she been off work to start making unprofessional gaffes like that? What had happened to her *brain*? 'I'm so sorry, I didn't mean to sound rude. It's just that I've worked with clients before who bring an architect up from London with ideas about . . .' Her gaze dropped to the notes she'd brought with her: they had a London architect. Of course. Probably a London audio specialist and a London lighting specialist too.

Gina closed her eyes and counted to five. She was running on three hours' sleep as it was. The previous evening she'd opened the first of her three wardrobe boxes to start sorting through stuff she'd never wear again, and handling clothes she'd forgotten she even owned had shaken out memories like bats. Shoes she'd danced in at other people's weddings. Dresses she'd worn on early dates with Stuart. Jeans still stained with beer from student gigs. Old skins that didn't fit, but that she'd kept because throwing them away felt like throwing away part of herself.

Three. Four.

Her wedding suit. Her apricot bridesmaid's dress.

Five.

When she opened her eyes, Nick was looking at her, amused. He offered her his hand, and this time she spotted the gold wedding band, the fine plaited leather bracelet. 'There's really no need to be embarrassed,' he said, seeing her awkwardness. 'I completely agree with you. This house needs someone who understands old properties. That's why Amanda wanted to get in a proper project manager, instead of struggling through it ourselves.'

Gina fumbled with her files, trying to free up a hand to offer him. 'Gina Horsf—' The name stuck in her throat. Again. She'd done it again. 'Gina Bellamy.'

Nick grasped her hand, shaking it firmly. His own was warm and dry, and she focused on it to distract herself from the blush spreading across her face. 'Congratulations,' he said. 'Just married?'

'The opposite, actually. I'm in the process of getting divorced.' She winced. 'Sorry. This really isn't going well, is it?'

'No, no. *I'm* sorry now. Although . . .' there was a faint

twinkle in the grey eyes '. . . maybe the congratulations still stand?'

'Maybe,' she said politely, and glanced down at her watch. Twenty-five to ten. 'Sorry, I was supposed to be meeting Amanda at half past so we should go in. I don't want to make a bad impression so soon. Well, *another* bad impression . . .'

'Why? Our meeting started at half past, outside, with a discussion of the exterior.' Nick swung the tool bag back over his shoulder and they set off towards the house.

'You haven't started knocking anything down already, I hope?' she said, with a nod to the bag. 'Before you've got permission and all that?'

'This? Just digging the foundations for the swimming pool in the cellar. I'm thinking it's easier to let the damp take over properly. Deep end's going to be where the champagne cellar is now.'

Gina opened her mouth, then realised he was winding her up.

'No,' he said. 'I'm putting a table together so I've got something to set up my printer on. I'm joking.'

'Don't try joking with the conservation officer,' she said. 'That's my first piece of advice. He doesn't respond well to humour.'

'He doesn't respond well to anything as far as I can see.'

'He responds well to logic and reason,' said Gina. 'And detailed knowledge of building regs.'

She knew Nick was looking at her with a wry smile, but she didn't turn her head. Instead, she concentrated on getting her face together and getting this job.

★ ★ ★

They didn't go in through the front door ('There's something wrong with the hinges. It's rotten, basically'). Instead Nick showed Gina round to the back of the house, over a paved courtyard garden to the long stone-flagged kitchen. The little herb beds were neglected, but she spotted ancient shells marking out patches for vegetables, old copper labels, a few cracked pots. Some cook had once filled the kitchen from the beds.

Gina could see figures through the musty windows: a man, whom she knew immediately from the tweed jacket was Keith Hurst, and a pale woman in a long cream cardigan with honey-blonde hair swept off her face in a perfectly straight fall. Film-star hair.

'Amanda, sorry, I've delayed your project manager.' Nick pushed open the kitchen door and ushered her inside. Most of the furniture had been removed, but the room was dominated by a massive oak table that looked as if it had been made in the house, and a black triple Aga at the far end. 'My fault. I was sharing my croquet visions.'

'Croquet is *so* far down our list of priorities,' said Amanda, at the same time as Keith Hurst said, 'Of course we do have records that croquet was played here before the war . . . Oh, hello, Gina.'

'Hello, Keith.' Gina smiled at him. 'Nice to see you again.'

He made a grunting noise that wasn't quite yes, and took a red hanky out to blow his nose loudly, a habit that Gina had almost forgotten until now.

Amanda Rowntree stepped out from behind the table, and Gina felt her attention sweep over her, from her knitted hat to her green boots. Amanda had assessing eyes. Cool and blue, with immaculate brown flicks of eyeliner, perfectly angled at the ends. 'Hello, Gina, I'm Amanda Rowntree,' she said, holding out a pale hand, with a chunky diamond ring that slipped round her slim finger as she shook Gina's. 'Thanks for coming. It's good to meet you.'

The voice was the one Gina remembered from the phone conversation but she hadn't pictured Amanda like this. She'd imagined a rather hard-faced executive with a grey suit and sleek bob, not a yoga blonde in cashmere and skinny jeans.

'Who are we waiting for now?' asked Keith, with a self-important check of his watch. 'I've got several sites to visit today.'

'Just the builder,' said Gina. 'Lorcan said he'd be here as soon as—'

As she spoke, there was a brisk knock at the front door.

'Perfect timing,' said Nick. 'Or psychic ability.'

'Which is exactly what you want in a builder,' said Gina, and Keith snorted.

'Good,' said Amanda, with a smile. She felt in her back pocket for a phone, checked it, then turned it to silent. 'Why don't we start the tour of the house at the front door? Seems logical. I've got to be at the airport by two, so let's get on.'

She swept out of the room, leaving Nick, Gina and Keith to glance at each other, then follow her like ducklings.

Amanda might not be wearing a suit now, Gina decided, as she hurried down the hall after Amanda's retreating back, but she almost certainly did when she wasn't there.

The Rowntrees' plans for the house were the usual mixture of common-sense renovation and wildly ambitious let's-chance-it punts that Keith intimated very firmly would not be permitted by the council.

The proposed extension to the kitchen, with state-of-the-art eco-glass and solar panels, met with sharp intakes of breath, as did the wooden guest chalet where the orangery had stood. The architect hadn't been able to make the meeting, which meant that Keith and, to a more diplomatic extent, Gina were able to be completely honest about his plans, something that she could tell amused Nick much more than Amanda.

Keith led the way round the house, photographing everything he deemed to be of historical interest, and making it plain to Gina, if not Amanda, that he'd noticed the single-glazed windows, the moulded details on the ceilings, the awkward beams – anything, essentially, that they might try to sneakily remove. Meanwhile Lorcan was honest about the structural work needed to fix various problems with the exterior; Gina already knew about the damp on the west side of the house, and the rotten battens under the oak panelling. And then there was the roof, the up-rated plumbing, the complete rewiring of the ancient ('possibly quite dangerous, to be honest') electrical system . . .

She watched the Rowntrees out of the corner of her eye, trying to get a sense of what they'd be like to work with. Amanda listened, occasionally asking for clarification of some term, and nodded, her blue eyes narrowed, as the information was laid out before her. Gina could tell this wasn't the vacant, panicked nod of the uninformed owner: this was someone who already half knew the answer. Detail-focused clients could be useful, in that they knew exactly what they wanted and didn't need to have all the options carefully laid out, but they could also be a monumental pain, if what they wanted didn't exist.

Nick, on the other hand, hung behind, apparently not listening, only to ask a question out of the blue, or to take a photograph on his phone of something Gina hadn't seen. He spotted interesting details, a shelf she'd missed or a sealed-up door, and when he snapped the picture, she noticed the ghost of a smile pass over his face.

It took them two hours to go through the house, from front door to back gardens, and by the time they'd finished, Gina knew she'd never have had the money to do what the Rowntrees had in mind. The house, though, would be transformed. In a positive, historically sensitive way, Gina stressed to Keith, who made no promises but didn't put up the brick walls he might have done, had she not been there to smooth over some of Amanda's more blunt suggestions.

Keith excused himself shortly after, leaving Gina and Lorcan to return to the kitchen with the Rowntrees to deconstruct what he'd said into some sort of workable plan, which Gina could then put into a draft schedule of works, and costs.

Nick ambled over to the espresso machine to make coffee for everyone except Lorcan, who had tea, while Amanda shuffled her papers at the table, her intelligent face furrowed with concentration as she processed the vast amount of information.

'So,' she said, and something in her voice made Gina uncap her pen automatically, ready to take notes, 'what do you think?'

It was a deliberately open question, and Gina forced herself not to leap straight in with too much gushing. 'I think you could make this house sing,' she said slowly. 'It's not going to be completely straightforward to carry out some of your ideas, on account of the listing, but sometimes that's good. It makes you think laterally.'

Amanda pressed her fingertips together and stared at Gina over the top. 'But be honest. Is that man going to make our lives a living hell, telling us to preserve every loo-roll holder in the place?'

'Keith? He's just the conservation officer. The final decision will be with the planning officer in charge. But it can be tricky, yes . . .'

'That's for the project manager to worry about, eh, Gina?' Nick put a professional-looking cappuccino in front of her. 'Sorry, no silver salver.'

'There are ways around things,' she said. 'But the bottom line is that if you wanted an old shell to put a modern house in, then this might not have been the one to pick. But I suppose it's a bit late now for that.'

'Yes,' said Amanda. 'About six months too late.'

'It's my fault,' said Nick drily. 'I fell in love with the wine cellars. And the potential. It's a project, isn't it?'

'It's a dream house,' said Gina. 'It needs owners with a bigger vision than just changing the wallpaper, and you've certainly got that.'

She wondered if there was something between the cracks in Nick's comment from the way Amanda stirred her coffee with a sort of grim determination, not meeting his gaze.

Without warning, Amanda looked up, fixing Gina with

her piercing interview eyes. 'Is there a reason it was so cheap?' she asked. 'The survey didn't seem too bad, but if there's some inside track on it with the council, then it's better if you tell us now.'

Gina shook her head. 'Nope. It just needs a lot of love. You can't cut corners with planning applications, and you're going to have people like Keith crawling all over the project, checking you're using sympathetic materials. That adds up. People round here don't have that sort of cash. Or time. It's nothing more sinister than that.'

'Shame. We were hoping for a ghost,' said Nick. He slid into the chair opposite Gina's. 'Nothing major, maybe a friendly cat.'

'Don't be ridiculous,' Amanda started, but it was Lorcan who spoke, taking everyone by surprise.

'I wouldn't rule it out.' He'd been leaning against the Aga, doing some calculations and sipping his tea. 'All old houses have a ghost or two, especially round here. Eh, Gina? Just depends how sensitive you are to them, I reckon. I wouldn't be surprised if you get a rustle of something upstairs.'

Amanda's head spun round. Gina spotted the half double-take when she met Lorcan's gaze, as if she'd only just noticed him. Despite his scruffy appearance, Lorcan was unusually lyrical for a builder: his best mate was a tour manager, and when he wasn't building houses, Lorcan was off all over Europe building stages for heavy metal bands, and lurking around Irish blues festivals.

'That's usually mice, though,' she said quickly, not wanting to put Amanda off. 'We can sort that out.'

'I hope not,' said Nick. 'What's the point of an old house without a bit of a chequered past? Might as well be living in some soulless new-build penthouse.'

He was looking at Amanda as he said it, but she was making notes and pretending she hadn't heard him. If Gina hadn't spent the last six months walking on eggshells herself, she might have missed it, but it was there, the echo of a stale row.

She didn't want to see it. That was the trouble with these projects; you often had to see the ragged plaster of the owners' relationship, as well as their house. 'So, would you like me to email you a rough schedule, with some projected costs?' she asked instead. 'If you've got meetings lined up with other project managers, that's fine.'

'There are no other meetings lined up,' said Amanda. She clicked her pen closed and picked up her coffee. 'I think you're just the woman for the job.'

'Brilliant,' said Gina, and realised it wasn't a very professional thing to say.

Nick smiled, and, after a tiny pause, so did Amanda. It was a friendly smile but it didn't fool Gina into relaxing.

Chapter Six

ITEM: lucky knickers from La Perla, black silk bikini briefs with tiny silver embroidered stars and black lace trim, size label cut out

Longhampton, 2005

Gina leans on the wall by the drinks table, nursing her glass of warm white wine, and wonders how much longer she has to stay at Naomi and Jason's housewarming party before she can leave without seeming rude. For a pair of twenty-five year olds, they're having a very grown-up party. The crisps are in a dip tray, and Naomi's coasters are much in evidence. But then everyone in Longhampton seems more grown-up than the flatsharers Gina's just left behind in Fulham.

If I stay here another hour, she thinks, I'll be in serious danger of having a conversation about mortgage rates. There isn't enough wine in the kitchen for that.

She's about to put the glass down, prior to making leaving noises, when Naomi sidles up to her in a new red dress – short, to show off her legs. Naomi has amazing legs. They're not long, but they're shapely, and end in very high heels. Jason can't stop staring at them.

'Stay,' Naomi hisses, out of the corner of her mouth, so the other three guests, sitting on the leather couch, like interviewees, don't hear over the polite sounds of Zero 7. 'Jason says the lads from football are on their way back from the pub.'

'I'm not into footballers,' says Gina, her smile fixed. 'And I've spent the last twenty minutes advising Jason's co-worker about planning permission for her loft extension. It's like being at work, but without the crazy fun times.'

'Let me get you a fresh glass,' says Naomi, loudly, and steers her into the kitchen. 'Stay another half-hour.'

'But I don't know anyone!'

'That's the whole point!' She over-enunciates the words to make up for the stage whisper. 'You've been in London for four years! This is how you meet people. And by people, I obviously mean men.'

'But I don't want . . .'

Naomi grips Gina's arms, her eyes fierce with the match-making intentions of the recently coupled-up. 'You're beautiful, you're funny, you're wearing a dress that we won't even see in the shops here for another eighteen months. You need to get out there and start dating.' A microscopic pause. 'Again.'

Gina narrows her eyes because in the kitchen everyone can hear you scream at your best friend. She knows Naomi isn't referring to her last relationship – a three-months-and-a-minibreak fiasco with Dr Adam Doherty, Unilever washing-powder researcher. Naomi means after Kit. It's been four years. They don't talk about Kit any more, but Naomi at least acknowledges his existence, unlike her mother, who refuses to refer to him at all. Janet's good at pretending things never happened.

Out of long habit, Kit's face slips into Gina's head, like a slide in a projector; she leaves it there a second, then consciously slips it out. She goes through phases of dating – she's not short of offers – but when you've been with someone who felt they'd been put on earth for the sole purpose of finding you, it's depressing to have to build up a relationship, dinner by dinner, dutifully researching each other, offering up likes and dislikes, like chess moves until one reveals something bad enough to checkmate.

'Not knowing people is *good*,' Naomi whispers. 'Believe me. You're a novelty. And you cannot leave me here with the IT department from Jason's office. I'm your *best friend*!'

'Ten minutes,' Gina mutters back, and at that moment there's a clatter at the door, and Jason roars, 'Lads!' as Naomi's face glows with relief under her highlighter and she takes the sizzling honey-roasted cocktail sausages out of the oven.

Immediately the party's atmosphere sparks into life, going from an awkward gathering of five strangers eating olives to something much more fun. Naomi's pretending to be cross with 'the boys' for being late, but Gina can tell that she's revelling in the puppyish teasing directed towards her and Jason. There are jokes about rolling pins and leashes, but it's OK because Jason is clearly happy to be under any or all parts of Naomi from the thumb onwards.

As Naomi hands out beer and sausages, the boys (*men*, Gina corrects herself) scan the room, and one or two glance her way. Gina doesn't know how to arrange her face, because she suspects Naomi is forcing them to look her way by saying things like, 'Oh, have you met my best mate who's moved back from London?' London, in Longhampton, is synonymous with snobbery, yet moving back means you've failed in some way. Lose-lose.

Gina wanted to love London, but alone without Naomi, or Kit, she couldn't find anywhere to fit in. And deep down, she didn't want to fit in: nothing felt right. So she's come home, in the hope that her life might start here instead. She smiles at Jason's mates. But the way they smile briefly, then turn back to their own group makes Gina's insides feel like they're peeling off.

She body-swerves another approach from Extension Woman, and goes back into Naomi's kitchen to pretend to look for a water glass, then considers going upstairs to the loo, but a couple she doesn't know are conducting an intense, nose-to-nose conversation on the stairs, gazing into each other's mouths while pretending to talk about *The West Wing*.

In desperation Gina goes back into the sitting room where the lads have pushed back the new couch and are now doing knees-up dancing to some Madness song, led by a red-faced Jason. *Madness*, for crying out loud, she thinks. Naomi hates Madness. She's always said they sound like a midlife crisis playing a saxophone. Jason and his mates are ten years too young for this.

Across the room Naomi grimaces, but it's all part of being in a serious relationship, as she frequently tells Gina in their long emails. Jason let her choose the wallpaper; she let him use the spare room as a home gym. God knows what she gets in return for letting him play Madness at their housewarming. Gina grimaces back but then one of the dancers stops and catches her rolling her eyes at him.

She looks away, mortified, because it would be the fittest one who caught her making that face, the good-looking one who's probably the captain. She doesn't know his name but it'll be something wholesome like Ben or Mark: Jason went to the other school in the area, Hartley High School, so all his mates feel like people Naomi and Gina know, even though they don't. This one would have been the lad Stephanie Bayliff or Claire Watson would have gone out with: he's got the Matt Damon cheekbones, teddy-bear-brown hair, the athletic frame of the sports all-rounder.

And the great legs. Gina can't help noticing. Great legs, gorgeous bum in jeans that actually fit, just-big-enough biceps under a shirt unbuttoned at the neck to reveal tanned skin.

She kicks herself for describing him in the same terms she'd have used at school. That's what coming home does to you.

He's not Gina's type at all – no glasses, no floppy indie-kid hair, not even a suit like Dr Adam Doherty – but something about his extreme handsomeness sets off a slow burn inside her. Gina's tried to persuade herself that she doesn't mind being single but according to the magazines, she should be having the time of her life, at twenty-five. And she isn't. This is the time of someone else's life – a nun, maybe. Or someone's mother. It's as if her worst fear came true: all the fun *was* concentrated in that blissful time with Kit.

And now he's coming over.

'Did I do something funny?' he asks, not angry but anxious.

His accent is local, with the lazy rural vowels that Gina's lost after years away. It's a gentle sound with softened *r*s. His eyes are fixed on hers, the pupils dilated, as if he finds her attractive, and she can't help noticing how long his eyelashes are.

She tries to summon up some repartee. It's not impossible, she tells herself. As Naomi says, he just sees the wrap dress, showcasing her best assets, and her hair in loose brown curls round her face, the dark red lipstick giving her rosebud lips, the expensive sheen on her high cheekbones. He doesn't know she's stayed in every night for the past seven months, watching soaps and learning how to tong with a hair straightener from back issues of *Cosmo*.

His expression takes on a hint of panic as realisation strikes. 'Are my flies undone?'

'No,' she says. 'Your flies are fine.' She pauses, then asks deadpan. 'Was that an attempt to get me to look at your flies?'

'No! God, no . . . not at all, sorry, I didn't mean . . .'

'I know,' says Gina. 'You're fine.'

He grins. 'Do you want to dance, then?'

'No,' says Gina, more definitely. 'And, anyway, you can't dance to Madness. You can only march on the spot. It's basically aerobics for men.'

He looks relieved. 'I hate Madness. Can I get you a drink?'

Gina holds out her empty glass. She was braced for some

deathless banter about her not dancing or him needing a teacher – but there wasn't any. Just an easy offer of a drink, the first step in the non-complicated chat-up routine. This is a lot easier than London.

Naomi's making faces at her from across the room, raising her eyebrows in that well-done gesture. Gina gives her a discreet two fingers from behind her hand – an old joke – but rearranges herself quickly when the man comes back with a fresh glass of wine.

'I'm Stuart,' he says, offering a hand. 'Mate of Jason's. We were at school together.'

'Gina. Naomi's best friend. Also at school together.' They juggle wine glasses and shake hands and Stuart grins at the cheesiness of it. He has a winning smile: his teeth are strong and white, his cheek dimpled. She feels another tug of desire. The music's changed: Naomi's obviously comman-deered the CD player and she's not known for her subtlety. Gina wonders if she *should* offer to dance; she's quite good, with a natural sway in her hips. She wonders how Stuart's hands would feel on her waist if she made him salsa.

'Don't make me dance,' says Stuart before she can speak. 'It's not pretty.' He lifts his eyebrows. 'Sit down?'

Why not? she thinks, and Stuart leads her to the sofa to chat, while his mates carry on pogoing inappropriately to Jennifer Lopez.

Why not? she thinks, half an hour later, as Naomi demon-strates the dimmer switch Jason fitted by turning the lights down low, and changes the CD to Katie Melua, throwing a moody blanket of slow music over the remaining guests. Stuart has to lean in to catch what Gina's saying over the music, and he smells of Hugo Boss, the scent that wafted from the boys' changing rooms at school. It tickles Gina, and she smiles. She can feel the firm muscle of his thigh through his jeans as he leans closer to her on the sofa, and she can't quite believe that she is being chatted up in this confident yet polite way. The outcome is not in question, and Gina finds that quite relaxing.

Chatted up. They're not at school any more. She's renting a place on her own. So is Stuart, probably. She shivers with desire, partly at the surprising realisation that she's now a proper adult, then laughs. She'd always assumed it'd be harder than this.

'Why are you laughing?' asks Stuart, anxiously.

'Because you're too handsome.' She's in that happy, cosy stage of drunkenness, the confiding stage where everything feels right. 'It's putting me off my conversation.'

He gazes at her. Gina thinks he's drunker than her: he looks serious. 'But *you*'re beautiful.' He leans closer. 'You've got skin like . . . like a peach.'

He reaches out and touches her cheek, not in a lechy way but as if he's curious to see what it feels like. Gina tingles all over as his finger traces her cheekbone, her nose, her lips. It's been ages since anyone touched her.

I probably shouldn't be drinking, she thinks. Mum would go mad. How am I getting home? No, don't worry. Safe here, with Naomi.

Her dry lips part as Stuart's finger traces down her neck, along the scoop of her clavicle, joined by another over the freckles in the hollow of her throat. The music is throbbing in Gina's head now, in time with the blood rushing around her body, waking up parts of her that haven't tingled in ages. She'd completely forgotten what it feels like to have someone's fingers reading her body. All Stuart's done is touch her, and she feels like water inside.

'You're like a peach,' says Stuart, wonderingly. 'Soft, like a peach.'

Gina stops herself telling him it's Palmers Cocoa Butter, and congratulates herself on her new adult mystique.

They gaze at each other for a moment in the sleepy chaos of the party, and then, without either of them seemingly initiating it, they're kissing with the one-night-only, hormone-driven single-mindedness of a pair of teenagers. Stuart feels and tastes and smells exactly as she'd thought he would, and she's letting go for the first time in years, falling into something that's completely obvious and straightforward.

Why not? thinks Gina, as Stuart whispers in her ear about getting a cab back to his. Why not?

Gina had vowed, before her first meeting with Rory Stirling of Flint & Cook solicitors, that she wouldn't be the clichéd vengeful wife when it came to her divorce. She wanted to be calm and mature, given that she had been considering separation before Stuart had made the decision for her, but even with a lawyer as reassuringly competent as Rory, thanks to Stuart's stupid demands, it was proving harder than she'd hoped to cling onto calmness, let alone maturity.

Friday was her third meeting, and Gina had really hoped

that this would be the day she would walk out with a firm date in her diary at which this foggy stage of her life would be over, and the new one would officially begin. Dates helped. She had already set herself the task of emptying the boxes in the flat by her birthday, 2nd May. One box a day, including the ones in storage, would be enough to get there, plus a few weeks to sell some things, at which point she could buy herself a fabulous birthday present, something so wonderful it would go straight onto the list of her hundred special things.

That morning, sorting out had put Gina in a very good mood. She'd given two bags of unused knitting wool, plus assorted needles and pattern books, to David, the tax accountant upstairs, whose wife made tiny hats for the hospital's premature-baby unit. Not only did the babies get hats, but now Gina never had to get round to learning to knit. She'd donated her unused Sodastream to the office kitchen, much to the delight of the web designers, and she'd left another bag of designer jeans she'd never diet back into at the dog rescue shop. Knowing things were going to better homes gave her a warm glow. But that warm glow vanished the moment she sat down in Rory's comfortable client chair, and heard what he had to update her on.

When she ran her eye down the list of items Stuart now apparently wanted in addition to the financial settlement, a sound that Gina didn't recognise had slid out of her. It sounded a lot like a clichéd wife. 'What?' she whined. 'He could have taken this when he moved out. I don't know where half of it is. I've given a lot of stuff away already too!'

'I know. It's tedious but, believe me, it's better that he gets it sorted out now than spends the next five years ringing you about his power drill.' Rory was only a few years older than Gina but he had the solicitor's gift of making everything sound reasonable, even when it wasn't. 'Try not to take it personally.'

'How can I not take it personally? It feels like he's reducing our life together to a series of . . . cash payments.' Gina flipped through the pages. It was ridiculous, starting out hurtful (he wanted more of the house profit on account of the 'months he spent supporting Mrs Horsfield while she was unable to make a financial contribution to the domestic finances') and ending up petty (the list of items he had now decided he wanted from the house). 'He didn't take a single photograph of us together, but he wants four glass bowls that we got on holiday in Venice eight years ago?'

'He's probably just seen Murano glass on the *Antiques Roadshow*,' said Rory calmly. 'Some people become very logical in the face of big emotional situations. We see it all the time. "What I'm owed". It's a coping mechanism, makes them feel in control of something. I'm sorry. As I said, don't take it personally. Easier said than done, I know.'

Gina bit her lip. This was one of the surprisingly painful side effects of divorce. A whole new Stuart coming out, one that she didn't even know: a Stuart who'd stoop to cheap shots about her illness and hide behind his solicitor. He'd never been like that while they were married. Or had he? Had she just tried not to notice? It was bad enough knowing he'd been running some kind of financial clock on the time she was off work.

Rory saw her expression. 'Don't dwell on it,' he said.

'Give him what he wants, if you can, and move on. It doesn't bring out anyone's best side, arguing over who bought what. If it makes you feel better, it's probably his solicitor driving all this, not him.'

The list blurred in front of Gina's eyes. She remembered buying the dishes Stuart wanted. He hadn't understood why she loved them so much; the artistry had meant nothing to him, and it was hard to imagine why he wanted them now. Unless he wanted to remember how romantic Venice had been, in the giddy early days of their relationship. The memory of that weekend snagged in her throat. It had started so romantically – champagne in the airport, the hotel that felt like a honeymoon suite, the exhilaration of visiting a city she'd always dreamed about going to with a lover. Where had that gone?

'We were happy sometimes,' she insisted pathetically. 'It wasn't always like this. Honestly. We did have *some* happy times.'

'I know,' said Rory. 'If you hadn't, this wouldn't be so painful now.' He pushed a box of tissues over the desk to her and she took one gratefully.

Flint & Cook's offices were very near the high street, and Naomi had promised to meet Gina in the café for a cake and debrief. As she wove through the bundled-up office workers shivering at the bus stop, Gina could see her sitting at the prized window table; Naomi was a splash of colour amid the OAPs, in a bright green coat, with a black sequined beret over her chestnut hair.

'Woah, you look livid, sit down,' she instructed, when

Gina shouldered her way inside. 'Don't speak. Not till you've eaten some of this carrot cake.' She gestured to the waitress for two coffees, and sat back.

Gina slid into the chair and took three deep breaths, then exhaled, trying to imagine the tension leaving with the spent breath. It was a calming technique she'd been encouraged to practise by her counsellor: 'Imagine your stress as a colour. What colour is it?' Today's stress was bitter, and an unpleasant orange, the same colour as Stuart's cycling gear. Gina exhaled, and imagined the air around her nostrils singeing with fiery plumes of her bad mood, like a cartoon dragon.

She was angry because, after an hour of picking over the financial bones of her marriage, she felt like a stranger to herself. The unhappiness had passed, and now it was the waste of time, more than the money, that burned at her conscience. All that, to end up as this bitter stranger.

'So,' said Naomi, 'edited lowlights, please.'

Gina drew a breath. 'OK, well . . .'

Naomi's mobile buzzed: a photo of Jason holding a laughing Willow popped up, and she hurriedly turned it upside-down.

Too late. Gina's stomach lurched. Jason and Stuart were exactly the same kind of straightforward, *Top Gear*-loving, football-playing blokes – but one was a happily married family man with a doting wife and a people carrier, and the other . . . wasn't. She and Naomi weren't that different – were they?

Naomi saw her wince, and looked aghast. 'Sorry,' she said. 'We're going to his mother's for dinner, just trying to work out logistics with the childminder . . .'

The coffees appeared and Naomi pushed the cake towards Gina. 'Just imagine what it'll be like when all this is over. Focus on Christmas. By Christmas you'll be a free woman, in that beautiful new flat, looking forward to a romantic New Year's break with some hot new bloke. I'm envious. I can think of two very eligible men off the top of my head who'd be thrilled to take your mind off all this. Just give me the nod and you can be meeting them over dinner at ours.'

'Christmas is ten months away. I'll probably still be getting texts about his sodding bicycle pump.' Gina scraped the cream cheese icing off the back of the cake. 'And no blind dates, please. That's so far down my list of things to do, it's on the next page. I don't know if I *ever* want another relationship.'

Naomi made a soothing noise. 'Don't say that. Maybe not right now but eventually . . .'

Gina took a long breath – 'Think blue, a healing colour, imagine your insides flooded with the waters of a lovely clean swimming-pool' – exhaled and forked the cake into her mouth.

'So where've you got to?' Naomi poured a stream of brown sugar into her coffee. 'Is the paperwork for the decree nisi in?'

'Yup, that's all going ahead. But Stuart's solicitor's making a big deal about the financial settlement. Apparently he's not happy about some details of the house sale.'

'What's to be unhappy about?' She widened her round eyes in disbelief. 'You sold the house, you've got the money in the bank. Half each. No?'

'No, apparently not. He feels he deserves more of it than me because he put his bonus into the mortgage and I was on sick pay for months.' Gina stabbed at the cake, which was crumbling in a very unsatisfactory dry way. Friday cake. Not fresh. 'It's so unlike him to be petty like this. He was fine about it at the time – or was he just lying about it? It makes me wonder what else he didn't really mean. And he keeps texting. Have I got this? Have I got that?' Gina bit her lip. 'I wouldn't mind, but every time the phone beeps, it's like he's reminding me that he's not texting to apologise. He's texting to get some *stuff*, as if I'm clinging to his old football kit and crying into it at night or something.'

Naomi wasn't saying anything. Gina glanced up. 'What are you thinking? You've got that face on.'

'Don't shout me down,' said Naomi, cautiously. 'But . . . you don't think he's doing this because he's hoping you'll get back together?'

'Sorry?'

'All those texts. He's got a solicitor, so why does he keep texting you? If he doesn't want to keep in contact?'

Gina put down her fork. In the middle of the night, lonely and disoriented, she'd wondered that too. Underneath all her other reactions, she couldn't shake the feeling that her mother was right: Stuart was a decent bloke; she should have tried harder. No one had the right to expect to be happy all the time. They'd been together nearly nine years. They'd got over the classic seven-year blip, largely thanks to her serious illness . . .

Then she thought of Bryony, and the supposed

murder-mystery weekend. Her ruined Christmas pretending everything was fine for her mother. Their wasted twenties.

'He doesn't love me any more,' she said flatly. 'I don't want to start thinking like that. Looking back, I don't know if he ever did love me. Not really.'

'What? You don't go through what he went through with you if you *don't* love someone.' Naomi looked horrified. 'Stuart adored you. And you loved him. That doesn't just vanish overnight.'

'It vanished enough for him to have an affair with a younger woman. God, he's such a *cliché*. Why couldn't he just get a motorbike like any other bloke?'

'Stuart was never known for his originality,' said Naomi. 'But don't start thinking he didn't love you. He did. You know that.'

There was a pause, as the idea of Stuart wanting to make things up sharpened like a photograph in developing fluid, taking on an unnerving credibility. Were the bowls a last-ditch attempt to remind her what they once had? He was proud. He wouldn't approach her outright and beg forgiveness. It wasn't his style. But then attaching romantic memories to inanimate objects wasn't Stuart's style either. Rory's *Antiques Roadshow* explanation was much more likely.

Gina shook her head. 'No. I had all this from my mum at the weekend. She thinks I should forgive him the midlife-crisis shag and beg him to come home. She's furious that I've derailed her plans for a pair of grandchildren and a house in the country with a pony.'

'Oh, she's not . . .'

'She played the "I don't want you to die a lonely old

spinster" card.' Gina felt reckless after an hour of trying to
rein in her self-loathing in front of Rory. 'She more or less
said that if I'd never met Kit I'd be happy with the marriage
Stuart and I had. Can you believe that? She's still blaming
Kit for everything. Never mind what I've done, or what *I*
wanted.' She covered her face with her hands. 'I don't
mind starting again, I can cope with that, but I wish I
didn't have to keep looking back at what I've screwed up.
It's such a *mess*.'

'Then let Rory handle it. It's what you're paying him for.'
Naomi sipped her coffee, then put it down, which meant
she was about to be very honest. 'Look, if it's any consola-
tion, it's a *relief* for me to see you being angry. That's what
divorcing people are meant to be like. Mean and bonkers.
You've been so calm so far, with your ruthless sorting and
your lists, I wondered if you were actually processing
anything.'

'Cheers.'

'No, I mean it. You've always been so amazing at listening to me ramble on about my problems, I wish you'd let
me do the same for you.' Naomi's eyes searched her face,
silently asking what else Gina was hiding from her, and
Gina felt her lips tighten. 'You should have said about your
mum. I could have done my impression of her. Would that
have helped?'

Gina half-smiled, and picked up her fork and mashed
some cake crumbs into the tines. 'I don't want to keep going
over the same old stuff. It's boring enough in my own head.
And I don't want to turn into my mother, stewing over
grievances from twenty years ago. I need to move on.'

'Move on, fair enough,' said Naomi. 'But don't underestimate just how far you've come in the last few years. How much crap you've had to deal with. That takes a lot of strength, Gina.'

Gina lifted her gaze. 'It doesn't feel like it. And what have I got to show for it?'

'You're *here*, dumbo.' Naomi looked incredulous. 'You're still here.' She looked as if she were about to say something else, then sighed. 'Tell me about your unpacking. Have you found that denim jacket I lent you about four hundred years ago?'

'No. But I've done ten more boxes since you were last over, and I've started making a list of those hundred things I'm keeping.'

The list was pinned to the back wall: a long roll of lining paper, with the items written in black marker pen, starting with '1. Blue glass vase (and flowers)' and running down, so far, to '15. My iPhone'. Gina liked the way it reminded her of something from a modern gallery, her writing getting bolder and curlier as the list crept down the wall. 'I've got a fair bit of space now,' she added. 'I can see half of a whole other wall and you can get into the spare room without turning sideways.'

'It's going to be gorgeous, that flat . . .' Naomi looked wistful. 'It must be like being in a lovely white cloud, lying on the sofa with a glass of wine and some music *of your own choice*. Not CBeebies. Maybe a novel. A novel! You must be doing so much *reading*! God, I miss reading. I miss going to the loo on my own most, but I miss reading just after that.'

Gina forced a smile. She wished sometimes that Naomi

would stop overstressing the grind of motherhood – she knew she was only doing it in order to make her feel better about not having had children with Stuart. It was the one topic Naomi had ever been less than honest about, and Gina sensed it was probably because the truth – that parenthood shone like a powerful light inside you, revealing hidden corners of your own soul, even with the worry and disruption – was prising open a tiny fissure in their precious friendship. Gina adored Willow and was honoured to have been made her godmother, but sometimes Willow's easy affection reminded her of what she didn't have. What she might never have now.

Sometimes Gina felt that looking at Naomi's life was like looking at her own from outside a window: she should be in there, with the husband, with the toddler. But she wasn't.

Naomi's mobile buzzed again. She turned it over, read the message, sighed and started to gather her things together. 'Sorry, I've got to meet Jason – he's just picked Willow up from the childminder and he's already having a meltdown about being late. I'll leave you to your beautiful cloud. Think of me watching the adventures of Peppa Pig while you're sipping a chilled Chablis and deciding which Scandinavian crime novel to read next.' She shoved her chair back and hauled her squashy leather handbag onto the table, decanting boxes of raisins and odd socks in search of her purse.

Gina had a sudden vision of her flat, set against the jangling cheeriness of Naomi and Jason's house: it'd be dark when she put her key into the lock, and silent, no television news burbling in the background, no sweet smell of garlic drifting from the kitchen. She'd have to bring it to life herself, only to go to bed a few hours later and do it again in the morning.

A childish loneliness gripped her, as if Naomi were off to a party she wasn't invited to.

'You don't want to come over and he can meet you at mine?' she asked, before she could stop herself. 'I've got a whole load of clothes to go to the charity shop, if you wanted first dibs.'

'Oh, I so wish I could but you know what I'm like. We'd put the kettle on, and get chatting, and then Jay'd turn up and be all *come on, come on*. He's only about five minutes away, so it's probably easier if I . . .' Naomi saw Gina's stricken expression, and hesitated. Gina wished she could delete her words in mid-air, pretend she'd never spoken. 'Oh. I can . . . maybe drop in for—'

'No, it's fine,' said Gina. She smiled too hard. 'Silly idea. It'd take you five minutes just to squeeze into the sitting room. Anyway, I'll be seeing you tomorrow . . . Are we still on for the Saturday usual?'

'Of course,' said Naomi. 'There's a new café opened over the road from our house, I've been saving it for us to try together. Come over.'

'OK,' said Gina. But Saturday morning was on the other side of a long Friday night.

The flat was as dark as Gina had expected when she let herself in, and colder. The lamps on the street below threw long shadows over the boxes crowding the sitting room, although there was a little more space than before. She moved quickly around the flat, breaking the silence where she could: she turned on the soft lamps, closed the horizontal blinds, put on the local talk radio station for some background voices while her soup heated on the hob. They were 'discussing' Valentine's Day, so Gina changed the channel to a play on Radio 4. She dithered for a moment about pouring a glass of wine from the open bottle in the fridge, conscious that she'd reached for it without actually wanting a drink.

Did she *want* a glass of wine? Gina frowned at it, as if it might tell her. Janet had never drunk at home, and had always been convinced Gina was on the verge of full-blown alcoholism because she'd cut loose a bit at university, which was only to be expected after an adolescence of sherry-less trifles and coq au vin with no vin. Janet's only squabble with poor Terry was over his fondness for one beer with Test Match Special.

Gina reached for the bottle, then stopped again. Was it just a habit? Did she want to be the sort of person who liked a glass of wine at home, which she'd got into with Stuart because all their friends did? It wasn't going to make anything go away.

What *do* I want? she wondered, in a sudden panic.

It felt as if every decision had to be re-examined, and the smaller the decision, the harder it was to work out, with no one else there to notice or comment or know. The answers that were floating up from Gina's subconscious were surprising her. Only having herself to please was strange.

She poured herself a big glass with a flourish, because

she could, then looked at it, suddenly scared by how much she wanted it, and poured it down the sink.

After supper, Gina curled up with her laptop on the sofa to start putting together the spreadsheet of costs that she was working out for the Rowntrees' project, but Lorcan hadn't replied to her text about the roofers, and without the Internet – still not set up – she couldn't do the research she needed. After half an hour, she gave up. It would have to be sorting.

The print-out of Stuart's list was on the coffee table. As well as the bowls he'd decided he wanted a pair of framed Tube posters Gina had given him one Christmas, and a powerful torch he'd bought with their combined supermarket points, and some WiFi speakers that had been in their bedroom. Nothing she particularly wanted, but annoying to find in the packed boxes.

Gina tipped some clothes out of a box, scrawled 'Stuart' on it, and dumped in four of his Dan Brown paperbacks as a start. Fine, he could have *everything* back. Each item she chucked into the box made her more irritated, but it was a nice clean anger, because she knew exactly what she was cross about: in this case, the way Stuart started either a Dan Brown novel or a Jeremy Clarkson collection on the plane to every single holiday, chuckling to himself then refusing to say what he was laughing at. This wasn't the confusing, diffuse pain that swept through her periodically: it was reassuringly specific.

Multi-gadget remote. Knife sharpener. *Wisden's Almanac 2009*.

And he might as well have his love letters back, she thought, turning to the box marked 'Study'.

Gina couldn't bring herself to throw out handwritten letters: they felt too much a part of the person, like locks of hair or baby teeth. She kept all the letters anyone had ever sent her in shoeboxes, stacked in a bigger box in her old study – postcards from her mum and Terry, notes from Naomi, jumbled together in manila envelopes.

The box was pushed into a corner by the door. Stuart hadn't written her many letters, but there'd been one or two sweet notes while she was in hospital; one in particular had been the closest he'd ever come to a proper love letter, scrawled in a waiting room where he'd sat, chewing his nails while she came round after her operation. It was short but precious because Stuart rarely committed his feelings to paper; she'd treasured it, but Gina didn't want to keep it now. It hurt her just thinking about it.

She reached into the big box and took out the first two A4 envelopes, one fatter than the other, neither addressed nor sealed. They brought her to an abrupt stop.

The first contained a small handful of sealed envelopes, addressed to Stuart, Naomi, her mother, Kit and a couple of other people. Goodbye letters that she'd never sent, but never wanted to get rid of either. Gina stared at them for a second, then put them back. Another day, when she was feeling more robust.

The second envelope was thicker, and it wasn't what she was looking for but Gina took a deep breath and tipped it out onto the pale carpet.

White envelopes, blue envelopes, all covered in the

handwriting of her early twenties, the studied arty script she'd used then with the curled *d*s and dashes. It made Gina feel uncomfortable to see it; it wasn't unlike her handwriting now, but there was something self-conscious about it. The letters were all addressed to the same person:

> *Christopher Atherton*
> *Brunswick House*
> *Little Mallow*
> *Oxfordshire*

Again and again. The postcards had been desperate, their message shouting from the back of the card. Even now, Gina couldn't help her eyes catching her own words even though she didn't really want to.

> *Having an <u>amazing</u> time in the big city. Today I saw the Pre-Raphaelite exhibition at the Courtauld which you'd <u>love</u>. I've bought you all the postcards. I'll send them. I think of you every time I see Ophelia, and wish we could see it <u>together</u>. <u>I love you</u>. I miss you. Gina x*

Gina cringed at her own gushing passion for the Pre-Raphaelites and their hyper-coloured reality and doomed women, draping and dying all over the place, with their bee-stung lips and the drooping eyelids. At the time, Gina remembered feeling as if it captured exactly how she felt, the helplessness of that all-consuming love bursting out of her, luscious and vivid, and withering on the vine in Hartley. Now, it just seemed superficial. It certainly wasn't any sort of death she'd encountered since. It embarrassed her to think she'd sent those images to Kit's house.

Gina's wasn't the only handwriting on the envelopes. Each line of Kit's address had been neatly crossed out, and her mum's home address in Hartley had been written beneath in fountain pen, with 'Return to Sender' under-lined three times. The anger in the writing still made Gina's heart race. It was elegant, looped copperplate, an educated hand, but there were points where the writer had pressed so hard the nib had splayed, leaving a hairline crack of fury running through the middle of the word. *Bellamy. Hartley.*

The letters were unread. They'd been returned unopened to her mother's house, but she'd kept on writing them. That was the point. She'd kept on writing.

With them was another little bundle of letters, addressed to her at home in Kit's untidy writing. Only a few, five, maybe six, sent while she was still at school. She didn't need to open those: she knew exactly what was inside. She knew them off by heart.

For a moment Gina considered putting the whole lot in the shredder, already full of two files of old bills she'd despatched the previous night. As soon as she imagined the precious letters mingled with the bills from E.ON something inside her lurched like the last-minute grab at the edge of a cliff. No. She'd carted these letters from one house to the next, hiding them in their envelope in her sock drawer, then her locked filing cabinet, but now – in this great sorting-out of her life – what was she supposed to do with them?

Give them to Kit, said a voice in her head. He's the only person who can throw them out.

She bit a hangnail but didn't notice the sting. Gina had seen Kit only once since the accident. That meeting hadn't turned out the way she'd hoped. If it were possible, it had actually made things worse.

She stuffed all the letters back into the envelope, and as she put it back into the box, she saw the shoebox with Stuart's letters in it, along with some keepsakes from their early days: a train ticket from their first date, a menu from a posh London restaurant from their second anniversary, some conkers. The conkers reminded her of a trip Stuart had taken her out on after one of her chemo sessions. He'd been gentle, protective, not letting her touch anything in case of infection. He'd picked up every single conker she'd asked for.

She held it in her hand, and squeezed it tight. Until she'd seen the conkers, Gina had nearly forgotten that. It had been a different sort of romance from what she'd felt for Kit, but still.

Gina slipped them all into a plain white envelope, wrote 'old letters for you to throw away if you want' and shoved them into the box between the speakers.

Then she hesitated. Was that the right thing to do? Stuart would just throw them out: he wouldn't want Bryony to see their old tenderness. And they were her letters, sent by him, read by her. Weren't they as much a part of *her* as Stuart?

She pushed her knuckles into her eyes. Was she doing what Naomi thought Stuart was doing – deliberately keeping in touch because there was still something there?

Gina put the envelope of letters back where it had been in the box. Maybe she would give the letters back to Stuart. But not yet, not in anger.

It was nearly nine o'clock. She made herself a pot of tea

in the kitchen, listening to the faint sounds of Longhampton's Friday night ramping up in the street below. It sounded fun . . . No, it sounded exhausting. And messy. Gina felt a sense of peace descend on her and the flat, and for a second, she was glad she had the place to herself. An unread Marian Keyes novel she'd found in a box, a pot of tea and a long hot bath. No need to make conversation, or force herself to go out to prove she wasn't past it, or ignore irritations. And a whole weekend stretching out ahead of her.

As she passed her list of a hundred things, Gina took the marker pen off the top of the box and added, '16'. Then she paused. What was it exactly? Her sofa? Her books? Her pot of tea? What was the object making this feel so right? She frowned. All of it was a bit floaty and she wanted to be specific.

She wrote '16. My reading sofa', but that wasn't quite it. It niggled at her for the rest of the evening, until she got up, crossed it out, and wrote 'Friday nights in'.

Chapter Seven

Longhampton District Hospital, June 2008

Dear Gina,

This is the longest afternoon of my life. When you come round, our life will have changed, and I know there is a long road to go down until you're back to normal, but one thing that will never change is us. I will be right beside you on that road, holding your hand whatever happens, because you're the most amazing, funny, beautiful person I've ever met, and my life is so much better since you shared yours with me.

With all my love, Stu x

Oxford, June 1997

It's nearly quarter to four in the morning and Gina knows she should be asleep but there's no way she can sleep now. It's not because she's drunk – though she is, a bit – it's because there's so much to take in that her brain won't stop, like a camera whirring and whirring, trying to press each image into her imagination for ever.

And also because she's intensely happy, so happy that she's scared she might never be this happy again. She needs to absorb every second so she'll never be able to look back and regret missing some of it.

It's what they say, isn't it? The happiest days of your life. That's *now*. Right *now*. Concentrate.

Gina glances at Kit, stretched out next to her in a secluded corner of the college rose gardens, his starched evening shirt open down to the fourth button to reveal the pale skin at the top of his chest, the first wirier strands of the hair that leads down his flat stomach in a fine line. She's used to seeing him in T-shirts, or jeans and boots, but he looks surprisingly right in black tie too, more rakish, more grown-up.

She looks away because thinking about the warm golden skin under the fine cotton shirt makes her tingle. Her pencil moves quickly over the back of her ball programme, taking in the careless arm thrown over his face, shading his eyes against the light, the lanky stretch of his leg. Gina can't quite get Kit's boyish energy right, the glow about him that makes her want to laugh because he's so perfect. It's not a perfection that can last. It's like a flower or a glass of champagne. The thought makes her panicky, in a dizzy, drunken way.

Kit always seems to know what she's doing, even with his eyes closed. He moves his arm, catching hers, caressing the soft inside with his thumb. 'You're allowed to grab five minutes' sleep before breakfast, you know.'

'Only lightweights do that.' She'd heard someone else say it as they were winding their way from one of the Persian tents, and liked the sound of it. Like the hired ballgown she's wearing tonight, Gina likes the feel of her borrowed personality: this Gina is smarter, more confident, less conscious of her mock results, which she suspects might be 'disappointing' on account of all the hours and hours she's spent on the phone to Kit over the past months. Or writing to Kit. Planning how to sneak off to meet Kit in Oxford.

Gina and Naomi are supposed to be visiting Shaun, Naomi's brother, again for more investigation of their Oxford applications, but the reality is that Gina is here at the Commem Ball with Kit, and Naomi is somewhere else in Oxford, doing something else, Gina's not sure what.

Kit offered to get Naomi a ball ticket too, as a chaperone, but Naomi declined. 'I've seen enough of you two mooching around like a pair of hipster cows,' she informed them. 'I'm not forking out a hundred quid to see you do it in black tie.'

The moon's white and round, though the sky around it is already light. It never crosses Gina's mind to be worried about being alone with Kit. Normally she's the worrying type but not with him. There's an old-fashioned honour about him, despite his worldly bohemian attitude, a decency that she knows her mum and Terry would love, if they knew about him, which, as yet, they don't. But they will. Soon.

And so they've had this amazing night, just them in their own Brideshead bubble. Kit introduced her to his friends, who seem nice; she'd met a few of them before on the two times she'd got away to be here with Kit (talking, talking,

talking). But they'd drifted off, and Kit and Gina were left alone to wander round this funfair of candyfloss and tents, piles of oysters and pyramids of blowsy lilies, rooms with string quartets and swing bands. It feels magical, as if she's stepped out of her boring world into a trippy fantasy – one that she might even be able to stay in. It stirs up a funny churning in Gina's stomach that's half excitement, half fear.

'This is the most incredible night of my life,' she says, without thinking.

'So far.' Kit doesn't open his eyes; he's had Finals, followed by ten days of parties. He's shattered. Then he opens one eye, amused. 'I mean, your life so far, not tonight so far. Did that sound sleazy?'

'It didn't.' Although now you mention it, Gina thinks, and shivers.

'Are you having a good time?' He sounds as if he's making himself talk to stay awake.

'The best.'

'Come down here and just shut your eyes for a bit. We'll go for breakfast when the big clock up there . . .' he waves vaguely in the direction of the quad clock without opening his eyes '. . . strikes the quarter-hour.'

'OK.' Gina isn't tired but she snuggles down next to him anyway, mainly to feel the warmth of his body on her bare back and shoulders.

They lie like that for a bit, listening to the sounds of the ball winding down in the distance, smelling the crushed flowers on the morning air. Kit's arms go heavy round her, and she feels more awake than ever. Physically, they've gone – she blushes, thinking about it – quite far, but they've never actually *slept* together. He's surprisingly gentlemanly about that. She thinks sleeping with Kit, literally sleeping, would be even more intimate than making love. Waking up with him, seeing his chest rise and fall, his eyelids flicker.

Sounds float up from the disco tent, a summer tune Gina decides will always now remind her of tonight. 'You're Not Alone' by Olive.

'This song? Will always remind me of tonight,' says Kit, as if he can read her mind. 'Of you.'

Gina smiles to herself and wriggles into his body. Sleepily, he responds, and then less sleepily. She feels something pressing into the small of her back, against the bones of her corseted bodice, and stops. Somehow his erection feels much more dangerous through the formal wool of his trousers than through his jeans.

She wriggles further, more deliberately, surprised at her own boldness, and Kit's hands begin to move where they're resting on her leg, shifting the net of her petticoat against her bare thigh. Gina reaches backwards, running her own hand up the length of his leg. She can feel the long muscle under the scratchy fabric. Strong, warm. They lie like that for a while, stroking and moving, but saying nothing, until Kit's breath becomes urgent, and he stops.

We're going to do this, she thinks, looking up at the round white moon with a top-of-the-rollercoaster thrill. It all feels right.

'Gina,' he whispers in her ear, pulling a long strand of dark hair out of the way, so his lips are right up against her skin. His breath is warm and champagne-sour, and he smells intoxicatingly familiar. 'Are you sure?'

'Yes,' she whispers back.

Kit pauses a second, as if giving her a chance to change her mind, and she pulls him awkwardly, wanting to show him that she really does want this, kicking off her shoe and sliding her bare leg beneath his. Kit rolls over onto his side, and their eyes lock for a long moment, his beautiful face framed against the sunrise-streaked sky above. Gina thinks of John Donne, but not about her A-level set texts.

Now she understands. This is what love feels like.

He gazes at her in wonder, and Gina feels beautiful for the first time in her life. Special and beautiful and powerful and completely safe. It's like flying.

'I love you, Gina,' whispers Kit, 'I could look at you for the rest of my life. And still never want to look away.'

Then he leans down and kisses her hard, his mouth sweet and hungry on hers, and everything else is lost in a rush of heat and darkness and the damp, sharp smell of crushed grass and wool and early morning roses.

The dog-rescue shop opposite Gina's new flat was getting the lion's share of her unwanted items, particularly heavy things like books and small furniture: it was nearest, and crucially, it was open at 8.00 a.m.

The shop's routine was now a marker in her own morning timetable. From her bathroom window, where she was usually brushing her teeth at 7.50 a.m. (shower: 7.40 a.m.; vitamins and Tamoxifen, 7.49 a.m., toothbrush, 7.50 a.m.), Gina could see the manager arrive with her dog. The stiff-legged Border collie sat patiently at the woman's feet as she unlocked the door, sniffed politely at any bags left at the entrance, then padded into the shop behind her. Sometimes it reappeared in the window where it watched for customers. It sat so still that Gina had assumed for a while it was a stuffed toy.

By her third donation drop-off, she'd learned that the collie was called Gem, the manager, who also ran the rescue kennels, was Rachel, and the older helper, Jean, couldn't get going in the morning without a good strong cup of coffee and a bacon sandwich. They all looked forward to Gina's donations as they were, according to Jean, 'a better quality of item'.

'Ooh, lovely, thank you, dear,' Jean said on Monday morning, not bothering to hide her nosiness when Gina heaved two bags of untouched paperback novels onto the counter. 'More books! It makes a change from the usual, what you bring in. Doesn't it, Rachel?'

Rachel looked up from unpacking a donation bag of nylon headscarves and hats. 'It certainly does. Although we also like your lovely chinaware and antique candlesticks. Hint, hint.'

'I've given up book groups,' said Gina, watching with relief as Jean unpacked her pile of unfinished Booker Prize shortlisted novels. 'It feels like a weight's lifted from my shoulders. Call me a philistine, but I've decided life is too short for a fourth attempt at *Ulysses*.'

Rachel pushed her thick black fringe out of her eyes and laughed. 'Life's too short for my first attempt. I'm saving it for my old age.'

'You wouldn't believe what we've been getting recently.

Perfectly respectable types who come in all prim and proper until you unpack their bag and it's full of . . .' Jean pulled a shocked face '. . . filth. Mind, they dash in and out pretty quickly, but I still know. I couldn't meet Mrs Nixon's eye at WI last week. Her poor Arthur . . .'

'Now then, Jean.' Rachel looked askance, but winked at Gina. 'Don't pretend you don't read them round the back!'

Gina smiled, but then had a moment of horror as she realised that the various charity-shop volunteers along the high street were probably building up five different pictures of her from the contents of her donation bags. Without thinking, she'd been directing different things to different shops: heavy books and small furniture here, home accessories to the Hospice at Home with the big display window, clothes to the Breast Cancer Care shop, who had more imaginatively dressed dummies.

As she left the shop for her office, Gina wondered what they made of her once she'd gone. If people analysed the bags like fortune-tellers, it was all in reverse: they'd be constructing her personality from books she'd never got round to reading. From clothes she'd never found the right occasion for.

She slowed down as something in the Hospice at Home window caught her eye. Out of all the charity shops in town, Hospice at Home had the best displays: it was dressed to look like a 1960s-inspired bedroom, and on top of a Perspex bedside table there was a beautiful silver bedside lamp, with a huge round metal shade.

That looks *gorgeous*, thought Gina. I wonder how much they want for it?

She was crossing the road to see, when she abruptly remembered that it was, in fact, hers. It was the touch-operated bedside light from the master bedroom at Dryden Road, and had gone straight from the packing crate to the GIVE AWAY box: Gina hadn't been able to look at it without hearing the *tap tap tap* of Stuart turning it down to read his cycling magazines in bed, rather than talk to her, and then the *tap tap* as he turned it off to slide over in the bed without making contact with her body.

She didn't hear any of that now. Weirdly, it just looked like a very expensive touch lamp, one that would work perfectly in the small spare bedroom of her flat.

Gina glanced at the ticket and winced. Twenty pounds? It had been a lot more than that, five times that, even in the sale.

She could remember the day she and Stuart had bought it, at Heal's on Tottenham Court Road in London. It had been a surprise weekend away for her twenty-sixth birthday; Gina found she liked London a lot more when she didn't have to live there. Stuart had booked the most romantic boutique hotel he could find, and they'd giggled about the hand-knitted hot-water-bottle covers – what sort of honeymoon hotel needed bed-warmers? Hotels seemed to bring out the best in their relationship: Stuart had handed over his credit card in Heal's while he was still in a dazed good mood brought on by a very late lie-in.

It's a nice lamp, Gina thought. Buying it was more vivid in her memory than the weekend away; she wanted it back. That couldn't be right. Could it?

A woman appeared in the shop window to rearrange the

display and caught Gina looking at the lamp. She raised her eyebrows jokingly and pointed at it but Gina shook her head with a sad smile. It wasn't coming back into her house. Let someone else get the benefit of its designer curves. Better that Hospice at Home got their twenty quid for it, before Stuart remembered they'd bought it and demanded it back.

At quarter past ten there was a knock on Gina's office door, and Sara, the wedding planner, stuck her blonde head in. 'Brought you a bit of cake,' she said, putting a plate on top of the filing cabinet. It had a chunk of salmon pink and white sponge on it. 'Had a naughty box of wedding-cake samples, and if it stays in my office I'll eat the lot.'

'Thanks!' said Gina. 'That's really kind of you.'

Sara raised her mug of coffee; it was a glitzy silver one of Gina's that never looked right with just tea in it. 'Meant to say thanks for the new mugs. To be fair, I was getting a bit depressed with David's Inland Revenue freebies. Who wants to be reminded of last year's tax deadline on their tea break, eh?'

'How'd you know they were mine?' Gina asked, still conscious of the charity-shop character-analysis issue.

Sara tipped her head. 'Aw, hon. They're very you. All of them. I knew as soon as I saw the "Keep Calm and Eat Cake" one.'

Naomi had given her that for her birthday. Gina wondered if she should be offended, then decided it was better to be known for eating cake than for tax reminders.

'While I'm here, your for-sale notice in the kitchen. Have

you sold that steamer yet?' Sara asked. 'I need to start my diet before the season gets going. It's the same every year, pure agony.' She sighed and patted her stomach, straining her pencil skirt to the limits of its ponte power. 'Very hard to keep brides on the straight and narrow with their low-carbing when you've got a bit of a tum yourself.'

Gina was about to tell her she could have it for a tenner, then changed her mind. 'You know what, Sara?' she said. 'Have it. I've got a juicer as well, if you fancy that.'

'Really?' Sara looked thrilled. 'How much do you want for them both?'

'Nothing. You're very welcome to them. Make a donation to charity, if you like. I'll bring them in tomorrow.'

'Thanks!' Sara's face was flushed with pleasure as she left, and Gina felt pleased too. It was nice. Nice to get rid of some junk, nice to feel it wasn't junk to someone else. If only everything leaving her house could be as useful.

When Sara had clip-clopped upstairs, Gina got up and retrieved the cake. She ate it with her feet on the window ledge, looking out at the canal. It was vanilla, with raspberry jam, and it tasted like a summer wedding.

By eleven, she'd made a timetable of the renovation stages for the Magistrate's House, and had started the first rough draft of the Design and Access statement for the consent application form when she realised she hadn't got a final answer from Nick and Amanda about what they were planning to do with the cellars.

She dialled the mobile number Amanda had left; Nick picked up.

'Hello, Nick, it's Gina Bellamy. This a good time to have a word?'

'It's fine. I was just . . . Hang on.' She heard some clunks and the phone was put down and picked up. 'Sorry, just juggling cameras. How are you?'

'Great, thanks.' Gina opened the file of photos she'd taken of the house's interior while they'd been walking around; she could already see how stunning the main hall would look once the panelling had been restored, ready for paintings and subtle wall lighting.

There was a lot to do yet, though. Lorcan had pointed it out while they'd gone round: the walls beneath the panelling were full of damp, which would have to be painstakingly cut out, the rotten battens removed and new seasoned wood patched in where it had decayed over the years. No one would know it was there once the panelling was back on, but it'd be sound, and *they*'d know: Gina liked that. Making the house solid, not just papering over the cracks.

She dragged her attention back to her spreadsheet. 'I'm just putting together a set of consent applications to get the ball rolling with the council, and I realised that we didn't talk about the cellars. You were going to let me know what your architect said about Keith's feedback.'

'Ah. We're still waiting on our architect. Busy man, by all accounts.'

'Busier than Keith?' Gina pretended to be amazed.

'They are two very busy men. Lucky for them that we've got all the time in the world, eh?'

'Well, quite.' She looked at her list. 'While you're there, did you decide whether you wanted to go ahead with the reclaimed oak flooring in the study and downstairs areas, or have me price up alternatives? And we need to talk about windows. I might have to get some measurements, if that's not going to disturb you today.'

'Sure. I've got Lorcan here, actually. He's doing some measurements himself. Something about lime replastering?' Nick dropped his voice. 'He keeps knocking on the walls, like he's looking for a secret door. Is that normal?'

'Yes. He's seeing if your plaster's blown. Or if it's solid brick or just plasterboard – some of it looks a bit modern, like it might have been a later addition.'

'Oh.' He sounded disappointed. 'I thought there might be some hidden tunnel down to the church or something.'

'You've been reading too many historical romances. Although the house was built by a wine merchant, so you never know, there might be a secret tunnel down to the cellars . . .'

'Aha! A wine chute, straight from the dining room to the inner cellar? I like the sound of that. Do you think we could get one?'

'I'll talk to Lorcan,' said Gina. 'He's built a couple of slides for me. I don't think a drink chute should be a problem. You might have trouble getting it past the conservation officer, though.'

Nick laughed. 'It's a practical modern addition. What time were you thinking of coming over? I'm here all day.'

She glanced up at the clock on the wall opposite; a dark gold 1930s starburst, bought with her leaving collection from the office. It was quarter past eleven. There were a couple of calls to make about Naomi's super-shed, and a few emails to return, but the rest of the day was empty. 'About twelve?'

'Great,' said Nick. 'I might have to nip out but Lorcan's here. You might get more sense out of him anyway. Fewer questions, at least.'

There was something about windows that Gina found fascinating, the connection, maybe, with previous owners who'd stood at them, looking out at the same view, but in different clothes, with different eyes.

The Magistrate's House window frames had rotted badly in the wet winters Longhampton had suffered for the past few years, and the sills were soft and spongy beneath the crumbling paint. When she got near enough to inspect them, Gina could almost shove her finger into the wood until it splintered like a chocolate Flake.

That's going to be expensive, she thought, as she took a few photographs of the detail, mentally tallying the cost of repairing twelve full-size sashes on the front and sides, with more decorative windows round the back, and that nice stained glass. Amanda could forget all about her eco-double glazing too: Keith Hurst was going to come down hard on any attempts to change the glass. He was passionate about preserving any original features, particularly historically authentic draughts.

Gina got a notebook out of her bag and wrote down, 'Draught proofing? Insulation? Ring Simon/Longhampton Energy Save'. It was her job to come up with Plan B, and Plan C, and if necessary Plan D, then make the client feel like it had been their Plan A all along.

Her boots crunched on the gravel that ran around the side of the house, as she went into the garden. The large north-facing drawing room at the rear of the house led onto a croquet lawn at the same level, which then dropped down via a flight of ornamental stone steps to a bigger flat lawn that could easily have passed for a small cricket pitch. Gina had found some photographs in the archive of four well-covered Edwardian girls playing tennis on it, in big hats and striped leg-of-mutton-sleeved blouses; she planned to email them to Nick and Amanda along with the proposed timetable.

Around the lawn smaller flowerbeds were now overgrown and knotted, and beyond that wilder land had run to meadow over the years. A few trees stretched their bare branches towards the pale sky. Gina was gazing at the stone steps where the tennis-playing girls had sat in awkward clusters with their mothers and beaux, wondering which of the big houses they'd come from, which well-to-do local families they'd married into, when she felt her phone vibrate in her pocket.

She pulled it out. It was a text from Stuart. She stepped back, unlocked the screen and braced herself for another petulant demand about loans.

I love you. Xxooxx

An unexpected acrid taste rose up in Gina's mouth, followed by a wash of relief that she was shocked to feel, given everything that had happened.

He was apologising. He was sorry. *He loved her.*

Naomi had been right. Her heart banged in her chest, up into her temples, as a rush of joy swept across her.

Gina often played this moment in her head, when Stuart realised what a huge mistake he'd made. She thought she'd be triumphant, and cool, or that she'd realise she didn't want him back after all, but now that it was here, those words in black fact, she was filled with a scrabbling desire to make it all right again. For things to go back to where they had been.

Her hands shook as she tried to compose a text in reply. But what should she say? 'Me too. I'm sorry'?

She drew a breath. What were the right words? Her mind was blank. Gina didn't want to get this vital message wrong, but she also didn't want to leave too long a gap, which could be interpreted as a snub, or worse.

The phone vibrated again, another text folding over the top of the screen like a note passed in class. It was another from Stuart.

Sorry sorry sorry. Ignore previous text. Meant for Bryony.

The rushing in Gina's ears stopped, and everything went silent. Shock squeezed her so hard she couldn't breathe, as a scarlet pain in her chest bloomed and spread like a slow-motion bomb, rising up around her in a cloud, spreading through her body.

She sank onto a stone wall, her legs weak beneath her, feeling nauseous. She knew this was disproportionate, but her reaction was out of her control. It was bigger than she was, an emotion she couldn't contain in her head. A distant voice told her to get out of sight of the main house, in case Nick or Lorcan spotted her.

She stumbled on the mossy stone flags, and scrambled

around to the other side of the house where walled fruit beds ran alongside the bridleway that led to the village. Tears were already seeping out of her, running down her face as her chest heaved. Gina tucked herself behind an ash tree and leaned her head against the bark, hating herself for the waves of misery that washed through her, knowing there was nothing she could do but let them come.

Gina wasn't sad for now: she was grief-stricken for the times Stuart had told her he loved her and meant it. She was grieving for the younger Gina who had been wasting her time, and she couldn't warn her; for the part of her that was lonely enough to want to go back, like an unwanted dog, even though she knew in her heart Stuart no longer loved her.

She heard Nick Rowntree before she saw him. It wasn't hard: his voice was sharp with annoyance and he clearly wasn't expecting to be overheard on the deserted footpath.

'No.' Long pause. 'No. Listen, I mean, no, will you just listen to what I'm saying? You said it was going to be two weeks at the start of the month. You know I've got this work to do for Charlie, and I need to . . . Amanda, I'm not saying that.'

Gina leaned against the tree, trying to mould herself into it. Please jog past, she thought, her chest shaking with sobs.

'So when are you coming back? . . . What? . . . Seriously? . . . Amanda, you know that's not the deal . . . Well, what am I— . . . *Amanda*. What am I— . . . Oh, don't start that . . .'

The voice was coming nearer. Gina heard the gate squeak and his feet on the gravel. Nick had detoured into the back garden: he didn't want to bump into Lorcan either.

Shit.

I should move, she thought. There was no way she could pretend she hadn't just heard what she'd heard.

'So what exactly *is* the point of this, then?' Nick's voice was stripped of the humour she'd heard before. He sounded defensive. 'Am I just some kind of project manager now? I thought that's what you'd hired Gina for. Or am I just there to manage the manager? You don't have to assume everyone's out to rip you off, Amanda. The whole world doesn't operate like lawyers . . .'

Gina panicked, not sure whether she could pass off lurking in the garden as some sort of buildings research. The sobs wouldn't stop: they were still gripping her lungs, even though her brain was now racing. There was only one way out – via the path Nick was crunching down.

'She's not provincial! And even if she is provincial, so what? In case you hadn't noticed, we've bought a house in the middle of nowhere . . . Hang on, there's someone in the garden. Hey! What are . . .? Oh. Hello.'

Gina stepped out from behind the tree. Nick was standing about three feet away from her, in his running shorts and an old T-shirt, his eyes fixed on her in surprise while Amanda carried on yelling into his ear. Gina could make out her voice. Furious. Barely stopping to breathe. Sweat had dampened Nick's hair, sticking a few dark curls to his forehead, and his face was flushed, from the run or the argument, Gina couldn't tell.

She held up her camera, hoping it would look like an explanation, but she could feel mascara clumping on her lower eyelashes, and she knew it was smeared. Her pulse was still hammering and every few moments a sob threatened to burst from her throat, the sort of annoying, hiccuping sob that she couldn't control, even if she tried.

'No. It's Gina. She's . . .' He smiled, looked as if he was about to make a joke, then realised she was crying and stopped. 'I'll call you back,' he said, and turned off his phone.

They stood staring at each other for a few seconds, unsure who should be most embarrassed, until Nick eventually spoke.

'Awkward,' he said.

Chapter Eight

ITEM: four glass Murano bowls, various colours,
made in Venice in the official Murano factory

Venice, 2006

Gina pauses by a quartet of glass bowls, each studded
with hundreds of tiny beads like multi-coloured floral
gems. Every shop in Venice seems to be selling Murano glass
but these are particularly intricate: the colours glow with
peculiar intensity – crimson, emerald, gold, midnight blue.

She loves the contradiction of them. Liquid, but solid;
delicate, but weighty. The skill of moulding the molten
strands of glass passed down from father to son to grand-
son, on and on. Holding the bowl is like touching their
fingers across the centuries.

'Aren't these gorgeous?' she murmurs.

Stuart's not even looking. 'They're OK.'

Gina presses her lips together, biting down the irritation
that's been rising since the walking tour of the hidden
churches this morning. You really find out what people are
like on holiday, she thinks. They've been together a year,
and she'd had absolutely no idea that Stuart moves his lips

while he reads. Gina noticed that on the plane on the way out. Now she can't stop noticing.

Don't be a hormonal cow, she tells herself. That's just PMT talking.

Because the rest of this minibreak *is* living up to expectations: Venice is everything Gina dreamed it would be from her History of Art A level. The hotel is tucked away and romantic, the sheets are about a million thread count, and Stuart's anniversary present to her came in a tissue-filled Agent Provocateur box. Dusk is falling over the squares she's longed to explore since she was a teenager, although she's unable to enjoy the glittering lights on the water because Stuart keeps reminding her that the place is full of pickpockets who'll steal her bag, given half a chance.

Gina realises that he's probably hoping they will, both to prove him right and to give him something to do.

She focuses on the pretty bowls, even prettier under the spotlight in the cabinet. They're the most beautiful things she's seen in ages and, better than that, they represent something. A tradition, a skill.

'Wouldn't they be a lovely memento of our first proper holiday?' Gina offers one to Stuart so he can feel its weight.

He holds it as if it were a cricket ball. 'What would you do with them?'

'Display them. Just have them in the house. They're beautiful. Beautiful things don't need to *do* anything.'

'Apart from collect dust.'

His stubborn refusal to see the beauty or the skill involved makes Gina snappish. He was just the same about the

Basilica San Marco. That wasn't PMT. He's got no excuse for that.

'Can you stop being so dismissive?' she hisses, aware of the owner hovering proudly behind the counter.

'I'm not being dismissive!' Stuart's face is creased with affront.

'You are. You've been really critical of everything.'

'I have no idea what you're on about.'

Gina watches him fiddling with a dish, as if determined to find a flaw in it. Normally, Stuart's very easy-going. But when he's grumpy, it's never about the thing he's outwardly grumpy about. His moods just escape through the path of least resistance, like volcanic lava, but without the heat and force. Stuart is more of a sulker. The Mount Etna of sulkers.

'What. Is. The. Matter?' she demands under her breath.

She doesn't even need to prod him. 'It's thirty-two degrees in Sharm, and Jason's just seen half the England cricket team on the golf course,' he informs her.

Oh, so that's what it is. The text from Jason earlier. He'd rather be in Sharm el-Sheikh with Jason and Naomi, out on an artificial golf course with the England cricket team.

Gina bites her lip. Sometimes it's easy being with Stuart: he makes her feel sexy and secure, and he says what he's thinking, eventually. But at other times, especially recently, Gina's found herself baffled by how little he understands her. Trying to explain *why* certain churches make her heart sing takes all the wonder out of it. Discussing them with Kit – or even Naomi who didn't do History of Art but is a part-time Catholic – only unpacked more magic.

Gina pushes that thought out of her head. It's not fair. 'Shall we go back to the hotel?' she says, keeping her voice even. She knows she should try harder to defuse this.

'Are you sure there aren't any more *museums* open? There might be one we haven't trailed round yet.'

She turns away. For that, she is having the bowls. She fishes her guidebook out of her bag and approaches the desk.

'*Scusi,*' she says to the shopkeeper carefully. '*Quanto sono queste ciotole?*'

'For you, five hundred euros,' he says, with a flourish.

Whoa. Gina had guessed they'd be a hundred and fifty at most. That's all her spending money for the holiday, and she's still got to get her mum and Naomi something.

'*Grazie,*' she says. 'A bit too much.' She turns to Stuart. 'Come on, let's go.'

'No,' he says stubbornly, and marches back to the counter. 'Bongiorno? How much for the bowls?'

The shopkeeper smiles and points to the price. 'Five hundred euros.'

'No, really, mate,' says Stuart, with an answering smile. 'How much?'

Gina feels awkward. She knows you're meant to haggle in markets but there's a way of doing it. A way of making it a respectful ritual, not a dismissive stand-off.

'I don't think you're meant to haggle in a *shop*, Stuart,' she mutters.

'You are,' he hisses back. 'I read it in one of your guide-books. They expect it.' He turns back to the shopkeeper. 'A hundred for the four.'

The shopkeeper looks stunned, then amused. He spreads his palm and says, slowly, 'Five. Five hundred euros.'

Gina tugs his sleeve. This feels wrong. It's spoiling the bowls. 'Stuart, please. I don't want them that much. Let's get some supper.'

He gestures to her. 'See? She's leaving.'

'OK. Four hundred,' says the shopkeeper at once.

Stuart gives her a quick, triumphant smile, and Gina feels foolish. 'A hundred and twenty.'

The shopkeeper laughs, but he's less confident now. There's something terrier-like about Stuart. She's seen it on the pitch: he never stops till he's got the ball, working harder than most players of his height and position would bother to.

'I do three fifty and that is my final offer,' says the shopkeeper.

'A hundred and twenty,' Stuart repeats. 'Come on. We've got the cash here.'

Gina can't watch. The fact that Stuart can't speak Italian and is making no effort to do so doesn't seem to matter to the shopkeeper, although for some reason it does to her. She hates looking like a crass tourist when this city makes her feel like a masked princess. Or it did. For a bit.

Why? she asks herself. Why does it matter? Stuart's getting her the bowls, like she wants.

He's not listening to her, that's the problem. He's doing what he thinks she wants, but he hasn't actually listened to *why* she wants it.

Stuart wasn't listening on the Murano glass-factory trip because he'd already decided it was just an extended sales pitch designed to part them from their cash. Which, Gina concedes, it partly was, but there was also something mesmerising about the ancient skill, the liquid glass, the colours. The idea of something fragile also being heavy and strong. Like love, she wanted to tell him, but she's getting the sinking feeling that it might be a metaphor too far.

'There!' Stuart turns round, triumphant. She sees the shopkeeper wrapping up four identical bowls, Stuart counting out a hundred and eighty euros and the shopkeeper theatrically counting it back. Then he hands the bag to her.

'Happy anniversary,' says Stuart, with a smile that Gina thinks means he's enjoyed getting some sport out of the weekend.

'Happy anniversary!' cries the shopkeeper. 'How long you married?'

'Oh, not married yet.' Gina shakes her head, and the shopkeeper wags his finger.

'You should! Both of you! *Belli, belli!*'

They are quite *belli*. They look like two honeymooners, Gina thinks, as they make their way across the square, lit up now with tiny lights strung between the street lamps like low stars. He's handsome, she's glowing. She could do a lot worse.

Her mother certainly thinks so. Naomi likes him. Everyone likes him.

I like him, Gina reminds herself.

Stuart puts his arm around her waist and she concentrates on how lovely Venice is. How lovely the hotel is, how romantic the four-poster bed will be. Gina leans her head on Stuart's shoulder, and they walk in silence in the warm Italian night air.

'I got you what you wanted,' he says, and if it hadn't sounded like a prompt Gina would have agreed.

'You did,' says Gina. 'But—' She stops herself.

'But what?'

They come to a halt, under a street lamp near the hotel, and Gina hears her voice carrying on: 'But do you have any idea what I love about them?'

'What do you mean by that?' The moment is teetering on the edge of something now. The canal water beneath the bridge glitters blackly with the reflected lights.

'I don't know. I just feel like . . . like you don't . . .' Gina can't find the right words and they're staring into each other's faces, the atmosphere thickening between them.

Gina suddenly has a very sharp thought: *His face is so familiar, but I don't know him at all.* What he loves, what inspires him, what scares him. If anything really does. It's fine, this relationship, but she can't see where it ends. Not in a 'we'll be together for ever' way, but because it doesn't seem to be going anywhere. They're getting used to each other, not sharing an adventure. This isn't what she wants for the rest of her life. And she's twenty-six. Her and Stuart – they're seventeen in pontoon, a nearly full-stacked Buckaroo. Not perfect, but then what is? The trouble is, Gina knows what is.

End it, says a clear voice in her head, and she has no idea where it's come from. *End it now, before . . .*

'I do,' says Stuart, his face confused with emotion. 'Whatever it is you think I don't do, I really do. I just . . . can't express it as well as you.'

Then before Gina can reply, he leans forward and kisses

her, and the kiss goes on for such a long time, Gina's back pressed against the cool stone wall of the hotel, that it pushes all the voices away.

Maybe we're eighteen, she thinks. Eighteen's worth sticking.

Stuart's **I love you** danced in front of Gina's eyes when she shut them, stark white, not black.

A mortified relief followed the pain. It was definitely over now – for both of them.

When she opened her eyes again, Nick was staring at her, his own embarrassment forgotten in his concern for her.

'Are you all right?' He looked so genuinely worried that she nearly told him, but her self-respect kicked in, just in time. You're at work, she reminded herself. He is a client, one whose wife thinks I'm provincial. Gina tried to distract herself with the rudeness of that and failed.

'I'm fine,' she croaked, but the sobs had turned into involuntary hiccups. 'Fine,' she repeated, frowning, only to hiccup again.

'You don't sound fine.'

Gina screwed up her face and flapped her hands at herself, willing it to stop. *Stop it. Stop it.* Naturally, that only made her sob-hiccup more. 'I am, it's just shock . . . Sorry, this is really embarrassing.'

Why do I even care? She thought, as her brain mercilessly flashed the words up again. *I don't love him.*

They stood without speaking for a moment or two, until Nick cleared his throat awkwardly. 'Um, Gina?'

She opened an eye. Nick was rubbing his chin. He winced, and ran the hand through his hair, damp with sweat from his run. 'You overheard what I was saying to Amanda,' he said.

Gina pulled herself together. 'For the record, I'm *not* provincial.'

'Of course you're not.' Nick looked sheepish. 'We hired you because you know this area. We don't want this house to look like something we could have bought in Fulham. Look, I'm sorry. I hope you don't feel . . .'

She blinked. Did he think she was crying because of what she'd heard?

'I'm not crying about *that*!' Gina blurted out. 'Not that I don't think it's bloody . . .' The hiccups overtook her again and she turned away with a groan.

His phone rang, and he grimaced apologetically while he answered it. 'Hello? Hey, Charlie, yes, I'm working on it right now. Yup, I'm at my desk doing it . . .'

Gina stared at Nick's running gear, trying to get her breathing under control. Her attention was drawn to the T-shirt: it looked like an old favourite, one that had been washed so often the faded cotton was paper-soft. His trainers were pretty battered, too. Part of the architect's plans included a high-spec yoga/Pilates studio for Amanda with special lighting and floor-to-ceiling mirrors, but Nick was clearly more of an old-school baggy-shorts-and-trainers runner.

Casual Nick and focused Amanda weren't the most likely

pair, she thought, but she could picture them in the Style section of a Sunday paper, him in bare feet, her in oatmeal loungewear, drinking aeropress coffee in their architectural kitchen, and talking about their unorthodox transatlantic lifestyle. Amanda, particularly, had that polish that made everything Gina said feel gauche.

'. . . by this afternoon? I can email you the jpegs and you can choose which ones you want me to retouch . . .'

Whatever it was, Nick and Amanda were together. She and Stuart were not. And now Stuart was rebuilding a life with someone else, starting again in that exciting romantic-text phase. Thrilling every time the phone bleeped. Gina turned the knife, tormenting herself to get the feelings out of her system faster.

When she looked up, Nick had finished his call.

'I've been at my desk all morning, honest,' he said. 'Were you waiting long?'

'I'd just arrived,' she said brightly. Pretend this never happened. 'So! Let's talk about your cellars!' Then she hiccuped, and groaned.

'Come inside,' he said, and jerked his head towards the house.

Nick left her at the kitchen table with a glass of water, and went off to shower. 'Back in a sec,' he said, without turning, and Gina was grateful. She sipped the water and the hiccups began to recede.

Upstairs, the hot-water pipes clanked as Nick ran the shower, and Gina could hear the distant sound of the builders' radio, some intermittent banging. Sunlight fell on the pitted kitchen table, a brief spot of warmth directly on her arm. She pressed her thumbs into the hollows at the side of her skull, and let the old smell of wood and damp and bare stone flood her senses until she wasn't thinking about Stuart at all, but about the house.

She didn't hear Nick padding back into the kitchen until he was right behind her.

'Can you do me a favour? It'll only take a minute.' Without waiting for a response, he held out three eggs, two pale blue, one opaque white. 'Can you hold these eggs for me? Cup your hands . . . No, like this.' Nick positioned her hands, curving one on top of the other until they made a nest. Gina watched, as if the hands weren't her own, as he carefully laid the eggs in the hollow.

She looked down at them, since she didn't know where else to look. They were perfect. The smooth satin curve of the shells made her own hands seem like a relief map of lines and cracks.

'There.' He straightened up, holding his hands over hers as if to set them in place. 'Careful. They're my last ones, so don't break them.'

Nick leaned back and, without looking, picked up an old-fashioned Polaroid camera that lay on a chair, its squat lens facing upwards. 'Already had a couple of incidents this morning. Turns out you can't hold fresh eggs and photograph them at the same time.' He paused, and took a quick snap. 'Is that a country saying? Don't answer that. Just keep very still. Brilliant.'

Gina breathed in and out, big, slow breaths that filled her lungs with the cool air. The tension in her chest was slackening. All her concentration was fixed on the three eggs filling her hands. She had the weird sensation of everything else outside her peripheral vision blurring backwards into nothing.

Nick ripped the photo from the camera, and stuck it under his armpit.

'Are these duck eggs?' she asked.

'Yup, from the farm over that hill,' said Nick. He peeled back the paper, frowned, then took another. This time the photo seemed to be right, because he put the Polaroid down and picked up his modern digital camera. 'Lovely, aren't they?'

He was standing directly above her, leaning round to get the light right; she could smell his freshly washed hair and the fabric softener on the clean white shirt. Her other senses seemed sharper now she couldn't move. 'One more. Lift your hand a little? Left hand? Perfect. OK. Perfect.'

The steady click and whirr of his camera. The distant sound of birdsong. The soothing, encouraging murmur of his voice. Gina's concentration focused on her hands until her whole body felt centred on the eggs, and an unexpected serenity settled over her shoulders, as if something was pressing down on her, very gently.

It went on for several minutes, the clicking and adjusting.

'Why am I doing this, please?' Gina asked, feeling she ought to say something. Her voice sounded loud in her head.

Nick answered without taking his eye from the camera: 'It's for a friend's website. She makes silver jewellery but the site's called Duck Egg Blue and she wants some photos. I don't know if she's ever seen a duck egg. I could probably have used three eggs from the fridge, come to think of it. Photoshopped them. Dur.'

Click. Pause. Adjustment.

Gina had never really looked at a duck egg before. Lots of her clients wanted duck egg blue kitchens, but this was prettier than any paint colour she'd sourced. Elegant, almost green. Too nice to eat.

'You should have got Lorcan to hold them for you. The contrast would have been better.'

'Ah, great minds. No, I tried it with Lorcan's hands, but apparently there was a bit *too* much contrast there. It looked like the eggs were in a chain mail glove. His words, not mine, I should add. It's my fault for leaving it so late. It's a good thing that you came over, actually – I used Amanda's hands for the test shoot but she's not coming back until next week.'

Click. Pause.

'Although you probably heard all about Amanda's itinerary,' he added. 'Out there.'

'I wasn't listening.' Gina kept her eyes fixed on the eggs. She had a strong mental image of Nick's face: wry, apologetic.

'Sure you weren't listening.'

'I wasn't. What does she do?' Gina asked, to change the subject. 'I don't think I asked before.'

'Amanda's a Mergers and Acquisitions partner in an American law firm. They fly her all over the place to hammer out deals. Her airmiles are insane, but she gets things sorted out in half the time anyone else can. Sorry, can I . . .?' A slight twist of the finger, a gesture that managed to be very intimate but detached at the same time. 'I'm sorry she's not around this week. I'm sure you've got questions for her. But if you write them down for me I can discuss them with her tonight.'

There was a pause, in which the other, unheard half of Nick's phone conversation hovered between them.

'Just so you know, it's completely normal to have massive rows when you're renovating a house,' said Gina, since she didn't have to look at him. 'Anyone who tells you different is either lying or they've forgotten. It's very stressful, finding out that someone you thought you knew has very strong views about, say, which way round a bath goes.'

'Oh, we know.' Nick gave a mirthless laugh. 'That's why I insisted we got a third party in to manage things. When we were doing up our last house, a vase ended up going out of a window during a discussion about dimmer switches. I was about ten seconds away from following it. I can't actually remember why we thought it would be a good idea to do up another wreck but there you go. I guess it's like childbirth. You forget.'

'Where was your last house?'

'East London. We bought a semi-derelict Georgian place in Clerkenwell that had been split into flats and got an architect to put them all back together again. Lots of glass and interior staircases, very stylish. Hot-tub-on-the-roof type of thing. Sold that last year and bought a flat in the Barbican, and started looking for somewhere more rural.'

That was exactly the house Gina had imagined the

Rowntrees in. She could see the kitchen now: four shades of white, lots of glass and no handles.

'Wow,' she said. 'So how did you go from there to here?'

'Well, it's got serious cellars for the bad home-brewing hobby I fully intend to take up, and I wanted a barn to make into a studio.'

'No, I mean, why would you choose Longhampton? Do you have family connections? Did you holiday here?' Gina was genuinely curious. 'It's not somewhere people often choose of their own accord.'

Nick looked up from his camera. His eyes were unusual: pale grey, like a wintry sky, and they seemed to look right into her. He wasn't scared of eye contact, but then, Gina reasoned, he was used to looking at people all day. 'Why are *you* here?'

'I grew up in Hartley. Have you been to Hartley yet? It has a garden centre.'

'You don't have a local accent, though. So you must have moved out and come back at some point.'

Gina hadn't realised it was so obvious. She wondered what else Nick Rowntree had noticed about her, and looked down at the eggs again. 'Sort of,' she said, as Nick gently moved her hands into a new position. 'It's not a bad place to live. But people don't tend to move *into* Longhampton unless they . . . well, unless they have to. For work. Or . . . family.'

'That's kind of the point. We wanted . . .' He stopped, reconsidered, then started clicking again. '*I* wanted to buy a house somewhere secret, where you can just step out of the world for a bit, not one of those Cotswolds villages that fills up on the weekend with all the people you're getting out of London to avoid. Somewhere with seasons, and proper weather. A house that hasn't had all the history modernised out of it. I've always wanted a house with a few ghosts.'

'Lorcan was joking the other day, you know. This house isn't haunted – if anything, I get a very happy feeling from it.'

'Do you? Is that your professional opinion?'

'Yes,' said Gina honestly. 'Most houses have one room that's the obvious heart, usually a big kitchen, but this has several – the kitchen's going to be amazing, the panelled sitting room's got that fabulous view of the lawns, that dining room is a fantastic entertaining space, the gardens are begging to be enjoyed . . . It's a house designed for people to live in. It feels lived in. In a good way. Don't you think?'

Nick looked at her as if she'd put something into words that he'd been thinking himself. 'I do. I don't want to lose that in the renovation. The fact that people have lived here before us.'

'You won't,' said Gina, and glanced down at the eggs. 'Is this what you do?' she asked, before the conversation got any more personal. 'Egg photography?'

'I usually do people.'

'What? Weddings?'

'God, no. I'd rather do eggs than weddings. Portraits. I was a news photographer originally.' The camera started clicking again. 'Spent ten years in London working for *The Times*, when they still had lots of staffers, couple of years freelancing in New York when Amanda was working there. I did a bit of food photography, bit of PR fluff . . . You know. You do what comes up. Some days it's MPs, others it's eggs.'

'I've never met a photographer before.'

'Well, we're just regular people, despite what you might read in the papers.'

She took a side glance at Nick, close-shaven and clean, in his jeans and loose blue shirt. His feet were still bare, tanned and smooth. Beach feet. Pretty brave on a building site.

'You might want to put some shoes on,' she said. 'Speaking as your project manager. Lorcan'll bill you for the time it takes to drive you to the surgery in town when you stand on one of his handmade renovation nails.'

'Good point. Let me just finish this.' Nick pulled a shutter half across the big kitchen window and made a channel of light fall on Gina's hands. It threw shadows across her fingers; she'd never looked so closely at her hands before or noticed the tiny lines under lines, like the hatching on a banknote, the soft pads of flesh. 'Sorry it's so dull. Won't be long.'

'It's fine. It's quite . . . relaxing,' she added, because it was. Something about the shape of the eggs, the light, the stillness had completely dissipated the shock of Stuart's text.

It doesn't matter, she told herself. Let it go. Let it be just another thing you're handing over to someone else, like the juicer.

Silence spread between them, knitting together her still- ness with his precise, economical movements, all around the eggs. Gina had the unusual sensation of floating in the moment, just enjoying the simple beauty of three fresh eggs. Their colour, their strength. Their satisfying smoothness.

I should say something, she thought. This is too weird. I didn't come here to have some kind of out-of-body experience.

'I'm sorry ... about ... earlier.' She stumbled over the words.

'Don't be. I hope I didn't interrupt some bad news.' Nick carefully raised her cupped hands a few millimetres and turned them towards the light. His touch was soft but firm, and made her feel part of the image, as much as the eggs.

'Not really. I got a text that wasn't meant for me.'

'From someone you know?'

'Unfortunately, yes,' said Gina, bitterly. Her brain was so relaxed that the words slipped out. 'Funny how you only find out how romantic your exes are after you split up, eh?'

As soon as she'd said it, she wished she hadn't. She didn't know this man. He was *like* her friend, the way he spoke, the way they seemed to have things in common, but he wasn't her friend.

'It's surprising the number of things you find out about people just after you split up,' he said evenly, without taking his eye from the viewfinder. 'Sometimes you think, God, if you'd been like that six months ago ... But then people change all the time.'

Gina didn't reply. She felt the mood between them balancing on an edge: one more comment would tip things into overshare. Just as she could smash the eggs with one tiny squeeze, she could completely screw up this very, very important contract with one more comment.

She bit her lip, hard.

Nick took a few more photos even though she couldn't tell what difference, if any, he was picking up, then finished. 'There, all done.'

He put the camera down and removed the eggs from Gina's hands. She rubbed them together to dispel the ghostly sense that lingered on them.

'Thanks for doing that.' His tone had gone back to normal. 'I don't suppose I can persuade you to put some rings and a bracelet on for me? She's sent over some really nice engagement-type ones, lovely little diamonds that you—'

Gina opened her mouth, but before she could speak, Nick flinched, and looked cross with himself. 'Oh, shit, no, I'm sorry. That was really tactless. I have no idea how that even came out of my mouth. I'm so sorry.'

'It's fine. Really.'

'Can I make you a cup of tea?' Nick gestured towards the kettle, and she nodded. A quick cup of tea wouldn't hurt. It would reset the mood. Then straight back to business, with the measurements and the windows. Her eye hunted around for distractions.

'I didn't know you could still get Polaroids,' she said, seeing the plastic camera on the table.

'You can't. Well, you can get new versions, but that's an original.' Nick was over by the counter; she could hear him opening and closing tins. 'Do you know how much film costs for that thing?'

'Er . . . a fiver?'

'Forty quid a pack. If you can find it. They don't make it any more.'

'What? Really?' Gina looked at the camera with new respect. It was an actual antique. 'So why do you use it?' she asked, over the sound of the boiling kettle.

'I like to make sure I've got the shot exactly right before I start shooting. And the Polaroid makes me concentrate on what's actually there, not what I can put in later.'

Nick wandered back and put the mug in front of her. Gina realised he hadn't asked her what she wanted to drink. She peered into the mug. Peppermint tea.

'Calming,' he said, seeing her expression. 'And also ideal for when your builders have finished off the last of the milk. That's one of the few things I learned from the London project.'

She sipped it. It was too hot but it was actually *exactly* what she wanted. Green and fresh. She reached for the Polaroid camera, which was bringing back some vivid memories. 'My friend used to have one of these.' There'd been a time when every party at Naomi's house had been a blizzard of Polaroids. Naomi's dressing-table was covered with browning photos Blu-tacked to the mirror, the white margins covered with biro scribble. 'You always looked like you were having fun. Very difficult to look good, though.'

'That's why I like them. They capture a moment, just as it is. Digital's like that in some ways, but you can always go back and improve it. Take stuff out, put stuff in. You can't tamper with a Polaroid. It's very raw.'

'Too raw,' said Gina. 'My nose always looked *huge* in her photos.'

'You were probably just too close to the camera,' he replied. 'That's a photographer failure, not yours.'

She laughed and cupped her hands around the plain white mug. 'It's probably a good job most of them ended up in the bin.'

Nick sat down on the other side of the table and clicked a few keys on his laptop, which had been whirring gently in the background.

'So, listen, about the cellars,' said Gina. 'I should maybe call your architect direct and ask him if he's . . .'

'Do you want to see the actual photos? Of the eggs.' He gestured towards the laptop. 'They've been downloading.'

'Oh. No. It's OK. I hate seeing photos of myself,' she said quickly. 'I never look like I do in my head.'

Nick's mouth twitched. 'I was only photographing your *hands*. You're not one of those women who thinks even their hands look fat, are you?'

'No.' Gina put the tea down. She didn't know how to express the jolt she felt inside when she saw a photograph that was supposed to be her, yet featured an older woman, with straighter hair and a sharpness about her face that she didn't recognise as her own. The woman she expected to see – dark, curly-haired, diffident, angling her stance to hide her thick waist – wasn't there. An almost-twin stranger was in her place. An actress who looked a bit like the original character, but not quite.

'Let's see, then,' she said, not wanting to have to explain all that to Nick, and he turned the laptop towards her.

It didn't look immediately like a pair of cupped hands. At first glance, the three perfect eggs seemed to be held in a textured nest, composed of hundreds of greys, the fine etching pushing the smoothness of the eggs into focus. It was simple but striking, the strength of the eggs and their dormant potential glowing in the centre of the screen, like something from a myth.

'Or . . .' Nick slid his finger around the track pad and a different image flashed up, this time with her hands as the centre of the photograph, almost religious-looking, lifting the three eggs up to the viewer like an offering. Again, Gina wouldn't have recognised her hands, but for an entirely different reason. They were pale and long, and the light had bleached out any lines so they resembled a marble effigy's, folded quietly over a sleeping chest.

They're beautiful, she thought, surprised, and glanced down at the hands resting on the table by the mug. They weren't actually in bad condition at the moment, but the ones in the photo didn't look like hers. They were elegant but powerful, the hands of a more dramatic woman, even without seeing her face. A saint. A young woman. An actress.

How could *hands* look so different?

'Or . . .' Nick fiddled with the settings, making her hands paler, playing with the contrast of the eggs, and suddenly Gina didn't want to see any more. She didn't know what it was, the ease with which he was changing her, the detachment of his observation. Or maybe that the mood wasn't quite what it had been half an hour ago. The sadness had returned.

It was as if a spell had worn off, and she wanted to go somewhere and cry. Cry properly, this time.

'They're lovely,' she said, reaching for her bag. 'Um, I've got to get back to the office, actually.'

'What?' Nick looked up, confused. 'I thought we were

going to talk about the cellar. Did I say something? Was it when I mentioned home-brew? That was a joke.'

'No, I just . . . I should call the architect directly and explain the situation.' It came out wrong, too brusque, and she felt bad. 'You're busy, and there's some other paper-work I can be getting on with. Better than Chinese whispers.'

Nick scrutinised her. 'Are you sure you're all right?'

'I'm fine.' Gina glanced down at her hands. 'Sorry, I don't know what it was. Something about my hands obviously freaks me out.'

My wedding ring, she thought. It was seeing that dint in my hand where my rings were, and now aren't.

She shouldered her bag and gathered up her notebook from the table.

'Here.' Nick touched her on the shoulder and she turned. He had something in his hand: the Polaroid. 'Would you like this?' he asked. 'It's actually rather beautiful, in that little square.'

Gina looked at the pearly eggs, cupped in her hands. It was beautiful. She could see it on the white wall in her flat, like a miniature.

Nick smiled. 'Consider it your model fee?'

'Thanks,' she said, and put it into her bag.

Chapter Nine

ITEM: a pair of cats' eye sunglasses

Derbyshire, September 2007

Stuart's back is sweating in the shape of a heart. One large damp heart forming in the top centre of his orange Lycra T-shirt.

Which is ironic, because hearts are the last thing on Gina's mind. Instead, she thinks, watching it grow larger and darker as they struggle up the fourth hill of the morning, I'd like to punch him in that exact spot. Bloody cycling holidays. Is he saying I'm fat? Or is courting cardiac arrest really his idea of *my* idea of a good time?

This is not what Gina had in mind when Stuart announced that he was sweeping her off for his birthday weekend. She'd offered to arrange it for him, thinking of Rome (he loves the bloodthirsty TV miniseries of the same name; she loves art and coffee), but Stuart insisted on doing it himself. 'It's going to be perfect,' he assured her. 'You'll love it.' It is perfect – for him. The B&B they're staying in even does organic full English breakfasts.

Gina thinks she should have guessed not to pack her

bikini when Stuart told her to bring suncream but didn't mention her passport. Still, she notes, already reordering today into a hilarious anecdote about her optimistic treat of a new pair of sunglasses that'll make Naomi laugh next weekend, at least the passport's in my bag. I can still make a break for it and go to Rome. How long would it take me to cycle to Manchester airport from here?

Gina eyes Stuart's muscular back, and her stroppiness melts a bit. Naomi would point out, once she'd stopped laughing, that men like Stuart aren't mind-readers. She should have told him Rome was what she wanted. Not outright, but maybe by leaving a few brochures out. Getting a *Rough Guide to Rome*. Dressing up in a bed-sheet toga.

But Stuart wouldn't have got the toga. He'd have wondered what she was doing with the laundry.

'Come on!' yells Stuart. 'Last push!'

A line of cars has been trailing up the hill behind them, the drivers' resentment boring into Gina's back like Xenon headlights. She can imagine what they're saying about them, Stuart in his cycling shorts and her with her brand-new helmet rammed awkwardly on top of her corkscrewing curls.

She forces herself to think of something else, just to get to the top of the hill. Naomi's official engagement party invite arrived before they left. What's she going to wear for that? The blue dress Stu likes? Something new? How much weight can she lose in four weeks?

Gina half regrets telling her mum Naomi's news: Janet has stopped hinting that Gina should think about settling down and has moved on to telling her direct. She's twenty-seven now, she shouldn't hang about. Tick-tock. Men like Stuart don't hang around for ever.

Burning lungs aside, Gina doesn't feel done with her twenties yet. Her life doesn't seem to have passed through any significant starting gate into proper adulthood, and yet all around her, friends are hurtling into premature middle age like lemmings. Baby announcements in the paper, everyone buying houses, the weddings of her few uni friends and, most recently, her first grey hair, found this morning in the unforgiving B&B mirror.

Her brain automatically calculates the numbers: if her dad were still alive, he'd be fifty-six this year. Terry, fifty-eight. Kit, thirty-one next month.

Thirty-one. Gina pokes the sore spot, pretending she's distracting herself from her aching calves. Married? Probably. With children? Two blond children with golden limbs and a cool taste in music and baby love-beads.

No. Probably not children.

The taste of this morning's fried breakfast rises up the back of Gina's throat. Baked beans, bacon, tomato and a sour sense of her own life disappearing down a different track, out of sight, while she goes on cycling holidays in Derbyshire instead of driving across Death Valley in a convertible.

A car honks behind her, then another, as if in psychic agreement, and Gina jumps so hard her foot slips off the pedal.

Mercifully, at that exact moment Stuart swings out his left arm and indicates that they should pull over at the panoramic viewing spot ahead. Gina finds a final shred of energy to reach the lay-by and tries not to look as the cars stream past them, back-seat passengers gawping. Her legs are burning. Only dignity stops her bending over and gasping for air like a landed salmon.

I need to get fitter, she thinks, staring at Stuart's lean thighs.

'There!' He offers her his water-bottle, gesturing over the rolling Derbyshire countryside with the other hand. He's not even panting, and the faint sheen of sweat on his tanned brow makes him look like an Olympic rower. Something heroic, anyway. 'Isn't that worth the climb?'

Gina wants to say, yes, it's beautiful, but the sweat running into her eyes has mingled with her suncream and is stinging. She takes off her beautiful Sophia Loren sunglasses and wipes it away.

'Are you all right, Gee?' says Stuart, peering more closely.

No. I'm not all right, Gina roars in her head. I'm worn out. I've been working solidly for seven weeks without a break because my boss is waging war on unauthorised double glazing and I'd rather have spent the weekend asleep at home, or at the very least at a spa hotel in York drinking cocktails, and I'll be thirty before I know it and we still haven't discussed what's happening when our lease runs out at the end of October . . . 'I'm fine,' she says, and takes a swig of water.

Water. Who knew it could be so delicious?

'Good.' Stuart smiles and his face is kind. 'You've done really well today, considering you don't cycle much.'

'Thanks.'

'Look, um, there's something I want to say.'

'Is it to do with my outfit? Because if you'd told me to pack gym kit I'd have . . .'

'No, it's not that.' He swallows. 'It's about us.'

Her stomach plunges. *Us.* He's going to finish it, she thinks. He dragged me up a hill, and got me so breathless I won't be able to cause a scene.

'Gina . . .' Stuart clears his throat and – oh my God – he takes her hand in his.

Gina's heart thuds in a different fast pattern. For the first time in ages, she really has no idea what Stuart's going to do. The whole point of Stuart is that everything is beautifully smooth and predictable. Like East Anglia. You can see things coming from miles away with Stuart. Her throat feels tight as he fumbles in the pannier on his bike.

No, thinks Gina. Surely not.

He drops to one knee, then lifts his face up to her with unexpected seriousness, and with the countryside spread around him, like a puckered green cloak, dotted with stone churches and toy-box farms, he looks like a tousle-haired landowner from a Gainsborough portrait.

A car honks behind them, and Gina feels sick at the speed at which this moment is hurrying her towards a decision, but at the same time giddy with a thrill she doesn't recognise.

'Gina, I want to spend the rest of my life with you. Will you do me the great honour of marrying me?' he says in a rush, and offers her a box.

It's spontaneous and romantic and everything Gina's always wanted in a proposal (apart from the lycra shorts, but she can forgive that).

'Yes.' She hears a voice, but doesn't recognise it as her own. She's floating somewhere above this scene, seeing the sweet film romance of a proposal on a hill in the English countryside. A car will stop soon to offer to take a photo of the happy couple, so they can keep it on their mantelpiece. Tonight someone will be telling their wife about the adorable proposal they witnessed on the way home.

'Yes?' he repeats, unsure, and her heart melts at the touching shadow of doubt in his voice.

Gina smiles. 'Yes.'

Stuart's face brightens with relief, and he's kissing her, his arms around her, strong and warm.

Gina tastes Boots' Soltan, and hears a car honk behind them, and she wonders if this is it, the moment the starting gun goes on her adulthood.

Yes, she thinks. It probably is.

For sale: Scott Sportster Women's hybrid bike £700
Lots of gears, knobs, what-have-you, barely used. Was a
present, cost £1500

'Obviously I'd need to take it for a test run before I make you an offer.'

Gina folded her arms, and steeled herself for the argument, the same way she steeled herself against builders who wanted to remove 'just this one beam'.

This man – he'd called himself Dave on the phone

– had been examining her pristine, top-of-the-range, ten-miles-on-the-clock mountain bike for half an hour now, making occasional *hmm* noises as if it were a clapped-out Fiesta in a back-street garage. She'd have booted him out as a timewaster twenty minutes ago, if he hadn't kept asking her very specific questions to which she didn't know the answers.

Gina hated not knowing the answers to questions, but she also hated seeing the bubble-wrapped bike in the hall every time she went out, reminding her of the chain (ha!) of events that had led her to this cramped upstairs flat-for-one. Stuart had bought it for her the day after they'd got back from the cycling holiday; they'd spent the whole afternoon in the cycle shop, which Gina hadn't minded at the time because she'd convinced herself that she needed to get fit for the wedding and cycling was as good a way as any.

Apart from one arse-aching trip round the Forest of Dean, it had never left their garage.

Just seeing that saddle stirred up a giddy mixture of regret and relief in Gina, and she had to fight an impulse to tell Dave to take it and go. But then reason kicked in: the bike was worth at least seven hundred quid, and seven hundred quid in her Something Beautiful Fund went a long way, especially since Naomi still hadn't got round to helping her with the growing pile of SELL items.

'I'm not accepting offers,' she said firmly. 'I know what it's worth.'

'Do you?' Dave looked at her, and so did the scrawny greyhound sitting between him and the door. It hadn't made a sound since arriving, and Gina was starting to be unsettled by its unblinking gaze. It had eyes like black marbles and a white throat like a bib over its brindled grey coat. She kept forgetting it was there; it seemed to have a knack of making itself seem very small.

Another reason to get this over and done with. She hadn't wanted a dog in her new flat either, but Dave had been going to tie it to the door and Gina couldn't let him do that. The high street was really busy.

'Yes,' she said, raising her chin. 'It's got thirty gears and Shimano hydraulic disc brakes. Barely been ridden. Kept in a garage.'

He rubbed his face. 'But I'd still need to ride it.'

'It's a woman's bike!'

'It's a present. For my girlfriend.'

'Good luck with that,' said Gina, before she could stop herself. 'You sure she wouldn't rather have a nice diamond necklace?'

Dave grinned and revealed a surprisingly nice set of teeth for a man who'd arrived with a skinny dog wearing a cheap-looking collar. Even so, she decided, this would be the last sale she conducted from her hallway. Something about the exchange was making her feel uncomfortable – something about putting a price on her own past, and being alone with a stranger.

She kicked herself inside. Stuart would be going ballistic if he knew she was doing this. So would Naomi. Not just selling the bike but letting people into her flat. It had been really stupid to give him her home address, especially now the people in the shop had gone home. From now on, buyers could meet her in the café over the road.

The annoying thing was that it was something her mother had been right about: when Gina had arranged to meet 'Dave' she'd sort of forgotten she'd be alone. Subconsciously she'd assumed Stuart would be there, like he always was when the electricity-meter reader came round, looming capably in the background, awkward questions at the ready. She'd only gone ahead with it to prove something to herself and now she rather wished she hadn't.

She glanced at the greyhound, and it turned its head away.

'I need to take it round the block and back,' Dave went on, 'check the suspension hasn't rotted.'

Gina put her hands on her hips. 'How will I know you won't nick it?'

'I'll leave Buzz.' He nodded at the dog.

She tried to think what Stuart would do now. Or Naomi. Neither of them was a pushover. Neither of them would accept a dog as collateral for an expensive bike. 'Haven't you got a wallet? Or car keys?'

'Ah, no, I never let my wallet out of my sight. Very dodgy people out there now, copying cards and that.' He looked boldly at her. 'Anyway, I can't cycle and keep hold of him.'

'That doesn't work for me,' said Gina. It was something she'd heard Naomi say. A lot.

There was a long pause. Then Dave sighed.

'Fine,' he said, reaching into the pocket of his cargo trousers and withdrawing a roll of notes. 'Here's a hundred-quid deposit. And my dog. Who is worth a damn sight more than that to me.' He slapped two fifty-pound notes on the post table, but the sight of the roll of cash reassured Gina:

at least he'd come prepared to pay. 'I'll be five minutes. We can negotiate about the rest when I get back. OK?'

'OK,' said Gina, feeling pleased that for once she'd done what Stuart would have done.

Dave wheeled the bike down the narrow passage and Gina held the front door for him. The dog made a move to follow but Dave swept the bike out and blocked the doorway with his leg. 'Oi! Buzz, stay!' He raised a finger, and the dog flinched. 'Back in five,' he said to Gina, and shut the door behind him.

The greyhound made a faint, sad whining sound and hurried to the door but Dave and the bike had gone.

'You stay there.' Gina made a 'stay' gesture and turned back to the stairs, trying to remember where she'd put the print-out of the bike from the Internet. She wanted to refresh her memory about some of the details before Dave got back and the haggling proper commenced.

To her surprise, the dog lay down by the door, and put his long nose on his paws, the picture of cowed resignation.

Gina wasn't keen on dogs. She wondered if she ought to drag the table across the bottom of the stairs to stop him following her up, but he showed no sign of moving. With a backwards glance, she dashed up to her flat.

When Gina galloped downstairs again, clutching the bike's guarantee and some paperwork, Buzz was lying exactly where she'd left him, his sleek head pointed towards the door. He was so still that for a second Gina wondered if he'd died, but then the narrow stomach rose and fell a fraction, and the whiskers on his long nose trembled with the out breath.

Gina felt a ridiculous awkwardness, as if she and the dog were two unintroduced strangers waiting for the host to return to a party. Was she supposed to interact with it? Or just ignore it? She didn't feel anxious about being attacked: Buzz didn't seem to have the energy to get aggressive with anyone.

She checked her watch: Dave had been gone seven minutes. That was long enough to get off the high street and maybe up and down one of the terraces running along-side. How far did people need to test ride a bike?

Don't answer that, she told herself, remembering the hours and hours Stuart had spent measuring her legs and making her stand on various bikes and talking to the sales assistant. At the time she'd joked that they were fitting her to the right bike, rather than the other way around, but neither Stuart nor the assistant had laughed. She'd given up, and tried to tell herself how lovely it was that Stuart was prepared to spend so much on a present for her.

Gina picked up the hundred quid and pocketed it, then put it back on the table. Then pocketed it again.

Something about selling the bike made her feel strange. It wasn't like selling Auntie Jan's unused coffee-maker from the wedding list. The bike wasn't just a bike: it was a possible version of her that she'd rejected. There had been a time when it was going to be at the centre of her life with Stuart. They were going to be that fit outdoorsy couple who went off with their matching bikes strapped to the roof of their VW Golf, and returned, pink-cheeked and happy, on Sunday night, to a lovely meal and a bottle of red wine.

Even as she thought how nice that sounded, Gina

boggled at her own powers of self-delusion. And yet, at the time, she'd truly thought that if she could just throw herself into the cycling Stuart would throw himself into something for her sake, like ghost-hunting or something, and they'd be fine.

He hadn't. And to be fair, she thought, she hadn't exactly thrown herself very hard into cycling. The short trip to the Forest of Dean, at the end of which she'd skidded on some leaves, crashed into a bush and sprained her wrist. And then, of course, she'd had the diagnosis and everything had gone out of the window. Then they'd had the wedding to talk about, then her illness and its gruelling treatment, then the recovery that had, at the time, seemed to be the making of them as a couple. The thing that bound them together. It was ironic, then, that as soon as that was all over and done with, so were they.

Guilt crept into the pit of Gina's stomach, followed by the usual rat-like scuttle of unwanted thoughts. Maybe if she'd pedalled harder, got fitter she wouldn't have been ill in the first place. Maybe if she'd been honest with Stuart instead of pushing those doubts down she wouldn't have . . .

That was stupid. A stupid, unhelpful way to think. But—

The letterbox rattled and Gina jumped, trying to get her haggling face together, but it was only a pizza leaflet being shoved through. The greyhound was up on its white-tipped paws in the blink of an eye. It was quivering, whether from nerves or excitement Gina didn't know.

'Sorry,' she said, trying to sound reassuring. Her voice sounded wobbly, even to her. 'That wasn't him.'

Lucy Dillon

The dog turned and regarded her with his dark, anxious eyes, then slowly sank down onto his paws, despondent.

Gina sank down too, onto the stairs, and waited.

Now it was there she couldn't get the image of herself on a bike out of her head, following Stuart up the hill in Derbyshire. She hadn't known then half the things she knew now. Or maybe she had. Maybe she just hadn't wanted to look too closely at them. Maybe she'd thought if she pedalled hard enough they wouldn't catch up with her.

When Dave had been gone half an hour, Gina called his mobile and went straight through to a generic voicemail. She rang again after another ten minutes had elapsed, left another, terser, message, and when an hour had gone by and there was no sign of him or her bike, even she had to concede that maybe there was a problem.

Had he had an accident? Had he got lost?

She didn't want to face the alternative, which was that he wasn't coming back, and neither was her box-fresh Scott sportster hybrid bike.

Gina fiddled with her silent mobile and wondered what to do. Stuart would be springing into action properly now. He liked it when things went wrong. It meant that all of his worst suspicions had been proved valid, giving him permission to start planning their way out of it.

A gloomy voice in her head told her she'd just sold her bike for a hundred quid and a scrawny dog. But that couldn't be right: he wouldn't leave his dog, surely. Men didn't leave their pets. Until recently, the only things that

190

Stuart had made any sort of fuss about keeping had been Thor and Loki: he'd instructed his solicitor about it.

Now the greyhound was starting to look agitated, glancing between her and the door, as if trying to communicate something.

'Do you need to go out?' Gina wasn't sure about dogs and their toilet requirements. Thor and Loki had shunned the litter tray in favour of the next-door neighbour's garden, something that had caused untold aggravation with Mrs Pardew. The last thing she wanted in her clean new flat was a dog puddle.

Faintly annoyed, Gina looked round for something to tie to the dog's collar, so it wouldn't run off. The only suitable object to hand was her long leopard-print scarf, which she looped around it. She steered Buzz towards the back door, which led into the small yard behind the optician's.

'There you go,' she said, dropping the scarf. 'Knock yourself out.'

With a quick backward glance at her, as if he was afraid of doing the wrong thing, Buzz scuttled into a corner and relieved himself against an empty flowerpot. The long, dark stream of urine that trickled down the concrete suggested he had been holding it in as long as possible. It went on for ages, and all the while he looked away, then back at her, apprehensively.

Gina's impatience evaporated. She felt sorry for the skinny creature, all angles and twitchy energy. The previous tenant had left a hose in the corner of the yard, so she used it to rinse away the pee. As she turned the water on, the dog cowered and immediately ran towards the gate that led on to the road behind the main street.

For a second, Gina wondered if he would find its owner if she let it go: she could follow it back to his house – and get her bike.

Or just let the dog go, and write the bike off to bad luck. Easy come, easy go.

But then she had a horrible vision of the dog wandering lost along the streets, searching for a master who hadn't given two thoughts to leaving it with a stranger, and her heart flexed in her chest. She'd never been able to stand the idea of anything being lost, or wandering; there were stories her parents had never read twice, after she'd spent four nights in a row crying herself to sleep over what might have happened to Paddington Bear if the Browns hadn't found him.

And it looked so skinny. Gina knew greyhounds weren't exactly tubby, but the rows of ribs were painfully apparent beneath the dull grey coat.

'Come on in,' she said, more to herself than to the dog. 'Let's have some supper.'

The greyhound watched Gina while she heated up a carton of soup from the deli, and didn't even try to steal any of the roll she warmed in the toaster, although she could see the leathery nose twitch with interest. Instead it lay flat against the door, not looking her way but flinching each time she moved.

It felt disconcerting, having a living creature in her space again. The cats had been an imperious presence in her house, invisible until Stuart came home, then materialising on his lap, cooing with adoration in a rather overdone manner, Gina had always thought. This dog seemed determined not to interact, yet she could almost feel his anxiety humming in the air.

Had he been left with strangers before? she wondered. Was he used to this routine? Something about the dog's meekness made her feel increasingly sorry for him, as if he had more reason to be scared of her than the other way around.

Gina poured her soup into a bowl, then opened and shut her cupboards trying to find something to give him to eat. Thor and Loki had their own shelf in her repainted and perfectly organised walk-in pantry. Thor ate only brand-name cat food; Loki was lactose-intolerant with a kidney condition. Not having to feed the cats was about the only thing that seemed to be saving Gina money in her new single life. It also saved her a fair amount of time and, she had to admit it, stress. It hadn't done her self-esteem any good to be rejected on a daily basis by two cats.

In the end she made the dog a bowl of Weetabix, which he gobbled down almost as soon as the bowl touched the floor, gulping and then licking the china clean.

Gina ate her supper and took a mug of tea through to the sitting room, where she turned the radio on (a play on Radio 4: plays were good for filling chunks of the silent evenings) and opened a box of clothes to sort through. To be on the safe side, she retied the scarf to the dog's collar, the other end to the leg of the sofa, but he curled up in a tight grey ball, his nose hidden in his speckled haunches.

Gina set out her sorting baskets in the space and started separating the contents into charity donations and eBay sales. When the play finished, she made herself a fresh cup of tea, and gave the roll she'd been saving for breakfast to the dog. The hot tea warmed her, but the eager, desperate way the dog gobbled the remaining roll made her feel warmer still, and then much sadder.

When she went to bed at ten to eleven, Buzz didn't move. He was pretending to be asleep so he didn't have to interact with her.

Not so different from being married then, thought Gina, and closed the door behind her.

Chapter Ten

ITEM: a Tiffany charm bracelet with the letter G,
a tiny enamel wedding cake, and a silver angel on it.
Inside the blue box, a few confetti petals and
a placecard holder, dated and signed
by Naomi and Jason Hewson

Longhampton, 2008

Gina isn't keen on the peachy, frothy strapless dress Naomi has selected for her role as chief bridesmaid but she doesn't want to say anything because Naomi is already in a heightened state of Bridezilla anxiety. The dress she was supposed to wear, selected and fitted months ago, has fallen victim to a dressmaker breakdown. With only four months left, they've got to find another one, in the sales. One more false move (viz., laughing when Naomi made her promise not to cut or dye her hair between now and the wedding; Naomi, it turns out, wasn't joking) might result in demotion, not just from chief bridesmaid but also from best friend.

Naomi's sense of humour has gone AWOL since she opened her first wedding file. She didn't laugh when Gina and Stuart – well, Gina mainly – suggested, completely deadpan, the double football-club wedding. It was only later, when Gina reassured her that she and Stuart were in no great rush to set a date, and certainly not within confetti-tossing distance of the Hewson-McIntyre nuptials, that she stopped twitching.

The trouble is, Naomi keeps assuming that Gina also has a four-inch-thick file of wedding plans and mood boards and favour samples, and Gina doesn't. Sometimes she wakes up and forgets she's engaged to Stuart, and when she does remember, she gets a rolling sensation inside her stomach that isn't the unalloyed bliss Naomi keeps insisting she feels now she's only fourteen weeks away from being Mrs Naomi Hewson.

Being engaged is fine for now. Nice, even. Yes, nice. Everyone's off her case, and Stuart's really getting into the renovation work they're doing on Dryden Road. Which is good, because they can't afford builders, and are scraping, stripping and steaming it all themselves. Gina's thrilled by how much Stuart's starting to love their old house. Up until now, he's been much keener on the executive estate Jason's looking into for him and Naomi's next home.

'Does it fit?' Naomi demands through the changing-room curtain. 'We can always get it altered – there's still just about enough time if you don't change shape *at all*. I'm only having one bridesmaid,' she explains to Barbara, the dress-shop owner. 'My cousins aren't the sort of girls you want walking behind you anywhere, let alone up an aisle. Plus, Gina's getting married soon herself, so she's not going to do one of those undignified leaps for the bouquet.'

'Hello? It's a curtain, not a sound-proof wall,' Gina points out.

'And she's my best friend in the whole world,' adds Naomi loudly.

She hoicks at the boned bodice, and two pale apples of flesh appear between her armpits and the corset. Nice. She shuffles her breasts around inside, trying to create the pillowy bosom Naomi's achieved in her beautiful wedding dress, and feels uncomfortably like a bad Nell Gwyn impersonator.

The last time Gina was a bridesmaid it was to her own mother, in the town-hall ceremony. Gina wore a Laura Ashley dress that made her look five, not eleven. Janet wore a two-piece Jaeger suit that made her look like the registrar. Terry wore a brown three-piece suit, but, then, it was 1991.

1991. Nearly twenty years ago. Time is passing in a very weird way, she thinks. It seems to pass more quickly in Longhampton than anywhere else.

Gina's been back now for three years, and she might never have been away. Sometimes, in the pub with Stuart and Jason and Naomi, someone mentions London – usually in the context of outrageous house prices, or criminal activity – and Gina has to remind herself that she used to live there. The dresses she wore to work are at the back of her wardrobe, and the numbers of her old colleagues at Wandsworth Council are still in her phone, but there's no trace of it inside her, apart from a sense of relief whenever Tube strikes are announced on the news. The weird thing is, Gina's not that bothered. She doesn't really want to think about those numb years. They're boxed up and parked at the back of her mental attic.

This is the start of her real life, she tells herself.

'How are you getting on in there? You've got to hoist your – pardon my French – boobs right up,' interjects Barbara. 'Do you want me to come in and help?'

Gina wriggles her shoulders back to redistribute her breasts so they're not quite as obscene, and takes a first proper look at herself in the mirror. What she sees is so different from what she's used to that she stops and blinks at her reflection. What with the diamanté-studded bodice and the net petticoat, this is more a ballgown than a bridesmaid's dress, and her face above the bare shoulders looks younger and lighter (Naomi has made her ditch her glasses and put in contact lenses for this trying-on session). Prettier.

That'd be the super-flattering soft lighting in the changing room, Gina thinks cynically.

But something about the way the corsetry is squeezing her shakes out an old sense memory of the last time her ribs were compressed like this, the feeling of warm air on her shoulders—

The dress Naomi has chosen is, without her knowing, nearly identical to the one Gina wore to her first ball with Kit. It brings it right back: dancing barefoot on the deserted lawn with the dew glistening on her red toenails, feeling untouchable in the bubble he created round them. That world where they were both still young and reckless and completely oblivious to everything that could go wrong.

Gina hasn't let herself think about that night for a long time, but with the bones of the dress squeezing her waist in exactly the same way as her dress did then, she can smell the early morning already heating up, the flower arrangements giving off their secret night-time burst of scent, caramelised candy-floss and shirt starch, Kit's aftershave and her own sunburned skin, undercut with the hangover creeping around the edges of her kaleidoscoping brain. And she misses it. Oh, my God, she misses it so much her whole chest is contracting – because it's gone. All those possibilities are gone.

She closes her eyes and lets herself yield to the desperate longing to go back. But she can't – it's not even that she wants that particular moment; Gina just wants to go back to the night of the accident and *not ruin things*. That's all she's ever wanted. To go back and let that life carry on the road it was supposed to, because who knows where they'd be now, if she hadn't spoiled everything?

Stop it, she thinks, furious with herself. Why are you thinking about this now? Why are you ruining this really nice day out?

'Are you OK in there?' Naomi jiggles the curtain. 'Come on out!'

Gina pulls herself together, and swishes back the curtain. She can tell from Naomi and the wedding dress lady's faces – the sudden, too bright smiles – that it's not right. She and the peach dress don't have the 'wow factor' they keep banging on about.

'It's *nearly* there,' says Barbara, encouragingly. She makes a scooping gesture. 'You need to hoick your boobs up. Here, let me show you.'

'No!' Gina steps backwards into the cubicle, nearly

ripping the curtain off its hooks. Naomi looks surprised. 'It's fine. I'll . . . Hang on.'

She pulls the curtain, and turns away from them, reaching into the corset to lift her handful of soft flesh higher up, and that's when she feels the lump, like a pea, buried in the lower side of her left breast. Her fingers linger for a moment, as if she could pop it like a spot.

Gina's hand freezes, and she holds her breath. Slowly, she removes her hand, and lifts the other breast up, irrationally hoping there'll be an identical lump there to explain the first. A gland or something. But it's fine – smooth and warm, the nipple nestling into her palm. Tentatively, she slips her hand around the left breast again, but this time she can't feel anything. The breath leaves her in a rush.

Probably just the corset. And she's about to start her period. Probably just that. That would explain the hormonal flashbacks, too, she thinks, relieved to have a reason.

Gina has an abrupt, stupid image of the Princess and the Pea. Surely if it was something bad she'd have felt it before. It'd hurt. This doesn't hurt. It's fine. Her fingers start to move there again, unable to resist. This time she can feel something.

'Gina?'

She pulls back the curtain and Naomi's expression brightens. Gina can see herself in the mirror behind them – tall, and dark, her cheekbones rounded under the light, and her breasts ice-creamy white above the corset.

Gina can't stop staring at her reflection over their heads, as if this new grown-up her is a ghost in the room behind them. She doesn't look ill – if anything she's put *on* a few pounds. Aren't you meant to start losing weight if you've got . . . lumps?'

'No wonder she's staring at herself!' says Barbara, approvingly. 'Where were you hiding *that* bosom?'

'You look beautiful.' Naomi's eyes fill and beneath the expensive haircut and designer scarf, Gina sees the teenager again, the girl who couldn't hold her vodka, who lied about liking Blur to impress Scott Rufford. She wonders what Naomi's seeing when she looks at *her*. How much has she changed?

She feels messy with emotions, and guilty that she's about to spoil what Naomi's wedding magazines say is a key bonding process for bride and maid.

'Are you OK, Gee?' asks Naomi, suddenly.

'Wedding dresses make everyone a bit teary,' says Barbara, all girls together. 'Your turn next, I hear.' And she winks.

'Yes,' said Gina, but the voice doesn't sound like hers.

In the morning, the dog was still curled up on the cushion by the door where Gina had left him, his long nose tucked into the sleek curve of his hind leg, making a tight knot of skin and bones. She was surprised by how small he was – in her mind, standing in the hallway, he'd been bigger. Now he looked like a kidney bean.

He was alive, because she could see the barrelled ribs rise and fall softly with each breath. She watched, counting the long seconds between each, noting the fine sprinkling of grey around his muzzle, the snowflake pattern of spots on his haunches. Although his eyes were shut while she stood there wondering what to do next, when she moved towards him they snapped open, and in a second the greyhound was on his feet, cowering slightly, his beady gaze fixed on her as if already fearing what her next move would be.

Gina didn't know much about dogs, but the submissive way its thin tail was curved between its legs made her feel ashamed of the irritation that had been bubbling in her head. He *was* bigger, standing up, but rather oddly shaped, with that broad chest and narrow hips and small, slightly prehistoric head.

'It's OK,' she said awkwardly. The greyhound shivered, though that might have been from the draughty hall; she could see the muscles twitch under his skin.

Talking to the dog was a bad sign. You've got to move it out before you start feeling guilty, she thought, as he – Buzz? Was that what the man had called it? – slunk into the kitchen. This is not your problem.

As the greyhound passed her, white-tipped paws making no sound on the laminate flooring, Gina could hear his stomach make a pathetic rumbling noise and knew she was going to have to feed him before she worked out what to do next.

Gina made Buzz another bowl of Weetabix, which he wolfed down before she had time to pour the milk on her own. Then, because he was still eyeing her plaintively, a nervous side glance that she couldn't bear to meet, she gave him a couple of digestive biscuits too, which he picked up and took under the table. He crunched them quickly and neatly, one eye on her the whole time.

While she ate, Gina ran through her own day in her head. She had an appointment to inspect the first stage of Naomi's playhouse-shed, which was taking shape in the joiner's workshop on the Longhampton Trading Estate, and from there, she needed to pick up some new paint cards from the renovation suppliers on the same estate; that gave her plenty of time to drop the dog off at the police station and report the theft of her mountain bike.

The only minor flaw in the plan was that she didn't know where the police station was since it had moved out of the town centre, and her Internet still wasn't set up, so she couldn't check online. Gina hadn't told her mother that. It fell into the list of tasks Stuart would have done, which she was definitely going to tackle soon. Being without the Internet was, in some ways, much less stressful than she'd expected.

Buzz watched her from under the table as she found the phone book in the pile of junk mail, then waited in a queue to talk to a human being at the station. It took a long time, and when she got through, the desk sergeant sounded harassed. Reporting the theft wasn't a problem – they'd send an officer after work to take her full statement – but the dog was. Apparently there was no room at the inn, literally, since they'd just raided a suspected drugs den guarded by no fewer than five dangerous dogs, all of which were now in the police station's emergency kennels.

Gina didn't want Buzz in her flat, but she didn't want

him in a kennel with dangerous dogs. He looked terrified enough already.

'What sort of dog is it?' the desk sergeant asked.

'Um, a greyhound?' Gina peered at Buzz. 'A whippet? I'm not an expert. He's skinny, anyway.'

'Is it dangerous? Snappy?'

'No, he's very quiet.' She checked her watch. She didn't want to be late for the joiner: he'd made noises about having to go out to cost a job at half past. 'Look, I just want to hand this dog over to someone who'll look after him. And I want to report a stolen bike, please.'

'To be fair, this is more of a matter for the dog warden. It's technically a stray dog you've got there . . . Let me give you a number to call. Have you got a pen?'

'What? Not an address where I can drop the dog off? Is he going to take long?'

'I can't say. He's usually out on call during the day, and it's a council department, so if you could keep the dog in your house until—'

'I can't do that! I have to go out.'

'Give me a moment.' The desk sergeant muffled a sigh, and in the background Gina could hear some frenzied barking. Did Buzz shrink under the table?

The phone came off mute. 'Right. Can you drop the dog off at the Four Oaks rescue kennels on the Rosehill road? They're one of the local overspill kennels for strays. I can give you directions and a number for them.'

'I know where it is.' Four Oaks Kennels was on the way out of Longhampton towards Rosehill. Gina had driven past the gold-and-green painted sign – the spreading oak tree

with paw-shaped leaves – often enough. It was the same spreading oak tree that was on the sign for their charity shop opposite her window.

She arranged a time for the constable to come and take down the details of the stolen bike, then hung up. 'Well,' she said to Buzz, 'you're going to be fine. They're very nice ladies up there – they do a lot of reading.'

His ears flattened against his head as if he were listening to her, and she felt surprised again at how unthreatening he was for a large, strange dog. Gina hesitated for a second, then reached out to stroke his head, but he shied away, backing into the sofa. When her mobile rang he flinched, and scurried to the door, tail rammed between his legs again.

Gina kept an eye on him as she answered; it was Tony the joiner.

'Hiya, Gina,' he said, and immediately she could hear the apology in his voice. 'Would it be all right if you came a bit earlier this morning? It's just that job I was going to quote for has moved and the lads are all out.'

'How much earlier?'

'Er, as soon as? I need to talk you through a few choices,' he said pointedly. 'As I recall the client was quite specific about some of the details. We're having a bit of trouble with some of these specs.'

Gina couldn't deny that. Naomi had had some quite innovative ideas about how the shed was to be divided between a three-year-old girl and a thirty-something bloke. A bespoke playhouse-shed was necessarily quite a complex design statement.

'OK,' she said. 'I'll be there as soon as I can but I've got to do a . . .' She had glanced out of the window across the high street and seen a very quick way of shaving half an hour off her schedule.

'That's not the most sensible lead I've seen but it's probably the most stylish,' said Rachel when Gina dashed into the Four Oaks shop with her latest donation. 'Can I interest you in a more traditional option?' She waved her long hand towards a rail of punched-leather martingales and handmade dog coats.

'No, thanks. Didn't I explain? I'm supposed to be getting rid of things,' said Gina. She dumped two bags of clothes on the desk. 'Here. I've got some clothes for you. Call it a sweetener.'

They were actually some of the clothes she and Naomi were supposed to be selling, but Naomi hadn't been round to help and Gina reckoned she needed to butter up the dog-rescue people a bit.

'Thanks! That's fab. I hope you're not getting rid of this handsome chap, though.' Rachel slipped out from behind the counter and bent to stroke Buzz's velvet ears. He pushed his narrow head into her hand, closing his eyes in a show of trust. 'You're a beaut,' she cooed. 'What are you called, eh?'

'Buzz. And he's not mine. I'm dropping him off with you.'

Rachel lifted her head in surprise. A hank of black hair from her choppy bob fell into her eyes; she pushed it back so she could fix Gina with an amused look. 'No, no. We do books, and old cardies, and jigsaws. Not *actual* dogs. You need to take him up to the rescue. Do you know where it is? Up on the hill, just past the big cherry tree?'

'I don't have time this morning. And I don't think I could get him into my car.'

Rachel stood up and brushed white hairs from her trousers. 'Beautiful as he is, I can't just take him in – there are procedures to go through. Who does he belong to? Did you find him wandering on the streets?'

'Some lowlife left him as collateral while he stole my bike last night. I phoned the police, and they told me to take him to the kennels so the dog warden can collect him and . . . do whatever they do with stray dogs.' As she said it, Gina wondered what the warden did with stray dogs. She had an unpleasant vision of *Lady and the Tramp*, and the pound truck. Another much-loved children's film that had given her nightmares, much to Janet's bewilderment.

'His owner just abandoned him?' Rachel's expression darkened.

Gina nodded. 'I don't know if he'll try to turn up and collect him – at which point I hope the police will nick the bastard, and hopefully get my bike back. If he hasn't sold it on already.'

'Bike, schmike,' said Rachel. 'Do you want this dog to go back to someone who'd leave him with a stranger? Do you have any idea what some people will do with a stray dog?'

Buzz had stayed stock still while they were talking about him, but out of the corner of her eye, Gina saw him sink to the ground, and curl up against a bookshelf, trying to make himself invisible. There was something pathetic about his eagerness to vanish from their sight that made her sad and angry at the same time.

Rachel must have seen it too, because her voice trailed off.

'So it's OK to leave him with you? Please?' Gina pounced. 'It's just that I'm already late for a meeting . . .'

'Fine.' Rachel flapped her hands. 'Leave him with me. I'll take him up there at lunchtime. But give me your number in case there's a problem.'

Gina's shoulders relaxed. She hadn't realised how subtly Buzz and his haunted eyes had lassoed her until the tightening band across her head suddenly slackened. She really didn't want to have to worry about something else, not when she sometimes forgot to make herself supper or spent whole nights lying awake.

'You're in safe hands here,' she told him, and untied her good scarf from his collar, then handed it to Rachel. 'Consider this a donation. It's Alexander McQueen.'

Rachel sighed, and looked at Gina as if she knew exactly what she was thinking.

Even in its early stage, the playhouse-shed standing in the centre of Tony's joinery workshop really was something to behold.

'Seriously, Tony,' said Gina, as they stood gazing at it, 'I could move in there myself.'

It was a shed of two halves. From the front, it was a pretty cabin, with pine shutters decorated with cut-out hearts, and tiny window boxes waiting to be filled with silk flowers; inside there was space for a play kitchen and a table for tea and a comfy chair 'for grannies'. That was one half. Round the back, however, another, much plainer, door led into a compact Man's Shed, with enough room inside for a leather recliner, a small television, a beer fridge and whatever else Naomi felt Jason needed to hide out with. The two rooms were separated by a sturdy dividing wall running down the middle, with a discreet serving hatch/observation window.

'Well, we got the two doors and the two halves thing solved,' said Tony, surveying it critically. 'Mind you, it's not going to be cheap, not with all those details your client wanted.'

'Don't worry about that. The budget's . . . generous.' Gina didn't want to think about how many of her own Christmas gifts Naomi had eBayed to pay for it. 'And the furniture's next, now you've done the main house?' she added.

The play kitchen was going to be Gina's own present to Willow: a mini Welsh dresser like the one in her own old house, and a table and chairs in the shape of toadstools to have tea on.

'Got one of the apprentices on it.' Tony folded his arms, amused. 'Started calling Kyle "the Elf", what with all the little chair legs he's been making.'

Gina smiled, and took some photos on her phone to send Naomi. Something about the playhouse was making her feel a bit broody, but she couldn't work out whether it was for children she didn't have or because, deep down, the little girl inside her was stamping her feet for an all-mod-cons Wendy house with real windows, and a proper black latch on the front door. Maybe a bit of both, she decided.

You'd have to have a heart of stone not to want your own scaled-down window boxes, complete with miniature roses.

Gina got home at five, determined to make a start on her project for the week: downloading all her music onto her laptop so she could sell or give away the CDs currently taking up two boxes' worth of space in her bedroom. She was fed up with having to climb over them to go to bed, and now the sitting room was starting to look clearer, she didn't want to get used to some level of clutter. The flat had to be *cleared*.

'Music' was item eighteen on her list. The additions were snaking down the lining paper now, some with a few doodles next to them, if Gina felt moved to it. She hadn't drawn in a long time. Now the whole wall felt like a giant sketch pad, tempting yet off-putting. The list was getting interesting, and she was trying to choose instinctively, rather than with logical reasons.

Some choices were practical – her laptop, her hi-fi speakers, her indulgent feather duvet, which was cool in summer and warm in winter – while some were deliberately impractical and sentimental: a framed photo of her mum and dad at Ascot, the lucky cat mascot Naomi had given her before her A levels. She couldn't choose just one CD, when so much of her life was soundtracked by her music collection, so she'd chosen all of it.

Gina slotted the first Beatles disk into her laptop to start copying it across, and thought how old-fashioned CD cases looked now. Some of these had been to university with her, some to her house share in London and others were really

Stuart's. Scratched, some with inserts missing, broken hinges. And yet the music was still clean and sharp. She did a rough mental calculation of how much hard cash had been spent on the contents of these two boxes and felt a bit sick. Still, if the charity shop got a quid for each of them, she'd more than paid for Buzz to have a few meals in the rescue.

She frowned. Buzz would be fine. And he wasn't her responsibility. She'd done the right thing, handed him over to the people who could look after him.

In the time it had taken her to sort out all the Beatles albums into a pile, *Revolver* had downloaded. Gina ejected the disk, clicked it back into its box and consigned it to GIVE AWAY and reached for *Rubber Soul*. There was something satisfying about downloading: it was going to fill up a useful chunk of quiet evenings, when she could tell her mother and Naomi that, yes, she was keeping busy, thanks.

She did some tidying while the Beatles' albums were being copied, but as she ventured into the Nineties, nostalgia started to slow Gina down. The CDs had been stored in floor-to-ceiling shelves in Dryden Road so she hadn't looked at the covers in a long time but now she did, and the memories came back as she opened each case.

Nick Drake. Lying in bed with Kit, listening to *Five Leaves Left* over and over while they kissed until her lips were raw.

Nirvana reminded her of revising with Naomi on the grass behind the rounders pitch.

Now That's What I Call Music! compilations with tracklists on the back conjured up entire long summer afternoons listening to the radio in her bedroom.

Radiohead, the Flaming Lips, Editors: the sounds of her chemo months. Complicated, textural music she'd never had time for when she was busy but which filled up her afternoons in bed while she was slowly resurfacing after the treatments, unable to move or think, and needing distraction from the pain in her bones, in her muscles. Gina put those to one side: she knew right now she'd never listen to Arcade Fire again because she'd be swamped with nausea.

She wondered what would be the musical memory for this phase of her life. You never really knew until the time had passed completely, and you heard something at random and everything came flooding back.

Alanis Morissette. Gina held *Jagged Little Pill* and ran her finger over the case, cracked where someone had stood on it at a party. It was the first CD she'd bought, from HMV in Longhampton, and it had sparked off her first proper teenage row with her mother, who seemed convinced that owning a CD with a parental guidance sticker meant that Gina was headed off the rails and into a life of drunkenness and tattoos.

Terry had tried to calm it down. At the peak of the argument, Janet had spat out something about Gina not getting this sort of behaviour from *her*, and the defiance had abruptly dropped away from Gina to be replaced with curiosity. What, exactly? As far as she knew, her soldier dad had had about as much in common with Alanis Morissette as she did. But Janet had clamped her mouth shut, claimed she had a migraine and stormed off to bed, leaving the questions hanging in the air.

Terry had persuaded her not to pursue it. 'She's just

worried about you growing up,' he'd said. 'Don't read anything into it. Some of those lyrics are a bit . . . angry, love.'

But as Gina had moaned to Naomi afterwards, what else could she do but read things into it when her mother never told her anything? She read in everything she could. You didn't get into the SAS if you were any old soldier. Your death didn't get a complete security blackout unless you were doing something dangerous.

And *how* was she like her dad? Were there genes in her that could be trained to kill, to stalk, to go charging into danger? Had he been like that all the time? How her mother, so neat and pretty, had ended up married to a man she wouldn't talk about was as much a part of the mystery as he was. Janet had only known Huw for four years. Less time than Gina had lived with Stuart.

Gina hadn't been listening to the tracks as they downloaded onto her laptop but on an impulse she clicked on 'You Oughta Know'.

All the hairs on the back of her arms stood up. She'd forgotten just how much anger was in that song.

The buzzer sounded, and Gina jumped as if someone had come into the room.

She turned off the music and fumbled with the entry-phone, trying to compose herself. Was it the policeman? Maybe Dave back with her bike?

'Hi,' said an unfamiliar voice. 'It's Rachel Fenwick from the dog rescue. Have you got a moment?'

'Yes, of course.' Gina pressed her lips together, pulling herself back. Rachel could take some of these CDs – perfect timing. 'Push the door, it's unlocked.'

While Rachel came up the stairs to the flat, Gina moved quickly around the room, straightening the three yellow cushions on her sofa, moving her laptop off the coffee table, relighting the hyacinth candle and turning on a couple of lamps. She found herself hoping that Rachel was calling to tell her that Buzz had been claimed, or was now settled in the kennels up the road. She didn't want him, but she didn't want him to be unhappy either.

There was a brisk knock at her door, and when she opened it, Rachel was standing in the doorway with two jute bags, both of which were filled with stuff. Next to her, on a lead attached to a brand new martingale collar, was Buzz.

Gina had a funny sinking feeling. So did Buzz, who cowered a little against Rachel's jeans.

'Hello!' Rachel raked a hand through her dark bob. 'I have good news and bad news. But mainly good. I think.'

'You'd better come in,' said Gina. Rachel seemed much keener to come in than Buzz did.

Chapter Eleven

ITEM: a tatty red A4 file of hospital notes,
referral letters, appointment cards, printed
fact sheets, Internet printouts

Longhampton, June 2008

Stuart hasn't stopped talking since they left the hospital car park, but the words are sliding past Gina's ears. Instead she's ticking off the familiar buildings on her side of the road: the row of Victorian terraced houses painted pink, yellow and fawn, the Neapolitan houses, as she's always thought of them, two Border Oak new-builds, then the church. The creamy magnolias in the garden of the big villa set back from the road, exploding with exuberance over the wall. And then the main run of houses peters out, and they're passing the old technical college, the Esso garage, heading back to half-finished Dryden Road, and the anaglypta they were going to steam off this weekend.

The outside world is exactly the same as it was when they passed this way a few hours ago, yet it feels as if it's pivoting in the opposite direction. The anaglypta will still need steaming. It's just that now she has breast cancer.

She tries it again in her head. Now I have breast cancer.

It still sounds as if she's talking about someone else. Someone braver, someone older.

Following her consultation with the Midlands' best breast surgeon, Gina officially has one small lump and some affected lymph nodes, all of which will be removed by Dr Khan at 3 p.m. on Friday.

'. . . and then he said it was a positive factor that it hadn't spread beyond those lymph nodes, which is something to focus on,' Stuart continues, as if she hadn't been there while Mr Khan was telling them exactly that. 'And then I asked him about hormone treatment, and he said because yours was oestrogen receptive, you'd be able to have Tamoxifen . . .'

Gina lets Stuart carry on talking, neatly sidestepping the word *cancer* as he goes. Recapping stressful situations has always been his way of dealing with things. He likes to feel on top of the facts, owning the options when they come out of his mouth this time round. In a way it's reassuring: being swept along on Stuart's train of practicality gives her the secret space in her head for the wider implications Gina knows he won't let her air.

How should she tell her mother? Janet gets hysterical in hospitals; she fusses like a demented hen, manages to make it all about herself. Better not tell her. Well, no, they'll have to tell her something: it'd be hard to disguise the chemotherapy.

Gina watches the art deco fire station slide by outside her window. And time off work. When to tell *them*? When to write letters, in case . . . Well, in case. And her stuff. There's so much stuff to sort out.

'. . . brilliant that the lump's so small. He said he didn't think you'd need reconstructive surgery. Not that that matters . . .'

Darker thoughts press in like clouds. It's not the size of the lump that freaks Gina out, it's that it's there at all. What has she done to get cancer? How did it start in her? Was it a trauma? Or stress? Has it always been there, waiting? Or has she caused it?

The Internet has not helped. Gina read some hideously judgemental blog about cancer being caused by suppressing emotions, forcing negativity down like coal, until it compacts into cancer. The words had felt as if someone had been yelling them in her head.

'. . . I can take some time off work to go with you to chemo, or my sister can come, as she's only a few streets away from the breast clinic . . .'

Stuart's not leaving any space for her to say anything, but Gina doesn't want to speak. It's as though he's talking about a friend, not her.

She mentally twirls around the spire of St Mary's Church and realises she's imagining herself flick-flacking from roof to roof of each house they pass, as she used to in the back seat of Terry's car. Gina pushes a fingernail into the fleshy web between her thumb and her forefinger to bring herself back into Stuart's car, into this moment. Into this new development that's actually happening to her *now*.

'. . . and you'll be almost halfway through your chemotherapy by my birthday in September so maybe we could go somewhere, if you're up to it . . .'

At last Gina's blood freezes with realisation.

Naomi's wedding's in September. The apricot-and-cream-themed wedding they've been planning for nearly a year while Jason and Stuart have been at cricket nets and the gym, and she'll be the spectre at the feast, the Bridesmaid with Breast Cancer, not even halfway through her treatment.

My hair, thinks Gina. My hair will have fallen out. Naomi will go mad. I'll totally upstage her if I follow her down the aisle with a bald head. Maybe I can get a wig.

The thought of Naomi's face when she has to tell her she'll be wearing a wig to her wedding makes Gina giggle hysterically, and Stuart finally stops talking.

'What did I say?' he asks. 'What's funny?'

She glances across and notices, with surprise, how drawn he is. Stuart's forehead is creased with concentration but there's a vulnerability around his mouth that she's never seen before, and she feels guilty: he'll have to bear this too. The chemo, the appointments, the strain of not being able to *do* anything.

'Is something funny?' he repeats, more uncertainly.

Gina hesitates. Stuart probably won't find it funny. But she tries. 'No, I . . . Just that I might have to wear a wig for Naomi's wedding. If my hair falls out.'

He frowns, then tries to smile. 'Why not? Think positive. We can get you a gorgeous wig – we can go to London, if you want. Naomi'll just be glad you're there.'

'She'll maybe want me to get an apricot-coloured one,' says Gina, hearing Naomi saying just that, chasing away the dread with a silly joke. 'To match the dress.'

'What? Of course she won't. And if she did, I'd tell her to get a bloody grip.' His voice cracks, as if he's about to cry.

He doesn't get it, thinks Gina, but at the same time she's reassured by exactly that, by Stuart's solid presence with his facts and his determination to win. To beat things.

'Oh . . . shit,' says Stuart, and pulls into the drive-through McDonald's.

They sit in the car park, saying nothing, and the tempting smell of chips floats into the car. Gina's surprised that it's still tempting. The radio's been on in the background, and she hears the gloomy opening bars of 'Chasing Cars' by Snow Patrol.

Stuart lunges at the off button.

'Don't,' says Gina, mildly. 'I've never liked that song. Now I've got a reason to hate it.'

They really don't know what to say to each other. There's too much. Too much they know they don't know. The car feels huge.

'You're going to be fine,' says Stuart, eventually, and there's a wobble in his voice, under the determination. 'We're going to beat this.'

Gina forces a smile onto her face. This'll be the easier way, playing the part of the brave patient until she believes it. Until it feels real. 'I know,' she says. 'One step at a time.'

'Gina.' Stuart grabs her hand over the gearstick and makes her look at him. 'I want to bring the wedding forward. Marry me this month. Before the chemotherapy starts.'

'But Naomi's wedding . . .' It's her first reaction; she knows it's stupid.

'Sod Naomi.' He looks outraged. It'd be funny, Gina thinks, if she could bear to laugh. 'You're the only thing that matters to me. I want to show the world we're a team, you and me. I love you.' Stuart gazes at her, handsome and resolute and only slightly scared. Knight-like. 'I *love* you, Gina.'

Did Mum feel like this when Dad proposed? Gina wonders. The feeling of being swept up in the arms of a strong, brave man who'll fight for you is so reassuring right now, even if it goes against everything she'd usually believe.

But this isn't usual. Nothing is usual any more. Her doubts about Stuart's minor failings seem churlish, snotty, compared with his fundamental decency. What's more important?

She buries her head in Stuart's shoulder, tearful with gratitude. He smells of Hugo Boss and the Persil she used to wash their clothes earlier in the week when she didn't definitely have cancer.

It still doesn't feel quite real.

'Okay,' she says. 'Let's get married.'

'The thing is,' said Rachel, 'it wouldn't be for long. A week at the most . . .'

'No, sorry,' said Gina, in case Rachel hadn't heard her the first time.

'. . . and I *promise* you there's no way I'd even be asking under normal circumstances, but you seem like a decent sort of person, and to be honest with you, he's literally got nowhere else to go.' Rachel raised her palms. 'We're so full I've got dogs in the *house*.'

'What about private kennels? I'll make a donation towards it.'

Rachel let out a quick, mad laugh. 'I *am* the private kennels. All our volunteer fosterers are full up. We've got as many dogs as we're legally allowed to take. I've rung around all the rescues in the county and I might be able to find Buzz somewhere by the weekend, but until then, even the police station can't take him. And I suppose the owner might come back, in which case you'd have to hand him over anyway.'

'I take it the owner hasn't reported him missing?' Gina was surprised to find that she didn't really care about the bike. It had gone. Fine. She'd never liked it. Somehow she was angrier about the dog: for the callous way he had been dumped with a stranger, and because she now felt responsible for him.

Rachel leaned down and cupped Buzz's ears in her hands, caressing them as if she didn't want him to hear. 'Of course no one's reported him missing. My husband scanned for a microchip but he couldn't find anything.' She glanced up, and added, 'He's a vet,' as if Gina might assume they had some kind of dog-scanning kit at home for fun.

She lifted the corner of Buzz's left ear, which was much shorter than the right now Gina looked at it. 'He probably had a tattoo on this ear, for ID, but as you can see, someone decided to remove it.'

Gina's skin crept. 'What? They . . .?'

'Chopped it off. Yes. A while ago – see where it's healed.'

'God, that's awful.' She flinched as the bloody image

flashed in front of her eyes – the fear. The pain. Buzz's fear of people seemed understandable now.

'It's not uncommon in failed greyhounds.' Rachel laid a long hand on his head. Buzz closed his eyes, and Gina could see the effort he was making to remain still. 'They're treated very badly sometimes. And Buzz isn't very big. I can't see him winning many races. We often get greys handed in half starved, just ditched in Coneygreen Woods. Tied to trees or just left to wander around to fend for themselves.'

'I still can't understand how anyone could just abandon their dog with a stranger, for the sake of a bike.'

'If it was his dog. Easy trick – get a dog from somewhere, pretend it's yours . . .' Rachel shrugged. 'Don't get me started, I could be here all night.'

Gina gripped her mug of peppermint tea. Be firm, she told herself, as she ached inside. Do not be pushed over. This is about you feeling abandoned, not some dog.

'So, I know it's a lot to ask,' said Rachel, 'but could you keep him here for a few days? Someone from Greyhound Rescue West of England might be able to take him but if you could just give him somewhere to sleep till then? An old duvet would do. They're incredibly easy-going, greys . . . Listen, I don't normally do emotional blackmail. It's very much my last resort.'

Gina sighed, and she knew Rachel would hear the sigh as a half-yes. It was what it sounded like to her. 'I'm not a dog person,' she said.

'Ah, well, greyhounds aren't your average dog!' Rachel's face brightened. 'No yapping. No digging. They like to sleep most of the time, and they're very tactile. I bet Buzz'll be curling up on your knee given half a chance.'

'Seriously?' Gina eyed the dog; he looked like a bag of bones. Not what she'd call cuddly.

'You just have to feed him,' she went on. 'Look, I've brought some food with me, and some instructions – I see you've got a backyard, so there is outdoor access – and give him a couple of half-hour walks. Greys don't need long walks. They're happy with short bursts.'

'Yes, but I work full time,' said Gina, playing her trump card. 'I don't have time to walk him.'

Rachel looked as if she'd been expecting that response. 'If you wanted to drop him off at the shop in the morning we could take care of him during the day. We've got a yard behind the shop and I sometimes bring my own dog in, and he just naps. I don't know if you saw him? The Border collie? He and Buzz have already met – they get on fine.'

Gina chewed the inside of her lip. Stuart would have said no half an hour ago. He wouldn't have made Rachel tea, as she had, or let her bring Buzz and his heartbreaking anxiety into her flat. Stuart never let anything unpleasant into their world; he stood at the threshold and repelled unpleasantness with logic and politeness. He'd have given Rachel fifty quid and firmly directed her out of their life.

While they were speaking, the greyhound was slowly relaxing his tense muscles against Rachel's buckled boot, matching the texture of his coat to the battered suede. Even in his skinny state, Buzz was more finely sculpted than any dog Gina had seen before. He had a weary nobility that reminded her of Elizabethan portraits of princes posing

with a hand on the head of their hunting hound, a bejewel-
led collar on its long neck.

But it's such a cliché, Gina told herself. Split up, get a
dog. It's what everyone expects you to do. Why not just
enjoy being on your own for a while? Spend some time on
yourself, don't allow yourself to be distracted by another
project.

'I hope you won't take this the wrong way,' said Rachel,
carefully, as if she was offering an observation Gina
might not want, 'but dogs can be wonderful company
when you don't want any *actual* company, if you know
what I mean.'

Gina met Rachel's gaze. She had very honest brown
eyes, framed with mascara, but crinkled at the edges. They
were eyes that had cried and laughed and didn't care that
much about crow's feet. Friendly eyes.

'Sorry?' said Gina.

'It just reminded me, the boxes, the new kettle . . .' Rachel
waved a hand round the room. 'Stop me if I've got it totally
wrong, but I've been here too, unpacking an old life into a
new one. It absolutely *sucks*. Everything about it sucks, no
matter what people tell you about fresh starts and all that
heal-yourself-sister bollocks. But dogs are great for broken
hearts. They don't give you advice, for one thing.'

Gina straightened her back. 'And how do you know I've
got a broken heart?'

Rachel shrugged. 'Because my house looked like this
when I moved in? No photos. Everything in new places.
And, call me Shirley Holmes, last week you donated fifteen
different books on how to leave a bad relationship and

variations on that theme. We've got an entire self-help section now, thanks to you.'

'That's . . .' Gina started to protest, then realised there was no point. She'd told Rachel everything about herself in her drop-offs.

'Brought back some memories, seeing those,' sighed Rachel. '*He's Not That Into You.* God Almighty. I *hated* that book. *It's Called a Break-Up Because It's Broken. Three* different people gave me that. I reckon they sell more to concerned friends than they do to actual dumpees. And they're all aimed at women, you notice.'

'Only women buy instruction manuals about how to end things without upsetting anyone,' said Gina. 'Men just get on with it.'

'Hah! If only it were that easy! In my experience, men prefer to manoeuvre you into doing it for them, then look all shocked and sad.' Rachel dangled her hands limply at the wrist, like pretend puppy paws. '"You're *dumping* me? Because I'm *sleeping with someone else*?" It took me about five years to work out that I should leave my ex. That's a lot of self-help books, believe me. So I know a woman trying to leave a relationship when I see one.'

Gina turned her cooling mug of tea round and round, not wanting to overshare but at the same time feeling warmed into confession by Rachel's exasperation. It felt wrong talking about divorce too much with Naomi: they both knew that Naomi wasn't really jealous of her freedom and time, and that Gina wasn't 100 per cent fine about it either.

'Sorry, I shouldn't be glib,' said Rachel. 'I know it's never straightforward. But it does get better. Just don't get a cat.

They just look at you like ... *meh. Here we are, the single woman and her cat. Great.* Now a dog will look at you like ... *how could he leave you? You're amazing.*'

Gina managed a small smile. 'You can stop selling the dog to me. I'll look after him. But just for a few days.'

She expected Rachel to cheer, but instead she looked down at Buzz, then raised her brown eyes with a cautious expression. 'I don't *sell* dogs,' she said. 'Not to people who don't want them. But – sorry if this sounds a bit woo, I don't say this to everyone, believe me – I just get the weird feeling this is right. Buzz has found you. I think you two will be fine together, for however long he stays.'

As Rachel spoke his name, the dog's head lifted and he saw Gina looking at him. He held her gaze for a second, then timidly tucked his nose back alongside his paws. Submissive. Unwanted. Resigned.

Gina blinked hard, twice, and frowned. Oh, bollocks, she was going to cry again. The music: that was what had loosened it. It was that unexplained, unspecific emotion that ambushed her when she thought she was in a clear place, the sudden swelling wave that roared up behind her, overwhelming her in a cloud of damp despair, leaving her weak and hopeless. Just like it had at the Magistrate's House, in front of Nick. She swallowed. She definitely didn't want another attack of hiccups.

'Are you OK?' asked Rachel, reaching out to touch her knee. 'Sorry, I shouldn't have said that. I used to hate it when ... Oh, no. I really didn't mean to upset you.'

Gina shook her head, then nodded. 'It's OK. 'S fine.'

'It is OK *not* to be fine, you know,' said Rachel.

She tried to centre herself: the white walls, the bold blue vase on the windowsill, the soft lamps, the hyacinth candle. Her place. Her new life.

Why wasn't it making her happy? When was she going to start feeling better?

'So . . .' Gina focused on the dog. 'So. What do I need to do?'

Rachel examined her face, saw that she meant it, and reached briskly into the nearest bag. 'I've made you a timetable to give you an idea. And I've brought everything you'll need.'

'You know I'm trying to clear this place out, right? I'm going to have to make you take three bags of CDs for this.'

'If you take the dog till Friday,' said Rachel, 'I'll personally carry all your junk over the road.'

That night, Buzz slept in the spare room on an old duvet, shut in to stop him causing too much damage. Not that it looked like he'd do any: he curled up immediately like a stone.

On the other side of the wall, Gina lay sleepless in her bed, aware of the living creature, silent and impenetrable, in her flat. She could hear her mother's voice, telling her she was making a mistake: dogs trailed germs round houses and bit owners while they slept. Stuart's voice, too, despairing at her pushover nature.

But at the same time, Gina felt something unfolding in her stomach like a butterfly. Buzz, a dog, a responsibility, was the first active decision of her new life. It might all go wrong. But if it did, there would be only her to deal with it.

There *was* only her now. The thought made her anxious or excited, she couldn't tell which.

It was impossible to sleep when her brain was spinning like this, rolling what-ifs round, sending her life down different paths towards different versions of herself. Gina stared up at the ceiling, and tried to imagine herself sinking into the mattress, being absorbed into the whiteness, a trick that sometimes worked, sometimes didn't. Tonight it didn't. She was in the middle of an energy surge, and her limbs felt jaded and restless. Her mind kept going back to the Magistrate's House, to the lists in her office, to the ExCel budget Stuart wanted, to the checklist Rory had given her to fill in about her finances; to where she might be now if she hadn't married Stuart, if she hadn't had cancer, if she hadn't met Kit. Different lives shooting off like side shoots on a climbing plant.

Gina sat up in bed, rigid with panic and energy.

Broadband. I should get the broadband connected, she thought. No one's going to do it for me. And I need to look up greyhound advice on the Internet. I can't ask Rachel everything.

She glanced at the alarm clock: 4.12am. The service provider was supposed to have 24/7 customer support. Probably a good time to jump the queues.

Gina threw back the duvet, and went to reconnect herself to the rest of the world.

In the morning, Buzz wagged his tail cautiously when she got up, and gobbled his breakfast in the corner of the kitchen that Gina had designated his, but he seemed relieved when she took him to the charity shop. He slunk behind the counter where Rachel's own Border collie sat, as still as a stuffed dog, watching the shop with his ice-blue eyes.

'Don't take it personally,' Rachel said, spotting her chagrin. 'He'll adjust. He's had a lot of upheaval, doesn't know who to trust yet. Men might be a problem – he didn't like my husband much. That didn't go down well, I can tell you.'

'He trusts *you*.'

Buzz was nudging at Rachel's pocket with his pointy nose.

'Yeah. That's because I smell of thirty other dogs.' Rachel pulled a sandwich bag out of her pocket. 'And I have magic kibble. Gem's just the same. Get kibble, watch the love flow, that's my advice.'

She slipped both dogs a nugget; Buzz hesitated, then took his quickly, as if he wasn't sure why it was on offer.

'He was all right last night?' Rachel glanced up at her.

'Fine. Not a squeak.'

'Then you're obviously doing something right.'

Gina shrugged and heaved her bag of CDs onto the counter. 'For you. But don't read anything into them. There's nothing to psychoanalyse about this lot other than that I had too much spare money in my early twenties.'

'I'm the last person to hold anyone's music taste against them,' said Rachel. 'If you pop back after five, we can give the dogs a quick once round the park – save you taking him out on your own?'

'Thanks. That'd be great.' Gina tried not to look at Buzz

as she left. It was bad enough feeling the sharp eyes of Rachel's Border collie following her out.

Gina thought about Buzz while she finalised the Rowntrees' schedule in her office, then emailed it to Amanda and Nick. She didn't normally take much notice of the dog-walkers, but today she admired a graceful pair of black greyhounds being walked along the towpath at lunchtime, and wondered if they were ex-racers too. She couldn't get out of her head what Rachel had said about them being dumped. How could you leave a creature that looked at you the way Buzz did, with all that pain and wisdom in those mournful eyes?

By the time she went to collect Buzz at five, she'd got quite emotional about the idea of giving him a cosy week's holiday, but when she bent down to fuss him, again he shied away, flattening himself against Rachel's legs and shivering.

She felt disproportionately foolish, crouched there, rejected by a dog in a shop.

'Ignore him,' said Rachel, shrugging on her coat. 'Less fuss the better. Just keep nice and calm and friendly.'

Gina let herself be led as much as Buzz as Rachel slipped a broad martingale collar around his neck and handed her the lead. She held it awkwardly. Buzz hunched his back.

They walked down the high street, with Gina ultra-conscious about where Buzz was, whether people might nudge him, or he might snap at toddlers or pushchairs. The lead felt tense in her hand, but Buzz trotted meekly until they got to the tall iron gates of the municipal gardens. Then, as they stepped into the quieter pathways of the park, his tail lost its rigid down sweep and he seemed to relax.

'There's a fenced area at the top,' Rachel explained. 'They can have a run around without getting in anyone's way. I don't think Buzz'll go anywhere, but I'd leave him on that lead. Let him know you're sticking with him.'

'OK.'

They walked along the path, the dogs between them.

'So, how long have you been in Longhampton?' Rachel asked, with a quick sideways glance. She had an easy way of asking questions that didn't feel like questions, just conversation. 'Is this a recent move?'

Gina hesitated, wondering what the answer actually was, where she started from in her new life. It felt less awkward than it had done when she'd first introduced herself to the Rowntrees. She supposed that was how it would feel, a little less awkward until one morning she'd wake up and this would be her new normal.

'I only moved from Dryden Road,' she said. 'I grew up round here.'

'Ah, not a big move, then. What do you do, when you're not giving all your possessions away to charity?'

Gina found herself telling Rachel about her job; it was much easier to talk about that than about herself. People generally liked talking about their houses, or moaning about the council, one or the other. Rachel was curious about the renovation work. Every so often she nodded a hello to someone else out walking a dog, but otherwise gave Gina the flattering impression that she was really interested in what she was saying.

It felt nice, unexpectedly so. Gina had never found it easy to make new friends – she really only had Naomi, and a few old workmates whom she met up with sometimes – but although Rachel didn't mention the self-help books again, Gina felt something was understood between them, and it was a relief.

Conversation moved on to the CDs she'd brought in, then to the kennels Rachel had inherited a few years ago. Once or twice Gina glanced down at Buzz, to check he was still with her, but he never pulled or tried to stop to sniff anything. He seemed resigned to their walk, not really enjoying it, his long thin tail curved down between his legs.

'Am I doing this right?' she asked eventually. 'He doesn't look like he's enjoying it much.'

They were nearly all the way round now. Rachel's collie, Gem, had never left her side, yet he'd been taking in every passing dog, every person, every plant along the way, his sharp eyes noting everything. Buzz seemed robotic in comparison.

'He's shut down, poor lad. They do it out of self-defence.' Rachel stopped and re-attached Gem's lead. 'It sounds cruel, but the best thing you can do with Buzz is not to make a huge fuss of him. Dogs need time to suss you out.

'Anyway,' she added, 'he'll be out of your hair by the end of the week. So don't beat yourself up too much if you're not best pals by Friday. I'm eternally grateful for this week, and so's he.'

Gina looked down at Buzz. He met her gaze, then looked down again, and her heart broke.

'Here's my ride,' said Rachel, jerking her head towards the muddy Land Rover parked on a double-yellow line by the entrance to the gardens. 'Better go before he starts yelling. He's not the most patient cabbie, my other half.'

As they got nearer, Gina saw in the driving seat a handsome countryish man with salt-and-peppery hair, his checked shirt rolled up at the sleeves to reveal strong forearms; in the back, cocooned in a child-seat, was a round-faced, dark-haired toddler, the spitting image of Rachel with her long straight nose. When they both saw Rachel through the window, their faces lit up with an identical beam, although the man went through a pantomime of outrage, stabbing at his watch with his finger and scowling unconvincingly.

'My boys,' said Rachel, rolling her eyes. 'George and Fergus. Fergus is the less grumpy one.'

Gina smiled, but a brief twinge of jealousy pinched her: it was always easier to be positive about starting again when you were back on the right side of the fence.

Rachel let Gem into the back of the Land Rover, but before she went round to the passenger side, she took hold of Gina's upper arms, and looked her right in the face. 'Listen,' she said quietly, 'I'm the last person to dish out relationship advice. I'm not even the best person to give advice about dogs. But one thing I've learned from spending a lot of time around dogs like Buzz is that they live in the moment. If they're fed, warm and walked, they're happy. And it's amazing how happy that can make you feel, too. You're doing a very kind thing for him. Be just as kind to yourself.'

She said it with such intensity that Gina felt like a spy being given some secret code information. She didn't know what to say in response.

But when she took Buzz home, and measured out the kibble that Rachel had given her, she hesitated over the boring tin of beans she'd started to open. Instead she made herself a pea risotto and ate it on the sofa with a glass of wine, listening to an Ella Fitzgerald album she'd forgotten she'd bought, enjoying each forkful as the smoky-sweet tracks of broken hearts and endless loves downloaded onto her laptop.

The CD finished, and she got up to put her glass and plate in the dishwasher. She hadn't heard a sound, but Buzz had crept nearer, still not too near, and was sleeping with his head on his paws.

Ella Fitzgerald, she thought, watching the lights over the town, the crescent moon rising over the roofs. This'll be my music to remind me of now. Mournful, soulful ... but hopeful.

Chapter Twelve

ITEM: a letter from Terry Bellamy

Matterdale Drive
Hartley
10th May 2001

Dear Georgina,
This is just a note to remind you that you'll need to put the Mini in for her MOT on 2nd June. I know you won't have forgotten, but you've had a lot on with your examinations and I just wanted to be sure. I'm an old fusspot, I expect you're saying! I gave her a once-over while you were home last time, so don't let the mechanics tell you she needs more oil, or spark plugs, or wiper blades because I replaced those, and she seemed to be running fine.
As always, if there's a problem with the garage, give me a call and I'll speak to them on your behalf. I often think about the two of us sitting in the garage while we were restoring old Minnie. You with your books, me tinkering away. Happy times.
Your mother and I are both very well. We're hoping to have a few days in Harrogate next

*month, if her migraines clear up. The warm
weather doesn't agree with her, but I think a
change of air's always nice.*

*I'm enclosing a little something for you to treat
yourself now you've got some time to relax. We're
both very proud of you, and are looking forward to
seeing you go up and get your degree in a few weeks'
time. Don't worry, we won't embarrass you with our
glad rags!*

See you soon, Georgina
All the best
Terry

Oxford, June 2001

Two days ago, Gina had sat her last finals paper and she's been in a pleasantly hazy state of drunkenness ever since.

For the first time in her life, it feels as if the pressure to be doing something has vanished. The sun's shining, time blurs, and one party wanders into another, then another. There are different lawns, different shady willows, the same jugs of Pimm's, and now the highlight of her week has finally arrived: Kit, coming from London with a bottle of champagne to celebrate.

When Kit strolled into the college gardens looking for her, Gina felt the red-faced rower who'd been trying to chat her up lean back in defeat. There's no point competing with this. OK, so he's come straight from his office wearing a suit, but it's rumpled, his linen shirt unbuttoned and his walk confident. The golden hair's shorter, but Kit still looks more like a charismatic young professor than a very junior venture capitalist, from a place somewhere between the self-conscious student life and the dry adult world.

In her three years at Oxford, Gina's never even been tempted by anyone else. No one else is like Kit. And now she's free to move to London with him and be a proper part of his world. Him in hers, too, of course.

They're lying on a secluded stretch of grass under the trees, and Gina's letting the sound of clinking glasses and blurred chatter, with the smell of flattened grass, suncream and Kit's city-heated skin, wash over her.

Gina's birthday trip to London with Kit for her twenty-first had been magical, but this – exams done, tension over, nothing left to go wrong – is better. I need to remember this, she thinks, in case I'm never this happy again - but she doesn't feel the answering grip of panic that she usually does. How many times has she thought that now, only to have something even more amazing happen?

This is just the start, she thinks, secure in her happiness. This is where it all begins.

'. . . talking to a guy who's developing this incredible new software in San Francisco which will totally revolution-ise . . . Gina? Are you OK?' He touches her nose. 'You look like you're miles away. Sorry, I know it's boring. Work.'

'No,' she says truthfully. 'I love hearing about your job. You're my sexy older man, don't forget. Go on, explain about hedge funds again.'

He rolls over onto his elbow, and Gina thinks he's

going to kiss her, but instead he has a question in his eye. 'Work's just a means to an end. What are we going to do now?' he asks.

Gina smiles tipsily. 'Well . . .' That could be anything. Kit is very imaginative.

'No, I mean, now you've finished your exams. Now you're free!'

A cloud passes across the sun. 'I don't know. Mum's been on my case about jobs again.'

'What? Didn't you tell her about the art foundation course?'

She sighs. 'Sort of. It just ended in a row. Terry tried to calm her down but she stormed off to bed with a migraine. She doesn't want to hear anything. apart from "I've got a job with KPMG." They know I did the civil-service entrance test.'

The truth is, Gina doesn't know what she wants to do next. Oxford was all she'd thought about for years, Oxford and Kit. Kit thinks she should go to art college, do a foundation course. When he says it, it sounds completely normal, a good idea, even. When Gina says it to her mother, it sounds ridiculously self-indulgent.

Kit traces the curve of her cheekbone. 'Well, they can't begrudge you a holiday, can they? You've worked so hard for your degree.'

'No,' she says, though she suspects Janet can.

'I've been looking into tickets for a round-the-world trip. You can get some amazing deals. Shaun's living in Sydney now, so we could stay there for a bit, and my cousin's in San Francisco . . .'

Kit waves his hand to indicate the limitless possibilities, and smiles the easy smile that still makes Gina's stomach flutter. Five years of weekends, wishing, letters, emails, bed, phone calls. Never long enough to get bored with that smile.

'You know how you think I look like a mole first thing in the morning,' she says, only half-joking. 'Are you sure that'll still be cute halfway across Death Valley?'

'Course it will. I could ask you the same about my snoring.'

'You don't snore,' she lies.

Kit stretches an arm around her, and Gina shoves the idea of her parents and the job fair and how she'll pay for the ticket from her head. He keeps offering to pay for her – he claims the only reason he's stayed on at the venture capital firm he interned at is to save up money to travel. It's not his fault he's good at it and they want to keep him.

'What do you reckon?' he murmurs. 'Australia? I can see you on the beach.'

It's a joke: Gina can't stand the sun. At least, she thinks Kit's joking. Is she a beach bunny type? Maybe she could be. She could be anything now.

'Or we could drive across America?' she suggests. At least motels have indoor loos. 'Just us, anonymous motels, autumn trees, the Eagles on the stereo . . .'

'We could do that,' Kit agrees, into her neck.

'What about a *Gone With the Wind* tour of plantation houses?' Gina loves big historical houses. She loves Kit's family home, a rambling, book-lined arts-and-crafts place. It's the kind to have secrets and history and interesting things under the floorboards, not like the Bellamys' over-clean house. The only downside is Kit's mother, Anita, whom she senses doesn't think she's quite in Kit's league. Anita, Gina suspects, would rather Gina was one of the up-and-coming actresses or novelists Kit went to school with.

'Mint juleps. I like the sound of that.' He nudges the soft skin behind her ear, and she melts into the grass. 'I've missed you,' he whispers. 'Are you going to come and stay with me for a bit? The guys are going away. We can pretend it's just us living there . . .'

Gina closes her eyes as his lips move towards her mouth, blocking out the sun and all rational thought; he kisses her.

Behind her eyelids, she sees herself driving in an open-top car with Kit, her long black hair flying in the breeze. She sees herself walking across a deserted beach in Australia. Dancing in a club in London, drinking wine in a French bar at midnight. If she's with Kit, she can see herself doing anything, because he can. The possibilities make her dizzy.

She keeps her eyes closed when the kiss abruptly stops and the sunlight returns in a bright glare on her eyelids.

'Gina?' says a woman's voice.

'Can it wait?' she asks flippantly.

'Gina.' Kit touches her arm and something in his voice makes her sit up. Her head spins. She's drunker than she thought: that last glass of Kit's champagne was one too many.

Miriam Addison, her pastoral-care tutor, is standing over her, shading her eyes with her hand. She's dressed for the garden party, but her expression is wrong, thinks Gina. Her expression is the one she wears when she reminds Gina that she's going to need to pull her socks up if she wants to get her degree.

'I'm sorry to interrupt,' she says, 'but can you come with me, please? There's something . . .' Miriam pauses. 'You need to call home.'

'Why?'

Miriam glances around. Half the guests at the garden party are staring at them, too pissed to care whether it's rude or not. Gina wonders what they think Miriam's telling her. Failing finals? Medical problems?

Maybe she *hasn't* got her degree. She feels sick.

'Come with me to the office,' Miriam says gently.

Kit sits up, suddenly serious. 'What's the matter?'

'Tell me now,' Gina says. 'Please. Just tell me.'

Miriam crouches down. 'I'm afraid your father's been taken to hospital,' she murmurs. 'He's had a heart attack. It's . . . not good news.'

'Her stepfather,' Kit is correcting Miriam, but in this second Gina's heart isn't making that distinction. She's seeing Terry in his chair the last time she was at home, trying to calm Janet, trying to pacify Gina, his pleasant face grey with distress at their silly row about the phone bill. He hadn't looked well then.

Gina feels herself falling down, down, down, even though she isn't moving. Without Terry, the migraines and moods will choke the house. She can see her mother's face, abandoned again. Her grief will be uncontrollable. 'Which hospital?' she says, but as she gets up, she stumbles, staggering on the daisy-free green of the college lawn. People can look: she doesn't care.

'I'll call you a taxi to the station,' says Miriam.

'No, I'll drive her,' says Kit, and turns to her. 'Gina. Where's your car?'

Minnie the green Mini, the car that Terry had restored for her while she was sitting her A levels, then taught her to drive in. Gina remembers him squashed gamely into the passenger seat in his brown suit, a fixed grin plastered over his anxiety as she crashed the gears and swore. Her legs give way beneath her.

Amanda's email accepting Gina's proposed schedule of works – and projected invoice – was as short and prompt as Gina's was long and detailed. It arrived at three o'clock, Amanda's time not Gina's, and was to the point:

> **This looks fine. Let's do it! Please get the ball rolling asap with planning, etc, and liaise with Nick re payment going forward, as per the terms set out in your email. I look forward to meeting up soon to review developments.**
> **Best, Amanda**

Gina had started the renovation timetable from the top, by booking a thorough structural examination of the roof. It wasn't quite as magnificent up close as it seemed from the long carriage drive; despite the massive chimneystacks at each end, hinting at stately fireplaces beneath, the actual roof was patched and uneven where the house had been extended over the years, and repaired more neatly in some spots than others. The surveyor had recommended a complete overhaul and, with the Rowntrees' breathtaking budget now in hand, Gina had called in the best specialist she knew.

A steel web of scaffolding had already been erected around the house, and today's meeting was to discuss making the lead valleys of the roof watertight, stopping the slow drip into the cavernous attics. Gina's notes had a whole section about the chimneys, starting with sweeping them free of birds' nests and the artificial blockages previous owners had stuffed up them for insulation. There was something about fireplaces, Gina felt, that brought a house to life even if you didn't use them. It was like clearing the house's throat so it could breathe properly.

When she knocked at the front there was no answer, so she picked her way past the heavy sacks of lime render stacked in the herb garden and knocked on the kitchen door. Nick was at the big table, working on his laptop, and looked as if he'd only just rolled out of bed. His dark hair was ruffled and flattened on one side and he'd thrown a beige fisherman's jumper over a pair of checked pyjama bottoms.

Gina wondered if she'd got the meeting time wrong, and was about to back away quietly, when Nick spotted her, shoved his chair back and beckoned her inside.

'Sorry, I'm just trying to get this done before the roof guy arrives,' he explained, offering her a cup of coffee from the half-full cafetière. 'I was up all last night editing photos. Lorcan's been here since eight – he asked if I was ill because I was in my pyjamas. Does everyone round here get up before dawn?'

'Yup. Welcome to the countryside. And Lorcan's got

more to worry about this morning with the roofer coming than whether you're up or not. Speaking of which, I was chucking out some stuff at my flat and I thought these might be useful for you.' Gina handed over some books she'd sorted from her most recent boxes – guides to renovating old houses she'd been given over the years. 'Don't take it personally,' she added. 'I'm not saying you need an idiot's guide but it might make things easier when Lorcan starts firing questions about joists and spurs at you.'

'Thanks.' Nick ruffled his hair and read the back of the first book with a wry grin. 'The idiot-er the better. My idea of DIY so far has been phoning for a plumber. But I'm a quick learner, you'll be pleased to hear. I wish I'd been more involved in our last place, but I was away so much with work.' He looked through the selection. 'These are a bit basic to be yours, aren't they? Or do you hand out homework to all your clients?'

The coffee was so strong the spoon was nearly standing up. It made Gina wonder how late Nick had been working last night, alone in the echoing house. 'No, they were Christmas presents. From my ex-in-laws. I don't think they knew what to get me. Everyone else got cupcake aprons and Mum's Diary, and that's not really me.'

'But this is your job. They didn't think you might be a bit beyond . . .' he squinted, amused '. . . *The Haynes Guide to Old Houses*?'

'It's just one of those things I no longer have to care about. Which is fine with me. I'm having a big sort-out at home, so if they're useful to you, you're very welcome to them.'

'A big sort-out. Sounds like the kind of iron discipline we need here.' He pushed a plate of toast towards her. 'Toast?'

Gina didn't normally eat breakfast with her clients but she'd been in such a rush to get Buzz to the rescue shop before this meeting that she hadn't had time for cereal. She hesitated, then took a piece. 'It's not really that disciplined. I'm a bit of a hoarder,' she said. 'But I've just moved to a much smaller flat with no storage – usual story, too much stuff and not enough room.' She chewed the toast to slow herself down. Nick was very easy to talk to. Too easy. 'I'm trying to get rid of anything that isn't either essential or important to me, and it's interesting – once you start, you find that actually . . .'

The words stuck in Gina's throat, as she realised she was about to say that *actually*, aside from diaries and personal letters that couldn't be replaced, she wasn't keeping as much as she'd thought she would. Stuart's box was by the door for the shopping list of things he'd requested via his solicitor; they weren't very personal, and one or two she suspected he'd put on the list because he thought she wanted them. Something about the pettiness of it had made her look twice at things she'd thought she wanted to keep herself.

It made the letters she'd kept seem even more important. That envelope of missives to Kit was still in the box, and Gina didn't want it to be one of the hundred things that defined her. But she couldn't shred them. Shredding them felt so final.

'Actually . . . what?' Nick was looking at her.

'Sorry?' Gina blinked, trying to reorder her thoughts

into something that was more appropriate for a client breakfast.

'When it comes down to it, what?'

'That actually they're not that important after all. Don't you get that when you unpack?' She reached for the milk. 'You spend hours putting things in miles of bubble-wrap, then get to the new house and think, Hmm, why did I keep this?'

'I haven't been allowed to unpack yet.'

'Well. You know what I mean.'

Nick sipped his strong coffee, and Gina thought he was about to change the subject and start asking about the roof, but he didn't. 'Personally, I think people get too hung up about *things* when actually what they should be stockpiling are moments.'

'Sorry?'

'Moments. Experiences. Not flashy ones like paragliding in the Grand Canyon or . . .' he made sarcastic air hooks with his fingers '. . . firewalking at the Burning Man Festival. Small everyday things, like – like being outside just after it's rained. Swimming in the sea. Arriving at a new railway station. Proper paintbox sunsets on summer nights.'

'Says the man whose job it is to capture moments so people can turn them into *things*. Like photographs. And magazines.'

He shrugged. 'Yeah, yeah. Be as cynical as you like. But I've spent a lot of time living out of suitcases over the past few years, and I can't say I ever missed any one thing in particular. I did miss having a really good shower. And I missed the feeling of getting into clean sheets.'

'Oh, clean sheets, yes. You can't beat crisp white sheets on a summer night. Or a warm blanket over the duvet on a cold one.'

'But is that the sheets? Or the feeling?' Nick looked at her quizzically over his mug.

'That's a bit deep for nine in the morning.'

'Not really. It's the whole point. Because once you've decided it's the *feeling* of the sheets, you can stop trying to chase the Perfect Sheets round the shops and just have the one set, instead of ten. Although,' he conceded, 'you might have to do more laundry.'

'You sound like you've thought about this a lot.'

'I had a big de-cluttering epiphany myself a few years back. When everyone changed over to digital, I went through a phase of buying every new bit of kit that came out. Didn't make me a better photographer, just made me a photographer with a bad back from carrying it all around. Once I decided to use one camera, natural light, my whole style changed. I went back to seeing what I was seeing, not letting the camera dictate it to me.'

He looked at her over the table, his grey eyes analysing her face, and Gina had the feeling he was seeing her as he'd seen her hands: spotting something beneath the surface, something she wasn't quite aware of.

Then his phone rang on the table, vibrating under a crumby plate and making the knife on it rattle. Nick glanced down. 'It's Amanda.'

They could both see that. A snapshot of a smiling Amanda in a red bikini and big Chanel shades, lying on a white beach next to a very blue sea, had flashed up.

It felt as if Amanda had just appeared in the room. The bikini was not how Gina usually pictured Amanda from her brisk instruction-filled emails.

Was that a honeymoon photo? Nick and Amanda seemed like the sort of couple who went on those Necker Island holidays. Gina caught herself.

'Do you want to get that?' she asked. 'I'll . . .' She gestured towards the rest of the house.

'No, stay there. It's you she'll want to talk to, not me. She's just checking I'm not up on the roof with a sledge-hammer.' Nick picked the phone up off the table. 'Hey, darling! How's Paris this morning?'

Amanda started talking at once. Gina could hear the tone of her voice, if not the words; she wasn't wasting time with chit-chat.

Nick's smile faded slowly. Then he put his elbow on the table and pinched the bridge of his nose. 'No, it's the roofer coming today . . . But, Amanda, we have to put in an application before . . . No, seriously, we have to . . . Amanda, Gina's here, she'll be able to explain it better. I'm not making this up, believe me.'

Oh, bollocks, thought Gina. The chatty mood had evaporated.

'Can you have a word with Amanda about Listed Building Consent, please?' said Nick, stiffly, holding out the phone to her. 'She's unclear about a couple of things.'

'Of course.' Gina braced herself. LBC hadn't exactly been a favourite topic when she'd been on the other end of the ranting; it was even less of a favourite now she had to explain it to frustrated clients. 'Hello, Amanda. How are you?'

'Hi. Good, thanks. I think Nick must have got the wrong end of the stick about this planning permission,' she said. 'He told me last night that it's going to take eight weeks before there's even a decision about whether we can go ahead with the kitchen build.'

'Eight weeks is the worst-case scenario, yes.' Gina rolled her eyes at herself. *Did I just say worst-case scenario?* Amanda seemed to bring back all the office-speak she'd trained out of herself since leaving the council.

'So what was the point of having that man come out to go round the house? I thought that was it. He can rubber-stamp it, no? He's seen what we want to do?' Amanda's tone was friendly but not happy.

'That was just a preliminary consultation. It's saved us some time because now we know roughly what the council is likely to approve, and Nick tells me your architect's amending his plans to take that into account. I've got the architect's details, so as soon as he gets back to me with new drawings, I can get the forms sent straight over, but while they're in the system, I'm afraid we can't really speed things up.'

'Really? I can't believe that.'

Nick was staring at her and when she glanced at him, he got up to put the kettle on for more coffee.

'I'm afraid it's standard. The formal notice has to go to parish councils, to neighbours and so on. It's to stop owners wrecking old houses when they aren't approaching the process as thoughtfully as you are,' said Gina.

'But we're not going to wreck the house. They've seen our plans – it's not like we're turning it into flats. I'm spending a *fortune* to restore the place. I don't see why we can't just go ahead, and then if they hate it, let them deal with it.'

'Amanda, I'm sorry, I can't let you – they can take you to court for unauthorised work. They can fine you thousands of pounds or, at the very least, make you tear down what you've done. We had the prison talk already, didn't we? And to be frank, my reputation as a project manager would be destroyed if Keith Hurst decided to make an example of you. Which is not beyond him. He really doesn't get out much.'

There was a pause at the other end. 'When you say thousands, how much exactly? Is it worth factoring it into the build budget and just going for it now?'

Gina frowned and tried to keep her voice level. In a way, she had to admire Amanda's sheer brass neck. 'That's not the point.'

'Oh, come on. I don't believe they'd mount a prosecution. That's just an empty threat. And it's *our* house!' Her frustration was audible. Amanda clearly wasn't a woman who was used to hearing no. Especially not a legal no.

'Believe me, they would. And they don't care that it's your house. Listed buildings are different. You're seen as a custodian, not an owner. I'm really sorry.'

'The reason I hired you is because I expected you to be able to handle this sort of thing.' Amanda let out an impatient sigh. 'I don't believe you can't fast-track it.'

'I'll monitor everything as closely as possible, I promise.' Gina had worked with some pushy property developers while she was at the council, but Amanda had a way of applying pressure she'd never felt before. She straightened her back, even though Amanda couldn't see. 'If you have a look at the schedule of works I emailed through, there's plenty that Lorcan can be getting on with while we're waiting for the go-ahead. Repairs don't need consent, so we've got the roofing specialist here today.'

'This is really disappointing, Gina.'

'I know, but in the long run—'

'Fine. Fine. I have to go. But if you can keep the pressure on, that would be appreciated.'

Gina found herself making agreeing noises, but before she could explain the rest of the week's schedule, Amanda had said goodbye and was gone.

'Wow,' said Gina, staring at the phone. The lock screen was a photo of duck eggs; the same duck eggs she'd had in her hands, she guessed. 'Did I handle that all right? I can't tell.'

'It sounded perfectly reasonable to me,' said Nick. 'In as much as any of this planning regulation stuff is reasonable.'

'No, I mean the time issue. I didn't realise there was a deadline on this. If there is, you'd better tell me now.'

The kettle boiled and he poured more water onto the coffee. 'There isn't, not particularly. Amanda just likes to get things moving ASAP – it's part of working in that field. Time is money.'

Gina wasn't sure that was the whole answer. 'She does understand that this sort of project doesn't move on normal schedules?' She gave him a square look. 'Some things will happen quickly, and others . . . Well, be prepared for rotten floors, and unexpected holes behind walls. I tell all my clients, you need a twenty per cent cash reserve and a forty per cent time one. Minimum.'

'Look, she's not going to be back for another fortnight.' Nick put the refilled cafetière on a pile of colour cards. 'This merger she's refereeing seems to be expanding daily, so I doubt she'll have time to make more than, ooh, three or four chasing phone calls a day.'

'Okay. Maybe ask her to condense it into one nightly email? Then I can respond properly.' Gina took a mouthful of cold coffee. Suddenly it didn't seem too strong any more. Her heart was pounding.

'It'll be fine. Honestly. Amanda's just very full-on. It's one of the reasons we had to build two offices into the last house. And buy the flat in the Barbican. I think we'd end up killing each other if we had to live together all the time.'

'Have you never lived together?'

He laughed. 'Once. For six months when her flat was on the market. Never again. We agreed that either we bought a second place, or one of us went into rehab or prison.'

Gina glanced over, surprised at the honesty of the admission, and Nick added, 'I'm joking. Sort of.'

'Still, this house should be big enough,' she said. 'A wing each?'

'That's the idea,' said Nick, but he'd turned back to the counter for the toast, and she couldn't see his face.

'Nick?' Lorcan appeared at the kitchen door. 'Morning, Gina. I've got Barry Butler here. About the roof? Ah, is that coffee? Grand.'

Gina poured him a mugful, then topped up her own. It

wasn't even half past nine yet, and she felt as if she'd been awake for hours.

'Has no one come for this dog yet?' Naomi asked, eyeing Buzz, who was curled up in his basket while Gina assembled the tea and cakes in the kitchen. He was doing his best to ignore Naomi, in the hope that he would be ignored in turn. But Naomi didn't ignore things.

'Not yet. Next week.'

'I thought the rescue woman was going to move him to a greyhound shelter?'

'She is, as soon as a space comes up. To be honest, he's no bother. He spends most of the day over the road. I just feed him, and give him somewhere to sleep.'

Gina put the tea tray in front of Naomi on the coffee table. She had hoped that her attention would be drawn to the bright clean lines of her nearly empty sitting room rather than to the dog in the corner. The boxes were now confined to the spare room (which they nearly filled, but still), leaving light to flood into the main living area. She'd put a big mirror on one wall, reflecting the grey-blue sky outside; the sill displayed three postcards on stalks, and the Polaroid of the eggs in her hands. The main blank wall, where her one amazing picture would go, still had only her lining-paper list, now decorated with a packet of gold stars she'd found in a box. No point in saving gold stars, Gina had decided. They formed glittering trails around her favourite things.

'Naomi? Cupcake? From the gourmet deli?'

Naomi was staring at Buzz's knobbly back with a

semi-disgusted, semi-fascinated expression. 'Are you feeding him enough? I've seen fatter supermodels.'

'I'm giving him this special greyhound food to build him up. Rachel says they're all skinny. He gets very nervous and apparently it stops him putting on weight.'

'You're starting to sound like you know a lot about this all of a sudden.' Naomi turned back to her with reproachful eyes. 'Don't get suckered in. You don't need a dog. They're a tie. You're getting rid of stuff, not taking things in. What about that holiday you were going on?'

'Oh, it's only for a few more days. I don't mind.' Despite herself, Gina was getting attached to Buzz. He demanded so little of her, and Rachel had been right: his silent company *was* just what she needed, to take the edge of her solitude. Buzz added a rhythm to her day that wasn't completely unwelcome in its new free-form state – he gave it a beginning and an end, and a walk around the park with her new friend.

'Any sign of your bike?' Naomi helped herself to the blue cupcake.

Gina shook her head. 'The police gave me a crime number, but they weren't very hopeful about getting it back.'

'That's outrageous. Don't they know what it's worth? Can you claim on your household insurance?'

'To be honest, Nay, I don't care. That bike didn't bring me any luck. I'm glad it's gone. It only . . .' Gina blew out a long breath '. . . it only reminded me that I wasn't the cycling wife Stuart obviously wanted. Now it's gone, I don't have to kick myself.'

Naomi looked at her sympathetically. 'Fair enough. I just wish you could have spent that money on your big treat. How's the fund coming on?'

'It'll come on a lot quicker when you get round to showing me how to flog my clothes.'

'Next weekend, I promise. Actually,' Naomi corrected herself, 'not next weekend – we're going to stay with my mother in Brighton. The weekend after that. We'll get the dummy round.'

'That'd be me.'

'Ha ha. Very good. But how's it going otherwise? You've got rid of loads. Are you not worried Stuart's going to see his old jackets in the window of the Oxfam shop?'

'No, I was tempted. But he's getting them back, in bin bags.'

'Is he asking for the rings?' Naomi asked nosily. 'You don't have to hand them over. I've seen it on *Judge Judy*. They're yours – people have them melted down and made into a divorce ring. Ooh, what about personal letters? Are you giving those back? That'd put a crimp in his love nest, unpacking a bundle of those.'

Gina smiled at the glee on Naomi's face, but then stopped. 'What would you do,' she said, 'if you had some letters that belonged to someone else? Would you give them back?'

'What? If I'd stolen them? Well, duh, Gina. Yes.'

'No, not stolen.' She hesitated again. 'Returned.'

Naomi put her cup down. 'Oh, no. Are you talking about those letters Kit's mum sent back? I thought you'd given them to him that time you saw him.'

'Don't look like that. No, I didn't. I was going to, but the moment wasn't right . . .' Gina winced. 'I thought maybe, now some water's passed under the bridge . . .'

'No!' Naomi looked incredulous. 'Get rid of them. For God's sake. Don't even think of going back to that mess. You had your chance to get it sorted out, and the pair of you managed to make everything just that little bit worse, so on balance, Gina, I would say, no. Do *not* send those letters back to Kit, do *not* arrange to see him, *stop* picking that scab, and move *on*.'

Naomi took a deep breath. She'd been speaking so quickly, her voice rising with each passionate sentence, that Buzz had abandoned his basket and retreated to the kitchen. 'Sorry,' she added. 'I've scared your dog.'

Gina didn't respond to the lame jokiness because Naomi clearly wasn't joking. It was hard to explain properly how she felt about the letters. She couldn't just throw them away – it would be like throwing out the part of herself that had written them. If he did . . . well, that was different. In the last house, there had been drawers to stuff them into. Here, every item that stayed was a choice.

'I just feel they're not mine to throw away,' she said. 'I want him to see them.'

'Why?'

'So he knows I wrote them.'

'He *knows*, Gina.' Naomi threw her hands in the air. 'But it was thirteen years ago. Why would he want to read them now? What's the point?' She sank back, and regarded Gina with surprise. 'Sorry, I didn't realise you were still so hung up on Kit.'

'I'm not hung up on him,' said Gina. 'It's more me. I just feel I have to tidy this up while I'm tidying everything else up. I feel . . . OK, I still feel guilty about it. I feel like all the bad luck in my life basically stems from not dealing with that situation properly.'

'What? You were a *kid*.' Naomi rolled her eyes. 'Who can honestly say they dealt with anything properly when they were twenty-one?'

'I wasn't the last time I saw him.'

'Well, he didn't exactly cover himself in glory then either, if you ask me.'

They sat and looked at each other, the highlights and lowlights of all the years they'd been each other's best friend flickering between them, too many for them to be anything other than completely honest with each other.

'Shred the letters,' said Naomi. 'Give them to me and I'll do it.'

'I can't,' said Gina, simply. 'That doesn't solve anything.'

'So what do you want me to say? Yes, go and see him? Because I don't think it's a great idea. Not right now.' Naomi gave her a sharp look. 'I'm not being funny, but it's going to look like you're using it as an excuse to get back in touch because you're getting a divorce. And even if it's not –'

'It's not.'

'– I guarantee that's how he'll see it. So give it a couple of months, then see if you're still desperate to hand the letters over in person. Wait until your decree absolute's through, at least.' She cocked an eyebrow. 'Any news on that?'

Gina sighed. 'It won't happen until the financial arrangements are sorted out. And that won't happen until Stuart gets that box of junk by the door and all the money he thinks he's due. Which could be a while.'

Naomi grimaced. She glanced around the flat, and spotted the list on the wall opposite. Gina watched as she levered herself off the sofa, and went over to read it.

'"One hundred favourite things",' she read aloud. 'Interesting.'

'It is.'

There was a pause as Naomi read on, occasionally laughing.

Gina grabbed the black marker pen from the pot on her desk, and went to join her.

'Shift over,' she said, and when Naomi moved, Gina wrote '20. Naomi McIntyre Hewson' at the end.

'A new entry at number twenty,' said Naomi, wryly. 'Below music but above, what? Tunnock's Tea Cakes?' But she bumped her hip against Gina's with affection.

Chapter Thirteen

ITEM: brown velvet Vivienne Westwood suit,
'guitar' jacket with nipped waist, and narrow
pencil skirt, size 12

Hartley, 2nd June 2008

Gina lies on her bed in her old room at home in
Matterdale Drive, after the world's gloomiest hen night
(Janet, Naomi and her, and a bottle of rosé wine at Ferrari's
in Longhampton) and stares at her wedding suit hanging
on the back of her door, like someone standing sentry over
her, making sure she doesn't do a runner.

The suit's cut so well that it doesn't really need a body
inside it. It's curvy and confident all on its own. Gina half
wishes she could put some kind of Sorcerer's Apprentice
spell on it and send the suit along to the register office
tomorrow morning in her place to marry Stuart.

Janet's mother-of-the-bride ensemble is hanging on the
back of her bedroom door: a hastily purchased dress-and-
coat combo from Longhampton's premier mother-of-the-
bride shop. It's muted, in shades of peach, and not what Janet
had planned to wear to her only child's wedding, but as Gina

overheard her telling the assistant, 'It's not what you'd call a completely happy occasion.'

Gina had leaned over at that point to explain that she wasn't pregnant, and the groom wasn't about to go to prison. Janet nearly fainted.

She manages a twisted smile at the memory. Her new recklessness is giving her a glimpse into what it must be like to be Naomi all the time. Fun.

They're doing some things the traditional way, though. Stuart has banished her from Dryden Road, and he's arranged everything from cars to food to the blue garter that was waiting for her when she got back from the salon this morning. He's even arranged for the hairdresser to come round to put her hair up into the last elaborate do she'll probably ever have. Stuart loves her hair: he's asked for curls and backcombing, the lot. Gina's a bit worried that, combined with the suit, she'll look like Sybil Fawlty, but it's a little thing to do for him when he's been such a rock.

It does cast a shadow over her heart, though, about how he's going to feel when all her long black curls fall out. As they will. In about six weeks' time.

Gina pushes the thought away. She's decided that, before she starts her course of chemotherapy, she's going to get her hair cropped. Properly Mia Farrow short, so that when it starts falling out it won't be such a shock. And it's something positive she can do. Anything more than that is just too hard to get her head around, and she finds her concentration sliding away, unable to take it in, as if the cancer's an iceberg she's too close to see.

This time tomorrow she'll be Mrs Gina Horsfield. She's

practised signing her name but it looks odd, the 'Gina' scrawled, the 'Horsfield' almost printed. It's like one of those dreams that feels like a very mundane waking reality, just before it lurches off at surreal tangents. Gina always scoffed at people who said, 'Ooh, it felt just like a dream!' but that's exactly how the last couple of weeks have been: no connection between one moment and the next, no clue as to which assumptions will turn out to be wrong, what strange new routine will suddenly become her normality.

She stares at the ceiling, trying to pin down how she feels. People keep asking her that. How do you feel? Are you OK? Cancer isn't something she imagined would be part of her life, especially not now, not aged twenty-eight. It's not what she's prepared for. She isn't brave; she isn't going to run charity marathons for Breast Cancer Care; she isn't going to look 'amazing' with a pixie hair-do. Other people do that. And who the hell is Gina Horsfield, anyway?

Her new life starts tomorrow. Gina doesn't feel ready. She hasn't finished with the old one.

And with that, she gives in to the temptation that's been eating away at her since yesterday. One last read of Kit's letters before that life vanishes. They're in a box with all her university memorabilia – postcards from Naomi, ball programmes, gig tickets, birthday cards from people she no longer sees. Earlier that day Janet had found her sitting in her old room, surrounded by her old life, and though Gina pushed Kit's letters under a yellowed student newspaper she'd worked on, she could tell Janet had seen them from the shadow of disapproval that crossed her face.

But so what? It's better than pretending the past never

happened at all, like Mum does. She can't make me ignore Kit the way she ignores Dad.

She reaches under the bed for the box and pulls it towards her, moving piles of old postcards until she reaches the bottom layers of stuff, where she'd tucked Kit's letters out of sight. But they're not there.

Panicking, Gina scrabbles everything out, spreading it across the floor – magazines, Christmas cards, lecture notes, lipsticks, pens – but they're gone. Her letters to Kit, returned by his mother, are still there. His to her are gone.

Something falls away inside her. There's only her mother and herself in the house.

Gina's ears fill with white noise as she marches downstairs to find Janet sitting in her armchair, next to Terry's empty one. She's painting her nails, the varnish a what's-the-bloody-point pale pink, as Naomi would call it.

'Mum,' Gina starts, but Janet interrupts her.

'If you're looking for those letters,' she says, without looking up, 'they've gone.'

Gina's mouth drops open. 'Sorry?'

'Those letters from Kit you were reading last night. They've gone. They've got no place in your new life.'

Blood pulses in Gina's face, hot and cold. 'What do you mean, they've gone?'

'I put them through Terry's shredder,' says Janet, primly. 'Don't worry, I didn't read any of them.'

A noise escapes Gina's throat that she doesn't recognise.

'It's for your own good,' Janet goes on. 'You're getting married tomorrow. It's the beginning of your new life. You don't want any bad luck lingering around from the past.'

'You had no right to do that,' breathes Gina, reeling at the loss. The first ever love letters Kit had written to her from Oxford, the ones that are still magical, the only love letters she has. 'You went through my stuff to find them . . .'

'As a mother you sometimes have to do hard things but, Georgina, there's no good looking behind you. You can't go back. If you want any kind of happiness in this life, you've got to live in this moment, not in the past. Believe me, I should know.'

Gina closes her eyes. Of course. The martyred widowed wife. It's not fair. It's not fair that her mother has no idea what a proper, magical, life-changing love feels like.

'It's very sad, what happened.' Janet's words are tight with self-righteousness, as if she's been preparing this. 'But Stuart's a lovely man. You've made that irresponsible, spoiled boy,' she still can't bring herself to say Kit's name, 'into some sort of fantasy. He wouldn't be half the support Stuart's being now.'

There are so many things Gina wants to yell at her mother that they're crashing against her brain like big moths against a lit window. There's too much: Stuart, the cancer, the wedding, the guilt that never properly leaves her . . .

'Why do you blame him for what happened?' It bursts out of her, for the first time in all these years. 'It was *my* fault!'

'It was *never* your fault.' Janet's voice cracks as she stands up, furious. 'Never! That irresponsible boy nearly destroyed my only child! And I will *not* stand by and watch you sabotage your chance at happiness now because of something that happened when you were too young to know what you were doing.'

Gina realises Janet is actually shaking. 'Mum,' she says, as the exhaustion of the last few weeks overwhelms her, but Janet refuses to speak. Her shoulders hunch, and she shrinks into herself.

They stand, facing each other, and Gina wonders if Janet is seeing an adult there, or her daughter. She's about to say something conciliatory – it's her wedding eve, for God's sake, she can hardly turn up tomorrow with red eyes – when Janet speaks.

Her voice has lost all its normal girlishness. She sounds like someone else, someone serious and angry. 'If you don't look me in the eye and tell me you understand why I destroyed those letters, then you shouldn't bother going to the wedding tomorrow, Georgina.'

Gina knows what her mother is saying.

Stuart is real, she tells herself. Stuart is caring, and dependable, and attractive, and he is *there*. He loves me. He loves who I am now, even with this disgusting disease that might kill me before I'm forty. This is it. This is who I am. Maybe it *is* better if the door to the past is shut.

She draws a long, shuddering breath.

'And I'll tell him,' Janet adds. 'It'll give me no pleasure, but I'll tell him. He's a good man. He deserves a . . .'

'All *right*!' Gina disengages herself. Her whole body feels too light.

What can she do?

Nothing. There's nothing she can do but go forward.

'I just want you to be happy,' says Janet, and her voice is so heartbroken that Gina stares at her in surprise.

She rubs tears away from her eyes, hard enough to smear

her mascara. 'It's the worst part of being a mother, watching your child make mistakes.'

Gina nearly says, 'I'm sorry I seem to put you through so many, then,' but she hasn't the energy for a row. She just wants this to be over. She wants to go to bed, and sleep, and not wake up in the middle of a dream.

As she left the house on Friday morning, Gina was surprised to feel a bit sad that this was the last time she'd drop Buzz off at the dog-rescue shop. It meant it was the last time she'd potter around the park with Rachel after work, chatting about dogs, between ball-throwing, and people, houses and the shopping shortcomings of Longhampton. Rachel was very easy to be with, even without the dogs to chat about: she was open and friendly, without ever probing too much. And, unlike Naomi, she had absolutely no views on Stuart, which was, at the moment, quite restful.

Buzz had been an easy companion too. He'd just about stopped flinching when the door buzzer went, even if he remained pathetically greedy about food. In fact, Gina was offering him the other half of her Friday-morning croissant when her mobile rang, and for a weird second, she thought it might be Rachel telling her off for spoiling the dog in the street.

It wasn't Rachel. Or, as she'd half expected, Amanda Rowntree.

It was Rory, her solicitor.

'Good morning, Gina.' He had a benign headmasterly

air, with his faint Scottish accent and precise diction. 'I thought I'd give you a ring to let you know straight away that I've some good news for you.'

'Is it that Stuart's decided to stop trying to get the last coppers from down the side of our marital sofa and signed the papers?' She tucked her phone under her chin while she juggled the lead and her bag.

'Actually, yes.' Rory sounded surprised. 'I got a call from his solicitor to say that the signed Acknowledgement of Service has been filed with the court, and we should be receiving a copy soon. If you come into the office this afternoon we can get on with preparing your affidavit, so it's ready to go as soon as the paperwork arrives.'

'But what about all that financial-arrangement stuff, about wanting a percentage of the deposit and compensation for the furniture I've got?' Gina stopped in front of the deli, confused. 'He's decided that *doesn't* matter after all?' She frowned. 'He's not going to turn round and make all these demands to hold up the decree absolute, is he?'

Rules. Stuart was always better at using rules to his advantage.

'Well, I can't say that definitely won't happen, but the impression I got from Mr Horsfield's solicitor was that he was keen to make it a clean break. With no unnecessary delay, was the phrase she used.'

'And what about that list of things he wanted? I've got a boxful of junk in my sitting room for him.'

'My advice would be to give it to him as soon as you can. It shows you're willing to co-operate. You can leave it here, if you want, and I'll have it sent to his solicitor.'

'Great,' said Gina. 'Well, that's . . . brilliant news.'

It was, wasn't it? She tried to catch the fleeting emotion that passed over her like a cloud: this was really it. Stuart hadn't made a last-minute bid for forgiveness. He'd been decent about it, in the end, but he wanted a life that didn't include her.

'Yes. Yes, it is.'

Gina detected a note of reserve in Rory's voice. 'You don't sound so happy about it. Is there a catch?'

'I don't think so, no. It's great news. I just . . .' He paused, and Gina could imagine him pushing the glasses up his nose, pressing his lips together in concentration. 'In my experience, Gina, and don't take this the wrong way, when one party does a huge *volte-face* like this, there's usually a reason.'

'Meaning?'

'Well, sometimes they just wake up one morning and think, Jings, life's too short to argue about who paid for the extension. I don't care that much now. And sometimes they get an interim invoice from their solicitor and think, Good God, it's cost me half as much as I'm going to get. I need to stop this madness.'

'That sounds like Stuart.'

Rory laughed briefly, then coughed in a way that Gina recognised. Less a cough, more a warning that something awkward was hoving into view.

'And sometimes,' he went on, 'particularly if there are other parties involved, they, ah . . . suddenly encounter a more pressing reason to sort things out. And that gets things moving faster than any stern letter from me could.'

Another strange emotion spread over Gina's skin, as she

was reminded of the 'other party' in all this. 'You think Stuart wants to get *married* again?'

'It's not my place to get involved in the personal side of things, but it does happen . . .' again, the awkward cough. 'I just thought I'd introduce the possibility, in case he decides to get in touch directly to speed things up.'

Gina tried to imagine Stuart being swept away by a sudden urge to get married, and couldn't. It wasn't that he wasn't a romantic – he never forgot their anniversary and always booked the same table at Ferrari's – but he didn't rush into things. And their wedding had been such a strained experience, she couldn't imagine he'd want to repeat it. She certainly didn't.

Unless Stuart wanted to do it better with Bryony. To replace that memory with a better one. Or he might have decided to emigrate? Gina could picture them biking round New Zealand. Kayaking and surfing and doing all the outdoorsy things she'd have hated.

'That's really thoughtful of you, Rory,' she said, 'but I expect he's just had some financial advice. Or maybe he's just trying to be nice.'

Rory made a sympathetic noise that was neither yes, no, and she hung up, feeling less happy than she should have been, given how annoyed she'd been by Stuart's earlier demands.

Then she felt a warm sensation on her left hand and realised Buzz was discreetly licking the croissant flakes off her fingers with his pink tongue. Something about the uncharacteristic naughtiness of it touched her. He'd never dared do anything so cheeky before.

When Buzz realised she'd noticed, he stopped, and reverted to trying to seem invisible. Gina almost wished she didn't have to hand him over to Rachel. It's good, she told herself. I've helped him a little way along the road. I didn't let him down. That's enough.

'Time to go,' she said, before she could let the little voice whispering in her ear get any louder. She picked up the bag with his bowl, his rug and the other junk Rachel had dropped off with him, then led him across the road to the shop and his new life.

At two o'clock, Gina reconstructed the painful collapse of the Horsfield marriage in dry legal phrases in Rory's office, then took the rest of the afternoon off. She spent an hour or so in the biggest supermarket, buying herself the most luxurious food she could find to celebrate the official independence now set in motion.

It felt good at the time, dropping treats into the trolley, but when Gina stared at her pile on the conveyor-belt, the chocolates piled next to the bottle of champagne, the smoked salmon next to the gourmet ice cream, it looked like an indulgent night in for a couple.

The check-out girl smiled conspiratorially at her as she scanned the luxury bath soak, and Gina had to force an answering smile, feeling like a fraud, but it was better than looking like a sad singleton having a binge.

She was on her way back with her bags when Rachel texted to ask if she wanted to call by the shop on her way home. Gina assumed she must either have left something in one of the bags or that Buzz had already found a home, but when she pushed the shop door open, Buzz was sitting there in a new collar, his coat gleaming from a fresh wash.

'Don't say anything yet,' said Rachel, but Gina had seen the happy flick of Buzz's whippy tail, and immediately felt terrible. He thought she was coming to collect him, and she wasn't. She was abandoning him, like his last owner had done. And the one before that, probably.

'Why? Doesn't he know he's going to a lovely new home?' she asked, joking to cover up her churning stomach.

Stupid divorce. Stupid ice cream for one. Stupid . . . everything.

'Well, that's the thing. Do you think you could be an angel and have him back for just a few more days?' Rachel's face was pleading. '*Honestly* a few days this time. I've got a foster place for him in Evesham but they can't take him until the middle of next week. Please? It would be so much less disruptive for him to stay with you.'

Gina let out a long breath. 'Fine,' she said, pretending she was going to say yes anyway. 'But just for this weekend. Definitely just this weekend.'

'Definitely.' Rachel's eyes twinkled. 'Come on, I know someone who wants to show off his new collar to his lady friends in the park.'

'How are things going with the ex?' asked Rachel, as they took Buzz and Gem into the park, and Gina found herself telling her about Stuart's unexpected change of heart.

It started off as an anecdote, about the patient manner in which Rory had translated her overwrought statement about Stuart's adultery into stiff legalese, but something about the sympathetic way Rachel listened coaxed out more and more, until Gina was admitting how stupid she felt, never knowing what emotional reaction would spring out of her next.

'And I should be glad,' she confessed, 'but I'm not. I don't understand how he's gone from being super-picky to rolling over, in the space of a week.' She stared up the gravel path, towards the hill where other dog-walkers were strolling in warm fleeces. 'That's what's so . . . weird. I don't even feel I know him well enough now to say, "He's doing this to be nice." I have *no idea* what he's thinking. It feels like I never did.'

'Maybe it's the new girlfriend pushing for a quick divorce,' said Rachel. 'Have you met her? Maybe she's holding out, Anne Boleyn-style.'

Gina shook her head. 'I don't know much about her at all. My best friend Naomi's husband plays football with Stuart, but Jason's taken some sort of vow of silence about what's going on. You know what it's like when mutual friends split up.'

'Awkward.' Rachel nodded sagely. 'Who gets custody of the mates, and all that.'

'In our case, Stuart did. They were mainly his mates to start with, so I can't really complain.'

Rachel and Gina had reached the top of the park, where a grassy space was enclosed as a free dog run. As usual, Gem sped off as soon as Rachel gave the sign, leaping and bouncing into the air with a small Jack Russell. Buzz slunk obediently into the paddock, but he stayed near Gina and Rachel, sniffing the grass.

'Just ignore him,' said Rachel, seeing Gina follow him with anxious eyes. 'My husband thinks he might have been abandoned up here before or he's got bad associations with running or something.'

'A greyhound? Bad associations with running? Don't they love it?'

'Depends what happened when they ran. Or after.' Rachel's face told her that she wouldn't want to hear the details, and Gina's heart contracted.

Rachel turned back to the dogs. 'Just ignore it, and let him get used to the fact that you're not going anywhere.'

'That's what I feel bad about,' said Gina, watching Buzz pacing nervously, tail between his powerful haunches. 'He's going to get used to me, and then he'll have to go again.'

'Don't think of it like that. You're teaching him to trust,' said Rachel. 'Really important. Now, throw this ball for Gem, and tell me more about your ex's midlife crisis. Do you think he's found God? Some of them do, you know. Or do you think he's got some new *thing*? The mid-thirties are a dangerous time for motorbikes and facial hair.'

'He's not into facial hair. Or motorbikes.' Gina hurled a manky tennis ball and Gem bounded off to catch it. 'He might get a tattoo, I suppose. If the tattoo parlour could produce all their hygiene certificates and qualifications.'

'Or, of course, the new girlfriend might be . . .' Rachel trailed off.

'She might be what?'

Rachel looked as though she wasn't quite sure whether to say what she was thinking, then said it anyway. 'She might be pregnant. Happened to a friend of mine – divorce was grinding along very slowly until suddenly it all went full speed ahead because he needed to put a deposit down at the Portland.'

'No, I don't think so,' said Gina.

'Why not?'

She opened her mouth to say that Stuart didn't want children, and realised it wasn't as simple as that. The stark truth didn't show either of them in a good light, if she could find it underneath all their excuses and reasons.

Gina stared down the long slope of the park. Until she'd come up here with Buzz she hadn't realised that the domed building in the centre was a bandstand. For some reason – maybe because until a few days ago she had never ventured there – she'd always assumed it was a war memorial.

There was a man at the bottom of the hill pushing a pram, a small dark woman walking beside it. He had tawny, ruffled hair, like Stuart. For an irrational second that made her stomach lurch, Gina wondered if it was him. If maybe he already *had* a child.

Rachel seemed to be waiting patiently for an answer, and Gina realised it was about time – for herself – that she actually formulated one, instead of ignoring it.

'We never seemed to get round to it while we were married,' she said.

'Men never would, in my experience.' Rachel prised the tennis ball from Gem's jaws, and flung it with a powerful overarm lob to the back of the paddock. 'George still claims he prefers puppies to babies. But then,' she added, 'to be fair, I never thought I wanted kids until I found I was pregnant with Fergus. I think I'd have been perfectly happy if I hadn't had children because I was already pretty happy with George, and I wouldn't have known any different. I was lucky it was wonderful in a different way.' She pulled a face. 'Although life's never straightforward, is it? What makes us happy this year might not cut it next.'

Gem bounded up with the ball in his mouth. He looked as if he was smiling. Rachel fondled his ears and chucked it again. Buzz didn't move. He stared intently at the ground, tail pressed anxiously between his legs. Gina noticed a man walking past with a terrier on the other side of the path, and she slowly moved so she was between him and Buzz.

After a second, the tail lifted a fraction and Gina felt her own relief mingle with Buzz's. She turned her attention back to Rachel, before she thought too much about it.

'Were you and your husband trying for a long time?' she asked. Rachel had to be in her early forties, as was her husband, and their son couldn't be more than three.

She laughed. 'No, quite the opposite – we didn't try at all. I only met George when I was nearly forty. Fergus was a complete accident. I'd just come out of a ten-year car-crash of a relationship, and George and I had only been on a handful of dates, if you can call them that. The relationship came later. Totally the wrong way around.'

'Really?' said Gina, before she could stop herself. That wasn't at all what she'd have guessed, from Rachel's outwardly together appearance. She looked like the sort of cake-baking, Range-Rover-driving modern mother, in her skinny jeans and padded gilet. Apart from the blue nail varnish. And the streaks of grey in her glossy black hair that weren't dyed away.

'I know.' Rachel's face creased in self-deprecating horror. 'In fact, our entire relationship is based on the sort of irresponsible behaviour you'd lock up your daughter for, but you know what? I'm not pretending it was sensible, but it turned out to be the best thing I could have done. Sometimes you've got to throw caution to the wind.'

'Yeah, if you don't mind what blows back in your face,' said Gina. It was always confident people who went on about leaping into the unknown and taking a chance on life. 'Sorry,' she added. 'I didn't mean to sound so rude.'

Rachel paused, weighing the soggy tennis ball in her hand. 'No, that's fair enough. Risks go both ways. But I'd never have chosen this life. If you'd told me at thirty, thirty-five even, that I'd be married, with a son, living in the middle of nowhere, I wouldn't have been surprised, I'd have been *appalled*. I was a Londoner. My boyfriend was married to someone else. I had a career in PR. But things change. Sometimes it's easier when it's out of your control because then you're just surviving. There's no sense of feeling you've chosen a potentially disastrous road . . .' She caught herself. 'Sorry, we were talking about you, not me. Did *you* want children? Was it just your ex who didn't?'

'I thought I didn't, then I did. Now I don't know.'

Gina knew she was being evasive, but she *didn't* know what the answer was. Every time she peered into herself, other people got in the way – Janet's nagging for a grand-child; the instinctive affection she felt for Willow; Stuart, and what a good dad he'd be. Above it all, her own ugly suspicion that life wasn't something you could rely on enough to bring a child into it.

'You've still got time,' said Rachel, encouragingly. 'You're, what? Thirty?'

'Too kind. Thirty-three. To be honest, I don't actually know if I can have children. I had chemotherapy about six years ago – I haven't really investigated what effect it might have had.'

'Oh,' said Rachel, abashed. 'Well, that's totally different. I'm so sorry I sounded flippant about the girlfriend having a baby.'

'No, it's fine. It's something I should think about.' Gina stared out across the neatly maintained gardens. The first green shoots were turning into leaves, and the beds looked like bright makeup palettes, with splashes of red tulips and yellow primroses. She made a mental note to get a window box for her wide gallery window and put some bold colour outside the white flat.

'I suppose,' she said slowly, 'if I'm honest, I am a bit torn about how I'll feel if Stuart does get his new girlfriend pregnant. If he decides to have a family with her.'

And not me. That the baby who would have been born with his eyes, his nose, his feet will now have another woman's hair, her smile, her chin. Not mine. Another window to look into and see someone else with my life.

'I'd be feeling sorry for her if she were,' said Rachel. 'Having a kid with a man who's still married? That's never a good start.'

'I wouldn't make it hard for them,' said Gina, decisively. 'I've got a list of clichéd things I swore I wouldn't do during the divorce, and being vengeful is right at the top.'

Rachel chucked the tennis ball one last time for Gem.

'Did your ex make a list, though? Because from what you've said it sounds like he's working through a cliché list of his own. Has he got a leather jacket yet?'

'No.' Gina considered: Stuart in a leather jacket. 'But it's only a matter of time.'

Rachel turned, raking her hair back with a hand. 'My advice, for what it's worth, is to let it all go,' she said. 'Be as kind as you can bear to be, and let karma take care of things. You can't grab hold of new opportunities if you're clinging to the past. You need those hands wide open.'

Gina reckoned Rachel had spent too much time amid the fridge magnets in the charity shop. 'You think?' she said.

'I know,' said Rachel, and hurled the ball – 'One last time, Gem!' – into the bushes. The collie raced joyfully after it.

Chapter Fourteen

ITEM: pair of hand-blown champagne flutes

Longhampton, June 2008

Gina sits at the table in the gastropub and tries to focus on all the sweet things Stuart is saying about her. His voice is rising and falling, and he's injecting a lot of effort into his delivery, but it's not really going in, mainly because everyone is looking at her and trying not to cry.

'. . . special woman . . . Knew as soon as I tried her cottage pie . . . For better or for worse . . . Matlock . . .'

I should be remembering this, Gina thinks, through a muzzy haze of pink champagne (she shouldn't be drinking but, come on, it's her wedding day). She stares at the flute in her hand, smooth and so fine she's scared she'll snap it. I won't forget how the bubbles in this wine are so perfect. Fragile but determined, directing drunkenness into her bloodstream while Stuart rambles on, filling up the gaps where Terry's speech would be, and where his best man's speech would be, if Olly had had time to get back from his holiday in Australia.

It still feels like it's happening to someone else. Even

though she's had the operation to cut the cancer out. Technically, it's gone. Realistically, it's only starting.

She waits for Stuart to come to the end of his speech, then rises to kiss him, to drink in the too-loud applause, and excuses herself to go to the loo.

Gina gets about ten seconds of peace before the door opens and Naomi comes in. There's a pinch between her threaded eyebrows that not even her new fringe is hiding. 'Are you OK?' she asks lightly. 'You're not feeling sick or anything?'

'I'm fine. Why are you looking so tense?' Gina asks recklessly. 'Is it because I've had a civil wedding and you've had to wear a fascinator?' Weirdly, she doesn't feel any compunction about being so direct with Naomi. Normally she bites her tongue, considering all possible offence, but now she's just saying exactly what she thinks to people. They seem to expect it – and it gives them something to forgive, some concession to make towards an illness that turns everyone she tells white, then blank with internal shock.

Naomi stares at her, and the ostrich feathers tremble on her head. They really don't suit her, and say more about Naomi's state of mind than anything else. Stuart's whistle-stop organisation hadn't given her much time to find the wedding outfit she'd dreamed about shopping for ever since they were teenagers. It feels like no time has passed since they were shopping for Gina's bridesmaid's dress, but it's already in a different chapter of Gina's life.

The appropriately mournful honking of Adele filters in from the bar as someone pushes the door open and goes into the Gents opposite. Gina doesn't blame Naomi if she's pissed off about her hat. The Vivienne Westwood suit isn't what she'd have chosen to get married in either, and she can't imagine she'll ever wear it again, but the assistant talked her into it, and for a second, it was exciting to be someone else, the sort of woman who blows eight hundred quid on a suit because why not? This is the best she's going to look for a while.

'I can't believe you can even think that!' Naomi smiles too brightly. 'Today's all about *you*. I don't care about my fascinator!'

'Then why have you got that face on you?' The champagne has gone straight to Gina's head; she probably shouldn't have had it. 'Please try to look happy. I feel like I'm at a party before the Battle of the Somme. Everyone looks as if they're about to burst into tears.'

'No, they're not!' Naomi's determinedly shiny mood is making everything she says come out with an exclamation mark. 'They're thinking about what a great couple you and Stuart make! Because you do!'

'They're not, Nay,' says Gina. 'They're trying to work out how happy it's polite to be in the circumstances. I don't blame them. Maybe this was a mistake. It's hard enough for me and Stuart. I mean, maybe it's *easier* for me and Stuart. At least we know what's going on.'

Naomi starts to speak, but her words come out as a gulp. She blinks, struggling to maintain the encouraging expression she's been wearing all day. In the salon, in the car, doing everyone's makeup round at Janet's – Naomi's been the one taking happy snaps, dishing out the compliments, cheering everyone along. It's not the elaborate wedding they'd planned as teenagers, but Naomi's done her best to keep up her end of the deal as chief bridesmaid.

'Don't, Gina,' she says, smiling brightly again. 'Come on.'

'Sorry.' Gina glances at the doors, worried someone will come in. Her mum, barely holding it together as it is, or Stuart's sister, who's very drunk. Everyone is drunk. They're all knocking it back to avoid talking about the elephant in the room.

The bridal elephant in a velvet suit and an ironically elaborate hairdo.

'Look, I'm really sorry about jumping in and stealing your wedding thunder,' says Gina, trying to make a joke of it, like they always do. 'There's still a few months to sort out a new bridesmaid, if you want. I don't want to be the bald bridesmaid who upstages you at the altar . . .'

Naomi turns away, but her control finally slips. 'I don't care about my wedding! I've told Jason we're going to move it till you're better, sod the deposits.' She yanks at the roller towel, making it crunch loudly. That silences the pair of them, and for a moment, they just stand there, staring at one another in despair, because all the normalities that their lives had pivoted on last month now seem like toy boats bobbing on a huge, unknown ocean.

'All I care about is you getting better,' says Naomi, in a broken voice. 'I don't want to lose my best mate. That's really selfish, isn't it? But I don't. I can't imagine making another friend like you ever again.'

Gina smiles, despite her brimming eyes. 'Don't tell Jason that.'

'He knows!' Naomi's own eyes are full. 'He knows what you mean to me.'

Gina reaches out to touch her arm, and Naomi struggles not to burst into tears. They both blink frantically to avoid mascara run, and the blackness of the situation gives them hysterical giggles, balanced right on the very edge of sobbing.

Gina's never felt more grateful for Naomi than at this exact moment; she's the thread that links all the parts of Gina's life together. Good bits, bad bits, secret bits, ugly bits. And knowing she does the same for Naomi gives her something to hold on to.

'We can't cry,' Gina half laughs, half sobs. 'If they see the bride and the chief bridesmaid crying it'll set them all off!'

'Don't worry, I used waterproof mascara. I knew this would happen.'

They blink and flap and try not to catch each other's eye because that'll be the end.

'The thing is,' says Gina, in a rush of honesty, 'I just want to get on with it now.' Now she's here with Naomi, she can get this off her chest. Stuart's being lovely, but she needs to be a certain way with him and with Janet. She finds herself reacting to fit in with their roles of supportive partner and devastated mother; it's easier to let their reactions shape hers. She fits into the space created by their concern.

If she thinks about how she actually feels, a cold black gap opens up inside her.

Gina grips the cold edge of the sink. 'Don't you think that . . . sometimes the universe balances things out?'

'What?'

'You know, we all get our share of good luck and bad luck, eventually.'

Naomi frowns. 'You're not making any sense, love.'

'I mean . . . I've been lucky, Naomi. When you think what *could* have happened to me . . . And it's like Kit's mother said, what goes around comes around. I—'

'No!' hisses Naomi. '*No!* That is such bullshit, Gina, and you must not think it.' She grabs her arm. '*Tell* me you don't believe that.'

But Gina does think that and secretly it's what's giving her the calmness people keep going on about. There can't be anything worse than this in her life now; the sword hanging over her head for what happened to Kit has dropped. And how much bad luck can one person have? Dad, Terry, Kit . . . Surely this is it now, for ever.

She just has to get through it. The thought of what 'it' might be makes the cavern open up again beneath her, and she wobbles.

'I'm going to be fine, Nay,' she says. 'We're going to get through this.'

Naomi looks as if she's going to throw up, but she forces another of her smiles, and together they go back into the private room, where everyone else's smiles suddenly reappear too, as if a switch has been flicked.

On Thursday, Gina heard, via Rory, that Stuart would be coming to collect his box of things from her flat the next day, after work.

She and Stuart exchanged brief texts directly about the collection time: he was going to call round on his way to football practice, but he made no reference to any reason for the sudden change of heart. In addition to the items he wanted, she'd decided to give him the set of Murano bowls. They were nice, and he'd bought them after all. Looking at them now didn't give Gina the pleasure they deserved; she wanted Stuart to have something beautiful to remind him of their marriage. Maybe one day he'd see in them what she had.

Gina was thinking about the bowls when she arrived at the Magistrate's House at lunchtime, wondering what sort of treasures had once been displayed in cabinets when the Warwicks had held court there. She headed round the back into the kitchen, drawn by the smell of toast. There was a crowd around the table, and as she knocked and let herself in, various heads turned.

'Ah, good,' said Nick. 'Someone who'll know what to do.'

Kian, one of the builders' lads, was sitting at the kitchen table, his head turned away from his outstretched hand. Lorcan and his apprentice carpenter, Ryan, were hovering behind him, looking worried, and amused respectively.

'What's happened?' Gina asked, reaching into her pocket for her mobile to call an ambulance. Kian's face was milk-white. 'Lorcan, I thought you were the designated first-aider on site.'

'It's not an ambulance job. We've just got a bit of a jewellery incident.' Nick stepped back and revealed that he was trying to get a ring off Kian's finger with a bar of soap. The camera on the table next to them was a clue as to what had just happened.

'Cold water,' said Gina at once. 'Ice cubes, if you've got them. And, failing that, we can try butter.'

Lorcan nudged the sniggering apprentice next to him. 'You heard the lady, Ryan. Bowl, cold water. Chop chop.'

Ryan went over to the brand new fridge-freezer, a lone white column of modernity in the ramshackle kitchen, and rummaged for ice cubes while Kian stared at his diamond-encrusted little finger.

'Suits you,' said Gina, and he looked mortified. Kian was one of the non-speaking apprentices.

'I'm afraid that's your hand-modelling career over, Kian,' said Nick. 'But if it makes you feel any better, I got some lovely photos.'

'Your regular hand model not back from Paris yet?' Gina raised an eyebrow, and something passed across Nick's face.

'No, but my reserve hand model has just arrived.' He raised a hopeful eyebrow. 'Would you mind ? It'll only take a few minutes.'

'It'll have to wait until we've had a chat about plastering.' Gina tapped her folder of notes. 'I've had a couple of quotes in from the contractors I showed round last week and I need to talk through some of the specialist repairs to the cornices in the—'

'Can we talk about them while I photograph some bracelets, please? I'm already late on this. I can't cope with you *and* Amanda *and* Charlie yelling at me.'

'Lorcan?' Gina looked at him. 'Aren't you yelling?'

'Me?' Lorcan pretended to be affronted. 'Do I ever yell? Listen, I can't risk any more of my lads to jewellery-related injuries so this one's all yours. That plaster isn't going to come off by itself.'

'It's already coming off by itself,' Nick pointed out. 'In most of the rooms.'

'Have you two been rehearsing this routine?' asked Gina, amused. 'Lorcan, if you get Ryan to make me some tea, I can ask Nick all about plastering while he's photographing.'

'I don't know.' Lorcan raised his hands at Gina. 'You models and your diva demands.'

'We're worth it. Milk, no sugar. ' And Gina let Nick steer her towards his makeshift studio in the drawing room.

Lorcan's team had already started to prepare the areas of the Magistrate's House that didn't require building consent for the first stages of repair work. The hall parquet was protected with plastic sheeting, and the stairs had polythene covers over their twisted oak banisters to shield them from the drills and barrows being marched into the downstairs rooms. Most of the panelling in the hall had been removed in sections so the old walls underneath could be patched up with new timber and fresh plaster where they'd decayed. Gina never ceased to be amazed at how simple even the most magnificent houses were beneath the polished wood and paint. Just lime and horsehair, wood and nails, like every other house.

The drawing room where Nick was working was shrouded in dust-sheets ('good natural reflectors'); he'd set up a trestle table with a couple of chairs in the wide bay window that looked out onto the far end of what would have been – and might still be - the croquet lawn. There wasn't much sun and the borders were overgrown but, even so, Gina's imagination supplied a padded velvet seat round the three sides of the window, with deep chintzy sofas, and tea on silver trays.

'I know what you're thinking,' said Nick, seeing the direction of her gaze. 'Window-seat? Right?'

'No,' Gina lied. 'I was thinking that I need to chase up the window specialists.'

She wasn't sure why that had come out. It was *good* that Nick had the same sort of vision of the house as she did. But either he seemed to have a knack of seeing into her head or she was very easy to read, and on days like today, with Stuart's visit playing on her mind, it made her feel self-conscious.

'But, yes, a window-seat would be amazing,' she agreed, unable to help herself. 'We could put radiators underneath and get Lorcan to build latticed covers over them.'

'I love that idea,' said Nick. 'Encouraging the croquet players from the comfort of inside when it's raining. Do you want to sit down? This'll take five minutes, then we can talk plaster. I promise.'

He cleared a space at one end of the table, stacking the camera magazines and letters into heaps, then pulled out a small velvet pouch and tipped a tangle of charm bracelets onto the table. He took a few shots of them in a pile on the white background. Then, at his suggestion, Gina slid them onto her wrist one at a time while he took close-ups of the charms and the links.

Nick murmured instructions, and she spread her fingers, picked up a cup, balanced her hand at an angle, watching the light fall onto her skin. As with the eggs, Gina had the strange sensation of seemingly seeing her hand and wrist for the first time.

Funny how that knobble on the wrist looks so delicate, she thought. When it's actually a reminder of the solid bone underneath.

'Nice manicure,' Nick observed. 'Going somewhere glamorous tonight?'

'Thank you. And no. The only thing in my diary is my ex who's coming round to collect a box of stuff tomorrow night.'

It had slipped out. She frowned at herself.

But Nick didn't react, just carried on clicking away. 'I see. Is it for his benefit? Does he notice things like that?'

'No. I always do my nails.'

'Why's that? Don't they get chipped, working in places like this?'

She hesitated. There was a reason why her nails were always neat, but it was personal: her favourite oncology nurse had encouraged her to wear dark varnish to strengthen her nails during chemotherapy – and to give herself something to do in all the hanging around. Her nails had split and ridged during the treatment, but Gina had persevered with creams and oils until they grew back. She never talked about her treatment at work: it had hovered over her like a label when she was at the council. But Nick sounded genuinely interested, and something about their closeness, yet lack of eye contact, made it slip out.

'I was advised to keep my nails covered with varnish while I was having chemotherapy,' she said. 'If they go black, it stops it being so noticeable too.'

'Really?' He didn't react to the mention of chemo, just nodded. It made her more inclined to go on.

'Yup. I liked having nice nails when everything else seemed to be falling out, or making me throw up. It made me feel less . . . grey.'

'I like that colour. What do you call it?'

'Parchment.'

'Appropriate.'

Gina picked up her mug of tea with her other hand and sipped from it. 'I like greens and blues but, as you so correctly observed, it's easy to chip on a building site, and I think it's important to be chip-free, as a project manager.'

'I agree,' he said, without taking his eye from the viewfinder. 'Although, in my old-fashioned book, you can't beat red nail varnish.'

'A red *nail*,' Gina corrected him, as he turned her charm bracelet, so the little heart charm was uppermost, nestled in the hollow of her wrist. A bright drop of scarlet enamel, like blood. 'The correct fashion term is "a red nail". Like "a bold lip" or "a smoky eye".'

'I'll remember that. Next time I'm photographing a top model.'

It felt intimate, Nick's close focus on her hands, their no-eye-contact conversation. Their voices had dropped not quite to a whisper but lower than normal, as if the camera were a third person they didn't want to distract.

And then he looked up, straight at her. His grey eyes

were merry, she thought, randomly – merry, like the Merry Monarch. Hooded, long-lashed Jacobean eyes.

Gina's mind went blank. Say something else about fashion singulars. She wasn't even a fashion person. All she could think of was 'a trouser' and that sounded . . . too flirty.

'So when did you have chemo?' He sounded interested, but not nosy.

'Six years ago. I had breast cancer. They caught it early, blasted me with the worst chemotherapy in the world, put me on Tamoxifen, and now it's in remission. Touch wood.'

'Glad to hear it. Touch wood.'

Nick moved as if he were about to raise his head, and Gina felt an urge to change the subject before he looked at her in a new way. She didn't want to see him examine her for signs he might have missed before.

'So, is Amanda back this weekend?' she blurted, the first thing that came into her head. 'She must be curious to see what's going on.' I'm getting enough emails about it, she added to herself. She assumed Nick was getting them too, as he was cc'd into most of them; something she found a bit odd.

'Sadly not.' Click, click. 'She's got a meeting with a different client in New York on Friday so she's going to stay in Paris an extra night, then fly out there. Easier than driving here, driving back, getting an early plane. It's OK,' he added, 'I've been Skyping her in the evenings, showing her what we've been up to.'

'And she's happy?'

'Very happy. Well, as happy as you can be when it's not very exciting.'

'I know,' said Gina. 'It takes a while to get to paint charts. So will you be spending the weekend pulling plaster off the walls?'

'Of course! Isn't that what everyone does at the weekend? No, I'll probably go back to London for a few days. Leave the plaster removal to people who know what they're doing.'

Gina wondered why she felt a bit disappointed by the reminder that Nick didn't really live here. This was just their country weekend place. Why should he stay here on his own?

'It's a good chance to catch up with all the friends Amanda's not keen on.' Nick waggled his eyebrows conspiratorially. 'OK, to be honest, I might stay here and pull plaster off the walls. Lorcan's shown me the special tool. It's surprisingly addictive. One more. Splay your fingers.'

He took a final photo of the charm bracelet, and Gina relaxed, picking up her tea out of shot. While she was sipping it, Nick lifted his camera and took a single photo of her. 'Sorry,' he said, 'I couldn't resist. You looked so funny. Here, I'll show you, don't panic.'

He turned the camera round so she could see the image. There she was, face half hidden by the white mug, her eyes above it, round and brown like a Manga heroine's, and her hand stretched out with the charm bracelet dangling languidly from her skinny wrist.

Her wrist wasn't skinny: it was just how Nick had shot it. Her, but not her. Her seen by someone looking at her and only seeing what was there.

'It's one of those moments I was talking about the other

day,' said Nick, seeing her expression. 'The first cup of tea after a boring photo shoot. Treasure it.'

'You didn't take a Polaroid,' she said.

'No, I didn't.' He paused. 'Do you want me to?'

'Um. Yes.'

But when he got the camera out of the plastic crate of equipment under the table, Gina held out her hand for it. He hesitated, then handed it over.

The last time Gina had taken a photo on a Polaroid had been at Naomi's fourteenth birthday party: it had been her and Naomi, crowding into the frame at arm's length, wearing Minnie Mouse ears. She'd stayed over because Naomi's brother Shaun had slipped them four bottles of Diamond White and Janet could detect alcohol on Gina's breath from the other end of the street.

'Say cheese,' she said to Nick, and he grinned obediently.

The camera whirred and clicked, and the flat slip of film slid out.

'I don't like having my photo taken,' he said, as she shook it around. 'And contrary to popular belief, by the way, you don't have to shake it. Like a Polaroid picture.'

'No?'

'No. The professional way to speed it up is to stick it under your armpit.'

'I'll remember that.' She stuck it under her arm, then checked the image: there he was, photographer Nick, photographed. Looking right up at her, his smile broad but more self-conscious than in real life. The empty house in the background and the off colours of the old film stock blurred the time period. There was something faintly Seventies about the drawing room now.

She'd framed the photograph well: he was plumb centre of the shot, his shirt neck open at the perfect angle to show the hollows either side of his throat. Gina hadn't noticed it in real life but as she stared at the photo she noticed the two tanned indentations, shadowed on his smooth skin, framed by the checked cotton. There was something very masculine about them. The bones under the skin again – delicate but strong.

'Good picture,' he said, leaning over to see, and she caught a whiff of the smell that had seemed so familiar the first time they'd met outside. It was like something she already knew. Probably just his shampoo, she told herself.

'Thanks,' she said.

The following day, Stuart rang the doorbell at dead on six o'clock, and Buzz darted into his basket in the corner of the kitchen, where he'd been hiding while she hoovered the flat.

'Don't worry, no one's coming to get you,' said Gina, and he flattened his ears, in a way she could now differentiate from his scared ear raise.

She pressed the intercom buzzer to open the front door, and rested her knuckles on her hips as she surveyed the sitting room. It would be a shock to Stuart: this was the emptiest, whitest room she'd ever lived in. Apart from the sofa and footstool, only the bright blue vase filled with red tulips splashed colour onto the paleness. There were a few boxes left to sort through but she'd shut them in the bedroom, out of the way. The last thing she wanted was for Stuart to start scratching through them now.

Importantly, though, Gina's flat felt like home. The sorting agony had been worth it. Everything here was hers. Not theirs. Hers.

She heard his feet bound up the stairs. Then he rapped three times on the door. Even though she was prepared, Gina suddenly felt nervous: this was the first time she'd seen him since they'd moved out of Dryden Road.

She opened the door and there he was, in his football-training kit, a bag slung over his shoulder.

'Hey.'

Gina didn't want to, but she couldn't stop her eyes sweeping Stuart's face for changes: his tawny hair was a little longer than she remembered, and there was a definite beard along his jaw, but otherwise he was completely as normal. He didn't look a lot different from the twenty-seven-year-old she'd met at Naomi's. Which was annoying. The least he could do, after what he'd put her through, was look as if he'd had a few sleepless nights. Instead, he had a faintly smug glow about him.

She forced a smile, and hoped it didn't look too tense. 'Hello. Come in.'

'Thanks for letting me come round,' said Stuart, politely, as he passed her, gazing at the white walls and the paintings she'd hung. He stopped at the window and stared at the vase as if he couldn't quite place it, then turned back.

Gina decided that she didn't like the beard: it made him look more football manager than star striker.

'I've put everything in there,' she said brightly, indicating the box on the coffee table. 'Including the Murano bowls.'

'Oh?' He raised a sarcastic eyebrow. 'The bowls your solicitor thought you couldn't find?'

Rory had been right, thought Gina. Financial settlements didn't bring out the best in anyone. Rise above it.

'I found them,' she said, simply. 'I thought about keeping two, and giving you two, but in the end I decided they should stay together, and that you should have them as a happy memory of that holiday in Venice.'

Stuart regarded her suspiciously. 'Right.'

'Because that was a happy time,' Gina pressed on. 'It was a nice holiday, and the bowls will always remind you of that afternoon. Seeing Venice for the first time, and eating ice cream in St Mark's Square and you . . . haggling.'

Stuart had started to look mollified, but he did a double take at that. 'Hang on. You're rewriting history again. You were *mortified* about that. You gave me a right earful about haggling, even though everyone knows you're supposed to. It was in the *guidebook*,' he added, with a trace of an old grievance.

Gina's determination to be gracious stuttered. Stuart always picked up on the tiniest things, then refused to let them go. 'I know,' she said. 'But when I look back on it now, I realise that it was very you. You were determined to get the best price and you did. I always admired your tenacity . . .'

You're talking about him like he's dead.

'. . . the way you never take no for an answer. It made all the difference when I was ill.' She glanced up and saw Stuart's expression had changed: he looked touched. She felt a rush of generosity. 'I want you to have the bowls, and when you use them, I want you to remember that we did have some happy times together. And,' it only occurred to her as she was saying it, 'that I was truly grateful for your stubbornness when it really mattered.'

This is about sending something into the atmosphere, she told herself. Like Rachel said, maybe I need to let things happen, instead of trying to control it all.

Stuart seemed at a loss. He'd obviously come prepared for an argument.

'Um, thanks. That's a nice thought.' He reached into the box and took one out; Gina had encased them in bubble-wrap, stacking them neatly together. Stuart undid one and held it up to the light, so the tiny dots of coloured glass shone like boiled sweets melted in sugar.

Gina had taken photos of the lights dotted along the canal at night but they hadn't really come out. The memory she'd wanted to capture was the promising dusk, the smell of grilled meat and the canals in the heavy night air. The oldness of the place. The bowls made her remember that.

'I'd forgotten how nice they were, actually,' he said, and glanced at her, his expression more like the easy-going one she remembered. 'No wonder that guy wouldn't back down. To be honest, ' his mouth tugged to one side, 'I got the exchange rate wrong in my head. I think I did beat him down a bit much. I checked when we got home and I reckon we underpaid by about a hundred euros.'

'What? No! You never said anything.'

'How could I?' Stuart looked sheepish. 'I'd made such a fuss. But come on. They're not bad, are they?'

'They're art, you philistine,' she said, only half joking.

He grinned, and Gina realised this was the first amiable

conversation they'd had in ages. It was tentative, and they were talking about their relationship as if it were a fondly remembered dead relative, but it wasn't bad.

'So . . .' Stuart glanced around the flat, more closely this time. 'Are you actually living here?'

'What do you mean? Of course I am.'

'No, I mean, it's so empty. Our loo had more stuff in it than this room.'

'I'm having a detox. You should try it.'

'Ha. As if. Is that . . .' His gaze had stopped at the kitchen, and turned incredulous. 'Is that a real dog?'

Buzz feigned sleep in his basket, pressing himself into the sides. Gina could see the signs of his nervous twitch, and kicked herself for letting Stuart, a strange man, into the flat. Buzz hated strange men.

'Not really. I'm just looking after him until he can go into kennels,' she said.

'How did that happen?' Stuart seemed amused. 'Loki and Thor will be livid when I tell them you've gone over to the dark side.'

'The *bark* side,' said Gina goofily, and after two beats, Stuart smiled.

Gina opened her mouth to tell Stuart exactly how Buzz had been dropped into her life then realised it probably wasn't a great idea to bring up the bike, not when things were going relatively cordially. Fortunately Stuart was already distracted by the Roberts radio sitting on the kitchen counter.

'This is mine,' he said, picking it up. 'Didn't you give me this for my birthday one year? It was in the bathroom.'

'No, it's mine,' she said. 'You're thinking of that DAB radio. It's in the box. It was on your list.'

Gina heard a faint sound from the kitchen, like a distant car engine being started, a low rumbling growl. Was that Buzz? She'd never heard him make a noise like that before. He rarely made a noise at all, other than the snuffly grunts he made when Rachel tickled his ears and the occasional click in his sleep.

'Buzz?' she said, and the noise stopped.

Gina turned back to Stuart. 'Anyway, I meant to say, off the record, thanks for getting the financial paperwork moving. I don't know what's prompted it, but . . . What?'

Stuart was rubbing his chin with his hand, as if working out how to say something awkward. 'Um, yeah . . . About that,' he said.

He's going abroad, guessed Gina. He and Bryony have decided to sell up and emigrate. That'd be why he hadn't bothered to take much stuff.

Stuart coughed and stared at the floor, but a faint smile flickered around his eyes. 'Um . . . not sure how to say this . . .'

'What?' She was starting to remember why remaining gracious around him could be such a strain. 'Whatever you've got to say to me, it's not going to be worse than "I'm having an affair", Stu.'

'I don't know about that.'

'Believe me, it won't be. Get on with it,' said Gina.

'Me and Bryony . . . Well, Bryony more than me . . .' Stuart looked up, and Gina could see he was enjoying the words, despite his reluctance to say them to her. 'We're pregnant.'

Gina had always loathed that phrase for its modern-parent smuggery, but now it made her feel nauseous. Something sour rose in her throat. '*She*'s pregnant,' she retorted automatically. 'Unless you've got some kind of man-womb you never let on about.'

He lifted his hands and dropped them, as if she'd just proved his point. 'You see? I knew you'd be like this.'

'Like what?'

'Bitter.'

'Bitter? Stuart, that's wit. *Bitter* would be some comment about, I don't know, you not even bothering to wait until you'd divorced your first wife before getting your next woman pregnant.'

'Look, it's not ideal but it is what it is. We're very happy.' His chin jutted self-righteously. 'Anyway, I didn't come here to discuss it. I just wanted you to hear it from me.'

Gina wanted to be cool and ask questions, but her mind was furious and red and blank. Naomi – even her best friend Naomi – hadn't told her she was pregnant until her three-month scan. Which meant . . . Gina's mind spun backwards.

'How pregnant is she?'

Stuart looked evasive, which told Gina everything. All at once, she didn't want to know details. Her chest felt as if it were about to cave in. 'You're such a sad old cliché,' she said. 'You're just like all those other man-children who hum and haw about kids, wasting years of people's lives, and then . . .'

'Fuck off,' said Stuart, outraged. 'Who was wasting time? It was *my* time that was being wasted too. You didn't even want children.'

It stung. 'That's not true!'

He glared at her. 'I was there, remember? I drove you to the clinic. And I sat there in that fertility office when you told the doctor you didn't want to go ahead with the embryo harvesting. You didn't want us to have children. Or, rather, you didn't want to have *my* children.'

'That wasn't—' Gina stopped herself before she said something she couldn't take back.

'That wasn't what?' demanded Stuart. He looked her squarely in the face, and the angry hurt in his expression made him look older. Older, and a stranger. 'That wasn't how you want to remember it?'

'That's not how it was,' said Gina. She clamped her lips together and tried to condense the blurry memory in her head into something sharp and specific but it wouldn't come together. There was too much she didn't understand herself.

Life pivots on such tiny moments, she thought. You get a split second to think how to deal with hugely significant situations and, *bang*, you get it wrong and everything goes hurtling off the wrong way. A minute ago things were going well. And now . . .

'Well, whatever.' Stuart waved a hand round her empty flat. 'Good luck.'

'That's it?' Gina's voice cracked. '"I'm having a baby with another woman, cheers for the bowls and the good times, good luck"?'

Stuart rolled his eyes. 'Seriously, it's impossible to talk to you sometimes. I *am* pleased for you. We've both got a fresh start. I'll be in touch.'

He grabbed his box off the table and made for the door, kicking it open with his foot and storming down the stairs.

Gina would have followed, maybe even chucked some old travel guides after him, but she couldn't move. Her legs felt like lead. Memories she'd shoved right to the back of her mind were crowding around her, the emotions unexpectedly very fresh again. She'd known at the time that she was only postponing the real pain for another day, but there had been so much else to think about then. There hadn't been room in her head to consider theoretical pain when real pain was being timetabled in three-weekly doses.

Now, though, the full impact of what she'd said, what she'd done, in the consultant's office in Longhampton hospital finally revealed itself. *Ta-da!* it said. *Here I am, and now you're six years older, and alone.*

Gina sank onto the sofa and put her head in her hands. She didn't cry but let the waves of emotion surge through her veins. She didn't know how long she sat there, letting the tide wash back and forth over the memory, but she stayed in the same hunched pose until her breathing returned to normal.

When she looked up, Buzz had left his basket and was lying by the door, watching it with his inscrutable black eyes. He wasn't waiting to be let out. He was guarding it.

Chapter Fifteen

ITEM: *Little Women* by Louisa May Alcott,
property of Georgina Jessica Pritchard, aged 8

Longhampton, 25th June 2008

The fertility specialist is kind, makes a point of talking to her and Stuart equally, alternating his gentle gaze between them both as he outlines the options available to them in the event of Gina's chemotherapy affecting their chances of starting a family.

Gina nods, and smiles politely. Stuart nods, and writes it all down, frowning as he links everything up with arrows and boxes, cross-referencing time frames and asking Mr Mancini to spell the drugs so he can look them up later.

It is, of course, fair, thinks Gina, trying to put herself in Stuart's shoes as his pen scratches across the ever-present notebook. It's Stuart's future son or daughter who may or may not be at risk from the chemicals that are scheduled to be pumped though Gina's veins, attacking the cancer and, sadly, other things in her body, like follicles and eggs. They're not fussy.

'. . . we can give you luteinising hormone-blocker injections to stop your ovaries working during the chemotherapy treatment, but again, that's not absolutely guaranteed . . .'

Except it's not strictly fair, is it? she thinks. Stuart can always go and have children with someone else. Another woman. She can't. This is her future as a parent they're discussing. As well as her future as a person. Gina tries to remind herself that it's amazing Stuart's thinking in terms of *them*, *their* family, but for once, she wants it to be about *her*.

Mr Mancini is explaining that her best option for motherhood is to postpone her chemotherapy while she takes a series of hormones *that might actually increase the cancer cells* in order to harvest some eggs, which Stuart can then fertilise, and the embryos can be put on ice until she's better.

So, for the mere chance of being a mother, she has to go through a pre-motherhood sacrifice and offer up her own body to chance and medical science.

Mum would love that, she thinks, staring at the baby handprint cast Mr Mancini has on his desk – to inspire his patients, presumably. It looks morbid to Gina, but at the moment, everything feels like a symbol of death. Trees, flowers, birds in the sky. The real test of a mother. How much do you want it? Are you willing to feed your own cancer to do it?

The answer should, of course, be yes. But Gina can't find that yes inside herself. There's just a worrying silence that isn't quite a no.

The worst thing about this conversation is that, for the first time since her diagnosis, Gina feels she has to make a decision. Not just about her future, but about the *sort of person she is*. So far, everything's been presented to her and the answer has been obvious. The doctors know more than she does about how to treat the cancer in her breast; where there have been 'choices', she's been smart enough to see that, realistically, there are no choices. Now, though, she has to decide something that will have a direct impact on a life beyond the treatment, and Gina doesn't want to look that far.

It's impossible to imagine children – nativity plays, parties, tooth fairies, exams – when she still can't get her head around the sobering fact that her own life might not now stretch out to the seventy, eighty years she'd taken for granted before. It might not stretch out another ten.

Across the desk, Mr Mancini pauses in his biology lecture and raises his eyebrows to check she understands what he's said. He's a reassuring man. But his outcomes are probably a bit more uplifting than her oncologist's.

'Of course, Mrs Horsfield, apart from your youth, you're in a much stronger position than many of the patients I see,' he says.

'Really?' says Gina. She can't imagine how her position can possibly be stronger. Because she came in quickly? Because Stuart is here taking notes? Because she's now Mrs Horsfield, not Miss Bellamy? That still sounds weird, but comforting, as if she's tucked under Stuart's capable wing.

'Well, you could opt to freeze a fertilised embryo, rather than eggs.' He glances between the two of them, the avuncular smile broadening. 'That has a much higher success rate. Afterwards, I mean.'

'But the procedure is the same?' Stuart asks. 'The hormone injections and the egg collection and so on?'

'It's just like IVF, essentially,' says Mr Mancini.

'We're familiar with that,' says Stuart. 'Not ourselves, obviously. My sister . . .'

Stuart's sister Melanie has just announced she's pregnant with IVF twins, due in January. The news has sent Stuart's mother into a fluffy whirl of grandmotherhood, over in Worcester. She's started knitting, and has cancelled her book group, ready to babysit so Mel can go back to work. Gina's tried to ignore the comments like 'Wouldn't it be nice to have cousins of a similar age?' until now because, deep inside, there's an unsettling blankness about her and Stuart's kids.

Janet, it goes without saying, is 'very pleased' and extremely jealous.

Oh, God, thinks Gina, as the second hand of the big clock ticks on above them. It wasn't that she actively *didn't* want to have children with Stuart, just that till now she'd been happy to leave it to chance. If it happened, it happened. He wasn't the man she'd imagined as the father of her children, but logically she knew he wouldn't make a bad one. He'd be great at the playing-football part for a start. It felt rude to write it off altogether. But she couldn't see baby Horsfields in her mind's eye, didn't quite believe they were part of her life's script, as university had been or getting her job.

Having a baby with Stuart will fix her in this person she is now. And that's not a bad thing, Gina reminds herself.

'We'll do everything we can to give you a baby,' Mr

Mancini assures them. 'We work closely with Oncology and, without wanting to get your hopes up, our success rates are currently second in the country. But we need your decision about embryos soon, so as not to delay the start of your treatment.' He raises his eyebrows and his pen, as if it's a given.

Gina can't find the right words. Luckily Stuart's there straight away, asking about dates, time frames. More drugs.

She can't think straight. Mr Mancini is asking a more intimate question of her and Stuart than the registrar did at their wedding. The registrar was only asking if she'd be his legal partner; Mr Mancini is asking if she'll create a human life with this man.

In fact he's not even asking. He's assuming Gina wants to. Because why wouldn't she? She's married to Stuart.

Gina's mind churns. The idea of freezing a moment like this is surely more complicated that it seems. What if Stuart leaves her? What if she leaves him? What if the chemotherapy sends her into an early menopause and Stuart leaves her and she marries someone else and her only chance of a child with that person is a half-Stuart baby?

The walls of the room are closing in on her, trapping her in this space, the parameters of her life rushing up at her. She doesn't want to feel so selfish, and scared, and alone, but she does. This isn't the life she's meant to have. She's being forced through the wrong door.

And Gina can't ignore the truth flashing in her head, so clearly she's amazed that Stuart and the doctor can't see it.

Gina doesn't want to lose her chance to be a mother, but she doesn't want to have a baby with Stuart. They get on

OK, but they don't love each other like she and Kit loved each other, and that's not enough for a child; she knows that now, with all the brutal clarity of someone with no time to kid herself. It wouldn't be fair.

What if someone else is out there who will wake up the dormant broodiness in her? She can't be the sort of monster who has *no* maternal feelings. Can she?

Freeze an egg, says a clear voice in her head. Freeze an egg, not an embryo.

'But what are my survival chances?' she asks, desperate for a more noble cloak to throw over the less noble feelings she's harbouring. *Stuart is a really nice man.* 'I don't want to get through the cancer, and have a baby, then discover it's come back and I'll be leaving the baby without a mother.'

'Don't think like that,' says Stuart. 'It's not going to happen. Anyway, the baby would have me. This isn't just about you.' He glances at Gina's shocked face. 'Sorry, that didn't come out right.'

'He's right,' says Mr Mancini. 'Don't think like that. Address the concerns, certainly, but think positively – you're young, you're fit, you've got a great support network.' He nods towards Stuart, who nods back respectfully.

Gina looks at Stuart, seeing him properly for the first time in weeks. He's strong and stubborn, loyal and not afraid to ask questions. Her mum thinks he's actually *too* good for her. The trouble is, beneath all the busy show of married coupledom, the dinners, the football weekends and the pub, Gina's not convinced Stuart loves her either. He just hates to admit he's wrong.

And wouldn't a man who really loved her be more

worried about the delay to her treatment? About the risk of putting a woman with oestrogen receptor positive cancer cells through IVF?

'I'm not getting any younger, Gina,' he says, in as light a tone as any of them can manage at an emergency fertility appointment in a cancer ward. 'I read a report saying that sperm quality declines after thirty-five too.'

'Then maybe you should freeze your sperm instead,' she says, trying to match his tone. 'I'll freeze mine, you freeze yours.'

It comes out wrong. She catches the exact moment Stuart understands what she's really saying, and it feels more painful than the fine needle biopsy they did on her tumour. It feels like a thin, sharp pain, punching into her chest.

Gina knows she's just punctured her marriage. No surgery in the world can fix this. She swallows, then looks across the desk at Mr Mancini and says, 'I think . . . I think I want to get the chemo started.'

If Gina hadn't been seeing Naomi for their regular coffee on Saturday morning, she might have phoned her to tell her Stuart's news. But instead she sat up until the light drained from the room, letting the new reality take shape and settle in her mind. What could Naomi do, anyway? she thought. Nothing. Rage now wouldn't help.

Buzz sat with her, and she felt comforted by his silent, unjudgemental company. Worse things happened, she thought, watching the slow rise of his chest. Buzz was proof of that.

In the morning, before Buzz's pre-breakfast walk, Gina was tidying the flat ready for Naomi to drop round prior to their secret visit to the shed-maker, when her phone beeped with a text:

Jason called into work – have got Willow. Can we meet in town? Sorry! Nxxxx

Gina normally loved seeing Willow, who had inherited her mother's chestnut hair and cheeky smile, and Willow adored her auntie Gee back. 'Eena' had been one of her first words, a memory that could reduce Gina to tears if she thought about it during a bout of PMT. This weekend, though, having to feel Willow's hot little hands reach for hers, and to catch Naomi's glances of maternal adoration would be tough, but Gina knew she had to get through it.

'Oh, nuts,' she said, and when Buzz looked up, she didn't even feel marvel at his 'really?' expression. Gina had long since abandoned her embarrassment about talking to the dog. She already talked to herself. Asking herself, 'Do I want this?' focused her decision-making with the never-ending wardrobe boxes, and the sound of her voice made the flat seem less empty. Buzz never seemed to mind.

'We'll have to be quick with the walk,' she informed him, and reached for the collar and lead.

The high street was quiet when she locked the front door behind her, and she and Buzz set off towards the canal, strolling along the leafy towpath, down by her offices to the Victorian iron bridge, and all the way back up, past strings of ducklings, joggers, other people with dogs who smiled and said hello as they passed. It was a longer walk than the thirty minutes Rachel had recommended, but Gina wanted to tire Buzz out; she couldn't take him to lunch, but she'd never left him alone in her flat before. She hoped he would sleep if he was worn out, not lie there worrying about when she was coming back. *If* she was coming back.

Maybe it was the first touches of spring in the air, or the different route, but Gina noticed that Buzz seemed to enjoy his walk a little more than normal: his steps were feather-light, he didn't shrink back as much when other dogs approached and he even sniffed a few times at the pocket she kept the treats in. And Gina didn't feel panicky without Rachel by her side to reassure her about her dog-walking: like Buzz, she felt relaxed enough to notice more, too – the paw prints in the muddy patches along the canal, and the matt china blue of the sky that would be exactly the right colour for the Rowntrees' dining room.

They got home just as the Saturday shoppers were starting to crowd the pavements, and Gina grabbed her things, ready to dash out to meet Naomi. 'Be back soon,' she said briskly. 'Basket, please. There's a Bonio.'

Buzz eyed her, then slunk to the basket, his tail firmly whipped between his legs. He curled up, resigned, and she had to turn on her heel quickly and leave before she had second thoughts.

She was halfway down the street when his sad pointy face haunted her so much that she had to go back for him. There maybe wouldn't be many more Saturdays together.

★ ★ ★

'We're late now,' Gina muttered to Buzz, as they hurried through the Saturday-morning strollers in the park. She was texting Naomi **Is it OK 2 bring dog? xxx** when she heard someone shouting her name.

'Gina? Gina!'

It was Nick. She almost didn't recognise him out of the Magistrate's House – it was like seeing someone from television in real life.

He wasn't wearing the usual checked shirt and painting jeans either. Presumably he was on his way somewhere smarter because he was dressed in dark new jeans and a soft cord jacket, with a grey shirt underneath, his dark hair freshly washed and brushed out of his eyes, the silver streaks at the temples catching the sun.

Gina waved, and he walked over, smiling at Buzz as he approached.

'He's fine,' she murmured to Buzz, feeling him lean into her leg anxiously. 'He's fine. He's a friend. Be calm. Nice and calm.'

'Careful,' she said to Nick, as he came closer. 'He's not great with men he doesn't know.'

'Wise chap. He's a he, then? I didn't know you had a dog. Hello. Hello, there!' Nick let Buzz sniff his hand, and carried on talking as Buzz tentatively investigated his messenger bag and jacket. 'What's he called?'

'Buzz. He's not really mine. I'm looking after him until the rescue find a space for him.'

'He looks like he's your dog.'

'I think he prefers anyone to his last owner,' said Gina.

Nick straightened. 'Are you on your way home or have

you just got here? If (b), would you like a coffee? I was just about to get one from the stand.'

Gina's phone buzzed. Naomi.

Dog OK if we can meet in park? Willow a bit whingey, don't want to risk café. Will be about an hour. Don't ask. Toilet related. Nxxxx

She glanced up. Nick was gesturing towards the mobile coffee stand by the gate.

'It's (b),' she said. 'And yes, thanks, coffee would be great.'

'And Sir?'

'Sir will probably try to eat whatever you're eating.'

Buzz leaned against her legs, a solid weight Gina had started to enjoy, and they watched Nick stride off towards the mobile coffee stand at the entrance to the park.

I wonder why I feel I know him from somewhere, she wondered. Is he *like* someone, or did I meet him once and not realise? Some party in London? Their worlds didn't seem to overlap in any way.

Whatever it was, there was something about Nick that made her feel unusually relaxed in his company. Maybe, Gina decided, it was because she *didn't* know him at all.

Nick returned with coffee and muffins, and they began to walk the longer lap around the park, looping up into Coneygreen Woods at the far end, where grey squirrels ran up the trees and small dogs stood at the bottom and barked at them. They stopped at a high point overlooking the park and the town beyond and sat down at the bench dedicated to 'our dear friends, Max and Sam', who were either a devoted married couple or a pair of Labradors, it wasn't clear.

'You didn't go back to London this weekend, then?' Gina asked, peeling the top off her coffee.

'Decided not to in the end. I had some editing to finish here, more pack shots for Charlie's website, and I've got a lot of series-linked telly to catch up on.'

'And there was the plaster. Admit it. It's like bubble-wrap. Once you start . . .'

'You've got me. Lorcan's letting me knock some walls down. He's coming round later with his sledgehammer.' Nick split a muffin and offered her half. When she shook her head, he gave half of her half to Buzz, who swallowed it in one. 'What are your plans for the weekend? Oh, no, wait – you were seeing your ex last night. How did that go? Did he notice your nails?'

'No, he did *not* notice my nails,' said Gina. 'He was too busy telling me all about how he's going to be a dad.'

'What?' Nick paused, his muffin halfway to his mouth.

'His new girlfriend's pregnant. Didn't say when, or how, but I'm not daft. There's been an overlap somewhere.'

'Wow. Was that a shock?'

'Thinking about it, probably no. All his mates at football have got kids, and Stuart doesn't like to feel he's missing out, getting left behind. He'll be a good dad, I'm sure.' Gina shrugged. Saying it aloud to Nick, like saying things aloud to Buzz, took some of the sting out. 'I can see him playing football with one. That was what he always used to focus on, the idea of playing football with his kids.'

Buzz nudged at Nick's pocket with his greying snout, and Nick slipped him another small piece of the muffin he was eating. Gina wondered if Nick knew just what an honour it was for Buzz to be stealing food from him.

'What if it's not a boy?' he asked.

'In that case he'll be the sort of father who won't let his daughter out of his sight until he's seen the boyfriend's bank statement and driving licence.'

'You're making your ex sound like a real prize. Look on the bright side. At least you won't have to spend the next ten years standing on the side of a pitch in the pouring rain while he does his competitive-dad act.'

Gina managed a small smile. 'True.' She knew how it would go, and she wouldn't have to deal with it. Stuart with breast-feeding guides, Stuart with checklists at parents' meetings. Stuart interviewing boyfriends. That was someone else's future now.

'I think what's weird,' she said slowly, 'is the idea that he's going to become someone totally different. A dad. Someone's dad. And I won't know him.'

'I dunno. Did you *meet* his dad? That's who he'll be. I think what parenthood really does is fast-track you into being your own mum or dad. I hear plenty of my friends go on about how it's totally altered their perception of their own place in the world, but give them a few years and they're *surprisingly familiar* . . .'

Gina bit her lip. Nick had unwittingly hit one of her own sore points: what traits of her real dad would any child of hers have inherited? Would a baby have made Janet unbutton some of those memories? Would being a parent herself have made her understand her own parents' blank relationship better?

'It's true.' Nick was staring out over the park below. 'I mean, Amanda – she's convinced that if she can just crowbar another baby into her life in the next twelve months, suddenly she'll be happy to walk away from her twenty-hour days and turn into some cheese-making super-homeschooler. I just don't think it's that easy.'

Gina had started to sip her scalding coffee but that sudden revelation made her stop. '*Another* baby? I didn't realise you had children.' She kicked herself immediately. Babies were minefields. They could be at school. They could be grown-up. Amanda and Nick could have lost a child.

'Sorry,' she added, 'none of my business.'

'What? Oh, no, don't be. Amanda has a daughter with her first husband, Kevin, in New York. Vanessa's at school there. It's tricky. She went through a phase of not wanting to see Amanda. I try to stay out of it.'

'You're not into kids?' Gina tried to angle the question tactfully; she knew herself how pointed it could feel.

'No, I like them. I just don't feel it's helpful for me to get in the middle of Amanda and Kevin. It's tricky. Two lawyers, you know? And a teenager.' He pulled a wry face and held up a spare hand. 'Shouty.'

Gina tried to imagine Amanda with a half-American teen daughter, and a former husband. She could see it more easily than the country Amanda with a baby on her hip. The family house in the countryside was starting to look more rational now: first find your nursery, redecorate it, relocate to the country, like a salmon going back upstream to spawn.

'So is that why she's so keen to get things moving here?' she said. 'House renovation first, then baby? Again, none of my business but it helps to know these things.'

'Well.' Nick shrugged and carried on staring out over the park below. 'Not officially. It's part of the plan, yes, but I'm not quite convinced that Amanda's reasons for having another child are exactly what she thinks they are.' He seemed to be choosing his words very carefully. 'I can't see her giving up everything she's fought so hard for at work.'

'Would you be the one to stay at home and do the child-care?' Gina felt as if Nick was almost leading her to ask questions, as if he needed to say things aloud to hear what he thought too. 'You can both work from home, can't you? Sort of.'

'Probably. I don't know. I wouldn't mind. I'm just uncomfortable with the level of *scheduling*. It's a human life you're talking about. I don't think you can plan it like a house renovation. You can't assume things. Amanda was young when she had Vanessa, only twenty-two, so obviously she wants to do things differently this time round, but she's thinking about it too much, and not enough. You've got to accept that you're not completely in charge any more.'

'You have to schedule everything,' Gina pointed out. 'Once you're over thirty-five.'

'It's not just that. It's ... expecting everything is schedule-able.'

Gina glanced at Nick to check his expression and was surprised to see him looking pensive, his grey eyes cast down at the path, the soft lower lip jutted out in thought. He'd shaved: the line of his jaw was smooth, not speckled with salt-and-pepper stubble as it often was at the house. She could imagine him now in the Groucho Club, or on a magazine shoot.

She tried to make her voice cheery. 'It'll all work out for the best. That's what people keep telling me. You can choose between "What's meant for you won't go past you" and "If it doesn't happen, it wasn't meant to be." There's a self-help platitude for every occasion.'

'Cheers.' He balled up his muffin bag and binned it. 'How's getting rid of all your stuff going? Flat empty yet?'

'More or less. I'm supposed to be meeting my friend in . . .' she checked her watch '. . . about half an hour so she can talk me through selling my clothes on eBay. I've been photographing them, actually – it's like seeing my own history in clothes form.'

'Really?' Nick seemed interested. 'You should make that into a little project.'

'I like the idea of a project,' said Gina. 'I've been thinking about what you were saying, appreciating moments, and I've started taking one or two photos. Nothing amazing, just moments that made me think, Yes, this is nice.'

'Show me?'

Gina hesitated, then got out her phone with the pictures she'd taken on it.

Buzz's long nose laid gently along his narrow paws, his eyes closed and nearly invisible.

The fern-heart shape in the froth of the morning coffee from the deli on her way to work.

The sky over the park.
The sky over the park with clouds.
The sky over the park with a rainbow.

'OK,' she said, 'so there are lots of the park. That's the thing about walking the dog. You start noticing the sky a lot more.'

Nick laughed. 'Everyone takes too many sky photos. What are you doing with these?'

'Nothing. Just taking them. Getting them out when I feel stressed.'

'You need to see them all together to get the full effect. The this-is-Gina's-happy-place effect. Print them out. But don't crop them or change the colours or anything. Keep them as exact moments.'

'Is this a photography class?'

'I wouldn't dare.' Nick grinned, and Gina was glad she'd bumped into him. She never seemed to have a boring conversation with Nick. Every time they spoke, something new occurred to her.

'It's working out better than the hundred things,' she admitted. 'That's stalled a bit. I thought it would be very profound . . . you know,' she put on a *faux*-pretentious voice, 'seeing my personality summed up in objects, but it's a bit depressing how boring the things I'm keeping are. I'm starting to think I'm just not a very interesting person.'

'I don't think that's true. Far from it.'

Gina cut him a sideways look, and caught Nick looking at her with a perceptive glint in his eyes, a half-smile on his lips. What was he seeing that she wasn't? she wondered, with a shiver.

She was saved from having to answer by the sound of Naomi's voice. She hadn't even noticed her approaching.

'Hiya! I thought we saw you up here!'

Willow was in the buggy, wearing the bright-red coat Gina had given her for Christmas and a pair of gleaming black patent leather shoes. When she saw Gina she reached out her arms and laughed. 'Gina!' Then her eye dropped. 'Doggy!'

Buzz slunk under the seat and Gina felt the lead go tight.

'Is Willow OK with dogs?' she asked. 'I think he'll be fine, but let's keep them well apart.'

'She's *too* good with dogs, believe me. Nanny Carole's got a doggy, hasn't she?' Naomi leaned over the buggy.

'Rotty,' confirmed Willow, solemnly.

'He's a Rottweiler. Don't say anything. Hello! I'm Naomi!' She offered her gloved hand to Nick.

'Nick,' he said. 'Rowntree.'

'Nick's a client of mine. He's the new owner of the Magistrate's House in Langley,' she said, gesturing between them awkwardly. 'Nick, this is Naomi Hewson, my best friend.'

'And dental-practice manager at the Orchards,' Naomi added. 'If you're looking for top-quality dental care. But I can see you floss already!'

Nick stood up and shook her hand, and Gina could tell Naomi was impressed from the smile that curled the corner of her mouth. It wasn't dissimilar to the toothy one Willow was directing at Buzz.

'The Magistrate's House, wow!' Naomi said. 'Gina *loves* that house, don't you?'

'*Do* you?' Nick glanced over. 'What have you been saying about my house, eh? It's all coming out this morning.'

'Nothing! What I think Naomi means is that my ex and I had a look around it last time it was on the market.' Gina glared at Naomi but Naomi was beaming at Nick.

'Is she being too modest, as usual?' she asked. 'Gina is the only person I know who can keep plumbers on schedule. And she's a *brilliant* interior decorator. She did our house and it looks as if we had someone up from London to do it. Amazing.'

Gina mouthed, 'Shut up!' at Naomi but to her horror, Naomi had gone into the hard-sell mode she recognised from the brief period in which she'd been single before Stuart, and Naomi had felt it her duty to talk her up to her single male friends.

Her blood ran cold. She had no idea what Naomi would say next, and there was no way she could shoehorn Amanda into the conversation without it being very obvious now.

Nick's face was deadpan. 'I haven't got as far as hiring an interior designer but I'll definitely bear that in mind. If she's as good with her swatches as she is with her spreadsheets, then she can do the whole house.'

Gina coughed. 'No, it's not—'

'Anyway!' He winked at Willow. 'I can see you three ladies have a date, so I'll leave you to it. Have a lovely walk.'

To Gina's surprise, but not Naomi's, Nick leaned over, touched her arm and aimed a friendly air kiss that nearly landed on her cheek. ''Bye, Naomi!' he said, blew a kiss to Willow, who blew one back, then strolled down the hill in the direction of the gates.

When he'd more or less gone, Naomi let out a long, whistling breath and sank down on the nearby bench. 'Excu-hoo-hoo-hoose me,' she hooted. 'I thought I was coming here to deliver a weekly pep talk about your divorce and I find you in the park with some gorgeous bloke. What's that about?'

'He's not some gorgeous bloke,' said Gina, sitting down next to her. 'He's a client. And up to this point, I'd managed to hide the fact that I wanted to live in his house, thank you very much.'

'Oh, come on. He doesn't care. He's flattered that the only tasteful person in this place liked it but couldn't afford to buy it. And I didn't know you did Saturday appointments.' Naomi jiggled her well-shaped eyebrows. 'You're a long way from Langley St Michael too. Or did he bring his binoculars?'

'I bumped into him. He bought me a coffee while I was waiting for you.' Gina put her head in her hands. What had that expression on Nick's face meant as he'd left? Was he wondering if that was the reason she was taking an interest in the house, because she'd wanted it?

'Well, I've said it from the beginning. There are worse ways to take your mind off a break-up than—' Naomi started.

'No.' Gina sat up, determined to nip this in the bud. 'Look, I know you're joking but *no*. It's not like that. He's married. We were just talking about his and his wife's plans to start a family, actually.'

'Really?'

'Yes. Really. He's an interesting guy. He's a photographer.'

'Don't tell me.' Naomi's eyes were twinkling, though her expression was serious. 'He wants you to pose for him?'

'I already have. Just my hands!' she added. 'I happened to be there. He needed a woman's hand. *Don't.*' She raised a warning finger.

'How have I missed all this?' howled Naomi. '*Why* have you been droning on to me about how you can flog off your twenty boring black dresses and missed out the bit about having your body parts photographed by a proper creative type who looks like some kind of stubbly-jawed model?'

Gina glanced down at Willow who was staring happily at Buzz. Buzz was staring at Gina's legs. 'There's nothing to miss,' she repeated. 'This is the first time I've seen him outside his house.'

'Well, you could do a lot worse.'

Their eyes turned towards the bottom of the hill where, in the distance, Nick was holding the gate open for someone with a buggy (of course), his other hand deep in his jacket pocket.

'Did you hear the *he's married* part?' Gina balled up the bag that her muffin had come in. In a way she was glad Nick was married: it meant they could maybe be friends, without any awkward overtones creeping in. He knew she knew about Amanda. Her divorce was now out there. They knew where they stood. She needed new friends.

'The best ones always are,' sighed Naomi. 'It's just the crap ones that get thrown back in. Speaking of which, did Stuart come and get his stuff last night? You didn't call.'

'I wanted to tell you in person. Bryony's pregnant,' said Gina. It came out surprisingly easily now. Nick's reaction had removed some of the pain, as had letting the thought breathe, instead of stuffing it away and ignoring it, as she would usually have done.

'What?' Naomi was getting something out of the bag for Willow but she spun round, mouthing the swearword she'd have used had Willow not been there. 'She's . . . Seriously?'

'Seriously. I wanted to see your face,' said Gina, wryly. 'Plus, I thought you might be able to fill in some more details.'

'I don't know anything about it,' said Naomi at once. 'Nothing! I'd have told you.'

'I didn't mean now,' Gina replied mildly. 'I meant, maybe you could find out. From Jason?'

'Oh. Right. Yeah.' She looked uncomfortable. 'I'll try. But Jason takes a weird line on repeating stuff he hears at football. I've tried to ask him things before, but he gets all changing-room brotherhood on me.'

'Actually, forget that, I don't know if I want to know,' said Gina. 'I don't have to, do I?' She probed the new sensation like a loose tooth, concerned that she might just nudge it out, and the desire to know every miserable detail of Bryony's baby would flood in, followed by humiliation and regret and guilt – the mighty triumvirate that roamed around her subconscious. I don't have to give this space in my head, she thought. Just like I don't have to give space in my flat to unreadable books or jeans that don't fit.

'Are you OK?' asked Naomi. 'Is it delayed shock?'

Gina shook herself. Not shock, just the dull disappointment that would hurt then fade, like a bruise. She made her attention turn to the first green shoots on the cherry tree that arched over the entrance to the park. Maybe she could photograph it every day when she came in with Buzz and Rachel. Like time lapse.

'Gina!' said Willow. 'Out, please. Doggy.'

From the other side of her leg, Buzz eyed the buggy with wariness, his grey nose twitching cautiously at the beam of love Willow was directing at him.

'Let's be very careful,' said Gina, to both Willow and Naomi. 'He's a shy doggy.'

'Gently,' agreed Willow. It was a word Naomi used a lot.

And they set off walking, very slowly and very carefully, around the park. Willow in the middle, with Gina and Naomi holding her mittened hands, the buggy and Buzz on the outside.

At the top of the hill, Gina lifted her phone over her head, and took a wonky but happy photo of them all.

Chapter Sixteen

ITEM: my wigs

Annabella: long blonde human hair wig
*Sophisticated and well-groomed, Annabella enjoys
lunchtime cocktails, the races, hedge-fund divorcees,
and tossing her head from side to side while laughing enchantingly*

Robin: dark brown curly crop
*Robin is bubbly but thoughtful, the sort of girl who
organises office birthday cakes, ideal for parties
when you want to look like yourself but with shorter
hair*

Matron of Honour, a pale apricot bob
*The perfect colour to match your matron-of-honour
gown for your best friend's wedding, if it's a sort of
apricot colour*

Longhampton, 1st July 2008

'I don't think any of these are going to be me,' Gina
whispers to Naomi.

'Not even this one?' Naomi holds up a very Eighties wig, the sort of cut Janet would have called 'perky'. Or 'jazzy'.

'Definitely not that one.' She grimaces. 'I'm having chemo, not going into news-reading.'

Naomi made this appointment for her the day Gina got her chemotherapy dates. Her first session is next week; the first of six courses, spaced at three-weekly intervals, to give her body time to recover from the chemicals that'll be dripped into her veins while she sits and watches one of the many boxsets that she's stockpiled on the advice of the patient support group. Stuart's marked the appointments on her calendar, with 'The End' in red. Gina can't think that far ahead. She's thinking in terms of *24* and *The West Wing*.

Naomi's taken charge of the cosmetic cheerleading side of the next few months. She took Gina to get the pixie-cut she's sporting now, so the hair loss won't feel so bad, and she's been boosting her with compliments ever since.

'I think you should go for a short wig anyway,' says Naomi, encouragingly. 'That crop suits you. Makes your eyes look huge.'

Gina's not sure. She feels very exposed. The back of her neck feels cold, and it turns out her ears are a weird shape, without the mass of dark curls around them. Her mother looked as if she was going to burst into tears when she saw it, and that was straight out of Naomi's expensive salon.

'I prefer the long ones,' she says, reaching for a model that looks exactly like her old hair, which she misses already. Tumbling dark brown curls, like Gina Lollobrigida.

'That is a very popular style,' agrees the assistant, who has appeared at Naomi's side. 'Very feminine.'

Dawn, their assistant in this fancy-dress session, has clearly done this before. She's sensitive to Gina's nerves, which, coupled with Naomi's cheerful honesty, means the hour passes quickly but not without a few laughs.

Gina sets aside a shorter version of her own hair, and a long straight dark wig for variation. She doesn't want to look at reds or blondes: she wants to look like herself. Herself with no hair loss.

But Dawn persists, showing her lighter browns, shorter cuts until Gina's curiosity is piqued.

'Have you never thought about being blonde?' Dawn asks, handing Gina an angular blonde bob. 'We get a lot of ladies with dark hair wanting a wig to wear for a change.'

'Go on,' Naomi encourages her. 'You've got pale skin. It'd work.'

Gina lets Dawn pull the wig over her hair, tugging it down around her ears until it fits. She tweaks and flicks the hair until it's natural, then lets Gina see in the mirror.

I look like Kit, Gina thinks, in shock. That halo of blonde hair, my eyes, my mouth – our kids would have looked like this.

Naomi and Dawn are making approving noises but Gina's properly spooked. She can't think about Kit right now. There are days when she never thinks of him, but since her diagnosis, she's been spending more time in hospitals and it's impossible then not to wonder where he is and what he's doing.

She pulls the wig off, and is almost relieved to see her spiky black hair beneath, like a newborn chick. 'Maybe something auburn?' she suggests, seeing Dawn's red face.

She doesn't want to seem ungrateful. 'I've often wondered what I'd look like ginger.'

The red hair is more of a success, and slowly Gina starts to engage with the effect the different hairstyles have on her, the way she smiles and looks at herself. Her eyes do seem enormous in her pale face, now all the focus is on them and not her hair. She's never studied herself so closely before. It's strange, noticing how large your nose is, how uneven your eyes are.

'Fringes are good,' Dawn tells her, 'because you might lose some eyelashes and eyebrow hair . . .'

'We'll be looking into false lashes,' Naomi butts in. 'I've got that covered.'

'And you can opt for human-hair wigs or synthetic . . .'

Gina's not sure she likes the idea of having someone else's hair on her head. Her own body is feeling less and less like hers as it is.

When Gina's lined up ten wigs on stands in front of her, Dawn leaves to deal with another customer while she chooses. 'Take your time,' she says kindly. 'You've got to love it, if you're going to wear it every day.'

'Thanks,' says Naomi. When Dawn's gone, she turns to Gina with a theatrical sigh. 'You know what's really unfair?'

'More unfair than cancer?' Gina demands. She can only be dark with Naomi. Their humour is outrageously dark now.

'More unfair than that. You look *stunning* in all those. If you get the blonde one, can I borrow it?'

Gina runs a hand over her crop. Her head's tingling. That's the trouble with reading up on the Internet about symptoms: you start getting them even before the treatment.

She wants to say, 'I don't need a wig, I'm just going to let my hair go,' but it's easy to say that, while it's still there, however short. Her hair's always been the most beautiful thing about her, and it's already gone. Gina doesn't miss it as much as she'd thought she would. In a really odd way, it was a silver lining to be forced into cutting it all off. It does suit her. And she'd never have had the nerve otherwise.

I'm finding out some really strange stuff about myself, thinks Gina, and she stares at her reflection in the mirror. She doesn't recognise the woman staring back, but that's not all bad. This woman is already surprising her with what she can bear, what she can do.

Naomi appears behind her, wraps her arms around Gina's shoulders and hugs her. Their eyes meet in the mirror, and Gina manages a smile.

Gina could translate Naomi's requests about Willow and Jason's super-shed but one thing she couldn't control was the weather.

As a sunny March tipped into a cooler April, the weather turned greyish and the work on the Magistrate's House was concentrated on the insulation and roof line, parts of the building where Gina had no real input. On the positive side, it meant she had more time to spent chivvying Tony's final details on the playhouse. The installation of Willow and Jason's finished shed was arranged with as much complication and secrecy as a moon landing. And only slightly less expense.

First, Naomi had to take Willow and Jason away for a three-day pre-birthday break at Center Parcs to give Tony the joiner time to get it dug in and set up. It wasn't a quick job – the electrics for Jason's beer fridge and reclining chair had to be run in from the main house, and Tony had finishing work to do on the roof, which had proper red tiles and a weather vane in the shape of Peppa Pig.

By Thursday morning, Naomi was supposed to be in the middle of an intensive programme of face-painting and general ballpark fun, but she seemed to be sneaking off every half-hour to send Gina texts. Gina was at the Magistrate's House, walking Nick through the renovation process for the linenfold panelling in the dining room when her phone beeped for the fifth time since breakfast.

Have you reminded Tony about the safety rails? Nxxxx

'Is that Naomi?' Nick asked, amused, as Gina fished the phone out of the back pocket of her jeans. 'What's she actually doing on this holiday, apart from texting you?'

'Texting me, mainly. Don't worry, I'm used to dealing with very demanding clients.' Gina frowned at the message. Jason must be having the worst birthday ever, she thought. 'Hang on, let me just reassure her that everything's OK.'

She texted back:

Would I skimp on the safety features for my favourite goddaughter? Everything very safe! xxx

'There. Sorry. Right, where was I? Linenfold panelling.' Gina ran her fingertips over the honey-coloured wood lining the walls of the dining room, skilfully carved to look like pleated material. 'Lorcan found this under a load of plasterboard – they must have covered it over during the war when the house was used to put up refugees. It's not in great shape now, but with a bit of love it could be stunning.'

'It's beautiful.' Nick traced down a panel by the door. 'Is it rare?'

'Very, round here. I haven't seen any as nice as this, anyway. It's Gothic Revival, I think, older than this part of the house – it might have been bought in from another house that was being broken up to give this room a bit of status. You can tell that it was designed to be the place where the Warwicks did their serious socialising. Look at the panels, look at the view. Imagine the table they'd have had in here. You could seat eighteen people, easily.'

'We should try to find some photographs of it in use,' said Nick. 'There must be some.'

'You almost don't need them,' she said, stepping towards the windows. 'It's one of those rooms that tells you its own story.'

Like the drawing room on the other side of the house, the dining room finished in a generous bay, projecting out into the garden, with three long windows looking over the croquet lawn. It was designed to show off a sweeping panorama of the countryside around the house: the gentle undulation of the hills dotted with sheep, the skyline punctuated with a few church spires. The view was framed by the fine proportions of the windows, and a massive

Gothic curtain-rail arrangement that looked as if it had been carved out of a series of ships' masts. No curtains were hanging there now, but the big rings hinted at heavy velvet drapes held in place with rococo gold tie-backs.

There was something proud about the view, Gina thought, offered to the diners along with their meal. It was spring now, but she could imagine that scene changing with the seasons – thick white blankets of snow, gold and copper splashes of autumn, different every day.

'That fireplace – did it come from somewhere else, do you think?' Nick indicated the massive stone hearth, with the solid marble mantelpiece above.

'Probably. But it's a good fit in this room. It gives it a real heart, real warmth, not just literal warmth. This house used to belong to wine importers – dinners were always going to be a big part of their lives. Just imagine this place at a family Christmas, lit with candles in the wall sconces and on the table, all the silverware glittering, the local great and good in evening dress, butler hovering in the background . . .'

She paused. Nick hadn't taken the bait. Since their first conversation about the croquet lawn outside, it had become something of a running joke: one of them starting to describe some real detail of the house while the other picked it up and turned it into the cheesy film version of English country life. But Nick was frowning at the fireplace.

'Are you planning to keep it as a dining room?' Gina prompted him. 'You could have some really wonderful dinners in here, lovely boozy weekend dinners that go on till the wee small hours . . .' She trailed off. She'd been about to make some comment about being sure Amanda and

Nick had the sort of friends who'd appreciate it, but something in his face stopped her.

'I don't know.' Nick ran a hand through his hair. 'Did Amanda email you about the rental idea?'

'What? No . . . Hang on, let me check.' Gina pulled her phone out of her pocket; there were five new emails, two of which were from Amanda, both headed 'Magistrate's House/Alternative Plans'. 'Oh, wait. I think she has.' She looked up. '*Rental idea?*'

Nick sighed. 'It's not set in stone – it's just an idea she's come up with about converting a smaller unit for private use, and doing up the rest to rent out as a holiday let, or one of those houses you hire for team-building conferences where you take it in turns to collapse backwards on your colleagues and put your back out. Or whatever they do. I haven't had colleagues since I worked in a camera shop during college.'

'So you're not going to live here now? Did I miss the memo about this?'

'No.' He shook his head. 'It's just something we were talking about last night. Amanda made the point that it's a big house, and we're not going to be here all the time. It makes sense, I guess. To think about it, at least.'

Gina bit back her first reaction, which was disappointment. More for the house than Amanda. Rental renovations never had the same heart as private residential plans. They were duller, safer. Made to suit lots of people a little bit rather than the culmination of one person's vision.

Nick was still staring at the panelling. She tried to work out what the studied blandness on his face was hiding. He had expressive eyes and a mouth that gave away his mood, good, bad or unimpressed, but his expression now was flat.

It was a big conversation for them to have had 'just last night' – and a fairly radical new idea. What about their plans to start a family? Did Amanda want to have her baby in America, near her daughter? In London? Or was it some kind of lawyer's business move to do with the planning permission?

Stop thinking you know these people, she told herself. You don't.

Gina cleared her throat, and tried to sound interested but not over-involved. It struck her, too late, that maybe Nick already thought she *was* over-involved, that what she thought was their running joke about the house's past might actually come across as her imposing her own renovation fantasies on *his* house.

'Well, it's a sensible thing to consider. You could convert one of the outhouses to be a self-contained flat, but it would put a different slant on my advice for the main house. We'd have to look at the critical path again, and there might be planning implications. Makes no difference to me,' she added. 'I'm happy to help you do whatever you want.'

Nick looked awkward. 'You can bill us for the extra work,' he said quickly. 'I don't expect you to revisit it for nothing.'

'It's not that,' said Gina. 'I'm just . . .' He *did* seem awkward, she wasn't imagining it. 'Sorry, I just got the impression that you wanted to live here. In the whole house.'

He didn't answer straight away. He tapped his fingers on the wood, playing it, rather than feeling for rot like Lorcan. 'I know it's a big house but the longer I'm here, the smaller it feels, if you know what I mean. Amanda hasn't really spent enough time in it to get a feel for . . . for what a personality it has. I think if she'd had some of the conversations we've had about the history of the place she'd start to see it less as a property investment and more as a home.' He paused. 'A family home.'

'Well, houses *are* just houses,' said Gina. 'You're the ones who make it into a home.'

Nick said nothing, and she didn't know what else to say, so they stared out at the garden, through the long panes of old glass. They were warped here and there, twisting the long hedges into curves.

'I was thinking,' said Gina, to break the silence more than anything, 'about that kitchen extension – you know, the one Keith said would be damaging to the fabric of the building? If you wanted an outdoor space for entertaining, why don't you put in an application to restore the summer house?'

Nick grasped the change of subject eagerly. 'I wasn't aware we had a summer house.'

'That big shed at the end of the main garden. If you were building it from scratch you'd need formal permission, but since it's already there, you could easily do it up. You're just repairing an existing structure for original usage. Croquet sets,' she added. 'And Pimm's.'

She was relieved to see a smile warm his face. 'And boaters. And white flannels. Who would do that, then? Lorcan?'

'No, I'd recommend the same guy I'm going to get to restore these panels. Tony's a specialist joiner, but he builds the most amazing summer houses as a side line. In fact,' an idea had jumped into her head, 'are you around this weekend?'

'Maybe. Why?'

'This might be on an entertainment par with pulling plaster off the wall, but do you want to come to a joint birthday party and shed opening on Saturday?'

'Naomi's famous shed? Isn't that a family party? I don't want to intrude.'

Gina didn't say that Naomi had already 'suggested' she bring Nick as a plus one. Three times. 'You wouldn't be intruding. It's just a few drinks, bit of birthday cake. Tony's going to be there for the grand unveiling so you can see what he's made for them and have a chat – he's basically built them a scaled-down version of what you've got here.'

Nick looked out into the garden. The roof of the Edwardian summer house was just visible at the edge of the terraced lawn; it had a little peak like a proper cricket pavilion, and crenellated roof details. 'But that thing's huge.'

Gina felt her phone beep with another text message from Center Parcs.

Too late for underfloor heating? Nxxxx

'After all the requests Naomi made,' she said, 'I'm not sure hers is a lot smaller.'

Gina couldn't have dreamed of better weather for the shed unveiling on Saturday morning. Keeping Willow and Jason out of the garden and away from the surprise had been harder than the military operation that had taken place the previous day, when Gina and the joiners had set up the whole thing, complete with working power lines for Jason's beer fridge.

Naomi led a protesting Jason towards the back of the garden, while Gina carried Willow on her hip. Willow was more excited about her 'surprise' and kept tugging at the pink satin mask Naomi had put round her eyes.

'To be honest, this is not the birthday treat I was expecting when you brought out a blindfold, Naomi,' said Jason, from beneath his black silk scarf. 'It's not a hot tub, is it? Because as soon as the football guys hear about it . . .'

'Better than a hot tub,' said Naomi, confidently. 'Although now you mention the football team, I might look into it. Gina?'

'I'll get the planning application forms,' said Gina. 'No, actually, forget I said that. It would start out as a hot tub and end up a swimming pool, knowing you.'

'Cake?' asked Willow. 'Cake in the kitchen!'

'Ssh,' whispered Gina. 'You weren't meant to see that. Cake soon.'

They were standing right in front of the shed now. Naomi looked at her, a conspiratorial twinkle in her eye, and Gina smiled back. It was good to be able to give something back to Naomi, to feel part of their family.

'OK, are we ready?' Naomi said. 'On the count of three. One . . . two . . . three . . .'

As Naomi pulled off Jason's scarf, Gina eased Willow's mask off her head, and laughed as the little girl's blue eyes went cartoon-round at the pink-shuttered Wendy house that had appeared by magic under the apple tree in her back garden.

'Do you like it?' She leaned her cheek against Willow's soft coppery hair. 'Do you want to go inside?'

'Blimey,' said Jason. 'It's nice, Nay, but it's a bit pink for me.'

'No, no – it's in two parts. You need to come round the back. Hold on, Willow, Mummy just wants to show Daddy his surprise too.' Naomi beckoned Jason round to the other side and, from the cry of blokeish delight, Gina guessed that the more manly shed-styling of the Jason half had done the trick.

Willow reached out and Gina put her down so she could run to the front door. She grabbed hold of the knocker and turned to grin impishly at Gina. 'Mind fingers!' she said triumphantly.

'Yes, mind your fingers. Shall we go in?' Gina opened the door and let her see inside – it was big enough to fit one toddler and one-and-a-bit adults, but from Willow's point of view it was enormous.

'Kitchen!' squealed Willow, pointing. 'My kitchen! Pink cups!'

'What's going on in here?' Naomi squeezed in at the same time as a serving hatch by the oven opened, to reveal Jason's face on the other side. 'Surprise! It's Daddy!'

As Jason supervised Willow making pretend tea for everyone from his serving hatch, Naomi nudged Gina, and whispered, 'This is the most amazing thing I've ever seen. It's even better than I hoped it would be.'

'You like it?'

'I *adore* it. Even Jason's got all emotional. He reckons Willow will be talking about this when she's fifty. It's the sort of Wendy house you remember your whole life.'

'Well, I'm thrilled that you like it. I'm honoured you invited me to the grand opening.'

'You're the guest of honour. You were the first person Willow wanted to ask when I told her we were having a party.'

'Don't.' She nudged her back. 'You'll make me cry.'

'I mean it.' Naomi's voice had a telltale sniff in it. 'I always knew you'd be a wonderful part of her life. It's a big relief to me to think that when she goes through her I-hate-you-Mum phase as a horrible teenager she'll have you to storm off to. Someone who loves her.'

Gina leaned her head against Naomi's; she knew her friend's eyes were brimming with tears, because her own were. They watched Willow pour pretend tea, her attention trained on the cups with an intensity that was pure Naomi.

'I'm so glad you're still here, Gee,' whispered Naomi.

'Me too,' she whispered back.

The other guests – Jason's and Naomi's parents, friends from toddler group, the neighbours – arrived at three, and after admiring the new addition to the garden, they quickly retreated into the warmth of Naomi's conservatory. Willow couldn't be persuaded to stop serving imaginary tea in the playhouse, but she was operating a very strict door policy, which meant that Gina wasn't allowed to leave, and only select guests were admitted.

Tony the joiner arrived in his Sunday best, and was honoured with an imaginary cake; he was outside deep in DIY conversation with Jason's dad, when Gina heard a tap on the front door of the playhouse.

She opened it, assuming it would be Naomi with some real tea, but it was Nick. He was wearing his navy peacoat and jeans, and his hair was more neatly styled than usual; Gina noticed the effort he'd made, and was pleased.

'Hello,' he said, peering inside. 'I hear this is where the best tea is being served.'

'It is,' she said. 'But you might not get any. It all depends on the hostess. Willow?' She turned to Willow. 'Can this nice man have some tea?'

Willow scrutinised Nick's face with a look that was more Jason than Naomi, then smiled sunnily and thrust a teacup at him.

'Take it,' Gina advised him. 'You're the first man she's agreed to serve all afternoon. And that includes her granddads.'

'I'm honoured,' he said, and reached out to take it with a charming smile.

As Nick sipped his pretend tea with due solemnity, Gina saw Naomi's red-and-white-checked dress pass the window, and then her flushed face was squashed in next to Nick's.

'I've come to release you,' she announced. 'There's a real cup of tea for you in the house. Hello, Nick,' she added, turning to him. 'Good to see you! Actually, Gina, before you move, let me take a photo of you and Willow.'

'No, it's . . .' Gina suddenly felt awkward, as Naomi got her camera out, but at the word 'photo' Willow had wrapped her arms around Gina's neck and was doing her big photo smile. Gina pulled a quick what-can-you-do face at Nick, and mugged along for the camera.

'Cheese! Aw! That's so cute!'

Nick tapped Naomi's arm. 'Want me to take a photograph of all three of you? Then you can be in it too.'

Gina started to tell him not to, but Naomi was thrilled. 'Would I like a proper photographer to do a quick portrait? Hmm, let me think. Er, of course! Hold on, let me get my husband. Jason? Jay! Come over here.'

'You don't have to do this,' Gina murmured, but Nick shushed her.

'It's no bother. You look so funny sitting at the little table, with that checked tablecloth. Like Alice after the Drink Me bottle.'

'Thanks. That was the look I was going for.'

Naomi had returned, dragging Jason behind her. 'OK, here's Jason . . . Jay, don't look like that. It'll only take a second.'

Gina slipped out of the Wendy house and went to stand behind Nick. She watched as he arranged the Hewsons into the best position, charming a smile out of self-conscious Jason, making a properly funny photo with Jason and Naomi behind the pretty windows while Willow stood proudly by the door. There was something attractive about the skilful way he kept them chatting and moving to stop them doing any 'photo faces' – she noted the tiny twitch of satisfaction in his expression when they all laughed at the same time and his finger moved imperceptibly, catching it.

This is a memory they'll talk about at Willow's wedding, thought Gina, and something tugged inside her, a feeling she didn't want to articulate because it was so unworthy.

That won't be me. That's going to be Stuart, and Bryony . . . and their own blonde child in the middle. Any other day, she would have been happy, genuinely happy that her friends were so blessed, so proud of their little girl. But today she couldn't fight the weird sensation of being on the other side of a pane of glass, watching other people playing her part in her life, and feeling further and further away, floating above herself, detached from the whole thing.

But this is where it starts, she told herself. Who knows what happens next?

'Gina?' Nick was nudging her to go back to the playhouse, to join in.

It brought her back to herself, and she shook her head. Nick's camera had a habit of catching something about her she wasn't always aware of. She didn't want to risk her own sadness showing through her photo smile.

But then Willow's chubby hand stretched out towards her. 'Auntie Gina!' She couldn't not go.

'Auntie Gina made the house for you,' said Naomi, as she arranged Gina in the centre of the photograph, on the little steps that led to the pink door. 'Isn't she clever?'

'You made it?' Willow looked awestruck.

'No, well, I . . .'

'Ssh.'

Gina felt herself being hugged and she smiled down at Willow, not at the camera.

Afterwards, Gina and Nick wandered back to the house for a cup of tea and a plate of food to eat in the garden. They sat on the wall next to Willow's sandpit, well away from a heated discussion about Jason's brother's planning-permission woes.

'Make sure Naomi gives you a copy of that photograph,' said Nick, breaking his birthday cake into pieces. 'It's one for the album.'

'I will.' Gina gazed across at the playhouse-shed. 'It was a lovely moment. Thanks for taking it for them.'

'How's your project coming on?' he asked. 'Your own happy moments?'

'Are you thinking of my hundred things? I've got a list on the back wall of my flat – I'm up to thirty-nine.' Gina stopped, then confessed, 'To be honest, it's kind of ground to a halt. It served its purpose while I was clearing things out, making me think about what I wanted in the flat, but I'm almost done now and I don't want to be writing "medicine cabinet" next to, I dunno, "music".'

'Actually, I wasn't thinking of that – more of those photos you showed me. The ones on your phone that you were going to print out.' He gave her a stern look. 'Have you? Or are you just filling up your phone with lots of cloud pics?'

Gina pretended to be outraged. 'I've been busy. I don't know if you've noticed but you now have eco-insulation in that roof of yours.'

'I thought so,' said Nick, and reached into his bag. 'Have this.' He handed her a carrier bag. In it was the Polaroid camera and some boxes of film.

'I can't take this – you need it.'

'I've found something else that does the same thing. I think you'd get more out of it than me.' He indicated the films. 'Make it your project – instead of a hundred things, take a hundred moments that make you happy. There are exactly nine boxes there, so you've got room for a few mistakes, but not many. Good discipline.'

'Thank you,' said Gina. A faint teenage excitement buzzed in her chest. 'You know, I've wanted one of these since I was thirteen.'

'Why didn't you get one?'

'It was an expensive gimmick, apparently.'

Nick grinned. 'Well, there you go. And here, I've got a couple to get you started. If you don't mind?'

He passed her a couple of Polaroids: in the first, Gina was accepting a cup of imaginary tea from Willow in the Wendy house. A warm orange glow surrounded them, and Gina's face was solemn, though her eyes sparkled above the cup.

The other photo was of her with Naomi, talking by the kitchen door. Gina hadn't noticed Nick take it, possibly because she was giggling and so was Naomi – proper unself-conscious double-chinned giggling. Naomi's hand rested on Gina's upper arm, Gina's head was tilted and her neck looked long and white against the red brick of the wall.

'Have you been watching me?' said Gina, surprised. Or flattered?

'What do you take me for?' Now Nick pretended to look affronted. 'A paparazzo? No, you said you were wanted moments that made you happy, and I knew you wouldn't be able to take photos of yourself so I took them for you. When *I* thought you looked happiest – with your best mate and your other little mate.'

Gina examined the white-framed images. The woman in her clothes didn't look like her. Or, rather, it didn't look like she usually looked in photos – a bit stiff, head held at an angle, shoulders hunched to hide her chest. In these, she seemed relaxed, longer somehow. Softer.

Maybe it was the old film: the photos could have come from a different time.

'It doesn't look like me.'

'It does. You're just one of those people who really change their expression when a camera comes out,' Nick observed.

'Am I?'

'Yup. In fact, you change your expression when you think someone's watching you, even when there isn't a camera around.'

'Doesn't everyone?'

Nick held her gaze. His grey eyes were curious, but gentle, moving across her face, reading it. 'Some people do it more than others.'

The moment stretched out between them, filled with the distant sounds of music coming from the kitchen, and pretend tea parties from the playhouse. Gina wondered if she should try to make her expression blank, but there didn't seem any point. Nick, she guessed, could already see what was in her mind: it wasn't so much that he was reading it as making her look at some of the thoughts she'd been trying to ignore.

He pressed his lips together, then said, 'Gina, there's—' just as another voice, a worried female one, said, 'Gina!'

Naomi was hurrying along the grass towards them, and Gina slid the photos into her back pocket. 'What? Are we out of imaginary tea?'

'I'm so sorry, I don't know what to do.' Naomi folded her

arms, then unfolded them. She looked angry and anxious. 'Stuart's just turned up. His car's outside. Jason told him not to come till five because you said you were going to leave by half four, but he's here.'

Something cold gripped Gina inside. Focus, she told herself. Focus.

'Did you invite both of them?' she asked.

'Of course not! Jason can invite Stuart if he has to but I'm not having . . .' Naomi trailed away as she turned her head towards the house and saw something that made her stop.

Stuart had appeared at the back door: a handsome half-stranger in his casual weekend jeans, the new beard. The new leather jacket.

Gina closed her eyes and willed her face to remain still, like stone, so she could hide behind it. I don't want to be a ghost in people's lives, she thought, with sudden determination. Having to slip away when Stuart arrives, him having to wait until I've gone. This is my life too. I have to be here, I have to face him. *Then* I can go.

It'll be awkward for him too, she told herself. I need to be the one who's gracious.

'Gina, do you want a lift back?' Nick jangled his keys. 'I'm heading off now – Tony's filled me in on summer houses. Got some editing to do.'

'Oh . . . no,' breathed Naomi, and Gina turned back to see something that made her stomach sink.

A young woman had appeared behind Stuart, clutching his hand in a proprietorial way. She was blonde, not particularly pretty, fit and tanned. But Gina wasn't looking at her longer-than-average nose or the swallow tattoo on her wrist: her gaze was drawn by the stripy T-shirt that emphasised the small but definite shape of Stuart's new life. Willow's birthday cake repeated at the back of Gina's throat, a sharp scratch of acid reflux.

The woman smiled hopefully, showing small, uneven teeth: it was a nervous smile, not a triumphant one, and Stuart started to smile too, but when he saw Gina's expression, it froze on his face.

It's over, Gina thought, as her chest filled with grief, but there was unexpected relief at the heart of it. She'd never have to wonder what it looked like again: Stuart and his new life without her. That was it. It had started: he was moving down a different path away from her.

Gina lifted her hand towards Stuart and Bryony and waved stiffly, forcing a smile to her face. Then she turned back to Nick, hoping the white noise inside her wasn't too obvious to his sharp eyes. 'A lift would be great,' she said, in a voice that didn't sound like her own, and she lifted her chin as she walked towards the garden gate, away from the house.

Chapter Seventeen

ITEM: a huge framed orange print of a *Gone With
the Wind* movie poster, moved from Gina's student set,
to her first house share, then to the guest
bedroom of Dryden Road

Little Mallow, October 2002

Gina is sitting outside the Athertons' house in Janet's
Fiesta, watching the bay windows for signs of life. It's
hard to see much because the trees provide a barrier and
the front garden is long. So far, she's spotted a couple of
shadows passing behind the curtains in the top left-hand
bedroom but that's enough to reassure her that someone
is in.

She's here because four weeks have passed without a
single letter returned to her mother's house. Janet's pleased,
but not for the same reason as Gina. No letters mean Kit's
maybe reading them, at last.

'I hope this means you can draw a line,' she observed,
but when Gina opened her mouth to explain that, no, far
from giving up, it was a very good sign, she had held up
her hands. 'We've all been through a nightmare, Georgina.

But there comes a point when you have to get on with your life.'

Gina doesn't see the point in trying to make her mother see that the life she wants is with Kit, and now that's half gone, she's stuck. Poor Terry is dead; Janet has no choice but to move on. But Kit isn't. Kit's still here. It's too awful to say aloud, but it's painfully clear to Gina that there's a big difference.

Their shared grief hasn't brought them closer. Just as Gina thinks there isn't a comparison between their situations, Janet is livid at any suggestion that Gina's loss is anything like hers.

Gina sits up in the car as the front door opens and Anita Atherton appears, in a calf-length grey dress covered with a long cardigan, a plaited leather belt slung around her narrow hips. Gina's timidly impressed at how stylish she looks, even in the current circumstances. Her long hair's swept into a bun, and she cuts a tall figure against the door, just as she did the first time Kit brought Gina home.

Anita pauses for a moment, then fixes her eyes on Gina, and starts marching across the garden.

She gets out of the car, wanting to meet her halfway, but Anita's quicker: she's at the gate before Gina can reach it, barring the way to the house. 'What are you doing here?' she hisses.

Gina summons up all her politeness and bravery. 'I've come to see Kit.'

'You've come to see Kit.' The voice is neutral but there's a fine sheen of anger shimmering around his mother, the way heat bends the air around a fire. 'Why?'

'To talk to him about my letters. I know he's been reading them. He's been getting them.'

'And what makes you think that?'

'Because . . . because I haven't been getting them back.' As she says it, Gina realises how flimsy her hopes are.

Anita gives a completely mirthless laugh. 'Or have you considered that maybe I've had better things to do lately than return them to you?'

Gina is floundering, desperate to say the right thing. But she doesn't know what the right thing is any more. Until this happened, she did. She had a good girl's knack for pleasing but now everything she says seems to be wrong, and she desperately doesn't want to offend this woman any more than she already has.

But he was *mine* too, she cries inside her head. My future. We should be in London right now. Or driving across America. Or swimming in Sydney.

The wind shivers through the trees around them, an early morning chill, and shakes some of the copper leaves from the branches. They float lazily down on an invisible breeze, all the time in the world.

Gina tries to make her face appealing. 'Can't I see him? Not even for ten minutes? Just to say—'

'To say what?'

Sorry? I love you? I haven't stopped thinking about you for a single hour of a single day?

Gina had prepared what she was going to say as she was driving there, but now she's faced with Anita Atherton's scorn, her impassioned speeches seem babyish, and she's ashamed but still determined to battle

on because with nothing to lose. she doesn't care how stupid she looks.

'To say that it doesn't matter what . . . that I love him . . .'

Anita's patience is running out. 'I think that would be the absolute worst thing for everyone. I meant what I said at the hospital, Gina. It's better this way.'

'Then just tell me how he is!' Gina begs. 'Please. I need to know. Doesn't he ask about me? Doesn't he wonder why I'm not writing to him?'

It's the not knowing that's driving Gina mad. No one will tell her anything. She has no memory of the sequence of events that abruptly curtailed the happiest day of her life, and now she doesn't even know what's happened to Kit. She's run through every possibility in her mind since the hospital: Kit partially paralysed but with the hope of recovery; Kit on crutches, learning to walk; and, her favourite, Kit still asleep like Sleeping Beauty, waiting for the torn muscles and nerves in his body to knit back together, to sit up in bed suddenly one day, right as rain. It does happen.

Gina swallows. What's been tormenting her in the middle of the night is the idea that he might have no memory of her, of their cinematic, once-in-a-lifetime love – the favourite songs, the gigs, the in-jokes, the laughter in her car, the experimental spag-bol dinners, the skinny dipping, the midnight phone conversations, the happiest, best years of her life that only Kit knows. She can look at Kit in any state and still love him, as long as he can remember that. Without it, without him, they're gone, and so is she, because Gina knows she'll never be as happy again, not without him.

Anita stares at her, pitying, then reaches into the deep pocket of her cardigan and brings out four of Gina's letters, held together with a red elastic post-office band. It bends them, creasing the paper as if they're junk mail. 'The reason you haven't had your letters back is because we've been away.' She sounds as if she's said these words too many times now, to too many people. 'We saw a specialist in California who works with spinal-cord injuries, and I'm pleased to say the signs are promising.'

'He's making a recovery?'

Anita's face twists. 'He's never going to walk again, if that's what you're asking. He's probably never going to live an independent life. He's never going to dance, or play real tennis, or swim. All the things he loved doing most. But he's alive.'

Gina didn't even know Kit played real tennis.

She was one of the things he loved most.

'But hasn't he asked about me at all?' she blurts out, and is ashamed at once.

Anita's shoulders rise up around her ears and her whole body tenses beneath the woollen clothes. She covers her face with her hands. Gina is left looking at the tight tendons of Anita's neck, and the hands that have aged so fast, the skin crêping. Her rings have gone.

After only a moment the hands are lowered and Anita fixes her with a bitter look.

'Please don't! He's important to me!' Gina is forcing out the words through the ringing in her ears. 'I know how you feel.'

'How can you know how I feel? You don't have the first

idea. Not until you lose something precious to you, and even then I don't know if you'd understand.'

Gina wants to say, Yes, I do. I lost my father. And my stepfather. And the love of my life. They're dead, and Kit's going to live. If she were older, more confident, she would say it but something in Anita's face makes her feel small and the pain just backs up inside her.

'It's because of you that Kit's where he is now.' Anita pauses, to let the words sink in. 'Don't come here again. And please. No more letters. Get on with your life.'

Gina's heart breaks inside her, a sharp, winding pain, and she can't think of a single thing to say as Anita walks back up the path and closes the front door behind her.

Gina stands there. *Because of me. All this is because of me.*

Gina woke on the Sunday morning after Willow's party with a headache.

It was raining outside, hard drops clattering loudly on the windows, but the headache was her own fault. After Nick had dropped her at home, Gina had tidied up two more boxes of junk, chucking out the entire contents without even looking at them, trying to avoid the mental image of pregnant Bryony, daddy Stuart, lonely old Gina. Meanwhile the knot in her stomach grew bigger and bigger until eventually she couldn't ignore it. She'd drunk a bottle of wine and sobbed with frustration on the sofa while Buzz hid in his basket, then fallen into bed fully dressed at about ten.

Now it was four in the morning, the rain was accompanied by distant thunder, and the crushing headache seemed to have spread over her entire body.

Gina stared up at the featureless ceiling and felt so lonely she ached.

Everyone else's life was moving on. Hers was stuck. It didn't help that she had to take her mother out later: their annual Sunday lunch on what had been Terry's birthday.

As she was mentally running through the few acceptable lunch venues (nowhere with loud music, 'garlicky food', dubious hygiene, etc.) Gina heard a soft brushing noise, and out of the corner of her eye, she saw the door open a crack, letting in a pale slice of light from the hallway.

She turned her head, but not her body, and watched as a long black nose nudged its way into the space, pushing it wider, to be followed by Buzz's narrow head and dark grey shoulders. Silently, the dog edged through the small gap, gliding on his noiseless paws like a ghost into her room, then hesitated, as if he was making sure she was really asleep before creeping in.

There was a distant rumble of thunder and Buzz cringed, then scuttled into the shadows of the room.

Gina kept still, but inside her heart was hammering. This was the first time she'd ever seen Buzz do anything of his own accord for himself. He was a totally passive creature, waiting to be told he could eat or go out, watching her for signs with those anxious eyes. At night, he'd always just gone to sleep in his basket – grateful, she guessed, to be inside. This was the first time she'd seen him dare take a tiny chance.

Something uncurled inside her, and she rolled over to let him know it was fine for him to be there. But as she moved, the usual shiver of fear rippled over the dog's coat and he shied back, ears flattened.

'It's OK,' whispered Gina. 'It's OK.'

They stared at each other in the morning half-light as the rain drummed on the big window behind the curtain. The whites around Buzz's jet eyes slowly disappeared as he read her face and saw only encouragement there.

'It's OK,' she whispered again, and with a quiet groan, he sank down against the door and tucked himself into a ball, his nose buried in the solid muscles of his hind legs. Close. But not too close.

Gina lay on her side and watched him pretend to sleep, then sleep for real, as the clock beside her bed edged out of the small hours and into early morning. The rain began to sound soothing. She was inside, warm, safe.

Without warning, at a quarter to six, Gina dropped off to sleep.

At some point in the thirteen years since Terry's heart attack, it had become a tradition for Gina to take Janet out for lunch on the weekend nearest his birthday, then over to the cemetery at St John's Church to put some flowers beside his headstone.

Stuart had never been included in the annual lunch: it was just Gina and Janet. And, in a strange way, the spirit of Terry. It was one day of the year when mother and daughter made more effort than usual to be generous to each other, in conscious memory of his years of quiet peacemaking.

This year, Buzz wasn't invited either, and to make up for his morning at home Gina took him for the longest of their walks, then treated them both to a Sunday bacon sandwich at the café that let dogs in. It was a particularly good bacon sandwich – fresh white bread, lots of tomato sauce, crispy smoked local bacon – and she stopped at the gates of the park to balance it on the brick wall so she could take a Polaroid of it with Nick's camera.

Gina had noticed plenty of things on the way there, but this was the first moment she wanted to use up a frame of film on. It wasn't so much the sandwich, she thought, warming the photo under her armpit to speed up the developing chemicals: it was everything. The softness of the morning air after the previous night's rain, the lingering drops on the leaves, the fact that she was only out at this hour because she was walking the dog, the fun of eating something messy and delicious outside. The whole thing was just . . . enjoyable.

Gina's head was still thick, but she was surprised by the glimmer of optimism she felt when she looked at the leaves, the sky, the sandwich. Small things, but satisfying; things she knew Terry would have appreciated, in his way. It was like the sun coming out, even though the clouds were still there.

She glanced down at Buzz, and smiled at the ketchup-stained muzzle peering up at her, a twinkle in his eyes as he licked his chops to get the final taste of bacon from between his gappy teeth.

Gina took another Polaroid of him, doing his doggy smile with the leafy park in the background. *That* was the moment.

As she and Buzz walked up the path towards the woods, Gina found herself half hoping she might see Nick. She told herself it was so she could show him that she'd started using the camera already, but it wasn't that: Gina wanted him to see her in a normal state, not the frozen-faced mess she'd been when he'd dropped her off at her house the previous afternoon.

Gina couldn't remember whether Nick was even in Longhampton today. There'd been some mention of London, of talking to Amanda about the summer house idea. She'd been concentrating in the car on not crying till she got home, and hadn't said much while Nick had chatted to fill the uncomfortable silence. He'd suggested a film but she'd got the distinct impression he was feeling sorry for her. She hoped she hadn't seemed rude.

She looked out for him as she and Buzz did their lap, but Nick wasn't among the weekend strollers in the park. Rachel was, though, accompanied by a couple of volunteers from the charity shop, and her husband, George. They were being towed along by two Staffies, a black poodle, a spaniel cross and a basset hound with ginger eyebrows, all sniffing and jostling each other. As soon as Rachel saw her with Buzz, she waved and headed over, followed by Gem, who seemed to be fighting the urge not to round up the straggling volunteers.

'Morning!' she said, beaming. 'Don't normally see you out and about on the weekend. Why aren't you in bed, for God's sake? Do you want to walk with us? It's our volunteer walk – everyone who takes a dog round the park gets a bacon sandwich back at the rescue. They're good sarnies. Some people even do two dogs and come back for seconds.'

'Would you believe I've just had one?' Gina checked her watch. It *was* tempting to join Rachel, to offload about Bryony and Stuart, but time was ticking on. 'I wish I could but I'm supposed to be taking my mum out for lunch. She's one of those mothers who virtually scrambles the police helicopter if I'm ten minutes late.'

'Next week, then? It's good for Buzz to socialise. And for you. Our volunteers are a nice bunch. Oh, and before you ask,' Rachel added, 'I've got to return a call about that foster place for Buzz in Evesham, so we're on the case, I promise. Shouldn't be too much longer.'

'Good,' said Gina, although she couldn't help noting that Rachel had said exactly the same thing well over a week ago now. 'Good, I'm pleased to hear it.'

Buzz was leaning against her legs, eyeing Gem cautiously.

'Has he stretched his legs up in the dog park yet?' asked Rachel. 'Offlead, I mean.'

Gina shook her head. 'I let him in, but he just stands there staring at me. I wish he would run. It's so sad, when you see other dogs belting around up there. They look like they're having so much fun, and something's stopping him.'

Rachel stroked Buzz's shorter ear. 'It'll come. When he's ready. You're doing a great job.'

'Really?'

'Yup. Brilliant. Listen, I won't keep you – see you tomorrow morning at the shop!' She smiled and jogged back to join the tail end of the dog herd heading up towards the wood.

Gina looked down at Buzz, who was watching Rachel's retreating red jacket. She wondered if he'd prefer to go with Rachel and the other dogs, but then he turned his head and looked up at her, ready to do whatever she wanted. Her heart melted. She hoped he hadn't heard the bit about the foster place.

I should have told Rachel about him creeping into my room, she thought, as they set off towards the gate, then was glad she hadn't, in case it was against some rule. She didn't want to get either of them into trouble.

'Isn't this a lovely day?' she said aloud, lifting her face to the warm April sunshine. While she was moving, noticing the reds and the yellows of the planted flowerbeds, she wasn't thinking about Stuart and Bryony. 'Much nicer to be out here than lying around in bed.'

I'm talking to a dog, she thought, as they passed a couple with a Scottie and exchanged smiles, and I don't actually care.

Gina had booked a table in a gastropub that Sara the wedding planner had recommended to her on the outskirts of Rosehill. The Sun-in-Splendour was making much of its lunch menu featuring Longhampton's locally sourced delights. More importantly, it wasn't a place Janet and Gina had been to with Terry. Lunches in those places, Gina had learned to her cost, ended up in a mournful list of everything that had changed for the worse, followed by tetchy corrections about events they each remembered slightly differently.

After Janet's ritual inspection of the loos, before which

no food was to be ordered in case there was questionable handwashing provision, the conversation settled into the usual series of questions and answers, starting with a round-up of other people's news and circling slowly into more contentious waters.

'How's Naomi?' Janet lifted the crust of her steak and kidney pie as if she wasn't sure what she'd find under it. 'Have you organised that shed she had you running around half the county for?'

Gina ignored the barb. Janet was very fond of Willow but blew hot and cold about Naomi, whose long-term loyalty would always be tainted by her brother's association with Kit. 'It's finished. It was unveiled yesterday at Willow's birthday party, and it's not just a shed, Mum. It's a multi-purpose summer house – I'm really happy with it. One door leads into a Wendy house, and the other leads into a shed for Jason. Tony did an amazing job. I'm seriously thinking about marketing it on the website.'

'I don't know why Jason needs a shed. He doesn't do any gardening. They should just have made a proper Wendy house for Willow.'

'They don't want to spoil her. And, anyway, Jason needs a place to get away from it all.'

'You can't spoil a lovely little girl like that,' said Janet, indulgently, then pulled a sad face. 'And how's Naomi's dad? Was he there?'

'He was. Just back from a golf holiday. Looking very tanned. For a Scotsman, anyway.'

'Still no partner?'

'No.' Naomi's parents had divorced when she was

nineteen; her mother Linda lived in Brighton with her second husband, Eric. Janet had maintained a supportive sadness about Ronnie McIntyre's single status ever since, even though he'd never looked happier. 'I don't think he will remarry now. He likes the freedom.'

'Well, he's never here, is he? And poor Linda.' She sighed. 'So far away.'

'Mum, there's nothing poor about Linda. She does salsa two nights a week, and only has to babysit once a month.'

Janet put down her knife and fork reproachfully. 'Babysitting your grandchildren isn't a *chore*, Georgina. It's something every mother looks forward to. It's the most wonderful part of having a family.'

'Linda's not that sort of granny. Naomi says she's already given them the money to go to Disneyland Paris on the condition that she doesn't have to go with them. Don't you remember what she was like when Naomi and I were young? Dyeing our—' Gina stopped herself just in time. 'Dyeing Naomi's hair for her? She'll be great when Willow's a bit older. A real fun granny.'

Janet sighed her all-purpose have-it-your-way sigh. 'Have you heard from Stuart?'

'Actually, Stuart was at the party,' said Gina. She'd argued with herself on the way over about whether or not to tell her mother about Stuart's baby, and had decided that she had to, even if it resulted in tears. It wasn't the best day to drop it on Janet, by any stretch of the imagination, but the teenager in her felt like shaking her mother's stubborn insistence that he could do no wrong.

'He probably wanted to see you.' Janet looked smug, as if she'd been proved right. 'That's nice. Did you talk?'

'No, it wasn't like that. He turned up with his new girlfriend.'

Her mother's face fell. Then, with a visible effort, she rallied. 'Well, it's good that you're all trying to get on. Very mature. Did you speak with . . . with the girlfriend?'

'She's called Bryony. No, I didn't, Mum.' Gina bit her lip. 'I think I might have tried to, if I'd known she was coming, but it was a bit of a shock. It turns out she's pregnant.'

Silence spread across the table, like a spilled glass of wine.

'Oh,' said Janet, and for the first time she looked furious.

'What do you mean, oh?' said Gina. 'Oh, that's nice? Or, oh, that's a shock?'

'I mean . . .' she cleared her throat '. . . I mean, that's shabby. Letting you believe he didn't want children, then going off and . . . doing that.'

'I don't think Stuart ever said he didn't *want* children,' said Gina. 'We just didn't have them. And it's probably just as well, considering how things have turned out.'

'But, Georgina,' Janet looked distraught, 'that's . . .'

This should be *me* being upset, said a lucid voice in Gina's head. I'm the one who's having to deal with all this. How come Mum's the one who gets to be upset? She doesn't know the half of it.

'There's no point getting wound up about it,' she said calmly, spearing peas on her fork. It was amazing how calm she could be when she was reacting against Janet's wailing. Maybe she ought to move home for a bit, she thought, just until all Stuart's revelations were done: she'd be incredibly sanguine, just to prove a point. 'It draws a line under things.'

'I will get wound up if it means you'll never have a family now.' Janet's knife and fork rattled on the plate. 'Not if that was your one chance before the – before your treatment.'

'Mum, you can't start thinking what if. What if I hadn't had cancer? What if I'd got pregnant and then been diagnosed? What then? Anyway, there's no saying I can't have children. I've got my annual check-up in a couple of weeks – it's something they can test then, I'm sure.'

Janet sighed. 'It's the least they can do. I think it's an outrage they didn't offer to freeze your eggs before the chemo. You should sue. *I* might. I've lost the chance to have grandchildren.'

'Sorry?' Gina put her fork down. They were heading into territory Janet had fastidiously avoided until now – which had made it much easier to keep her decisions about her fertility private.

'I was talking to Eileen Shaw from the gardening club. Her daughter's just been diagnosed with what you had, and she's being rushed in to have her eggs frozen before they start treatment. I've been reading up on it.' Janet eyed her daughter. 'It depends on the type of cancer, I understand. Whether they can do it.'

'I don't want to talk about things like that over lunch,' said Gina, firmly. 'Would you like some chips? They're hand-cut gourmet ones.'

Janet sniffed. 'But it's a medical . . .'

Gina shook the chip basket at her. 'Chips? Mum?'

She pursed her lips, and took two of Gina's chips. 'Hand-cut chips. What else are you meant to cut them with?'

Gina pushed the thimble of tomato sauce towards her, but she knew she'd only bought a little time. The trouble was, once she started telling her mother the cold, hard truth, where would she stop?

This wasn't the day.

Terry Bellamy,
1949–2001
A much loved son, husband,
stepfather and friend

Terry's headstone was in the far corner of the cemetery, next to an old sycamore tree that scattered propellers over the neighbouring graves like confetti. It was a simple gold inscription on a plain granite stone. Nothing fashionable or attention-seeking, but solid and weathering well, much like Terry himself had been in life.

Gina looked at it, and thought, *Thank you, Terry*, the same thing she thought every year. Thanks for being the invisible oil in the engine of our family. I'm sorry I didn't say thank you more often at the time. I'm sorry I screwed up your final hours, although I suppose, in a sense, it meant you could slip away quietly, without any fuss, which is what you'd have wanted.

Although, she wondered, was it really? At the end, you wanted the people you loved around you, holding your hand and making you feel you were a vital link in a chain of affection, that you mattered, that you'd made a mark in the sand, even for a second, before you slipped into oblivion. Terry had been politeness itself to the nurses, the ward sister had told them. That had been the last mark he'd made.

Gina looked up. The view from St John's wasn't the prettiest: lots of other graves, and then a rather scrubby field. Not the most inspiring place to spend eternity.

I'd like to be scattered in that view from the dining room of the Magistrate's House, she thought. In that rolling bosom of fields and woods and open skies, near the apple orchards and the sheep farms, somewhere life goes on, season after season, renewing itself constantly. Not trapped in a graveyard, waiting for my annual visit.

Janet sniffed to signal that she'd said her own silent prayers, and dabbed her eyes with a tissue. 'He was a good man,' she said, as she said every year. 'I wish we'd had longer.'

Gina put her arm around her mother's waist, and squeezed. Janet had only been married to Captain Huw Pritchard for four years whereas she'd been Mrs Bellamy for ten. Terry had been the one who'd dealt with teenage tantrums and revision and driving lessons and hot flushes and mousetraps.

'I know,' she said, and felt her mum lean on her for a moment. Janet was small, and felt smaller in her pink wool swing coat. I'm all she has left now, Gina thought, and her chest tightened. They were both pretty much back where they'd been before Terry had come on the scene.

'Can you do the flowers, Georgina?' Janet offered her the paper-wrapped bunch. 'You do these things so much better than me,' she added, in a transparent but well-meant attempt to be pleasant.

Gina crouched down and stuck the flowers they'd brought into the holes of Terry's flower holder: white carnations, Mum's favourite, and cloud-like gypsophila to fill in the gaps. She worked quickly and neatly, snapping the stems to make a ball of white petals, a summer snowball on the plain granite.

'Very nice. Makes him look loved,' said Janet, when she'd finished.

'Because he was,' said Gina. 'Well loved.'

After a moment's appreciation, she stepped back, and they walked down the long path together. Janet put her arm through Gina's, and a different sort of atmosphere settled between them. A happier, more conciliatory one.

'I'm sorry about before, Georgina,' she started, rather self-consciously. 'I didn't mean to make you feel worse about this business with Stuart having a baby. It's only because I don't want you to miss out.'

Gina started to say, on autopilot, that she didn't feel as if she was missing out, but she stopped herself. If Janet was trying to be honest, she should too. 'I know,' she said instead. 'But it's difficult, Mum.'

Now Stuart was removed from the equation, Gina didn't know how she felt about children. For a long time she'd just felt grateful to have beaten that round of cancer; any more seemed like tempting Fate. And something with Stuart had always stopped her broodiness.

Suddenly she wasn't sure what she thought. It made her light-headed. The new horizon of possibilities, balanced on the other side by the pinprick reminder she had every morning when she took her Tamoxifen. Life wasn't infinite. It wasn't endless. She didn't have all the time in the world. Maybe she should be more grateful for what she did have.

'Of course it's difficult.' Janet patted her arm. 'Having a child . . . it's like cutting out your heart and letting someone carry it around with them for the rest of your life. But you don't even think twice about it. All you ever want is for them to be happy. It's . . . Oh, I can't explain it very well. You're a part of me.' She blew her nose with a loud parp. 'You always will be.'

And a part of Dad. The thought went through her mind, and the mood was soft enough that Gina found herself saying what she was thinking for once, instead of biting it back. 'Mum,' she said. 'Is there a reason we don't go and put flowers on *Dad's* grave?'

Janet tucked the tissue back up her sleeve. 'Because he's not buried anywhere. He was cremated and scattered.'

'There isn't a memorial stone?'

'No. He always said he didn't want a grave for people to cry over. He was a soldier, Georgina. They're tough like that.'

'Is there a plaque in the regimental HQ, though?' Gina persisted.

'No.' Janet was walking more quickly.

'But if he died on duty . . .'

'He died while he was with the SAS. That's why we've got no details. It's security.'

'But . . .'

The mood had changed again. They were by the car, and

367

as Janet went to get into the passenger side, Gina saw the tight set of her lips. 'Georgina, if I could bring myself not to ask, I think you could too.'

'But he was my dad.' It came out before she could stop it. 'I don't see why it's so awful to want to talk about him. Terry never used to mind. It's not like it affects what I felt for Terry.'

Janet stopped and glared over the roof of the car. 'Today, of all days. This is Terry's day, not . . . Huw's.'

Gina was about to argue back, then thought, *Shut up, Gina.* That had been a good moment there, and she'd spoiled it.

Janet stared at her, her lips pressing together as if she were struggling with a thought that wouldn't come right in her head. The wind picked up, rustling the leaves around the churchyard, lifting her blonde curls. She was wearing her best pearl earrings, the ones Terry had given her for their wedding.

She's still really young, Gina thought. Fifty-six. Far too young to be widowed twice – before she was even fifty. Far too young to be reminded about *two* graves, for God's sake. An impulse to do something nice came over her.

'Do you want to go and get an ice cream?' she asked. 'Banana split and all the trimmings?'

It was something Terry had always suggested after a run out – taking what he called 'the long cut home' via the Italian ice-cream parlour by Longhampton station. Sometimes the offer was made with indulgent good humour, more often in desperation over the sound of mother-daughter sniping.

Janet stopped frowning, and her expression softened.

'Yes,' she said, with a smile that made her look younger. 'And a scoop in a coupe for me.'

Gina heard Terry say it into the rear-view mirror, his kind eyes smiling at her in the red leather back seat.

'A scoop in a coupe it is,' said Gina, and got into the car.

Chapter Eighteen

ITEM: a hospital wrist tag

Oxford, 12th June 2001

Kit's in a private hospital. It's very different from the NHS A&E department to which they were airlifted after the accident, but the second Gina sets foot in the echoing foyer the taste in her mouth comes flooding back – the calmly rushing staff, the smell of disinfectant and human fear.

She grips the carrier-bag with her offerings in it: magazines, some grapes, CDs of their favourite music. She wasn't sure what to bring, what Kit might be up to enjoying, because no one will tell her exactly how he is, but she didn't want to bring anything that gave the wrong message. She wants her presents to say, *You're going to be fine.*

The presents have to say that because Gina can't believe anything will be fine again. Her brain is foggy with grief and shock, not helped by the codeine she's on for her broken collarbone. Nothing feels real, but that's not a problem because she still hopes that at some point she'll wake up and this will all have been a dream.

She shuffles on the plastic seat outside his room and adjusts her shoulder brace, which is digging into her bruises. The nurse went in five minutes ago and hasn't come out. Gina wonders if they're having to cover Kit up, or prepare him, and a cold sensation runs across her skin.

The nurse reappears and she leaps up with a wince.

'Sorry to keep you waiting – we're short-staffed today.' She's a young trainee nurse, flustered with too much to do. 'I can't find Mrs Atherton. I think she's been sent for a lie-down by the doctor. She hasn't left since Christopher was brought in.'

Gina's secretly relieved: she's not sure she can handle Anita's grief on top of her own. She doesn't know what to say. She hopes just talking to someone who loves Kit too might be a comfort. 'It's OK,' she says. 'I can keep him company.'

'Are you family?' The nurse is checking her notes.

Everything in Gina is screaming, *No, I'm his girlfriend*, but some Naomi-ish instinct makes her say, 'Yes.' She has to get inside that room. Even it means lying.

'That's fine then,' says the nurse, and opens the door. 'Just till your mum gets back. Ring the bell if you need me.'

'Thanks,' says Gina, and she goes in.

It's a big white room, full of light, and there are vases of flowers everywhere. Pink lilies, orange roses. Jarringly bright in the whiteness, not smelling of anything. In the middle of the room is a white hospital bed, surrounded with cold metal machines, and inside, tucked up under the blanket like a six-foot tall child, is Kit.

A cold hand clutches Gina's innards and grips her so hard she's scared she's going to lose control of her bladder.

His eyes are closed and circled with dark shadows. His long lashes seem even longer now he's so pale, but his beautiful hair's been shaved to a pale golden suede for wires to be attached under the stretchy bandage that covers part of his head. He doesn't move when she comes in. But the machines keep humming and flickering, and Gina stares at his chest until she sees it rise almost imperceptibly, then fall, holding her own breath until she see his.

Her head fills with loud, violent emotions that she feels too small to contain. It's so *unfair*. She's never seen Kit so still. Even when he was asleep he seemed to glow with energy. Now he's there, but he's not. He's different.

'Kit,' she breathes, perching on the chair by the bed. 'It's me. Gina.'

Of course there's no response, and Gina hates herself. What did she think? That he would spring up, that she would wake him with a kiss? Already the hope she's been nursing for the past days seems like the relic of a stupider time: Kit *looks* lucky not to be dead, as she overheard her mother say, while she was slipping in and out of anaesthesia.

Her eyes skim the room, looking for clues about his condition. The monitors seem linked to everything. He has breathing equipment, as well as a heart monitor; that can't be good.

Gina notices that there's no stubble on his soft jaw. It only takes a day or two for a scratchy layer to speckle his smooth skin. One weekend they'd spent the whole time in bed and she'd joked she'd seen it grow. Someone's been shaving it for him.

Her heart aches with irrational jealousy and she touches his hand. It's cool.

'Kit, I've brought you some music,' she whispers, reaching into her bag. 'I've made you a compilation of all our songs, in case you can hear them. Well, I *know* you can hear them. And I'll come every week, and read to you. Whatever you want. Travel guides, if you like. I've made a list of those plantation houses we were going to visit on our driving tour. We can still do that.'

Tears are running down her face at the cruelty with which that dream was crumpled and tossed aside in one careless second.

'I'm here,' she whispers. 'I'm not going anywhere. I promise. We'll get through this. You're strong and I'll do everything I can and—'

The door opens and Gina hears an audible gasp – she turns, realising it's not the nurse.

Anita Atherton, Kit's mother, is standing by the doorway, staring at Gina with a look of such absolute fury and disgust that her skin feels as if it's burning.

Gina opens her mouth, but already she knows she was wrong about Anita too: there's no way Anita wants her comfort. She looks about ready to kill her.

Her hooded brown eyes are boring into Gina's the way Kit's did, with the confidence that comes from Oxford conversations and smart dinners with well-connected friends. Gina hopes Anita can see her love for Kit, but she's terrified the woman can see her gnawing fear too – that she won't be strong enough, that she'll fail Kit in the same way she's failed her mother, drowning and cut-off in her own overwhelming grief. A grief she had stirred up even more by her actions.

She juts her chin. Be brave, she tells herself. You're doing the right thing.

'Please leave,' says Anita, polite but determined.

'Can't I stay five minutes? I've brought him some music, some things to keep him connected. I can read to him, if you want, while you're taking a break . . .'

Anita is across the room in a flash, and takes hold of Gina's upper arm, with a grip that would hurt if Gina was taking any notice. She looks down at the hand stupidly. Anita's long fingers are banded by rings – gold and diamonds and artistic lumps of semi-precious stones. She'd been fascinated by them at the dinner table, that time Kit had her to stay; the way they flashed and sparkled as Anita's hands waved in witty debate with her guests.

'I'm sorry, but no one would answer my calls,' Gina babbles. 'I can come at a different time if this isn't convenient.'

Anita is marching her to the door. Gina can barely believe it. 'It's *me*,' she says, bewildered. 'It's Gina.'

'I know. Please leave,' says Anita, in the coldest voice Gina has ever heard.

Gina takes one last long look at Kit, tucked in the white bed, and remembers it all: his smooth chest, and his confident hands, never still, making every nerve in her tingle, jumping together at gigs, crushed in the moshpit, talking and talking into the night, their conversations ebbing and flowing between deep, urgent kisses and then silent exploration of each other's bodies, waking and sleeping together.

The smell of his sweat and the heavy warmth of his arm thrown over her, never wanting to let her go.

That's all gone. Like a book that's finished, the characters are still in her head, but there will be no more story. It's over. Gina wishes she knew what to do now, in these precious last seconds, but she doesn't. They've already gone.

Anita is closing the door in her face.

Weeks had now passed since Gina had reported her bike as stolen, and there was still no sign of it turning up. More to the point, no one had come forward to claim Buzz, so he was officially handed over to Four Oaks as a stray to be rehomed.

Although, as Rachel observed, Buzz was looking less and less like a stray each day. He spent Mondays and Tuesdays in the Stone Green Projects office with Gina, supposedly to help his slow rehabilitation with strangers, but really because his quiet company under her desk while she worked made him the best kind of office mate, barring the occasional digestive indiscretion. At lunchtime Gina turned off her laptop instead of working through, and they stretched their legs together along the canal, where the tall green nettles were getting lush in the warmer weather and the ducks were even prettier close up than when she'd watched them through her window.

At night, Buzz still crept into her room after she'd gone to bed, not before, and curled up by the door to sleep. Gina was sometimes woken by the sound of him scrabbling and kicking as if in a nightmare, his muffled whimpers cutting straight through her, but they seemed to be lessening as his ribs became sleek and the snowflake patches of white on his grey coat began to shine. She'd begun to stick her Polaroids on the back wall of the sitting room, alongside the list of a hundred things, and already Gina could see the difference between the first picture of Buzz – him sleeping with his nose laid carefully along his paws – and the latest of him happily licking tomato ketchup off his nose.

It made her happy to think she'd helped bring the light back into his eyes, but also guilty that at some point Rachel would find a home for him and she'd have to let him go.

It hadn't taken much for Rachel to persuade Gina to become his official fosterer, and as part of the deal she had to take him up to the vet for his microchip, vaccinations, and any other care George the vet thought he'd need to persuade someone to adopt a third-hand failed greyhound.

George had the sort of reassuring countryman presence that could have calmed a rampaging elephant but even so, Gina could see Buzz was quivering as George ran his hands over the greyhound's legs, feeling for old injuries. Every so often, Buzz would glance in her direction for reassurance, and his fearful expression tugged at her heart.

'Is he in reasonable nick?' Gina stroked Buzz's trembling haunches while George pulled back his lips and pressed his gums. 'I think he's put on a bit of weight since I got him.'

'I can see – that brindle's really starting to come out in his coat. Pretty snowflakes too, very unusual. You'll be a handsome chap before long.' George stroked Buzz's narrow head. 'Well, his teeth are pretty terrible and we'll have to start from the beginning with vaccinations but he's not the worst greyhound I've seen.'

Gina's mind shied away from what that might mean. 'Are they all as nervous as him?'

'No. Normally greys are pretty easy-going. Poor Buzz must have had a rough time of it for him to be so scared of men. But he'll get there. I reckon he's about five, so he's got a good seven or eight years of better life to enjoy. Worth waiting for, eh, lad?'

Gina stroked Buzz's knobbly spine and felt him lean into her, a sign of affection that she'd started to enjoy. She'd rescued him from that old life. Cheap, for the price of a bike she'd never wanted. 'Rachel said he might have been badly treated in the past. Shouldn't he be with someone who knows how to deal with traumatised greyhounds?'

'He seems to be doing all right with you,' said George. 'Just keep doing what you're doing.'

'But I'm not doing anything.'

He smiled, and his craggy face softened into a surprising sensitivity. George had kind eyes; Gina found herself being soothed in the same way that Buzz obviously did. 'Sometimes,' he said, 'nothing's absolutely the right thing to do.'

Gina had just got Buzz clipped into the car harness now fixed to the rear seat of her Golf and was about to set off home when her phone rang.

It was Nick. As she picked up the call, Gina inwardly hoped there wasn't a new problem over at Langley St

Michael. She and Lorcan had spent most of that morning talking to a specialist electrician about the best way to tackle the ancient wiring system that coiled around the Magistrate's House, like electric cobwebs. Lights had a habit of blowing all round the house, and nothing seemed linked to anything else on the enormous antiquated fuse box.

Amanda's architect was proposing an elaborate system of recessed spotlights and remotely controllable dimmers that the electrician had immediately explained wouldn't work, and might not meet building regulations. Nick had been fascinated by the technicalities, and Gina had left Lorcan explaining it to him in his patient Irish accent, drawing big diagrams on the back of some lining paper. Gina was pretty sure it was going to cost a small fortune, and whether or not Amanda would be prepared to pay it for a rental property, she didn't know.

'Hello,' said Nick. 'Are you still at the vet's?'

'Just finished,' she said. 'Did Lorcan manage to explain the magic of electricity to you?'

'Hello? Lighting is something I actually understand, missy,' said Nick. 'I feel as if I owe it to the house to know what I'm doing to it.'

'At least you know what you're paying for.'

'Yeah. Um, on that note . . . I know you're on your way home, but do you think you could possibly come over and have a chat on Skype with Amanda? She's got a free hour between meetings and wants us to walk her round the house so she can see what's been done so far.'

'OK,' said Gina. They'd managed to do a fair bit, but the work at this stage was slow-going preparation, and most of it wouldn't be visible to Amanda's eye. It certainly wouldn't tally with the amount of money it had cost. At least when clients were on site they could feel damp plaster and see the skips filling outside the house. 'When's she calling?'

'She's going to ring when she's free, but she's aiming for lunch her time.'

'And where is her time this week?'

'New York.'

It was several weeks now since Amanda had been in Longhampton for longer than a flying visit, although she'd replied to Gina's updates and queries promptly by email. The meetings in New York had expanded, she explained, but she made no mention of her daughter or her ex-husband. It was another strange aspect of Gina's growing friendship with Nick that she knew one Amanda from what he told her, and a very different Amanda from the emails and brief phone conversations. And, more worryingly, while Nick seemed to be settling into the house, it was harder, from the dispassionate way Amanda talked about the 'project', to imagine her living there at all.

Gina pushed those thoughts aside: none of her business. 'So six, seven?'

'If you could come over about six, it'd be brilliant.'

She glanced at the car clock. 'Nick, you do realise it's a quarter to six now?'

'Is it?' He sounded surprised. 'God, so it is. Sorry, the electrician had the Wi-Fi down most of the afternoon so I've been trying to catch up with some work. Can you come over now? Is that too soon?'

Gina looked over to the back seat where Buzz was curled

up in his harness, braced for the journey. He was quite a good traveller, lifting his grey muzzle up to the open window and closing his eyes in the breeze.

'It's going to take me . . .' she did some rapid mental calculations '. . . about twenty minutes to get home from Rosehill, then another ten minutes to feed Buzz, then get back out to you, so . . .'

'Bring Buzz with you,' he said easily. 'If you think he wouldn't mind a bit of mess.'

'*You* don't mind?'

'No! What's to mind? I'd quite like the look of a greyhound around the place. I'm sure it was on one of Amanda's mood boards, a pair of greyhounds. And they're quite heritage, aren't they? Elizabethan? They're probably on some council list of approved dogs for the building.'

'Yeah, you'd never get a Labradoodle past Keith Hurst.' Gina smiled. 'Fine. I'll be with you in about twenty minutes, then.'

'Thanks. I really appreciate it.' Nick paused, and she could see him pinching the bridge of his nose. 'Just so you're prepared, Amanda was talking about the latest invoices and the rental idea again.'

'I'm always prepared,' said Gina, but she was glad she still had all the files in the boot.

Lorcan was still there when Gina arrived, rehanging the heavy back door on its hinges with one of his apprentices.

'Shouldn't you be at home by now?' she asked. It was gone six. 'Won't the lovely Juliet wonder where you've got to?'

'She's baking a million cupcakes for someone's wedding. I've been told to stay well away till the icing sugar's settled.' Lorcan stood back and gestured to the doorway. 'How's that, then?'

The door hadn't been much to look at a few days ago, but now, with the layers of thickly applied paint stripped away, the fine details of the beading had reappeared. It was a classic Regency door, with six beautifully proportioned oak panels, and Lorcan had had it sanded in his workshop, ready for painting. Under the layers of cheap white paint there were traces of a rich holly green, the original door that had been opened by butlers and dashed through by girls in petticoats.

'I've sent the knocker for cleaning,' he added. 'That'll look grand, nice big lion's head, it is.'

'Looks fabulous.' Gina ran a finger over the newly smoothed wood. 'But haven't you got more important things to be doing than doors?'

He raised an eyebrow. 'I've heard Nick on the phone, telling Mrs Rowntree what we've been doing, and I reckoned something she can actually *see* might give her a better picture of how things'll be when they're finished. You can flash your iPad all round that roof space and she's going to have no more idea than Nick about how much better it all looks. At least with this there's a bit of interest.'

'I know.' Gina had been going over the past weeks' work in her head, searching for interesting nuggets to spice up the rather dull insulation facts. There weren't many. 'And we can't start any of the big plans until the consent comes through – and from what I've managed to find out, they're going through the application with a fine-tooth comb at the council, which isn't going to make her very happy. It's not going to be finalised for at least another fortnight at the earliest.'

Lorcan gave Gina a look she'd seen many times before. 'Whatever they're paying you, Gina, sure it's nowhere near enough.'

'Ah, so *now* you want to go home,' she said. 'No, honestly, it's fine. Go on.'

'Nick can explain it perfectly well.' He handed a bag of tools to Kian the apprentice and sent him to tidy up outside. 'He's asked me if I'd give him some plastering lessons. Says he wants to feel like he's had a hand in putting the place straight.' Lorcan rubbed his chin. 'Normally the last thing you want's some random client let loose on their own house, but you know what? I reckon he'd actually be pretty good.'

'What'll I be good at?' Nick appeared behind them, carrying the builders' crumb-strewn tea tray. He smiled at Gina, but he looked tense already: she'd noted a faint line between his eyebrows.

'Plastering,' she said. 'Look, Lorcan's already letting you carry the tea tray. Took Kian three months to be allowed to do that.'

Lorcan patted the sanded door. 'What do you reckon? It's come up really nice.'

'Perfect,' said Nick. 'Exactly what a back door should look like. Well, apart from the paint. Maybe needs a bit.'

'See? He's an expert already,' said Lorcan, at the same moment as the incoming FaceTime tone rang out on the iPad Nick had balanced on the tray.

Amanda's face flashed up – not her red bikini, Gina observed. This looked more like a business headshot: she was glaring sternly from a grey background, her hair pinned into a Hitchcock ice-blonde pleat.

'Ah. I believe that's my cue to depart,' said Lorcan. 'I'll see you two tomorrow.' He gave a quick salute to the pair of them before striding off towards his van. To make sure he wasn't dragged into the conversation, he got out his phone and started making a call.

Nick glanced at Gina, flashed a quick smile, and pressed the answer button.

'. . . you can't see properly here but we've re-insulated, and replastered all the attic space with the eco insulation the architect recommended,' said Gina. 'I've got photos of the work in progress that I can email. And some of the wool, if you want to see it?'

Nick wafted the iPad in the general direction of the sloping ceilings in the attic. There wasn't much to see, apart from the smooth pinky-grey plaster that was now dry and ready for painting. To Gina it looked like a big 'done!' tick; to Amanda, she knew, it would look like a flat nothing.

'Wait? Is that scaffolding all round the house?' asked Amanda.

Nick stopped wafting the iPad.

'Yes,' said Gina. Her voice echoed in the cavernous empty space around them. 'The roofers are up there sorting out the lead valleys. There's plastic sheeting covering the bits of rotted woodwork where they've taken off the tiles and started replacing the joists. It's repairs mainly – we need to wait for the official go-ahead to tackle that ornamental skylight because it's part of the consent application.'

'Still no word on that?'

'No, sorry. But I'm on it.'

'Can't you hurry them up?'

Gina pressed her lips together. It was all very well Nick standing behind the iPad at all times: it wasn't giving her much chance to relax her face between bouts of impatient questioning from Amanda. Her tone was polite but even brusquer than normal; she obviously hadn't had a very good morning so far. 'It tends to work in the opposite direction,' she said. 'The more you hurry them up, the slower they like to go. They think you're trying to hurry them past some dodgy detail.'

'That's ridiculous.'

'Sadly not. I used to work with these people. It'll take as long as it takes, but while we're waiting Lorcan's getting a lot done. The first-phase jobs are well under way, and I've got the specialists lined up, including the electrician.'

'Yes, I wanted to talk to you about the electrical quote Nick mentioned this afternoon. It seems extraordinarily high.'

'That's not final,' said Gina. 'Stephen's going to send me a breakdown, so we can discuss it, maybe with the architect as well. He quoted a ballpark figure because there's always going to be some margin for unknowns in a renovation like this, but with a house this size, and the amount of work you want to do on it, you really need to start from— Hello?'

She thought Amanda was being unusually quiet, and realised the screen had frozen. Then it went black.

Gina looked up at Nick. 'She's gone.'

'What? She's hung up?' He turned the screen round, and groaned. 'Oh, you know why? The power's off again. The Wi-Fi's down.'

It was still light outside, the sun slowly fading out of the pale blue sky, leaving the bare floorboards bathed in a sweetish yellow, streaked with shadows from the scaffolding. They were like bars across the room.

'Has it been doing that all day?' asked Gina.

'To be honest, it's gone off a few times since I moved in. But then that electrician bloke did have a good meddle with the fuse box this afternoon.' Nick folded his arms, tucking the iPad underneath. 'He may have disturbed the three particles of dust holding the connections together.'

She reached for her phone. 'I'll call Lorcan. He might not have got home yet. He's not an electrician but he knows how to fix fuses.'

Nick reached out and touched her arm lightly. 'No, leave it. The poor guy's been here since eight this morning. Let him get some supper. It often comes back on by itself.'

'Shouldn't we ring Amanda's mobile?'

'No. Let's *not* ring Amanda's mobile.' He tipped his head towards the stairs and started walking towards the landing. 'Let's go downstairs and have a drink, and wait for the power to come on again. She'll be back in a meeting at two her time, so if she doesn't call by seven, she won't be calling at all.'

'Well, I suppose it proves the point about needing to rewire from scratch.' Gina followed him towards the staircase. 'I was hoping I could put that electrician's quote into perspective for her. It must seem like a hell of a lot of money for nothing you can see.'

'You should see the figures Amanda deals with every week,' said Nick. 'Millions of dollars, bandied around like loose change. Come on, I need a glass of wine. It's been a long day.'

As they descended, Gina trailed her hand down the polished oak rail that swept round in a sinuous curve above slender wrought-iron balustrades. She loved the idea of the thousands of hands that had trailed along it, just like hers was now. Natural polish smoothed by thousands of fingerprints.

'These are going to be breathtaking stairs,' she said, 'when you get the disgusting carpet off them, and have them treated. Proper your-carriage-awaits stairs.'

'Or sliding-down-the-banister stairs. Into the eight-foot Christmas tree at the bottom . . .'

Nick turned the corner on the landing part of the staircase. As he glanced up, his eyes twinkled from the shadows, and something moved inside Gina's chest. There was an energy in his plans for the house that she couldn't help responding to: he wanted to live here, to make the rooms sing with activity, the way she had when she'd looked around it herself.

It came into her mind with perfect certainty: I'm going to give Nick the witch-ball.

She could already picture it, suspended like a green moon in the hall. Its mysterious glamour fitted this house so much better than her own calm, white flat. What could creep up on her in that modern flat, compared with the fabulous spirits and shades here?

'What are you smiling at?' he asked.

'Nothing,' said Gina, and smiled more.

Buzz was waiting for them in the kitchen, where he'd been shut for his own safety.

Gina could tell he'd been pacing round and round, and when she appeared he whipped his skinny tail round like a helicopter and looked pathetically relieved to see her.

'I was going to have a pizza, but clearly that's not going to happen now.' Nick opened and closed the fridge door. 'Do you fancy some cheese and biscuits?'

'I'm staying for supper?'

'Well, I'm going to open a bottle of wine, so we should probably pretend to have something to eat with it.'

'Um, OK. Thanks. That'd be great.'

'Do you want to sit down?' He gestured towards the kitchen table, which was piled high with interiors magazines, paint cards, letters, pens and coffee mugs. The jumble felt jarring to Gina, after the cleared spaces of her own home. She fought an instinct to go through it with a recycling bag.

'Don't tidy up,' he added, putting a wine glass in front of her. 'Just sit.'

'I have no intention of tidying up. I've clocked off for the day. And I have to drive back, don't forget,' she pointed out, as he half filled her glass.

'Then don't drink it all. Or let me get you a minicab.' Nick twisted the bottle expertly to stop the drip. 'At least Amanda liked the door, eh? Smart move. Maybe that's the tactic – get Lorcan started on the windows as a diversion-ary tactic for the electrics.'

Something in his voice made Gina feel she had to say something. 'The whole point of having a project manager is that you and Amanda don't have to do the good cop/bad cop thing. I'm on your – *plural* – side. I want this house to be right for both of you. But it's quite hard, if you both want different things from it.'

Nick didn't reply at once. He moved around the kitchen, getting plates out, knives and forks from the dishwasher, placing them at the end of the table with the least mess on it. Cheese (expensive, from the deli in town, wrapped in greaseproof paper), oatcakes, farmers'-market trackle-ments, pickles. 'I'm sorry if we're making you feel uncomfortable,' he said, after a while. 'I didn't realise that was how it was coming across.'

Already Gina was regretting what she'd said; once it was out of her mouth she realised it wasn't really about the house at all. It was edging into territory that wasn't her business. 'Look, she's busy,' she said. 'I can tell. Maybe we should have another regrouping meeting about this rental idea. A proper chat.'

Nick looked at the food, then at the disorganised table. He began piling the cheese and plates onto the builders' tea tray. He indicated towards the main house. 'Let's go and eat somewhere I don't have to look at any interiors magazines.'

The library had been covered with dust sheets, ready for the panelling to be removed from the walls for treatment, but in the meantime Nick had clearly chosen it as his escape room, possibly because of deep red walls and the cosier proportions. A squashy sofa had been placed in the centre of the room, with a coffee table in front of it, and in front of that there was a stack of black technology: a huge flat-screen TV, a DVD player, speakers, camera chargers. The multi-coloured wires snaked around the dust sheets, like a map of the London Underground.

Nick put the tray on the coffee table, picked up his wine and settled himself in a corner of the sofa. It was huge, and even though Gina sat at the other end, she didn't feel awkward about their nearness. Three other people could have fitted between them and, anyway, there was no other chair in the room.

Buzz had followed them in and, after a moment's observation, lay down at a safe distance, his muzzle resting on his paws.

'That's the first dog I've ever seen that didn't try to get up on the sofa,' said Nick. 'Or go for the cheese. It's smelly enough. Ah, hang on.'

He got up and returned with a couple of altar candles, which he lit and placed on the carved wooden mantelpiece, set over a more manageable fireplace than the ones in the main rooms. 'So I don't have to get up again if the lights don't come back on,' he explained.

'And your iPad? If Amanda calls back?'

Nick checked his watch. 'She's not going to now. She'll be in her afternoon meetings.'

Gina stopped slicing a piece of Cheddar. 'Seriously, though, I can make some calls and get someone out to have a look at the electrics, if you want. Last chance?'

'Yes. I'm sure. I've got torches.' Nick sank back into the sofa with a sigh. 'And if they don't come back on, it can wait until Lorcan gets here in the morning. I've had enough for today. Could you please cut me some Cheddar too? On an oatcake?'

Gina passed some cheese over and sank back into the sofa. It was extremely comfortable, and she felt her whole body relax into its cushiony embrace. The wine helped. As did the softening light from the windows, the candles' brightness intensifying in the dusk.

This is nice, she thought, surprised by the happiness wrapping around her. She hadn't felt happy like this in a long time. Not actively happy-happy, as she'd been in the park with Buzz at the weekend, a different sort of happy. More . . . content. Like there wasn't anything else to worry about.

'You're about to say something about the house,' said Nick. 'I don't want to talk about the house any more today. Let's talk about anything else.'

'OK.' Gina thought: there were lots of things she wanted to ask Nick. 'Tell me about your favourite photography assignment. What was the most interesting job you've been on?'

'Ah.' He smiled. 'Good question.'

Nick had good stories, and genuine gossip, and he didn't mind recounting anecdotes in which he was the idiot, the guy who had the wrong lens, the snapper who fell for the wind-up. He reeled off people and places without name-dropping, but Gina noticed that Amanda didn't seem to feature in any of his stories, except as a reason for him being in a particular place or with certain friends.

The light slowly faded from the room, and the candles

burned on the fireplace as they drank the wine and picked at the cheese. Nick asked how Gina's photographic project was going, and the conversation turned to photographs he wished he'd taken (of his mother, before she died, mainly), then to regrets in general.

'I try not to believe in regrets,' he said, topping up their glasses. 'Or, at least, I only regret things I didn't do, not things I did.'

'That's what all the best fridge magnets say. Fridge magnets never regret anything.'

Nick leaned into the cushions, like a cat stretching. 'Surely once something's done, it's done, and that's it. You move forward from it, instead of thinking, What if *this* had happened, or *that*?'

'But that's assuming that what's happened is all done and dusted. Sometimes the thing you regret changes too much for you to pretend it didn't happen.' She stared into her wine. 'Sometimes it changes who you are. You can't put that behind you, not without losing a part of yourself.'

He waited for a moment, then asked gently, 'So what's your biggest regret, then?'

'I ruined someone's life,' said Gina.

Chapter Nineteen

ITEM: a train ticket, return from Longhampton to Oxford, 1st July 2008

Oxford, July 2008

Gina scans the café and feels nauseous with nerves. Not only does she not know what Kit looks like now, she doesn't know exactly how disabled he is. Will they have to seat him somewhere specially accessible? Will he be able to feed himself?

Her ignorance shames her. She's only realising now how much she doesn't know. Kit gave little away in his email, just agreed a date to meet here in Oxford where he lives. Naomi didn't want to help her track him down, but unwillingly, after some pleading, she did, finding his address through her brother Shaun.

'Is this really the right time to get back in touch with Kit?' She'd gestured despairingly at the pile of appointment letters from the oncology unit on the kitchen table, filed and notated in Stuart's handwriting. 'You've got enough to think about.'

'I have to see him now,' said Gina. 'I need to sort things out.'

It had seemed so important then, but already Gina can feel this meeting slipping out of her control, away from the brave little speech she'd been running through her head since she'd made the decision to give him back the letters she's kept for so long.

They're in her bag, tied with red ribbon. Gina's been doing a lot of sorting-out lately. These past few nights, in the strange period between her operation and the full-on assault of the chemo starting, she's been thinking a lot about what would happen to her things if the cancer's worse than the doctors say. The thought of Stuart finding these letters, or Naomi burning them, makes Gina feel sick.

Kit's the only person who can decide what to do with them. They're his.

And, yes, a tiny part of her still wants him to know that she wrote. There's a younger Gina somewhere, a Gina she left behind, who needs to know that he knows so that part of her life can be tied off.

She spots him sitting by the window, and for a surreal second, Gina's heart thuds in her chest, still sore from the operation. Kit looks fine – he looks more than fine, he looks almost no different from the way she remembers him. There's no hideous injury, no supportive chair. He's wearing a white shirt with a loosened tie, and his blond hair is shorter but still tousled. The same Kit but sharper, more grown-up.

She hurries across the café, weaving through tables, eagerness making her clumsy. This would be ironic, she thinks, bubbling with relief. So *Romeo and Juliet*. Kit's actually fine, but they're meeting again because now *she*'s the one who's sick. No, she corrects herself, she's not sick. She's in the system. The cancer, and the affected lymph nodes are out. It's all been caught in time. The chemo will start in four days. She's going to be fine. Put through the mill, but fine. Don't think of the alternative.

'Kit!' she says breathlessly, then stops, two feet from the table. The dream shatters, the needle screeches off the record.

'You don't mind if I don't get up?' he asks drily, gesturing to the lightweight wheelchair he's sitting in. It looks expensive, and high tech, but it's a wheelchair, nonetheless.

'No, no, of course not.'

There's some awkwardness around the kisses.

Oh, God, she thinks, ashamed of herself. How could she have imagined this would be anything *other* than awkward? They aren't the same people they were then; they're like actors out of character, familiar but with wholly unexpected lines coming out of their mouths.

It takes Gina several minutes to stop thinking about Kit's eerily still body in the hospital bed the last time she saw him. It's amazing he's as animated as he is.

She doesn't remember asking how he is, but he tells her: he's running a website that co-ordinates holidays for disabled travellers and their carers; he lives just outside Oxford. He's been all over the world in the past few years because although he'll never regain use of his legs he doesn't see that as an obstacle, just a challenge, and, yes, he's married, of course, with two children, Ben and Amy.

A knife lands in Gina's chest at the casual mention of his family, his children, but she ploughs on, smiling.

The stranger on the other side of the table with Kit's voice and Kit's face makes her wonder, in a dazed, detached way, whether he's seeing the old her, or the grown-up Gina she's become. Apart from her wedding ring, she's no different. She hasn't done anything, none of the things she'd said she would. Kit has. He's done more.

Eventually, when Kit's CV has been thoroughly explored and Gina has pushed a disappointing Caesar salad round her plate, he pauses and looks at her with an expression that she can't read.

'So,' he says, 'what's this really about?'

'I wanted to see you,' she says.

Kit makes a here-I-am gesture, sweeping invisible crumbs down his front. This new chippiness makes Gina inwardly tearful. It's not what she remembers, but what right has she to expect that?

'I wanted to see you because I've . . .' This is the first time she's had to tell someone outside her immediate family that she has breast cancer. She emailed the HR manager at work about her sick leave. Gina presses her tongue against her teeth to focus herself. 'I've been diagnosed with, um, something pretty serious.'

'Really? And you thought you'd look me up because I might have some pearls of wisdom for you about hospitals?'

'No!'

Gina struggles to get her thoughts into a dignified order, but they scatter around her, blowing away.

He hooks an eyebrow, the first trace of the old Kit, but this time he seems angry, not amused. 'So what do you want me to say? Just because I'm in a wheelchair, it hasn't turned me into Confucius.'

'This isn't easy for me,' she blurts out, and knows immediately that it was the wrong thing to say. And then, once the floodgates are open, the wrong things start tumbling out. 'I wanted to say I'm sorry, that I honestly wanted to be there for you. And even if I didn't understand then, I think I do now and—'

Kit raises his hand, and his eyes are very tired. 'Gina, you don't understand. Let me tell you just how much you don't understand.'

And over the course of thirty agonising minutes, in which Gina is struck completely dumb, he does just that.

It's only when she's back on the train, shell-shocked, and reaching into her bag for the last packet of tissues that she realises the letters are still there. She didn't give Kit the letters.

She's horrified and relieved in equal measure.

Nick leaned forward and held her foot for a moment, in apology. The intimacy of the gesture stopped her in her tracks. 'Before you speak, you don't have to tell me,' he said. 'I'm sorry, it was an intrusive question.'

Gina swallowed. 'No, it's OK.'

He let go and sank back into the cushions, an unhurried expression on his face.

Gina hadn't told Stuart about the accident for a long time: she was scared he'd see her differently afterwards. He said all the right things, but Gina had always wondered if she'd slipped a bit on the pedestal Stuart liked to keep her on. He was quite black-and-white, especially about drinking. Another reason Janet had loved him so much.

Now, though, it felt different. She *wanted* to tell Nick: she felt instinctively that his perspectives were different, and he didn't know her. It seemed more important to be honest with him than to reveal this old self that felt so separate now.

'When I was twenty-one I was in a car crash,' she began slowly. 'It was my fault. My boyfriend was driving my car. It was an old Mini that my stepdad restored for me – it was beautiful, but no airbags.'

'Ouch,' said Nick. 'Was it a write-off?'

'Complete write-off.' Gina mimed crumpling up a piece of paper. 'He took the worst of the impact and ended up in a wheelchair. He still *is* in a wheelchair. That's a regret you can't just leave behind. There isn't a single day that goes by when I don't think about it.'

'But if he was driving, why was it your fault?'

'Because I was too drunk to drive.' She stared at the fireplace, feeling the whole story rising in her chest as if it needed to come out of its own accord. 'I'd been drinking too much anyway. I went through a bit of a party-animal phase at university – I thought it made me look cool. It was the ladette time, you know, Jack Daniel's for breakfast, cowboy hats. My dad – my biological dad – had been the life and soul of his regiment, by all accounts, so I suppose I thought I was making a connection with him. I didn't know much else about him.'

Nick said nothing.

'But I wasn't really the life and soul. I was shy – everyone else was either much cleverer or much posher than me. Most of the time I sat in my room and panicked about when they'd finally rumble me and come to kick me out. But when I'd had a few jars, I was *hilarious*. I used to go to gigs all the time, starting off with Jack Daniel's and Coke in a pint glass. The one thing that stopped me going completely off the rails was my boyfriend, but I only saw him at weekends. He was older than me, already working.' She paused. It felt weird to introduce the idea of Kit to someone new: he existed so much inside her head. 'He was called Kit. Short for Christopher.'

'How did you meet him?'

'I met him at a gig in Oxford while I was still at school. It was the real thing, for both of us. He used to come and see me at weekends, or I'd go to London to be with him. I know those sorts of relationships don't often work out, but it worked for us.'

Nick tilted his head, assessing. 'Must have been pretty serious, then.'

She smiled, knowing what it must sound like. 'I know everyone thinks their first love is *amazing* but Kit and I were one of those irritating inseparable couples. Soulmates. I felt like I'd come home when I was with him. His family were all creative – they had a beautiful house in Oxford, like something from one of those Richard Curtis films

where Mum's an artist and Dad's a famous academic . . .'
Gina's eyes travelled around the panelling, shadowy and
flickering in the candlelight. 'I suppose this house reminds
me a bit of theirs.'

She'd never made that connection before. This was
the house she and Kit would have had, if the version of
her life in which she married him and had several blond
and angelic children had happened. Not her and Stuart
at all.

'I bet it *wasn't* like this house,' said Nick. 'This house is
falling to pieces, and will soon be a residential retreat for
business types doing team building on the croquet lawn.'

Gina levered herself up on her elbow. 'What?'

He flapped a hand at her. 'Forget it, I didn't mean to
interrupt. Carry on.'

She sank back. 'I don't know why I'm telling you this.'

'Because I asked. And I'm interested. Go on. You were
telling me why you think this accident was somehow
your fault.'

Gina closed her eyes. 'Because I should have been
responsible. I put everyone in a shit position. My stepdad
had had a heart attack and he was rushed to hospital. Mum
fell to pieces. She needed me there. I was supposed to go
straight away, but I'd just got back from a garden party and
I was hammered. I'd been drinking Pimm's from a bucket
with a straw. Kit said he'd drive me.'

'Was there something wrong with the car?'

'No.'

'Did you distract him while he was driving?'

'Not really. I mean, I don't know, I was probably a bit

399

hysterical. Terry was one of those people I thought would just live for ever, you know. I didn't realise how much I loved him until . . . until it looked like I was going to miss saying goodbye.' She blinked. 'And I did miss him in the end. That's a regret.'

'But it was an accident? What happened?'

She turned her head away. That was what had tormented her for years: *she didn't know*. 'I've got no memory of it. I remember leaving the place where the car was parked, but that's it. I was in hospital for a few days under observation but I got away with a broken collarbone, whiplash, concussion and some scratches. Kit didn't. He was in intensive care for weeks.'

Nick let out a long breath but didn't speak, leaving space for Gina's words to spill out into the sympathetic silence.

'So, basically, in the absence of any other evidence, it was my fault. If Kit hadn't got into that car, he wouldn't have had the accident, he wouldn't have wound up paralysed and he'd have had the amazing career he was supposed to have. But he didn't because of me.'

'*Not* because of you,' said Nick, quietly. 'He survived, though?'

'Yes. I wasn't allowed to see him. I wrote to him after the accident but his mother sent every single one of my letters back.'

'Why?'

'She didn't think I was strong enough to deal with the future he had. So I wrote for such a long time to prove to her that I was, and she just kept sending them back. Then when I had my cancer diagnosis, and I thought I was going to die, I tracked him down and took the letters to give back to him in person.' Gina ran a hand through her hair. It was weird explaining this to someone who didn't know her and Kit, and their story. It sounded . . . a bit melodramatic, frankly. 'I wasn't thinking straight. Well, you don't, when you first hear you've got cancer. I had this feeling Kit and I had reached a sort of karmic balance – I'd got my comeuppance for the accident now.'

'Whoa. And?'

'Well. It didn't go the way I'd thought it would.' Gina's cheeks felt hot. 'He told me that I should come back when I'd actually had some treatment and understood what I was talking about.'

'Harsh,' said Nick.

'Well, looking back, he was probably right. I thought I understood, but in a way the treatment isn't the hardest part to get your head round. It's how you feel the day *after* the last session. When they're done with you, and you're on your own. No more specialists or experts to ask. Just you, but you're not the same person you were before. That's the hard part. It's over five years since my last treatment but every morning when I take my Tamoxifen, it reminds me that I'm not the same person I was before.' Gina stared at the fireplace, barely aware that she was talking. 'It's funny, isn't it? Some things just change you outright. It's not like a slow evolution, it's like . . .' She snapped her fingers, unable to find the right words. 'The second I woke up in hospital after the accident, I knew the life I'd had before had gone, but I was desperate to hold on to it. I suppose that was why I kept writing to Kit. I wanted to keep it alive. Same with the cancer, same with the divorce. You look back and it's definitely you in all the photos, but it's not you. It all feels fake. You have to keep starting again.'

'Is that such a bad thing?'

She sighed. 'I don't know. There's less and less time left to get it right.'

The words hung in the air between them, spreading like ink in a glass of water, colouring the atmosphere a darker shade. Gina didn't feel she had to explain more: the expression in Nick's eyes was sympathetic and sad.

'You never felt like going back after your chemo and telling Kit how rude he'd been?'

Had Kit been rude? He'd had reason to be.

'There didn't seem much point. And, to be honest, I was a bit crushed by the whole experience.' Gina was glad Nick couldn't see her face: her eyes were filling with tears. 'What made it worse was that while I'd been pissing about in dead-end relationships, working for the council, he'd set up his own travel company for disabled people *and* got married *and* been named Oxfordshire Business Achiever of the Year. He'd actually managed to do more with his life despite being in a wheelchair than I had in more or less perfect health. Something he was kind enough to point out to me. I mean, it's better in a way, that I *didn't* ruin his life but . . .'

Nick laughed out loud. 'He sounds a peach, this guy. That can't have helped your state of mind, days before your treatment for cancer.'

'No. It didn't.' She managed a smile. That had been what Naomi had said. *What an arse.*

Nick paused, waiting for her to say something else. When

she didn't, he said, 'But how long ago did all that happen? Ten, twelve years? It shouldn't still matter now, surely.'

Gina took a sip from her wine glass. It was good wine, nicer than any she'd had before. She thought about asking Nick what it was, then decided not to bother, in case it was so expensive she'd never buy it. 'You know when you trip over something, and you stumble to get your balance, and you do a sort of I'm-not-falling-over-honest run, in case people are watching? That's how I feel like my life's been. Ever since I didn't quite get the life I'd thought I would I've been staggering forward but . . . not neatly. Everything's just a reaction, to try to catch up with where I think I should be. I shouldn't have married Stuart, for a start.'

'Why not?'

'Because that was a classic stagger.'

Nick sighed. 'You know, it might be the wine, or it might be because it's been a long day, but I'm going to have to ask you to explain that. I mean, not if you don't want to, but . . .'

Gina drew a deep breath. 'Stuart and I were fine together as boyfriend and girlfriend. Everyone kept telling us what a great couple we made, but there was always a sort of . . . gap between us. The sort of gap you can fill with lots of holidays and projects? I kept meaning to break it off so we could both find people to make us properly happy, and then I got cancer, and we were engaged already, and he felt obliged to bring the wedding forward so no one would think he was abandoning the sick woman.'

Or in case I died.

'You do tend to project quite a lot in your relationships, don't you?'

'What do you mean?'

'Well, does your ex think he married you because you had cancer?'

'I don't know. But he's very polite, Stuart. He'd never tell me if he did.'

'Look.' Nick put his glass down on the arm of the sofa and gazed at her. 'There's no point reviewing decisions you made at the time from the perspective of where you are now. We'd never do anything. If marrying Stuart had been such a mistake, someone would have stopped you. Naomi or your mum. Or someone.'

'Oh, come on,' Gina scoffed. 'Do you know anyone who's stopped a wedding? Apart from in *The Graduate*.'

'Well, no. OK. But no one gets married thinking they'll split up.' Nick picked up his wine glass and topped it up. He was drinking faster than she was. 'You get married because it's right at the time. For the people you are at the time. You hope that you'll grow at the same rate, and you'll have your lives in common but . . .'

'But?'

'But it doesn't always work like that. Sometimes you grow apart, not in the same direction. But when you come to make a decision about whether to get out or not, you stop thinking about the moments, whether you're happy in the moments, and start looking at it as if your entire marriage is some kind of precious tapestry you have to preserve at all costs. It really isn't. That nice holiday you had in Hawaii in 2009 isn't going to keep you warm if you're not talking and haven't had sex for all of 2013, is it?'

Gina had a sudden mental picture of her relationship with Stuart embroidered into the Bayeux Tapestry. A lot of boring trips to the big Sainsbury's, their annual holidays to sunny places, then the drama of her cancer, the medics, stitched like Norman soldiers, rushing about her prone form, Stuart presiding over them. It made her giggle.

'What's funny?'

'You,' said Gina. 'I've got you so involved in bloody renovation work that you're even thinking about relationships in historic conservation terms.'

He smiled crookedly. 'I'm not sure renovation's always an option.'

She reached out for her glass. It was empty.

'Oh, God,' she said, staring at it. 'How did that happen?'

Nick looked at her from the other side of the sofa. His face was even more handsome in half-darkness, the downward slope of his eyes emphasised by the pearly candlelight. He didn't speak, but carried on reading her face with a familiar hint of a smile in his expression.

Gina felt something stirring in the middle of her chest. Wine always made her feel wistful and a bit flirty, and even though there were several cushions between her and Nick on the sofa, she was suddenly very aware of his solid form near her, the warmth of his bare feet, the dark traces of hair at the base of his ankle.

The silence grew, and the atmosphere changed with it, more than if they'd been speaking.

For God's sake, Gina! yelled a voice inside her. *Stop it! Get up! Go home! Call a cab!*

But it didn't feel inappropriate. It felt relaxing and right, as if she'd just opened her head to someone for the first time in years and they'd understood.

Nick could be a good friend, if nothing else, she told herself. They had lots in common. He didn't sound too happy about his relationship tapestry either. That Hawaiian holiday sounded quite specific. Not that it was any of her business.

'You know what I think?' he said, with a tentative smile.

'Do tell, Dr Freud.'

'I think you're waiting for someone to forgive you, and it's pointless, because the only person who can do that is yourself. It's done. Go back to Oxford, and go to all those places and see how everything is exactly the same, and the world didn't end because you made a mistake. And you should see this love of your life, who laid a guilt trip on you at the worst possible time, and tell him—' Nick stopped.

'Tell him what?'

'Tell him that you're—'

Gina's ears twitched. There was a noise, coming from downstairs, an old-fashioned American telephone noise.

'Is that your mobile ringing downstairs?' she asked, even though they both knew it was.

It rang. And rang.

The mood shifted and changed, like a flimsy soap bubble. One wrong word and it would burst. Nick's eyes didn't leave her face; she couldn't tear her gaze from his.

Gina summoned up all her self-control, imagining it rising like a twister inside herself. 'I think you should get that,' she said.

Nick held her gaze for a second longer, then said, 'You're

right. I'd kick myself if it was the council phoning about the listed building consent.' And he levered himself off the sofa and put his glass on the table.

Gina closed her eyes and sank back into the cushions as he left the room. She was tired, and the wine had gone straight to her head. Half a glass more would have tipped her over into tipsiness.

There's no way I can drive, she thought, fighting back sleep. He'll have to call me a minicab. It's not late. I'll just close my eyes for a second.

Downstairs, she could hear Nick's voice rising and falling. He wasn't shouting but there was no laughter in his voice. Was it Amanda?

It could be anyone. Nick probably had hundreds of friends, journalists, photographers, London media types; he lived in a different world when he wasn't here. She didn't know him outside this house. And yet she felt as if she did.

Maybe I *should* go back to Oxford, she thought. It wasn't so much about giving Kit the letters back as . . . what? Letting that door close properly this time? Like seeing Stuart with Bryony, it would be painful but it would mean an end to the imaginary scenarios.

Buzz got up, came a little closer to her, then grunted as he settled back down. Gina dropped her hand to feel his velvet ears, hot and soft. His biscuity smell drifted up, a sign that he too was falling asleep.

This is nice, she thought, and drifted off.

Gina was woken the next morning by sharp sunlight flooding in through the uncurtained sash windows. It was so bright she felt as if she was on stage, under the full barrage of spotlights.

She blinked and sat up, screwing up her eyes against it. Nick had thoughtfully covered her with a duvet and removed her shoes, but otherwise she was fully dressed and, apart from a slight muzziness around the eyes, not even hung-over.

I must have been tired, she thought. Two glasses of wine and I pass out on someone's sofa?

The pile of technology opposite her was blinking with a selection of red and blue lights, which suggested that the power had come back on in the night.

What time was it in New York? Was there a chance Amanda might Skype at any moment to pick up where she'd left off? What time was it here?

Gina reached down for her phone, and checked it with a groan: it was half past seven. Lorcan and the workmen were early starters, and if she didn't get a move on, there was a chance they might catch her here. She didn't want that. She wasn't even sure she wanted Nick to see her this morning.

The only thing Gina hated about being drunk was not quite knowing how she was coming across to other people. It hadn't mattered when she drank as a student because everyone else had been as out of it as she was, and they were all just trying to look 'fun'. But it was different now. Through her rosy red-wine haze, she'd seen something in Nick's face the previous night, when he examined her with those grey eyes that saw things she didn't know she was showing.

'Come on, Buzz,' she whispered, and collected her things as quietly as she could.

Gina let herself out of the house by the kitchen door, and picked her way through the cool dew of the herb garden, the morning air smelling very green. It was refreshing, and for a second she wished she had her Polaroid with her. Then she decided it was better that she didn't.

Chapter Twenty

ITEM: an antique silver locket with a folded fortune
cookie slip inside, reading 'It is never too late,
just as it is never too early'

London, May 2001

Gina thinks she's never seen anything as beautiful as the
sun fading across the London skyline, making the
pearly dots of the street lights stand out like sequins across
the curled streets and roads. It's so lovely, she almost feels
like crying.

'Happy birthday,' says Kit behind her, his arms wrapped
around her. He clinks his mini bottle of champagne against
hers. 'To the most beautiful woman in London.'

Gina glances towards the sign on the pod that specifically bans food and drink from the London Eye, then at the
other four people in it, studiously ignoring each other.

'Ignore that.' Kit hugs her tighter, hiding her bottle from
the security camera. 'This is a special occasion. Anyway,
there's much worse we could be doing up here than toast-
ing your twenty-first birthday.'

He turns her round, and Gina melts into Kit's kiss, letting

herself sink into this perfect moment. It's a relief to close her eyes and just feel, after the last few hours of relentless sensory overload.

Oxford is magical, but London is something very different. Gina's been to London many times since Kit started working here, but it still gives her a giddy sensation in the pit of her stomach. It's like being in a film. Everything is loud and bright, new and familiar at the same time. It's not the famous buildings that fascinate her – Big Ben and the Houses of Parliament, which they passed on the bus – but the plethora of real, scabby history everywhere. Creepy Victorian alleyways, the unnoticed third-floor Juliet balconies, the remnants of neon signs and horse mounting blocks; the art deco traces under high-street fascias, and the ghosts of old Underground architecture. Ghosts of people's lives, clinging to the buildings. Gina's eyes can't take it in fast enough.

Kit had sent a train ticket and a card 'entitling the bearer to one Magical Mystery Birthday Tour of London'. Since she arrived at Paddington, he's swept her around Fitzrovia, where he works; Chinatown, where they slurped noodles at high speed in a clattering café; Soho, for martinis in a crowded bar; and now they're on the London Eye, hovering high above the South Bank. Below them an electrical blanket of lights and red buses and black cabs and trees and streets. London. A million possibilities. And in the centre of this spider's web of new things, Kit is holding out his hand to show it all to her, happy to be sharing it.

He turns her back around, so she's facing out of the glass pod towards the river, and she leans against him, wrapping his arms around her. He rests his chin on her head, and it's nice to be able to hear what he's saying. The cocktail bar was so loud, lined in stainless steel, full of shiny-faced people shrieking. Gina's used to loud bars – the student union is always rammed – but the jostle was fierce, workers squeezing full value from their early evening before catching their trains home.

Here, at last, they're alone. Ish. The brief pause before they head off to a gig at Brixton Academy, then a Persian curry from a new place Kit's found, then bed.

'Having a happy birthday?' he asks, kissing her hair. His voice is hoarse from yelling.

'It's the happiest day of my life.' Gina leans back. 'You must have spent ages planning it.'

'Not at all. The hard part was deciding what not to do. There's so much else I wanted to fit in. Sure you can't stay an extra day? I could pull a sickie . . .'

'I wish I could. But I've really got to revise.' Gina's exams are looming over her, now so close that she can't actually fit the reality of them into her head. Like a huge iceberg, or the Titanic, just a sheer face of facts and stress. She deserves one day in London with Kit but two days makes her feel sick and panicky.

'Aw, sure? I wanted to take you to the National Gallery. There's an amazing Holman Hunt retrospective.' He's talking over her head, gazing out at the city below. Then his voice drops. 'So, do you think you could live here?'

Gina shivers with excitement. They haven't explicitly discussed what'll happen after her finals. Janet hopes she'll do a law conversion course 'because there's always work for lawyers'; Terry is careful not to hope anything other than she'll come home now and again, and not max out her student loan too catastrophically.

One thing Gina does know, though, is that she's not going back to Longhampton. Not now Kit's opened the door to a louder, faster, more colourful world. London scares her, and she's not sure how she'll fit in, but now she's seen it, Longhampton seems even greyer. She's somewhere between the two. Their pod rises higher over the river and she's surprised not to feel more freaked out by the height. The glass feels so safe.

'Yes,' she says. 'But I don't know what I'd do. Are you still going to be here?'

'If you are, of course I will be.' Kit is still in his venture capital job; every time he talks about leaving, he says, they give him another technology project to work on. 'I was thinking about cashing in my savings and travelling, but I'm flexible. We can do anything we want to. No ties.'

He squeezes her as he says it, and his hug releases a little butterfly of anxiety inside her: finals next year are Gina's last official hoop. After that, there are no more. All decisions, all choices are her own. Unlike Kit, she doesn't really relish the thought of that. How will she know if she's made the right choice? How will she know if she's chosen the right job, the right flat?

At least she knows she's got the right man. That's something.

'You've gone quiet,' he says.

'I'm just looking at the view.'

Millions of houses spread out beyond the thick steel

ribbon of the river. Gina imagines millions of people inside them, all slotted into routines of alarm clock, bus, work, home, sleep. And those routines slotting into bigger routines of date, marry, baby, school. The cogs ticking on and on, pushing you further into your choices, only to flick you into a different channel when you least expect it. Like it did for her mum.

The prospect of real life entices and terrifies her.

'Look,' says Kit, suddenly. 'We're at the top.'

The pod stops for a moment and Gina feels weightless, teetering not on the edge of London, but the edge of the limitless world opening up to her.

Everything's possible, good and bad, and only she can decide which way it'll go. Can I do that? she wonders frantically. How am I supposed to know if I've got it right? When will I know if I'm wrong? 'I wish we could press pause on this second,' she blurts out. 'And be this happy for ever. Here. Just us.'

'Why?' says Kit, amused. 'Everything's just about to happen. All the amazing things out there are waiting for you to find them. This is when you'll really start to live.' He nuzzles her neck. 'When *we*'ll start to live.'

Gina wants to believe him, but something inside her is resisting, telling her it's not so sure it's that simple. It would have been nicer, she thinks secretly, if he'd told her that in her cosy, shabby turret bedroom back in college, surrounded by her posters, and her vases, and her flowers. In the bed they both know so well, curled up together, breathing each other's sleepy, familiar breath.

Here, in the glass bubble over the Thames, it feels as if

there's someone else with them – the sophisticated, complicated city that Kit fits into so smoothly and Gina's slightly scared of. She already feels nostalgic for her university days and they're not even over yet.

Let go, she tells herself, as the pod begins its slow descent. Have faith in yourself, and let go.

She imagines herself swallow-diving from the top, a long graceful plunge into the murky river of royal barges and police launches.

'Gina, you can do anything you want,' Kit whispers in her ear, as if he can hear her doubts. 'You have no idea how incredible you are because you just see something and you do it. It's one of the reasons why I love you.'

Gina's whole spirit lifts as it always does when Kit tells her he loves her, and for a moment she believes him: that the world is opening to her, and the right thing will somehow rise up and make itself known, through her doubts.

This is the start of my adult life, she thinks, and kisses him until the wheel stops at the bottom for them to get out.

Gina had hoped the last box she unpacked from her old house would turn out to be symbolic, and maybe contain some mystically apt item that would sum up the past few months.

With every box that was emptied and folded up, her flat had become lighter, and so had she. For the first time in her life, Gina felt absolutely no desire to fill the spaces that emerged around her. Instead she enjoyed arranging the few objects she'd kept, looking at them properly in different places. There was room for her to spread the Sunday papers on the floor and read them at leisure while the sun streamed in through the picture window and Buzz snored raspily in his basket.

But the final box didn't contain anything very interesting. It was marked 'spare room' and it was stuffed with the random contents of the chest of drawers in their second guest bedroom. Old ripped jeans, odd socks, T-shirts 'for painting in', and Stuart's work shirts with worn collars that she'd always meant to learn how to mend. Not even a forgotten tenner in the pockets.

Gina tipped the lot into a black bin liner and took it down to the fabric recycling bank by the supermarket. And she didn't have a moment's regret about it – which, she realised on her way back, was the mystical sign she'd been looking for.

She'd discovered an ability to throw things away.

Her original plan, back in the grey days of February, had been to finish the unpacking by her birthday on 2nd May, but as it turned out, she'd done it with ten days to spare. Admittedly, there were a few racks of clothes that Naomi was supposed to be helping her to sell, and she knew she had to do a second, more ruthless edit of her wardrobe, but the wall that had once been blocked with boxes was now cleared, and decorated with her growing list of a hundred things, and the Polaroids she was taking. The spiderweb of words and images looked so good that Gina wasn't even sure she wanted to buy a big picture to hang there.

A Hundred Pieces of Me by Gina Bellamy.

- *Buzz lying paws up in the sun.*
- *The misty view from the top of the park first thing in the morning.*
- *White ducks on the dark river.*
- *An early morning bacon sandwich.*
- *My silver pedicure.*
- *The soft lilac blanket from the household shop on the high street folded over the foot of the bed.*
- *A blurry photo taken while jumping around the flat to 'Jump' by House of Pain* – it was supposed to represent dancing but she wasn't sure if it worked. Gina liked it, though. She liked the experimentation of it.

Instead of buying things to fill her flat, Gina was now obsessed with the square photos and their white borders. The Polaroid camera went everywhere with her. It had the weird effect of making her look for moments of happiness instead of waiting for them to happen. Three scarlet ladybirds on a green leaf by the river reminded her of the sun on her hair, and the secret dark green smell of the overgrown foliage as she and Buzz brushed past; a moment she'd never have noticed without Buzz or the camera.

There were forty-two photos on her wall. The forty-third, she hoped, would be of her birthday cake, because this birthday was going to be her best, even if she had to spend it alone.

In fact, maybe that was the whole point.

Gina's birthday present to herself was a day off work, and the three things that always made her happy: an early morning walk, lunch with her friends, and a really big cake from the deli.

Buzz's present was a longer-than-usual trot, all the way round the towpath past Gina's office and up through the Georgian streets of Longhampton towards the park, where the cherry blossom was cascading sugary petals over the wrought-iron gates of the gardens and the lilacs created an avenue of pale scent as she walked in.

Gina stopped for a moment to enjoy the explosion of pale pink, the sun filtering through it, and fixed it in her mind as a possible colour scheme in the flat. One bedroom wall could be that pale pink. She could do that every year, just for cherry-blossom time, where the sunlight would catch it. And it could be gold for Christmas, Aegean blue in August. Anything she liked.

She was still turning colours over in her mind's eye as she returned to the flat to get things ready for her little lunch party. Naomi had taken the day off too and was coming over with Willow, as was Rachel. She wanted to thank them, as much as anything, for getting her through the last months: with all the fairweather friends the divorce had weeded out, she was even more grateful for the ones who remained.

There was only a brief moment when Gina opened the front door to find just two birthday cards – from her mum and from an ex-work colleague who'd shared the same birthday as her – that she felt the weight of making her birthday special for herself, just like she now had to make everything special on her own, but even that evaporated when Willow burst through the door an hour or so later, followed by Naomi bearing even more bags than usual and, more or less at the same time, Rachel.

Naomi gave her an indulgent night cream ('face it, we're getting on'), and Willow had made Gina another mug with her handprint on it, a bigger one this year.

'You have to use it.' Naomi wrestled it off Gina, and poured tea into it immediately. 'No sticking it in a cupboard or on display. If it breaks, we'll make you another.'

'Of course,' said Gina. 'Even if I had a cupboard to stick it in, I wouldn't. I'm all about the using.'

Rachel brought wine and flowers and an embroidered martingale collar for Buzz 'from the girls in the shop', which again Gina put around his muscular neck as soon as it was unwrapped. There was a brass disc attached to it, ready for a name, and it was seeing the blank surface where an owner's details should be that nudged Gina into a decision she'd been toying with for a few days.

She looked up from where she was crouching by Buzz's side. 'Rachel, there's something I wanted to ask. About Buzz.'

Rachel paused, chocolate cake halfway to her mouth. 'If it's medical, ask George. I know about as much as you do.'

'No, it's about his foster place.' Gina took a deep breath and leaped into the first big decision of her new year. 'I want to adopt him,' she said. 'I've been thinking about it, and he likes it here, and I can't bear the thought of him having to adapt to another person now. Do I . . . need a licence or some sort of formal . . . whatever?'

Rachel put her plate down and clapped her hands in delight. 'No! Oh, wait, you need a formal home check.' She pretended to look around the room, under the sofa, behind a giggling Willow. 'Any cats . . . any dangerous hobbies . . . any wild animals? No, this seems to be *the perfect home*. Congratulations, I now pronounce you owner and dog.'

Naomi clapped Willow's hands together and they cheered on the sofa.

Gina's heart expanded with happiness and she slipped an arm around Buzz's barrel chest, wondering if he could tell what had just happened. He leaned against her. 'What about an adoption fee?'

'Nah.' Rachel waved an airy hand. 'Do you have any idea how much your donations have raised in the shop? Way more than we'd charge you. Consider it our gift to you, in return for your gifts to us.'

'Oh, I like that,' said Naomi. 'It's a karma balance. Happy birthday!'

'Smiling doggy!' said Willow, pointing at Buzz.

Gina looked: his top lip was pulled back from his gappy teeth in something very near a smile. But the real smile seemed to be shining from Buzz's dark eyes as he looked straight back at her, and the trust she saw in them made her own eyes fill. *From now on this is your birthday too*, she thought, wishing the words into his graceful head. *The day your life with me started.*

With Willow playing on the big chair, while Buzz watched her from a safe distance, Rachel and Naomi chatting on the sofa, Gina's flat felt small but full of life. It didn't take much, she realised. You didn't need lots of friends, just good ones.

She took the Polaroid camera out of her bag and quietly snapped the scene: her new friend, her best friend, her goddaughter, her dog, her birthday cake, her flat. Having a lovely time, filling her home with their friendship.

When the print developed, Gina wrote 'Happy Birthday to Me!' on the white border, and went to stick it to the wall. Right in the middle of the collage.

After they'd left, Gina was putting the plates in the dishwasher when the intercom bell rang. Thinking it must be Rachel or Naomi coming back for something, she pressed the button. 'What did you forget?'

'Gina? It's me,' said a man's voice. 'Can I come up?'

It was Stuart.

Gina felt a clench of resistance. She hadn't spoken to Stuart since his surprise appearance at the Hewsons' party. Rory was handling the financial paperwork, and though she'd just about got her head around the fact of the baby, Gina didn't want Stuart to spoil the gentle warmth of her birthday mood with some thoughtless request for yet another forgotten wedding gift, or worse, some sort of ham-fisted apology.

'I'm just about to go out,' she lied.

'Won't take a minute.'

Come on, Gina. Don't be churlish.

'OK,' she said. 'One minute.

'Really one minute,' she told Buzz, as Stuart's feet thudded up the stairs at a run. 'Then we'll take some cake to Nick. Good reason to go out.'

Buzz's ears twitched forward, then back again, but instead of skittering into the kitchen as he would have done a few weeks ago, he lay down by her feet, eyes fixed on the door.

When the knock came, Gina took a deep breath and opened it.

'Happy birthday,' said Stuart. He was holding a bunch of flowers – a carefully non-romantic selection from M&S. The lilies were balanced with several ornamental thistles. 'I was going to leave these, but since you're in . . . I can say happy birthday in person.'

'Thanks for remembering. It's sweet of you to take the afternoon off work to drop them off,' she said, trying to be light.

He looked awkward. 'We're, um, on our way to the hospital, actually. Check-up.'

'Oh.' She must have flinched, because Stuart seemed to check himself

'They're apology flowers too, to be honest. I wanted to say sorry,' he went on. 'About turning up at Jason and Naomi's the other weekend. We shouldn't have done that, not without warning you.'

'You're Jason's friend too,' Gina started, but he held up a hand to stop her.

'No, it was stupid. I shouldn't have brought Bryony. I don't know what I was thinking. We were on our way back from her mum's, and I suppose I just thought, maybe if you met her, we could just, I don't know, have a beer and . . .' Stuart's voice trailed off, and he shrugged at the ridiculousness of what he'd just said. 'I'm sorry.'

It was because he was happy, Gina realised. He was in that blissed-out state where nothing outside his bubble registered. Stuart had been a bit useless at anticipating other people's feelings at the best of times; he wasn't malicious, just a bit . . . unimaginative.

'Should I take it as a *compliment* that you thought I'd be fine about being ambushed by your pregnant girlfriend?' she said, and it didn't come out as jokily as she'd meant it to.

Stuart's eyes searched her face, trying to work out how sarcastic she was being. 'Well, yeah. To be honest. You seemed almost relieved when we decided to split. I thought you'd be, like, fair enough. I didn't want him. I thought you might be glad that someone else did.'

'That's what you thought?' It amazed Gina how much more observant she was about Stuart's personality now they'd split up. He really did decide how things should be, and then set about making them fit into that view. It was just that she'd always been happy to make herself fit; she didn't have to do that anymore.

'Yes! Come on, you were barely talking to me at the end.' Stuart raised his palms, as if she were being unreasonable. 'I couldn't say anything right. It was like you were determined to find a problem with everything I said. And, for what it's worth, Bryony and I didn't *plan* this baby. It just happened. But I'm glad it did. It forced us all to move on. We could have stayed like that for ever. At least this way we've both got a chance to start something new.'

Anger bubbled inside Gina, a knee-jerk resentment at his criticism, but it didn't stick. Underneath the voice of reason pointed out that he was right. They could have stayed in limbo for years, each needling the other to do something bad enough to break up over. What kind of victory was that?

It was easier to hate Stuart when he was a curt text or a

four-page legal demand. When he was just decent, familiar Stuart standing in front of her, the world's most awkward love rat, she couldn't. Gina looked at him, and his awful new beard, and his half-excited, half-terrified demeanour and couldn't be angry any more.

There had been good times for her and Stuart – the way he'd looked after her when she'd been ill, for one thing. The happy hours they'd had renovating the house, the weekends away. It would be childish to ignore that, to justify the way it had ended. She'd been lucky that he'd been there for her when she'd needed someone reliable and solid.

I'm not even angry with him for cheating, thought Gina. I'm angry with myself for not loving him enough. And what's the point in that? Why regret what you can't change now?

Stuart was braced for her response, and at the sight of his apprehension, the fight went out of her. Something in his face reminded her of Buzz. He was expecting her to be cruel, when he used to look at her with adoration. 'The wife', he'd loved calling her. Half joking, half not.

'I'm sorry,' she said.

He was thrown. '*You*'re sorry?'

'I'm sorry that it didn't work out.' Gina swallowed. 'I'm sorry you had to live through a complete nightmare with my cancer, and I never really said thank you.'

'What? You don't need to thank me for that.' Stuart seemed bemused. 'What else was I going to do? I loved you. I hated watching you suffer. It did my head in. If anything . . .' He frowned, then rolled his eyes. 'What the hell? It needs to be said. I always felt guilty that I didn't spot it before.'

'Now *that*'s ridiculous! If I didn't notice, how could you?'

'I should have felt . . .'

'Don't.' Gina raised her hands: this was what had wound her up all those years, his determination to take charge. 'It was my body. I should have noticed something wasn't right.'

'Does it matter now?' From the expression on his face, Stuart wasn't just talking about the cancer.

'No.' She tried to smile. Her emotions were blurring. 'We did our best. I hope you'll be happy. I hope you'll make each other happy. With . . . with the new baby and everything.'

'Thanks. I appreciate that.' Stuart squeezed his forehead, as if trying to rub out a headache. 'I'm just sorry if . . . You said I wasted your time. I'm sorry if I did. I hope you haven't wasted it.'

'It was your time too,' she said. 'And it wasn't wasted. Everything gets us to where we are now, right?'

She stretched out her hands. Stuart took them, folding them in his own, and gazed into her face as if he was looking for traces of what they'd once seen in each other. For a second, Gina caught a glimpse of the Stuart she'd first fancied at Naomi's party: a twentysomething football hero with nice jeans, no chat-up lines, and denim-blue eyes that would make him a handsome old man.

He squeezed her fingers. She recognised the old tenderness, and then it was gone, their history, slipping under the waters like a stone.

'Can you be sad and happy at the same time?' she said, her voice cracking.

'Dunno,' said Stuart. 'I'm not as good with words as you are. Come here.'

425

They stood and hugged goodbye without calling it that, and Gina felt lightness shiver through her, the same lightness she felt when she walked into her airy, empty flat at the end of a long day.

Thirty-four. This was what grown-up felt like. It wasn't so bad.

It had just gone three o'clock when Gina drove out to Langley St Michael and her mood lifted with every song the local station played. The sun was shining enough to warrant sunglasses for driving, she had half of the enormous birthday cake in a tin, and her dog – her very own, very first dog – was harnessed to the back seat of her car, pointy nose lifted to the gap in the window, eyes closed in sheer bliss.

There had been no comeback as yet from the detailed email Gina had sent Amanda in response to some of the queries she'd raised in her Skype conference, mainly about the roof and the letting issue. She'd been over several times since the power-cut night to liaise with Lorcan about various building schedules, and Nick had seemed fine when she'd called in. Friendly, cheerful. Just as normal, in fact. But, then, she'd been deliberately normal too.

Gina wasn't sure whether she was relieved or slightly disappointed. Relieved, she decided. Just about.

Nick was sitting out in the rear courtyard with Lorcan, his two lads and the roofers when she pulled into the circular drive. They'd obviously knocked off for the day, and were enjoying a cold drink in the sun.

'Hey!' Nick raised a can of Coke to her. 'Come and join us!'

'Half three? You've finished early, Lorcan.' Gina made a show of checking her watch. 'What time do you call this?'

'It's Friday. We've finished those joists and we're waiting on the new lead. No point starting the next phase till Monday now.'

'Slacking.' Gina pretended to sigh. 'And you're encouraging them, Nick. What can I say? Don't let them bill you for a full day. Have they tidied up?'

'This is what you pay her for.' Lorcan looked amused. 'The whip-cracking.'

'And she's very good at it. Except I can't help noticing she's very late herself.' Nick squinted up into the sun.

'This is my day off, I'll have you know. I only came to bring you a bit of birthday cake.'

'Ah, that's more like it,' said Lorcan, as Gina put the cake-tin down on the wall next to them and started cutting slices.

'It's your birthday?' said Nick. 'You didn't say!'

'I'm not big on birthdays,' said Gina. 'I'm not twelve. And before any of you suggest it, it's not a significant one.'

Nick made a pshaw noise. 'That's no reason not to treat yourself. Where's that greyhound of yours? Did you bring him?'

'He's in the car.' She hesitated. 'I should let him out – it's getting warm. Do you mind if I bring him round? He's a bit wary of men. In groups.' She glanced at Lorcan.

'Ex-racer?' His face was sympathetic, and she nodded.

'I getcha. Listen, we'll tidy up, then make a move. Monday morning, eh, Nick?' Lorcan picked up his slice of cake and got to his feet. 'And a happy birthday to you,

Gina,' he added, giving her a smacking kiss on the cheek. 'May you have many, many more to come.'

Buzz seemed happy to be back at the Magistrate's House, and strained on his lead as she took him round the gravel path to the back of the house, where the lawn stretched out like a green skating rink, as big as a couple of tennis courts together. Nick was already sitting on the stone steps with another cold Coke for her and a washing-up bowl of water for Buzz, which he thoughtfully placed on a step up so the greyhound didn't have to bend down too far. Gina unclipped his lead, and let him stretch out by her feet, the white snowflake patches on his coat shining in the sun.

'So, did Lorcan actually say the lead wasn't coming for the roof until Monday, because . . .?' she started, but Nick put a hand on her knee and squeezed it. Not in a sexy way, in a 'please, no' way. It was an easy, friendly gesture. He held it for just a second, but it was long enough for a tingle to run through Gina's leg.

'Can we *not* talk about the house?' he asked lightly. 'I've had a whole day with Lorcan discussing the pros and cons of recessed lighting, and a whole night arguing with Amanda about en suites. I just want to sit here with my cold drink and enjoy the garden.'

'Isn't whip-cracking what you pay me for?' said Gina.

'Like you said, it's your day off. It's your company I'm enjoying now, not your timetabling expertise.'

Before Gina could process the compliment, Nick chinked his Coke can against hers. 'And happy birthday. May this year be considerably better than the last.'

'That's not going to be hard. I could get shingles and it'd still be better than last year.'

'OK.' Nick turned to her, and looked her straight in the eyes with his unsettlingly straight gaze. 'May this year be the happiest year of your life, with everything you wish for, and some surprises on top. How's that?'

Gina smiled, and the wish hung in the air between them until she broke the moment by glancing down. 'It's not been a bad first day so far,' she said. 'I've had cake, I've got a dog, I've had flowers and an apology from my ex . . .'

'Oh?'

She nodded. 'We had a conversation we should have had a long time ago. You were right about regrets. They're unfair. I think we've drawn a line.'

Nick smiled. 'Good. You look happier.'

'Do I? I think maybe . . .' She jumped as Nick made a sudden sideways movement.

'Ssh,' he said, and she thought he was going to touch her, until she realised he was reaching for the Polaroid camera sticking out of her bag.

Gina turned to where he was looking and saw that while they'd been talking Buzz had made his way down to the wide lawn, which was bathed in afternoon sunlight. He was trotting as if testing the grass. Then, as his paws hit the smoother surface, he began to run, faster and faster, until he was racing around the outer edge of the lawn, all four legs stretched off the ground, covering the distance with effortless speed.

Gina held her breath, overwhelmed with the beauty of it. She'd never seen Buzz run before, and the power took her by surprise. He was a machine of muscle and sinew, graceful and economical. How long had he been penning up that energy? How long had he wanted to run, and not dared?

And why now? Was it something in the design of the gardens, or did Buzz know, somehow, that he was safe with Gina, that he could finally run free and wouldn't have to fear being abandoned again? Her throat closed.

I will never leave you, she thought fiercely. I could never leave something as beautiful and alive as you.

Nick caught one, then two, full-stretch bounds, but eventually he put the camera down.

'I just want to watch him,' he whispered.

Buzz seemed to be powered entirely by joy, flexing his racer's muscles for the pure delight of running. No traps, no muzzle, no harsh handling, no deafening track noise. Just grass under his pads and sun on his back. The weeks of proper food, augmented by the odd tin of sardines, had brought a deep sheen to his brindled grey coat, and although he was slight, the power in his front legs was plain to see as he arched and stretched, his ears flying backwards and his almost prehistoric jaw open in a smile as he sprinted in wide, ecstatic circles.

Tears were slipping down Gina's face. 'I've never seen him run like that,' she whispered, afraid the sound of her voice would distract him.

'You never let him off the lead?' Nick's breath brushed her neck.

'He never wanted to go.'

They watched the greyhound run until he slowed down to a gallop, like someone waking up from a dream. As Buzz turned the final corner he seemed to see Gina, and she stood up. Without taking his eyes off her, Buzz trotted over, panting heavily, his long pink tongue lolling out from the gap where he'd had his rotten teeth pulled out.

Gina crouched down to stroke him, and the greyhound reached up to her, laying his long head against her neck and closing his eyes. She could feel the power of the warm muscles, and the thud of his racing pulse, and the hot quick breath on her ear. Buzz suddenly chattered his teeth very close to her neck, and for a second she thought he was going to bite her, but instead he made a series of delicate, precise clicking noises.

It was something Rachel had told her about, on one of their walks around the park, something she'd only seen a greyhound do once.

'It's called nitting,' she'd said. 'They do it instead of licking. It's a sign of affection.'

Gina put her arms around the dog's neck and thanked someone somewhere for the best birthday present of all. Even anxious, scrawny dogs could still run for fun, when the sun was out and no one was watching them.

She felt Nick's hand on her shoulder, and let herself absorb the moment as much as she could, with her eyes closed and her heart open. Gina didn't want to see anything, or try to photograph it. She just wanted to remember what it felt like, inside her heart.

Chapter Twenty-one

✦

ITEM: silver platform shoes that always make
me (a) feel slim, and (b) want to dance

Longhampton Football Club Annual Dinner, August 2009

Gina peers at herself in the mirror and wants to cry. The green silk dress doesn't look anything like it did on the model in the website. And the model wasn't even a human being. Somehow this very expensive dress is managing to be too baggy and too tight at the same time.

But my shoes are fantastic, she thinks, staring at her feet, which look fabulous in the high platform sandals. The peep-toe reveals her metallic red toenails, little red jewels. Toenails, back to normal, at last.

It's an effort to stare at her feet. Gina's eyes keep flicking upwards to her chest, to see if her breasts look balanced in this dress, with its busy pattern, or up to her hair, which she still hasn't made a final decision on.

Her hair's long enough now to pass off as a radical cut, rather than the regrowth from her chemo. It's 'elfin', with longer strands around her ears, exposing the skin at the base of her neck and framing her big eyes. Not that she's feeling particularly elfin right now, thanks to the steroids – another side effect of cancer that no one likes to mention.

Gina runs a self-conscious hand through it, making strands stick up. It's grown back coarser and straighter than before, and Naomi keeps insisting that she looks like Audrey Hepburn. She doesn't, of course. She looks like Liza Minnelli during a fat phase or, more generously, Liz Taylor. But it captures an elusive thought that keeps floating round Gina's mind like a stray white feather: *I'm not the same person I was before this.*

It's not helpful, not when all of her and Stuart's energy is going into getting everything back to where it was.

'Are you nearly ready?' yells Stuart, up the stairs. He's trying to be patient, but this is a big night. 'We're going to be late!'

It's the football club annual dinner and awards night. Gina doesn't want to go. Her final treatment finished in February, and after a few weeks off to recuperate, she's back at work. She's still weary to her bones, but Stuart's getting some award for most capped player, most goals and most valuable club contributor, and since he's been the most amazing support to her, she wants to be there for him.

She's well aware that everyone will be thinking that too. *There's Gina. Doesn't she look great? Back to normal. All cured. How lovely, her and Stuart, such a supportive couple.*

Time is pressing on. The cab will be here soon. She's not delaying. She's definitely not delaying.

'If you're trying to decide what to wear, I can make the decision for you!' he yells up the stairs. 'But hurry up.

Whatever you wear you'll look beautiful,' he adds, as a slightly too late afterthought.

Gina glances at the clothes draped over the spare bed, a mess of hangers and tissue. She bought five different dresses in the summer sales, increasingly expensive ones, trying to find an outfit that will say, 'I'm fine!' for her. Something energetic and confident.

Apart from the extra stone, and the shorter hair, she looks the same from the outside, but inside Gina feels totally different. In the last year, she's been scared, fearless, lonely, humiliated, bombarded with technical information that she's absorbed in an instant: she's heard a different voice talk to the nurses, to Naomi, to herself. That person is sharper than the old Gina, but right now, she's very tired. Just for tonight, she wants things to be back to normal.

Stuart's feet bound up the stairs and he's there in the doorway of the spare room, filling it with his James Bond black tie.

The dinner jacket makes him look older, but sexier. Gina feels a burst of admiration for her husband, in his unfamiliar outfit. He's like a film star tonight, freshly shaved and hair tousled, his smooth good looks a little tired round the edges with the after-effects of this long, long year. All the other WAGs will want to touch him, kiss that clean-shaven cheek. It's just Gina who doesn't.

'Whatever you wear you'll look . . . Oh.' He stops. 'Are you wearing that?'

'Yes,' says Gina, immediately on the defensive. 'What's wrong with it?'

'Nothing.' Stuart's face clouds, as he struggles to find the words that will convey his thoughts without triggering a collapse of her precarious mood. 'It's just . . . Um, it's a black-tie do.'

'So? This is black tie. It's Issa.'

'It's quite . . .' He gestures around his neck, where his bow tie is. To Gina's irritation, it's not black silk, hand-tied, but a bright blue-and-white ready-tied job on elastic, the club's colours. 'High-necked?'

'That's the style.'

They look at Gina's reflection in the mirror, and she realises how high-necked it is. How frumpy with the necktie that looks like it's strangling her and the wild tropical print that she chose so her contours would be hidden. She looks like someone's spinster aunt at a wedding, bundled up in a curtain.

'Don't you normally wear, you know . . .?' He makes V-neck gestures over his pressed shirt front. 'More plungy stuff? What about that nice red dress? You know how much I love that.'

Gina does. Every time she wore it, in the first year of their relationship, they never made it out of the flat. However, it doesn't fit now, and she's not sure she wants to wear it anyway.

'I don't really feel comfortable in low necklines,' she says. 'I feel like people are looking at my . . . me.'

'They're not, but OK,' he says quickly. 'That's fine. Wear what you feel most comfortable in.'

Gina's torn inside between wanting to wear something sexy and familiar so Stuart'll fancy her again and, in doing so, wake up her narcoleptic libido, but she's scared that if she does he'll realise that that girl's gone. Not just the hair, but the playfulness has gone. The confidence, the patience.

'And are you going to leave your hair like that?' Stuart adds, a beat too late again.

She meets his eye in the mirror and is seized with a sudden irrational fury that he can't read her mind.

'So what do you want me to wear?' she demands. 'That red dress, and a wig?'

'Why not, if it makes you feel like your old self?' He raises his hands as if he can't see what the problem is.

'Because I'm not my old self, Stuart!'

There's a long pause, in which Gina can hear them both trying not to drop the tiny bombs that will blow up the last fraying links anchoring them together. What was there, she wonders, before the cancer and the house? What did link us together? The minibreaks?

It wasn't the conversation, she thinks bitterly. There have been times when she's tried to untangle the complicated feelings of guilt and fear that occupy her mind, but Stuart's jumped straight in with a 'think positive!' or 'don't get all morbid'. The medical care was just the start. It's not over. Not the way he wants it to be.

'Maybe you should go without me,' she says. It comes out more martyred than she'd intended it to; she genuinely thinks it might be better if Stuart went on his own, had fun, instead of worrying about her all night. He's done nothing but worry about her for months. He deserves a night off, and she deserves a night off from being worried about.

'You don't want to be there?' He turns away, then glares at her. 'Why didn't you say something before now?'

If Stuart understood me, Gina thinks, he'd laugh away this irrational, frightened mood that's got into me. He'd find a dress that I liked *and* he liked, flatter me into it and promise we'd leave by eleven. He'd make me feel it didn't really matter if I stayed and had a bath but it would make his night to have me there.

If I understood him, she thinks, I'd be able to make him see all that. But I don't know how to without him feeling I'm criticising, or that I think he's not doing enough. We don't know each other at all, and we don't even care.

This isn't how it was supposed to turn out.

A car honks downstairs: the minicab. Not any old minicab: Gina's surprise for Stuart is that it's the best minicab in Longhampton – a Bentley.

He looks at her. 'Are you coming, then? Yes or no. Decide now.'

It would have jolted her into a yes before. Now, she feels resentment answer for her.

'No. Go without me. You'll have a better time.'

'For God's . . .' He shakes his head. 'Fine. I won't be late.'

Gina begins to tell him not to leave early, but he's already thundering down the stairs.

Slowly, she takes off the four-hundred-pound Issa dress, still with its tag attached, and puts it back with the other four in the box, then shoves it on top of the wardrobe.

'Oh, you're not selling that, are you?'

Naomi pointed in amazement at the green silk maxi

dress Gina was arranging on the tailor's dummy, ready to be photographed. It still had the swing tag on it and she winced at the price.

Gina had ordered and returned a lot of clothes in the months after her final radiotherapy sessions. Her old clothes didn't fit, thanks to the weight she'd put on, and in any case, she wanted to see something different when she looked in the mirror. The trouble was, she didn't know what she wanted to see so most of her impulse buys ended up going back. The Issa one, the one that made her want to burst into tears, had stayed on top of the wardrobe and when she found it again, it was too late to get a refund.

Gina tied the pussycat bow, stood back and took a photo of it on her phone. 'Yup. I'm never going to wear it.'

'Aren't you? Why not?'

She looked at Naomi sardonically. 'Because I'm unlikely to take up ballroom dancing now, and I can count the number of black-tie dinners I've been to in the last year on the fingers of one finger.'

'Fine.' Naomi sighed, then touched the sleeve reverentially. 'But it's gorgeous. You've got such a great eye for colour. You sure I can't offer you . . .'

'It's two sizes too big for you! No. Just get on with writing it up, please.'

It was a Sunday. Jason had taken Willow to visit his parents in Worcester, and Gina and Naomi were finally going through the pile of clothes Gina had set aside to sell; the money would go on insurance and general greyhound-owning gear, of which there seemed to be a limitless supply. So far that morning, Gina had photographed two black

Vivienne Westwood dresses, a complete ski suit Stuart had encouraged her to buy for a skiing holiday they'd never had, and several wool coats.

It was odd, seeing her clothes in isolation. Even odder, hearing the descriptions Naomi was coming up with for them. It made Gina sound like a very different person. The sort of person who apparently went from office to black-tie function on a regular basis, accessorising all the way.

Naomi was still looking at the dress, playing with the tie. 'If I'm being honest, it's not your usual style, this. Did you buy it for something in particular?'

Gina sighed. 'It was that weird time after my treatment finished. I thought that if I bought enough dresses I'd want to go out. I wanted Stuart to see me as an independent person again, not the pukey, crying, moody invalid we were both getting a bit sick of.'

'Oh, Gina. He never thought of you like that.'

'It's fine,' said Gina. 'It's just a dress. It wasn't a few months ago. It was a huge guilt trip. But now it's just a dress. And it's a dress I can turn into dog insurance. So, come on. Work your sales magic.'

Naomi chewed her lip. '"This fabulous vintage Issa dress . . ."'

'It's not vintage. It's only five years old.'

'That counts as vintage. "This fabulous vintage evening dress, from the Duchess of Cambridge's favourite label, Issa, will be your go-to event statement piece for years to come."' Her fingers clacked on the keyboard. '"Featuring timeless detailing and a flattering cut that will have you pulling this luxe gown out of your wardrobe for any smart occasion.'''

'Oh, you're very good.' Gina looked at the screen. 'It's the sort of description that made me buy it in the first place.'

'Stop it, I'm tempting myself. And everything must go, right?'

'Right.'

While Naomi was filling in the specifications, Gina took photographs of the label and other details. It was soothing, doing something productive, and – she had to admit – made a change from chasing Nick's building work. She'd spent nearly all the previous day getting quotes from plasterers in preparation for the next phase of work on the Rowntrees' house; the timetable was now extending towards Christmas.

Christmas. She paused, struck by how quickly time had passed since she'd moved into this flat. Last week – in the middle of the night, to be exact – she'd plucked up the courage to email Kit, to discuss handing over his letters. It had been something Nick had said, about going back to see the town, rather than just Kit, that had made up her mind. Gina wanted to go back so she could close a door properly. Looking back, it had never just been about Kit. It had been about that precious time, living alone, learning, drinking, being free; all of that was still there, tied up with guilt about Terry's death, and she needed to let it go.

Kit had returned her email the next day, and Gina was meeting him tomorrow, in a café in the middle of Oxford. And in a way that was good, because the nerves were taking her mind off her annual check-up at the breast clinic that afternoon. That had come round sooner than she'd realised too.

Naomi looked up. 'Problem?'

'No, just . . . thinking about work.'

I'll tell her about seeing Kit after I've been, Gina thought. It'd only complicate things now.

'How's it going at the house?' Naomi finished typing and got up from the laptop. She wandered over to the wall of Gina's photographs, and inspected the new ones with interest. They were spreading out across the white space, like leaves on a tree, joined up here and there in clusters when she hadn't been able to pick just one – three of Buzz, a couple of different cappuccinos, the sky over the park in different weather – white puff cumulus, mauve-tinged herringbone streaks, inky-blue rainclouds.

'Good, thanks. Well, sort of good. I still haven't heard any more from Amanda about whether they're going to let it or live there themselves. Actually . . .' Gina frowned, thinking aloud '. . . she's gone unusually quiet. She must be busy - normally there's at least one detailed email a week, but I just get one line responses from her these days. I haven't had one of her lists since . . .'

Since the follow-up to the Skype conversation over a fortnight ago.

'She obviously trusts you to get on with things.'

'Yeah. Well, I hope so.' The alternative was too stressful to consider: that Amanda had lost interest in the house and was looking into offloading it.

'By the way, I think you've made a mistake on this photo,' said Naomi.

She'd picked one off and was waggling it at her: a Polaroid of the herb garden where bright lilac chive flowers bobbed under the blackcurrants and mint bushes – Gina had blurred the image to try to capture the slight cloud of green fragrance that rose up as she brushed past.

'You've written "the smell of wet herbs" on here, but I think what you meant to put was "hot man in shirt sleeves",' Naomi observed. 'Shall I change it for you?'

Nick was caught in the corner of the frame in his blue shirt, the sleeves rolled up to reveal his tanned forearms. He was talking to Lorcan out of shot, and his face was animated, his mouth lifted at one side, mid-smile, his hand pushed into his dark hair as he laughed.

Gina blushed. 'It's the herbs. The smell of the herbs. He was just . . . in the background.'

It was true and it wasn't. Secretly Nick was as much part of that moment for Gina as the herbs or the rain. His interest in the house, his jokes, his intent way of listening to her gave the place a special atmosphere. It was a way of sneaking Nick onto her wall, past herself and her conscience, because during the time she spent chatting to him, talking about the house over peppermint tea, explaining the secrets of the building, she was lit with an energy she hadn't felt before.

'You're blushing.'

'I'm not.' She got up and joined Naomi at the wall of photos. Without speaking, Naomi pointed at two, three, four photos where Nick's face or hands were part of the background. And one of him full frame, offering her an old red brick with a charming smile.

'That's meant to represent my love of old local materials,' said Gina, weakly.

Naomi snorted. 'You can call it what you want. I call it a very good reason to go to work right there. He's gorgeous. And an artist. And nice. That's a combo you don't see very often.'

'And he's married. And my employer.'

'Tsk.' Naomi threw her hands into the air in a details-details gesture. 'That doesn't stop you looking. It's nice to look sometimes. It must be like going to work with a Rembrandt in the front office.'

Gina stuck the photo back on the wall, next to one of the rosebeds in the park, where the scent changed from one end of it to the other. Something she'd never have noticed without Buzz to walk her past.

'You're not saying anything,' observed Naomi.

'There's nothing to say.' Gina smiled brightly. 'Except it's just a shame that the nice ones always get snapped up first.'

'There's a girl on the other side of town who said the same thing about Stuart Horsfield.'

'No!' It came out more forcefully than she meant: Gina didn't dare let the furtive middle-of-the-night thoughts take on any solidity. 'No,' she added, more gently, 'it's just a nice summer crush and . . .'

'So it's a crush!'

Gina turned away, then turned back. There wasn't much point in trying to keep things from Naomi. 'I'd rather it wasn't. Nick's a nice guy, and I hope we'll be friends when I've finished working on his house. But I don't know what's going on with him and Amanda. I don't want to ask.'

Naomi looked more serious for a second. 'I'm not saying you should have an affair with a married man, of course

443

not, but I'd rather see you have a harmless crush on a nice guy than be the I'll-never-have-another-relationship woman you were a few months ago.'

'Did I say that?'

'You did.'

Neither of them spoke for a moment. Then Naomi picked up a bag of clothes by the door. 'Do you want to do these, then we'll get some lunch?'

'No, that's going to the hospice charity shop at the hospital. I'm going to drop them off in the morning.'

'Is it tomorrow?'

Gina nodded.

'Sure you don't want me to come with you?'

'I'm sure. It's just the annual check-up – mammogram, chat with the doctor, routine stuff.' Gina tried to keep her voice calm because she knew Naomi was listening for wobbles. She liked to keep her diary full around her annual check-ups so she didn't think about the date too much, but this year, the days seemed to have padded themselves out, and she hadn't worried as she usually did. More than that, wobbles or not, she wanted to go alone. It felt like the next step. 'I'll be fine.'

Naomi tipped her head to one side. 'If you change your mind, I can take the morning off. I can easily nip up. Or meet you after?'

'Honestly, no, it's fine. I'm treating myself to a massage afterwards. Stuart and I always used to go out and buy something for the house from that reclamation place, but I thought this year I'd do something for me.' Gina nodded towards the new space around them. 'Something I won't have to dust.'

'Well, if you're sure.' Naomi frowned.

'I'm sure.' Gina reached out and squeezed Naomi's arm. 'But thank you.'

'You'd do the same for me,' said Naomi. 'What are friends for?'

The next morning, Gina left Buzz with Rachel over the road, and set off for the hospital.

She couldn't pretend even to herself that the drive to Longhampton Infirmary didn't make her heart rate rise. The line of larches up the hill. The Neapolitan houses in their colourful row. Then the concrete Spar shop by the estate, and the left turn into the hospital grounds – the seconds counting down until she'd be there. The sensation of clinging to those seconds floated up again and Gina had to remind herself that she'd been there before, three times now, and in an hour or so, it would all be over again for another year.

The familiar smell of the hospital brought back more memories as she walked through the over-bright corridors towards the oncology unit but Gina made herself focus on what was happening now. She noted they'd changed the colour scheme in the waiting area to a soothing pea green, that there was a new coffee concession, that someone had got rid of the scratchy abstract paintings down the corridor and replaced them with a mosaic rainbow.

The local hospice ran a shop around the corner from Oncology, and Gina was pleased to drop off her last bag of donations – things she'd been saving especially for them. Not all her sorting had happened in one go: there had been various items that had been hard to put in one box or another, but as she winnowed the possessions in her flat, she'd slowly felt the bonds loosen on the final items and now she was ready to let go of these last ones too.

The blue cashmere pashmina that she'd covered herself with during her chemo sessions; the soft headscarves Naomi had ordered from America for her when her scalp was still downy and she'd felt self-conscious; some real hair wigs; a pair of sheepskin slippers. Soft things that had given her a little bit of comfort during the raw days that had dragged on and on. When Gina looked into the bag, she had a clear vision of her old self, a girl who'd been braver than she'd realised at the time.

'I hope they help someone else,' she said, when she handed them over to the volunteer in at the shop, and she felt better knowing they would. Giving away those memories was a step forward for her. It didn't mean they hadn't happened. They'd always be inside her, whether she had the evidence or not.

The waiting room was full of couples, as usual – mothers and daughters, husbands and wives – but Gina noticed a few more single women than she had in the past. She settled into her seat with an interiors magazine but she'd barely had time to open it before a nurse appeared at the entrance.

'Mrs . . . um, Ms Bellamy?' She looked around and when she saw Gina, she smiled and beckoned her forward.

The butterflies surged in Gina's stomach but she smiled back, and followed the nurse into the mammogram room. On her own.

★ ★ ★

The massage therapist at the new holistic spa was very good, the oils were soothing and the background music was pleasantly unwhale-like, but in hindsight, Gina wondered if maybe a massage hadn't been the best idea as a post-check-up treat.

She lay on the couch, trying to focus on relaxation, but instead she ended up thinking. About the check-up (she'd scoured the expressions of the nurse and doctor for any twitches but had seen nothing). About her body (whether anyone would ever touch it again, besides massage therapists). About the inside of her body (and what it looked like after the chemo, whether or not her ovaries had started producing eggs yet).

To stop herself thinking about the tests, Gina allowed herself to think about Nick, away from Naomi's keen gaze. His quick grey eyes. His casual precision with details. His ability to prod her imagination into action. His dark hair, the way he pushed it off his face when he was thinking. Fine, she acknowledged to herself, with a guilty thrill, it was a crush but there was something stronger underneath it. A similarity between them that Gina knew he felt too. In a few months, Nick had gone from someone who felt like a friend to someone who actually was a friend.

I've just got to make sure that stays when the crush wears off, she thought, and felt a kind of bittersweet pleasure that she could be so rational.

The hour was up too soon, and when she was dressed and heading for home, after collecting Buzz from Rachel, Gina found herself feeling tearful, as if the massage had squeezed all her emotions to the surface. The happy wagging of Buzz's tail when he saw her arrive was nearly enough to set her off. He needs me, she thought. I make a difference to his day.

Her phone rang as she was crossing the road opposite her flat.

'Just bossy old me, I'm afraid,' said Naomi. She was trying to cover up her concern, but Gina could hear it. 'I waited as long as I could. How did it go?'

'Fine.' She wiped her nose with the back of her hand.

'Are you crying? Oh, my God, Gee. Where are you?'

'I'm in the high street. I'm just . . . emotional.'

'You stay there,' said Naomi. 'I'm coming to get you. You're having dinner with us tonight.'

'I've got Buzz with me.'

'Well, obviously he's invited too.' Naomi snorted. 'Willow would never forgive me if she missed a chance to have dinner with the smiling doggy.'

Dinner at the Hewsons' was always noisy but fun, even though now it started at six and finished with Willow's diva-like departure from the table at seven, with kisses blown in every direction.

Jason volunteered for bath duties so Gina and Naomi could talk, and when Buzz had settled himself in the kitchen, they went through to the cosy sitting room Gina had helped Naomi decorate.

'But it all went fine at the hospital?' Naomi kicked off her shoes and curled into the soft leather armchair. She peered anxiously at Gina. 'I know it's upsetting whatever they do.'

'I think so. They just ran the usual tests, asked if I'd had any new symptoms, checked my meds.' Gina turned her coffee mug round in her hands. 'It's not that. I just . . . I can never help thinking about what things *could* have been like. If I hadn't had Stuart there to support me, or if I hadn't had you. It makes me realise every year how lucky I am.' She raised her eyes to Naomi's. 'Most of the time, I forget how horrible it was, but when I go there, it comes back – how *scared* I was. Not the pain, just the sick feeling of not knowing what was coming next.'

'Listen, there's nothing wrong with taking a moment to remember all that, so you can really appreciate how strong you were, but don't dwell on it,' said Naomi. 'This year's your five-year appointment. And that's . . .'

'It's not a guarantee of anything. It just means it's in remission.' Gina tried to put the churning sensation in her stomach into words. It had retreated during supper, when Willow had shone her sunny smiles over the table, but now, alone with Naomi, rainclouds seemed to move across the back of her mind. 'I had this feeling, when I was leaving, that I shouldn't waste any more time, just in case. Didn't I promise I would *do* stuff when I got better? And what have I done? Really?'

'What? You *have* done stuff. You've set up your own business. You've got divorced and moved house. What else were you supposed to have done? Climbed Everest? Cut yourself some slack, woman.'

'No, I mean . . .' Gina's voice trailed away as the reasons slipped out of reach. Things were fine now. She did feel stronger, more in control of what happened to her, but she felt so far behind everyone else.

What is it that I feel I haven't done? Gina asked herself. Why do I feel there's something missing when I have a flat, a business? I have friends.

She thought of Buzz's tail, wagging with delight when he saw her. I want to mean something to someone, she thought. I want to be a vital piece of someone else's life too. It gave her a metallic pang inside.

'Tell me,' said Naomi. 'Come on, what's up?'

She shook her head and smiled uneasily. 'I don't know. It's the hospital. It just makes me jumpy. Every time I leave that place I can't even have a headache without worrying that it's a sign of secondaries in my brain.'

'Well, that's understandable. But look at you. The picture of health! I haven't seen you looking so good in ages. It's all the time you're spending outside staring at that roof in Langley St Michael.' A mischievous look came into Naomi's eyes and she lifted a finger. 'Aha. Don't tell me this is a ploy to make a move on Nick Rowntree under the guise of not wasting any more time.'

'No!' Gina was outraged. 'That is an appalling thing to say! In fact, of all the appalling things you've said about my breast cancer, that is almost certainly the worst.'

'Although not the most untrue.'

'It *is* untrue.' At the thought of Nick, Gina felt a wave of wistfulness sweep her, the same sadness she'd felt as a teenager, knowing she'd never see Joy Division play live. 'It's the wrong time, and in the wrong place. It's a shame. But you're right, in a way. I did come out of there this afternoon thinking I should start telling people how I feel more. You never know what's going to happen.'

'They shouldn't make you walk through A&E, for a start. That big pregnant mammal statue thing's enough to finish anyone off. They should put something nicer near the front, I reckon. Not sure what, though.'

'When were you in A&E?' Gina rolled her eyes. 'Did Jason's knee go again?'

Jason's knee was prone to 'going' during football matches. His various strappings had won their own award one year at the annual club dinner: Best Supporter.

'What?' she demanded, when Naomi didn't answer immediately. 'Come on. Tell me.'

'Um, we have news.' Naomi wriggled in her chair. 'Argh, I can't not tell you any more! It's been killing me! I wanted to wait until everything was fine with you, you know, today's appointment, but . . . guess what?' She drummed the arm of her chair.

At once Gina knew, but she played along. Excitement struggled with the distant leaden feeling of being left out. She forced it to one side.

'What? You want another shed? Give me time to get over the last one, please.'

'No, stupid. You're going to be an unofficial auntie again!'

Gina clasped her cheeks in pretend shock. 'You're having a baby?'

'Yes!' Naomi's face flushed. She looked about fourteen – excited and nervous and radiant. 'It wasn't planned exactly but . . . yes! He or she's due in January so this Christmas is going to be *soooo* boring.

'You're okay, aren't you?' she added, hastily. 'I know it's not great timing with Stuart and everything.'

'Of course I'm okay!' said Gina. 'I'm thrilled. Honestly. C'mere, give me a hug. I'm so, so pleased for you.'

They hugged in the middle of the room, and as Gina squeezed Naomi more gently than usual, her head crammed with thoughts. She was so *lucky* to have a friend like Naomi, who could make black jokes at the right time, and knew her well enough to be honest. She was starting from scratch again now, a single woman in her thirties with Tamoxifen and a business loan, but at least she had Naomi and all the love the Hewsons gave her.

But. But . . .

Underneath her arms, Naomi's shoulders rose and fell jaggedly, and when she looked, Gina saw she was crying. That was when she realised she was too.

'Why are you crying?' Gina sobbed.

'I don't know.' Naomi gulped and held her at arm's length so she could look her in the eye. Her expression was contorted with emotion. 'I'm just so glad you're still here. I'm so glad Willow gets to grow up with you around, and the new baby'll have you in its life too. I always wanted a sister growing up, but you've been so much better than that. Thinking about you at the hospital today – it's just been reminding me all day about how close we came to losing you.'

'But you didn't,' said Gina. She laughed, a squelchy sound because of the tears. 'I don't know why we're crying. There's nothing to cry about. I'm fine.'

Naomi wiped her eyes. 'It's the bloody hospital. I always come home and cry after my smear test. There's something about being up there that reminds you how easily things can go wrong.'

'And the probes,' said Gina. 'No one likes having their parts probed.'

Naomi laughed, and wiped her nose. 'No, that's true.'

They looked at each other, their smiles smudged with tears, and Gina knew it wasn't going to be easy, juggling their friendship with another baby, another demand on Naomi's time and love. But they'd work out a way of doing it. Theirs was a friendship that stretched forwards as well as backwards. It would stretch in any direction it needed to, in order to keep them together.

Chapter Twenty-two

ITEM: a thick sheaf of coloured printed garden-party
invitations for various drinks parties in New College,
Oxford from 1998–2001, hole-punched in the corner,
tied up on a yellow ribbon

Oxford, June 2001

No one has ever driven Gina's Mini apart from her, not
even Kit, and the seat doesn't go back quite far enough
for him to fold his long legs in comfortably.

But Gina's drunk too much to drive, and she's in no
state to concentrate even if she wanted to, so Kit squashes
himself in and tries to adjust the mirrors and the seat so he
can at least get it out of the tiny parking space Gina's
managed to find.

'Careful!' she says automatically, as he comes within a
whisker of scraping it against the Land Rover behind.

'OK!'

'Sorry, sorry.' It's just that she can't bear the thought of
any damage occurring to her car, if Terry isn't there to fix
it. She makes a wild bargain with the universe: if the car can
stay perfect, Terry will too.

The traffic out of town is painfully slow, and Gina can feel herself wanting to sweep the cars out of their path with one powerful backhand swipe. It's the Pimm's. Or, she concedes guiltily, not that she'll tell Kit, possibly the speed she took to wake herself up. She regretted it as soon as it was done, but it's done now. Precious minutes are ticking away, and she has no idea what's happening with Terry. He could be dead already. He could be waiting for her. Clinging on to say goodbye. That would be just like him. Waiting.

All the times she made Terry wait flash before her. Outside school discos. At the station. At Christmas.

'Why is it so slow?' She nearly weeps.

Kit's hand reaches over and covers hers. Not hard, given that the car's so small inside that his left knee is rammed against the handbrake. 'I don't want to say relax, but it's going to take us a certain amount of time to get there, and that's all there is to it. We're on the way.'

'I know.' Gina swallows. She wants to be calm but her body won't co-operate. Her heart's racing. 'I know.'

'Is your Auntie Sylvia going up to the hospital now?'

'Yes, she was just waiting for me to ring back.' Another thing to feel bad about: Auntie Sylvia having to hang around by her mother's telephone table instead of rushing to her brother's bedside, just because selfish Gina drank fishbowls of Pimm's at a garden party.

Oh, God. Is this her fault somehow? For not going to a university closer to home? For wanting to be nearer Kit?

Gina wonders if the guilt will stay with her for ever, like a scar, if she can't get home in time to see Terry. Her brain is making weird connections, the sort that seem very profound when she and Kit are stoned and listening to Radiohead but which now scare her. She feels like an astronaut, returning from outer space to the earth too fast. Her home world and her university world have always seemed like different universes, and she's been different people in them. They've never crashed into each other like this. The consequences have never occurred to her.

'Shit. Mum'll go mad if she realises I've been drinking,' she says aloud, hearing her voice slur.

'You'll have sobered up by then. I should give my mum a call when we stop for petrol,' says Kit. He has to shout a bit over the raw sound of the little engine. 'Let her know I won't be back.'

'Does she know you're with me?'

It's no secret Kit's mother hasn't grown to like Gina over the years. It's not that Anita dislikes her, she just doesn't think the relationship is going anywhere. She's made that clear on the infrequent occasions Gina's met her and she's affected surprise that Gina's still on the scene.

Kit pauses too long, and she knows that, no, Anita Atherton doesn't know where he is.

'Kit!' She glances at him – too quickly, sudden movements make her feel nauseous.

'No, it's not like that.' He frowns, and changes down to overtake a slow-moving pensioner. The Mini howls in protest at the unusually proactive driving. 'I'm supposed to be at a wedding this weekend, one of Mum's cousins, in Hampstead. I said I was going up to Oxford to see some mates, and that I'd be away till Monday.'

'You could have just told her you were with me.'

'I thought it would be easier on you if I didn't.' He glances across, anxious that she sees that he means it. 'I didn't want to get into an argument about which is most important, family or you. Obviously it's you. But she'd probably pull out some distant relative who could get me an interview at Deloitte and we'd be back into the job argument again.'

'Well, if we're going travelling, will you tell her you're with me then?'

'Of course.'

They drive for a bit, and then he glances back, a cheekier twinkle in his eyes. 'Does that mean you'll come?'

Gina's heart thuds. 'Guess so.'

It's as easy as that with Kit. Decide it; do it. When she's with him, she's the kind of girl who thinks like that too.

And then her stomach lurches again. 'If Terry pulls through.'

'He'll pull through,' says Kit. 'The quiet ones are the strongest.'

'I don't want to lose another dad,' she says, in a voice that sounds so small she's not even sure she's said it aloud.

She sees Terry in the garage, oily fingers fixing this car. Her, taking him for granted. Why does everything break?

Instead she looks down at the map. They need to get onto the A40 and from there it's straight home, but the Mini isn't used to fast roads: it shakes worryingly and the steering wheel vibrates. The few times she's taken it on the motorway, Gina's stuck to the slow lane where she can feel the car tramlining on the lorries' tracks.

'Can you stay?' she asks. Kit's starting an internship at

some banking firm on Monday; it's very prestigious. He beat hundreds of people to get it. Anita's telling everyone, apparently, even though Kit wanted to do something 'more media'.

'I wish I could,' he says. 'Maybe tonight. But I'll have to be back on Monday. You know, for work.'

'OK.'

'Gina,' says Kit. He's fiddling with his right hand, steering with the flat of his left wrist as he tries to get something off.

'Careful,' she says, as they get perilously close to the centre line.

'I'm fine.' He grabs the wheel again. 'Hold out your hand.'

She does and he drops something into it. Something warm and heavy. It's his ring, the gold signet ring he wears on his little finger. It was his granddad's.

Gina looks at Kit, heart in her mouth. Is this . . .? Does he . . .? She wishes she wasn't so drunk, that she was more ready for this moment rushing up at her.

'Gina,' he says, glancing sideways, looking for somewhere to pull over, but there are no lay-bys on this stretch of road.

'Kit, be careful,' she says. 'Please be careful.'

'I am.'

Gina is holding her breath. It's all too loud. Too fast. This isn't how it's supposed to happen. She wants this moment to slow down so she can appreciate it.

The road clears, and Kit turns to her. He's smiling. Gina thinks she's never seen him look so handsome, as if he's been carved out of marble.

'Gina, I love you,' he says. 'And I want you to wear this and remember that—'

Gina never hears the end of that sentence because without warning a tractor pulls out of a turning ahead, and as Kit fights to avoid it, the little car spins.

And spins and spins and spins, like a space shuttle returning to earth too fast, until it leaves the road and smashes into a tree, scattering glass and metal and smoke across the grassy bank.

Kit's ring bounces into the footwell of the car, then falls into the sheared-off wheel arch, and from there onto the churned mud where it's crushed by the weight of the crumpled Mini grinding it into the earth.

He was waiting for her when she arrived. Gina didn't need to scan the restaurant to find Kit this time: he'd chosen a table near the entrance and was facing the door so he could catch her eye when she walked in.

She thought he seemed older than the last time she'd seen him, more solid and flesh-and-blood. The fineness of his features had settled into a sandy handsomeness, his hair paler and a little longer. He was still in a suit but it fitted him better, less like the suit of armour it had been last time. His wide-spaced eyes and long nose were very Oxford, she thought. Kit had finally turned into the Oxford academic his mother had hoped he'd be.

He raised a hand. Gina detected a trace of anxiety in his expression, replaced by a tentative smile when she waved from the door. It surprised her to see him anxious, after how sharp he'd been last time.

'Hello,' she said, as she slid into her seat, with no kisses. 'It's nice to see you.'

As usual, Gina had thought a bit about what she was going to say on the train, but the hour she'd just spent walking through the streets of Oxford had swept everything out of her head. She hadn't expected the melancholy nostalgia of seeing the familiar landmarks with a new set of students running through them, drunk and euphoric at the end of their exams. New shops she didn't recognise next to old sandwich bars and academic outfitters; London chains where she remembered independents.

It was as if she'd never been there, or as if she'd been there in a dream, floating through, leaving no trace. Sad, and reassuring at the same time.

'It's nice to see you, too,' said Kit. 'I did wonder if I'd ever see you again. After the last time we met. I'm sorry.'

'Oh, look, that was my fault,' she started. 'It wasn't the right time to see you. I'd just had some . . .'

Kit put his hand on hers, and they both flinched at the contact, then smiled awkwardly.

Gina didn't pull hers away; he didn't move his. Eventually he patted hers and broke the contact. She felt a shimmer of sadness mixed with relief.

'Let's get it out of the way. I'm sorry for being so rude and self-righteous when I saw you last. You were ill. I was . . . horrible. It was unforgivably mean and I regret it.'

'I didn't say anything the way I wanted to either.' She fiddled with the spoon in front of her. 'It probably came across as offensive, looking you up just because I was ill myself.'

'Actually, that wasn't what made me so mean,' said Kit. 'I was going through a really driven phase. You weren't the only person I steamrollered.'

'Yeah, yeah, it's not you, it's me. That old cliché,' said Gina, without thinking, and he smiled wryly.

'I discussed it with my therapist afterwards – what exactly made me so angry with you. I think it was just that I didn't want to hear you say sorry. You were so desperate to say sorry. It's the one word I couldn't cope with at the time. Sorry meant it was your fault, and it wasn't.'

Gina looked up. Kit's brow was furrowed with awkwardness, and suddenly he seemed far more like the man she'd known, the boyfriend who'd taken such delight in discovering new things with her.

He took a long breath, then blew out his cheeks, as if gathering his thoughts in the right order.

Gina said nothing. It didn't feel odd to launch straight into this conversation, with no polite preamble about the weather or work. It felt as if they'd been waiting thirteen years for the right moment, and now it was here.

'It took me a lot longer to come to terms with the accident than it did to recover physically,' he said. 'Everyone blamed everything else – you for being drunk, the car for being too old, the traffic, the weather, British roads, everything. Everyone who came round to see me had someone else to blame. In the end, I saw this very perceptive counsellor who said that as long as I thought like that I was never going to let go of it and move on with my life because I'd always be the victim.'

'But it *was* someone's fault,' said Gina. 'It wasn't an Act of God. If it was anyone's fault it was mine.'

'I don't think so.'

'Your mum does.'

Kit shrugged. 'I'm sure your mum thinks it was mine. Mums need someone to blame and they're never going to blame you. Dad agreed with the counsellor. His counsellor said something similar. We spent a lot of time in counselling, my family. Did you get any?'

Gina shook her head. She'd had two sessions with a woman who was very sympathetic, then tried to make it all about her dead father, something Gina didn't feel was helpful. Janet had refused all offers of counselling and thrown herself into gardening and keeping Terry's half of their bedroom exactly as it was.

'Is that why she sent my letters back? Did you even know I'd written?'

Kit picked up the teaspoon on his coffee saucer. 'To be honest, I told her to do that. I didn't want to be reminded that I'd screwed your life up too. I thought it was better that I just didn't see you than you come once a week, then once a month, then twice a year.'

'But—' Gina started.

'You were twenty-one,' said Kit. 'And I couldn't even get my head around never walking again. I couldn't think about what I'd just lost. Mum only told me much later how long you wrote for, though. I felt terrible. Thinking of you writing and never getting a reply.'

The news made Gina feel cold. It went against every-thing she'd always assumed: Kit really *had* turned away from her. He hadn't wanted her letters.

'But if *you*'d told me not to write, I'd have stopped,' she said. 'I assumed your mum was keeping us apart because she hated me for ruining your life.' She winced. 'God, that sounds so melodramatic now. So self-centred.'

'It's not. You were romantic. Your letters always felt like hearing you talk, you put so much of yourself into them. But I guess I didn't want to be reminded of all that, once that life had gone. And come on. We were kids. If you can't be melodramatic then . . .'

'Sorry,' said Gina. The letters were in her handbag now. Should she even mention they were there? When she'd emailed to arrange this meeting she hadn't mentioned them; now she was beginning to be glad she hadn't.

Kit was talking again. 'While we're doing apologies, I'm sorry you got a hard time from Mum. She was over-protec-tive to begin with – she did as much as she could herself, but we had to have nurses in, and physios, the whole lot. I feel bad about it now because I got this reputation for being brave and positive about my disability, but that was mainly because she didn't let anyone see me when I was an angry mess.' He looked rueful. 'I was a really angry mess. But I didn't want anyone to see that because everyone kept going on about how brave I was. I felt like I'd be letting them down if I was anything else.'

Gina finally felt a tug of recognition. 'I know. My mum doesn't really have a clue about how bad chemo was because Stuart, my, um, my ex-husband, never let her see.

He was the only person who sat through it with me. Him and Naomi. She still thinks I made a bit of a fuss – I remember her asking how I was feeling when I'd just left the house after three straight days of throwing up every time I moved my head. I told her that the last round had been so agonising that I'd actually wondered how much worse dying would feel, and she told me I'd get nowhere with that attitude.'

Kit flashed the understanding grimace of survivor humour Gina knew too well from the occasional support group she'd been to after her discharge from the cancer unit. 'There's always someone who was *literally* about to die until he *literally* decided to pull his socks up, right?'

'Or took herbal remedies. Or started drinking nothing but pomegranate juice.'

'Yeah, magic pomegranates, thanks. Someone tell the NHS.'

He managed a laugh, and Gina felt the ghost of their old familiarity. Like the buildings outside, it reminded her of an older time, a different one. Something that had been nice when it was alive, but was gone.

'Should we get something to eat?' he asked. 'Since we're here?'

The waitress had been circling their table for a while and was now approaching again. Kit gave her a 'Two minutes?' signal that spoke of lots of lunches out, and turned back to Gina, his eyebrow raised.

'Um . . .' She struggled for a moment: she hadn't meant this to be a long meeting, just long enough to hand over the letters, but it hadn't turned out as she'd expected. Kit wasn't angry or bitter like last time, and part of her did want to stay.

Maybe if she stayed, she'd know whether or not to give him the letters.

'I'd like to catch up,' he added. 'You threw in an ex-husband there that I don't remember hearing about.' He smiled, and something about the hopeful look in his eyes, as if he too wanted to close the circle, tipped the balance.

'It's weird, isn't it?' she said, when the waitress had gone with their orders. 'Coming back.'

'How do you mean?' Kit regarded her over the top of his coffee cup.

'Well, Oxford. It's like a backdrop to a play. It's so unchanging and beautiful. Every new student who arrives thinks they're special, but really you're just passing through. Nothing changes because you're too small to change it.' Gina groped for the right words. 'I don't mean to sound negative. It wasn't a bad feeling, just . . . When I walked through college, I think I expected to be blown away with memories, but in a way it was a relief when I wasn't. It was just a very lovely place. Where someone I once was, was once.'

He smiled. 'The idea is that *you*'re the one who's meant to be changed by college, not the other way round. Unless you're Shelley or Margaret Thatcher or someone.'

That wasn't what the old Kit would have said. He'd have put himself in the same bracket.

'That's probably true,' she said. 'If it was *too* nice, we'd never leave.'

465

'I suppose it's different for me – I've been here all the time,' said Kit. 'My office is just down the road.'

'Do you get used to seeing all the new students and thinking, Oh, my God, they look so young?'

Now he looked wry. 'No.'

'Good,' said Gina. 'They made me feel very old today.'

'You don't look old,' he said. 'We're not old.'

'We are, though. We're at that point where we really should know what we're doing. It struck me walking down here – in my head I felt like one of the students, but they probably looked at me and saw a grown-up. When does that stop?' Dur, she thought. What a dumb thing to say to a married father of two, with his own business. *Stop projecting.*

'I'm sure you know what you're doing,' he said gallantly. 'Did you say you'd started your own business last time I saw you? What was it again – interior design?'

The salads arrived, and the mood changed, as Gina let Kit lead her through a description of her job this time. He seemed particularly interested in the Magistrate's House, in the building-consent side of things, and in the added value the Rowntrees' renovations would be putting on it. He was surprisingly knowledgeable about building regulations, having converted his listed vicarage into a wheelchair-friendly home, and they chatted about the house, the gardens, the options available to Nick for his studio.

The common ground made things smoother, and as they talked, two old friends joking about the intran-sigence of conservation officers and how to deal with damp, the image of an unbroken Kit and a more artistic,

Oxford-polished version of herself floated tantalisingly in front of Gina's eyes.

Would they have married? Would they have stayed here in Oxford and had angel-haired, musical children, gone home to visit Gina's mum, driven past the Magistrate's House and fallen in love with its potential? Would they have been the ones renovating it, with Kit's City salary, and her interior-design skills?

Or not, she thought. Despite the accident, or because of it, the moshpit-happy creative Kit had grown up into this man who wore suits and talked about tax relief on home offices. And what about her? Would she have taken her 2:1 and got some milk-round job in a bank or a legal firm, instead of accidentally setting up the one business that she was really good at? Would she and Kit have grown snappy with each other as the easy, carefree days of their relationship slipped further and further away and they turned into people they didn't recognise? And would she ever have been good enough for Anita?

She felt cold at the thought of living in a slowly dying dream, as the memories faded around them. Somewhere, years in the past, a tipsy Gina lay back in a punt as Kit pushed them away from the bank, and let the sunshine bleach her closed lids, oblivious to anything else but that happiness. Time had preserved that as it was. First love in amber.

'So . . . the business sounds great.' Kit looked up from his salad when she fell silent. 'How about other things – have you got kids?'

It snapped her back to reality.

'No,' she said. 'It didn't happen for us. What with one thing and another.'

He didn't get the clanging hint. Instead he gave her what Gina and Naomi called a 'new dad' look. 'It's not too late for a family, you know. There are lots of routes to parenthood. We're thinking about a third. That or a really big dog.'

'I've just got one of those,' said Gina. 'Although I think my mother would prefer a grandchild. Like I said before, she never really got her head around what the chemo actually did to the bits of me that didn't have cancer. She prefers to pretend things haven't happened.'

Kit speared the last bits of avocado on his plate, then put his fork down. 'You know, you should talk to your mother. Be honest, you're both adults. It doesn't do your relationship good to have gaps like that.'

'There's a lot she still won't talk to *me* about,' said Gina. 'Like about my dad.'

'Still? Seriously? After you've been through cancer, she still won't talk about him?'

'I think she's just one of those people who can only deal with a certain amount of emotional detail.'

He jutted his lower lip in a 'You sure?' way. 'You'd be surprised. Parental love is stronger than anything else you ever experience. Talk to her.'

Gina felt a faint irritation, and part of her was pleased because it had been going far too well. 'Not everyone has this saintly parental love I keep hearing about.'

'It could be a defence mechanism. She's had a lot to deal with over the years.'

'Well, if it is a defence mechanism, she should patent it

468

and flog it to the MoD because it's proved pretty resistant to my questions for the past twenty-odd years.'

The waitress was back, hovering beside them. Gina wondered if they were getting swifter service because Kit was in a wheelchair or because he was cutting a strikingly handsome figure in the café. Probably the latter. She'd almost forgotten he was in a wheelchair at all. The longer she spent in his company, the more his new charm emerged: it was a more conscious, harder-edged version of his old easiness. The suited version.

Would I fall for it? she wondered.

Would I, not *am I*.

'Coffee? Pudding?' said Kit.

Gina shook her head. 'No, I should make a move. If I leave the dog too long with the sitter he gets all excited and thinks he's moving in there for good.'

She still hadn't decided whether or not to give Kit the letters. They felt increasingly irrelevant but she didn't want to go home with them in her bag. And she couldn't leave them in a bin.

Kit signalled for the bill, then looked at her, as if he was trying to find the right words.

'I was glad when I saw your email this time,' he said. 'I didn't like the way we'd left things but I didn't feel it was my right to be in touch. I wasn't sure what you wanted to say – I was worried you were going to tell me the cancer had come back, and you wanted to give me the tongue-lashing you meant to give me last time, before I laid into you.'

Gina smiled. 'No.' She found herself reaching for her handbag, and the decision was made for her. 'I wanted to give you these. I've been moving into a smaller house and I found them – I couldn't throw them away.'

She put the letters on the table in front of them, tied up in their red ribbon. A solid bundle of memories, sitting between them, like something that had come up from the *Titanic*.

'The famous letters,' said Kit, half humorously. 'Really?'

'All of them. You don't have to read them, obviously, but . . . if you're going to bin them, then at least wait till I've gone.'

She watched Kit's face for a reaction but he was staring at them, a smile playing on his lips as if he couldn't decide whether to be flattered or horrified, given what he'd said before.

'They're our memories,' said Gina. 'Joint responsibility for them. I kept them. You can decide what to do with them now.'

'And what about my letters to you? Do I get those back?'

'Sorry. Mum threw them out before I got married.' Gina didn't need to say why. 'Bar the ones I kept in my old French dictionary. She never looked there.'

Kit touched the stack of envelopes reverentially, then picked them up, weighing them in his hands. 'You wrote a lot of letters.'

'I had a lot to say.' She paused. 'I loved you a lot.'

He didn't speak at first. He seemed to be struggling with more emotion than she'd seen so far under the smooth adult surface. Then he looked up, and his expression was unguarded, illuminated with snapshots of wild parties and late nights and first fumbling kisses. It wasn't because Kit wanted to relive those moments with her now, Gina knew, it was more that her presence was releasing the memories from a locked part of his mind where they'd been hidden away for years. Only she understood: those memories only existed with her. She and Kit were opening the door and letting them fly away.

'I know it's a lifetime ago, but it'll always be special to me, you know,' said Kit. 'All those things we did together. Even if I don't think about it a lot, it's still there.' He touched his chest, just above his heart. A familiar Kit gesture. Sweet. Slightly pretentious. 'Part of me.'

'I know. Part of me too.' Gina smiled. 'It was exactly what first love's supposed to be like. I'm glad it happened.'

He reached across the table, took her hand and held it this time. They sat like that for a long moment, saying nothing, until Kit cleared his throat and looked momentarily uncomfortable.

'There's one more thing I want to say before you go,' he said. 'I nearly wrote to you myself but every time I wrote it down it just looked so bloody pious. I think it's one of those things you have to say aloud.'

'Do you?' Her skin tingled, as she braced herself for something awkward.

'Yup, I do.' Kit held her gaze. 'When I saw you last time, you said it was your fault, the accident. I should have told you that it *wasn't* your fault. Or at least it was as much mine as yours. I could have got us both a taxi to the station, and taken you home on the train, and you'd have said goodbye to Terry. But I didn't. I wanted to drive you there, because I loved you – I'd have driven you even if you hadn't been pissed. I wanted to be the hero who got you home. And instead you missed him.'

Kit looked torn. Gina realised he'd been carrying that thought around in his head for the past thirteen years: she was the first person he'd been able to tell. Her hand tightened around his, and she had to force herself not to say, 'It's OK,' because she knew that wasn't what he wanted to hear, not really.

'There's no *fault*, Kit.' Her voice choked in her throat. 'We are what we are. Forgive yourself.'

He raised his eyes to hers, and an understanding passed between them. Gina felt a weight lift from her chest, and she realised it was the guilt of wanting to change the unchangeable. There was no point: it was what it was. Without warning, the accident, the bitterness towards Anita, the helplessness of loving into a painful silence – they were just scenes on the tapestry of her life. They'd happened, she'd been through them, but they no longer pinched her with the same physical regret.

She didn't want to go back. She wanted to go forward.

Kit smiled brokenly, and Gina blinked away tears. They were two adults again, two people who might be friends or who might never see each other again. Whichever way, they were linked by something that had made both of them what they were, for better or worse.

'I have to go,' she said, getting her things together. 'I really need to catch the three o'clock train.'

'I'm going to stay here a while. I might have a coffee. I've got some reading to do.' Kit put a hand on the letters and pulled them over to his side of the table. 'Don't worry,' he added. 'I've got plenty of work too.'

'Don't tell me whether you throw them away or read them,' she said quickly.

'I won't.' He tilted his head, the last in-joke. 'But thank you for writing them. I hope there are sketches.'

Gina smiled again, then turned away as an entirely new feeling swept over her. She actually wanted to get back to Longhampton.

Chapter Twenty-three

ITEM: a seashell necklace from a beach seller in Thailand

April 2007, Koh Samui, Thailand

Gina is now hotter than she's ever been in her life, to the point where she can actually feel the shell on her necklace imprinting itself onto her factor-thirtied skin.

Jason and Stuart have gone off to some kite-surfing activity, leaving Naomi and Gina on the hotel deck, where guests can choose to be shaded under umbrellas or expose themselves to the sizzling rays of the Koh Samui sunshine while Beach Ambassadors float about with trays of green drinks.

Gina's under an umbrella with a book. Naomi is basting next to her with her headphones in.

This isn't really Gina's idea of an ideal holiday (no old houses, no trains, quite a lot of lying around followed by bouts of grumpy tennis) but Jason's mate at BA got them a deal on the package, and Stuart offered to treat them with his bonus. Hard to say no, really. Gina hates the wounded look Stuart gets when she tries to explain that she'd be perfectly happy with a week in France. He thinks she's making a point about saving up for a house deposit; she's just being honest.

Gina gazes at the sea, through her duty-free sunglasses, as it glitters and sparkles in the distance beyond the hotel's decking. There's something tactile about its blueness: it could be glass or a huge pool of blue jelly. She feels a sudden urge to touch it, to see if it would be solid under her fingers.

She rolls onto her side. Naomi is lying flat on her stomach, trying to get her back the same colour as a Caramac. It's ambitious, given her pale Celtic colouring, but she's determined. So far, she's the colour of early rhubarb.

Gina leans over and pulls out one of Naomi's ear-buds. It seems she's listening to some sort of I Can Make You Calm CD, not music.

'I want a swim,' she announces.

Naomi's head lifts groggily. 'What? In the infinity pool?'

There's an infinity pool in front of them, perfectly clean and turquoise with a regular ripple every three seconds. No one's been in it in all the time they've been on the deck.

'No, in the sea.'

'Why?'

'Because I want to see if it's the same kind of sea as the one we have at home. Full of jellyfish and six-pack plastic.'

Naomi sits up and re-adjusts her triangle top, which has spent more time undone than it has tied. 'I didn't buy this bikini for swimming in, you realise. It actually said on the label that it's not meant for water-based activity.'

'I'm not asking you to swim home.' Gina stares out at the water, twinkling invitingly at her. 'I just want to feel it. I've never swum in the sea before.'

'I think the sun's gone to your head,' Naomi grumbles, but she gathers up her stuff anyway, ramming the straw Stetson over her chestnut mermaid plait and finding the complimentary hotel flip-flops, as Gina heads off down the beach towards the sea.

The sun's much hotter away from the shady decking, and Gina can feel the rays tingling on her skin. The fact that she only has thirty minutes before she burns makes it all the more urgent, and her feet slip on the soft white sand as she hurries towards the aquamarine shallows.

She gasps with delight as the first ripples of water lick her toes.

The sensation is gorgeous and she dashes in, loving the splashes that tingle on her shins. It's a private beach, and there's no one else around, so Gina undoes the sarong covering her hips and throws it back up the sand, plunging in so the water covers her knees, her pale thighs and her stomach. It's a delicious sensation, and it makes her feel naked, despite her swimsuit.

For a moment Gina stares out to sea and feels a surge of complete freedom, as if there's nothing between her and the edge of the world. She pushes on, the water now a solid weight against her legs, rising up her body, and all she can see ahead of her is the horizon, a dark blue line against the perfect cloudless Thai sky, and something inside her seems to be rising to meet it.

The sand is smooth and slippery under her feet, falling away as she carries on until she's on tiptoe, straining her calf muscles to keep in contact. With one final push, she lets herself fall into the clean embrace of the sea, like a dancer falling into the arms of a partner, and her face is submerged under the salty water, her hair floating around her as she pushes off.

Under the lazy waves it's cool and light, and it's the light that seems to fill her eyes and nose as much as the warm water. Gina's senses explode with a thousand simultaneous messages, all of which she wants to capture but can't. Instead, she sinks into the moment, feeling the power of her arms and legs as she pulses them against the heavy weightlessness of the sea, and it occurs to her that maybe this feeling of being completely connected to every muscle, every nerve in her body is what Stuart loves so much about his cycling.

But she's floating like an astronaut, not sweating and panting against gravity, and pure elation fills her. I'm *alive*, she thinks. I'm a human being, made of water and blood and muscle and bone, and I'm alive, here in a place on the planet I'd never imagined I'd be. I bought a ticket, I got on a plane, and here I am. I *can* travel on my own.

Everything is unfamiliar, except herself, and here in the water Gina suddenly sees the point of her sturdy legs, her long arms, her skin, her feet, and she's grateful for it all.

She kicks hard, and she's above the water again, shaking her head to get the sea out of her nose. The sun's hot, but her body's cooler: another gorgeous sensation.

Naomi swims up to her carefully, a cheeky grin on her face, her pink shoulders visible above the clear water. 'Can't swim too far,' she says. 'My bikini bottoms are already offending the fishes. Sea to your liking?'

Gina smiles beatifically, closes her eyes and lies back,

raising her face to the sky. She feels free, and limitless, and ready to embrace all possibilities. 'I love it,' she says.

***

Gina stared at the timetable for the coming weeks' work on the Magistrate's House and knew she was going to have to ask Nick direct: what was going on behind the scenes that she wasn't being told about?

In the space of a few months, Amanda had gone from breathing fire down her neck about delays in the consent application to not replying to any of Gina's last three emails about the house, all of which had had, Gina thought anyway, fairly interesting news about the lost objects the builders had found in the walls as well as more technical updates about the roof. Gina needed a few decisions to pass on to Lorcan, but her queries had met with nothing.

The phone calls had stopped too; there hadn't been another Skype conversation since the night of the power-cut. There hadn't even been a response to her excited forwarding of the Listed Building Consent for the whole rebuild programme – Nick had cracked open champagne for her and the builders on site the afternoon it had come through. Payments were still made on time, but the beady interest had, it seemed, evaporated.

She tapped her pencil against her teeth, no longer seeing the boxes, instead seeing Nick touching the fresh plaster, asking her question after question about his house. He was more fascinated by the place's history than ever. She had tried to broach the topic of Amanda's silence with him, hinting at workloads, wondering when she'd like to visit, but it was awkward. Nick barely mentioned her unless her name came up in direct conversation. And the closer their friendship got, the less Gina felt able to ask about something she didn't really want to know about: the state of his marriage.

She frowned at her neat flowchart of jobs for the rest of July, August, September, trying to visualise the house knitting back together with each week of plasterers, electricians, builders swarming over the wooden floors and high-ceilinged rooms, but it didn't give her the pleasure it usually did. There were too many questions lurking behind the building work.

Was Amanda negotiating to sell the house on? Did she want to live here? Weren't they happy with what she was doing?

Gina stared unseeing at her own plans. Amanda had warned her at the start that she wasn't going to be very hands-on, but her silence now was different.

Something was definitely up because now Nick had gone silent. He hadn't returned her last message about flooring for nearly three days. It had been a slightly spurious message – what she'd really wanted to tell him about was her meeting with Kit, and how positive it had made her feel – but even so, he never usually took so long.

Gina rang his mobile, but there was no answer. She tried again, still nothing. Just his cheerful message on the voicemail.

A cold feeling pooled in the base of her stomach, and she grabbed her car keys. It was time for a site visit.

★ ★ ★

When Gina reached the end of the long tree-lined drive to the house, she was surprised to see Lorcan sitting on one of the low walls outside, talking on the phone with his black eyebrows crunched together in stress.

It was only nine o'clock and already the sun was scorching the dark green leaves of the box hedges. Two of Lorcan's lads were sitting in the back of the van, texting and reading the paper out of the sun, and the roofers' van was parked next to it. The roofers were sunbathing on the croquet lawn.

'Morning!' she said. 'Shouldn't you be up on the roof or something?'

'Ah!' Lorcan looked relieved to see her. His curly black hair was flattened, a sign that he'd been pressing a hand nervously to one side of his head while making multiple phone calls. 'Finally. Someone who might know what's going on.'

'Where's Nick? Still in bed?'

'Not here.' Lorcan shook his head. 'I can't get hold of him. There's no one in the house, his car's gone, and he's not answering his phone.'

'Really?' Gina checked her watch. 'Are you sure he's not gone for an early run or something?'

'Nope. I've got a set of keys. There's no one in there. Place was locked but it's empty.' He paused, then said, reluctantly, 'I had a look round, in case he'd had an accident, but nope, nothing. He wasn't here yesterday either. I didn't mention it because it was your day off but I haven't been able to get hold of Nick since Monday.'

'Since Monday?' Gina's bad feeling intensified. Nick never went away without telling them, or at least joking about bringing them exotic delicacies from that there London. 'That's a bit weird.'

'Isn't it. I was just about to call you. Are they away?'

She reached into her bag for her phone, to see if there were any messages. Nothing. 'Not that I know of.'

Lorcan frowned. 'Could he have gone on an assignment?'

'I think he'd have told me. I mean, I think he'd have let us know,' Gina corrected herself quickly. 'Let me try him again.'

But there was no answer. She left another message, then turned back to Lorcan.

'Um, well, I guess . . . just carry on,' she said. 'I'll try to get hold of him, and update you when I can.'

He gave her a shrewd look. 'What do you reckon? Done a bunk? Inland Revenue on his tail?'

'No, no.' Gina didn't want to believe that. 'It's maybe a family emergency. I'm sure it's nothing dramatic. I'll let you know.'

'And where are you off to in the meantime?' Lorcan asked, as she turned back to her car.

Gina had a rebuild to quote on in Rosehill, another playhouse-shed to oversee for a friend of Naomi's, an interior-decorating project to discuss for a café in Longhampton. But if she were being honest, she was only interested in one job right now. 'Might take the dog for a walk,' she said.

Buzz was pleased to see Gina back early, and they went for a stroll around the shadier side of the park, where they met Rachel, looking cool in big Jackie O sunglasses, with Gem. Gina took a Polaroid of a chilly can of Diet Coke with condensation beading glassily on it, but it didn't make her feel any less sticky, and it didn't stop her mind turning worried circles either.

She was back at home in the flat, having some lunch – why not? she thought – when her phone rang.

'Hi,' said Nick. 'I've got about ten missed calls from you.'

'And the rest.' The relief at hearing his voice caught her unawares. 'Where've you been?'

There was a pause, then a sigh at the end of the phone. 'Long story. Can you come over to the house this afternoon? I need to catch up.'

'About three?'

'Great. Thanks.' He didn't even bother to make a joke. 'I'll see you then.'

Gina put the phone down thoughtfully. Buzz was watching her from under the kitchen table, his nose laid on his paws. Too hot, said his weary face.

'I'll be back later,' she told him and, almost as an afterthought, picked up the witch-ball by the front door. It didn't belong in this modern flat. It belonged somewhere older, somewhere spirits were more likely to be.

Nick was waiting at the newly painted front door of the house when Gina arrived, leaning on the frame and making such a neatly angled picture that she would have Polaroided him if she hadn't been carrying the green glass witch-ball.

'What's that?' he asked, nodding at it. 'If you're planning on putting that under my mattress, even I might spot it.'

'A witch-ball. For detecting evil forces trying to creep into your house.' She smiled but had to hold the smile when she got near enough to notice what a ragged state Nick was in.

His jaw was dusty with silvery stubble and his eyes had that gritty up-all-night appearance Gina knew well. Although his linen shirt and jeans were fresh on, he looked grey and exhausted, as if he'd caught a quick nap just before she arrived.

'You can only give them away,' she went on. 'I'm giving it to you. Well, to the house. In case the ghosts are getting upset by all the building work.'

He smiled bleakly. 'You might be a bit late on that score.'

'Why?'

Nick gestured for her to come in, and she followed him into the dust-sheeted hall, prepped ready for the specialist plasterers to start the detailed renovation of the loops and swags of the elaborate moulded ceiling. He sank onto the broad stairs, and Gina sat down next to him.

'What's happened?' she asked. 'You look terrible. If you don't mind my saying so.'

'Ha.' He rubbed his eyes. 'Haven't been to bed in a few days. I've got some news. Did you get Amanda's email?'

'No.' Gina reached for her bag, to get her phone to check, but Nick stopped her. She looked up, surprised to feel his strong fingers brush her wrist, however lightly. They made her skin tingle with a bright sensation.

'Sorry.' He lifted his hand apologetically. 'I just ... I'd just prefer you heard it from me.'

'Is it the house? Are you selling?'

'No! Not at all. It's ... me and Amanda.'

'Oh,' said Gina.

Moving? Baby? She didn't know which she wanted to hear least.

'OK.' Nick rubbed his face with his hand. 'Right. I don't know how to put this. Amanda and I have decided to separate. She's filing for divorce from me – I've volunteered to be unreasonable. Photographers often are, apparently. We've been in London since the weekend trying to work out how to handle it but, for the time being, she's going back to New York, and I'm staying here.'

'Here here, or *here* here?' Gina pointed to the parquet floor of the hall, then felt stupid.

Nick pointed at the floor. '*Here* here. I'm finishing the refurbishment, then we're going to reassess. So your job is safe.'

'I wasn't worried about my job.' She met his gaze. Nick's eyes were bloodshot, but still sharp. She wanted to touch him, to pat his arm comfortingly, but wasn't sure she should. 'Are you OK? What happened?'

He shook his head. 'Nothing's happened. Well, no – you happened.'

Gina's heart chilled. 'What? Me?'

'Don't worry, not *you* you. It was talking to you the other night, about regrets and moving on – it made me realise how *un*happy I was. And how *un*happy Amanda was. I realised we were wasting time, and none of us has time to waste, have we?'

Nick hadn't moved his gaze from her face since he started speaking, and Gina felt a low, slow heat building inside her. She tried to put up some kind of barrier to hide the confusing sensations filling her mind, but she couldn't.

It was as if Nick was reading everything about her, then and now, and things she didn't even know she was thinking.

'Amanda is determined to have a baby, and I don't want to be the dad who sees his child every two months via flights to New York. Babies don't stick relationships together. She's been "investigating her options" so it's safe to assume she's got plans laid already. With or without me.'

'And you?'

Nick said nothing but gazed at Gina for a long moment; she could read everything from the spark that flickered in his weary eyes when he looked at her.

'Do I have to say?' His lips were dry, from hours and hours of talking, and they cracked a little at the edges. Gina felt a tugging desire to run the ball of her thumb over them, then kiss them to feel their roughness against her lips, to have that mouth that said such intelligent, funny things exploring her own.

She nodded.

'I've fallen in love with someone else,' he said. 'Someone who makes me absolutely determined not to waste a single second of my life away from her.'

For a stomach-dropping instant she wondered if he was talking about someone other than her, *that he'd met someone else*, but his eyes never left hers, and the grey irises grew darker and softer as if he were trying to print her face on his mind, like a photograph. Nick's voice was breaking but he couldn't stop talking in his husky whisper.

'I met someone who's made me notice all the small things, as well as all the big things, that I like about my life.

I want to make her happy. No,' he corrected himself, 'I want to be happy *with* her. She makes herself happy.'

Gina managed a smile. The moment was stretching out, not flitting away from her. She tried to slide herself into it instead of hovering above it, framing it with her imaginary Polaroid.

'Even happy people can always do with some help.' Her own voice was husky now, echoing in the empty hall. They were whispering for no other reason than to make their own little world smaller in the big house.

Nick turned on the stairs, his long thigh pressing against her hip. Her senses were filled with his familiar Nick-smell, a mingling of washing powder, cologne and the musky maleness of his skin. Gina had surreptitiously sniffed every washing powder in Waitrose, trying to identify the right one; when she'd found Fairy non-Bio her heart had done a secret flip. But it had only been a tiny base-note of the scent that had seemed so familiar to her from the morning he'd walked up behind her outside. If it was a colour, she thought, it was dove-grey, sleepy but strong, the colour of Georgian walls, something she wanted to wrap around herself.

Nick took her wrist again, but this time he circled it gently with his hand, caressing the knobbly part with his thumb.

'You're bringing this house back to life,' he said softly, more to her wrist than to her face. 'And the way you do it is so thoughtful it moves something inside me. The way you show me what to fix, what's rotten, what needs replacing. What to cut out, what's precious. You have no idea how incredible you are when you're running your hands over some oak, or telling me the story of some stone.'

He lifted the wrist up to his lips and kissed the blue veins on the inside. A million shivers of electricity ran up Gina's arm, tingling into every part of her.

Nick was giving her every chance to stop this, she thought. He was giving her a moment to say, 'No, this is too weird, too soon, too unprofessional.' But it wasn't any of those things. It felt completely right, as if every other wrong step in her life had been leading to the centre of a dark green private maze in the middle of this falling-down, magnificent house.

Gina turned, giving in to the longing to feel the dry heat of Nick's lips, and pressed her mouth against his. He hesitated briefly, then she felt him slide a hand around the small of her back to pull her closer. The kiss was sweet and soft for a moment, then Gina's lips parted and it became something more urgent and yielding as her own hands reached for him, wrapping around his back, then tangling into his hair.

They kissed as if everything else had vanished around them, and Gina felt a sense of utter happiness she'd never experienced before. It was like floating, weightless, the same euphoria she'd once felt in a tropical sea, of being completely supported but at the same time lighter than air.

She felt a buzzing in her back pocket. 'My phone's ringing.'

'Ignore it,' Nick murmured into her neck, pressing kisses into the hollow where her scent gathered in the hot weather.

'That's not very professional. What if it's Keith Hurst?' She laughed into his mouth.

'Oh, go on, then . . .' Nick released her, but only far enough for her to get her phone out of her jeans. He carried on burying his nose in the soft skin behind her ear while she answered it on the other side.

'Stop it,' she muttered happily, batting him away. 'Hello?'

'Is that Georgina Bellamy?'

'Yes.' Something in the voice made her sit up straighter. It was an official voice, one that rang a distant alarm bell in the back of her mind.

'This is Catherine Roscoe from Longhampton Infimary breast clinic. Is this a good moment to talk?'

Gina pulled away properly, and put a finger in the other ear to hear better. Reception was mutinously bad in the old house. 'Um, no, but go on.'

'I'm sorry. It's regarding the annual appointment you attended on Monday – I wonder if you could come in and have some further tests this week?'

'This week?'

'Yes, we'd like to schedule them as soon as possible. Are you available tomorrow lunchtime?'

Gina's insides hollowed out. Tomorrow lunchtime. That wasn't a routine test. That was urgent. That was . . .

'Yes,' she said, and her voice sounded strangled. She coughed. 'What time?'

Nick was staring at her, already conscious that something wasn't right. He frowned, silently asking what was wrong, and Gina turned away, unable to stop the childish rage at the wrongness of it. She squeezed her eyes tight shut, bowing her head to ward off the emotion crushing her as if it might go away.

Not now. Not now, she begged the universe. Not now she had just found this man, this incredible feeling of joy. Please, not the hospital.

'Could you manage twelve o'clock?'

'Twelve o'clock,' she repeated mechanically. 'And do I need to bring anything?'

'No, that'll be fine.' The nurse carried on talking in her soothing manner, about tests and directions and car parks, but Gina wasn't listening. The blood was roaring in her ears.

Further tests. At best, a new kind of cancer to carve out and scorch with chemotherapy. At worst . . . Her mind turned away from the bleak fact, which her eye had skimmed in so many leaflets, but she made herself think it. At worst, a recurrence of the old cancer, somewhere else. And there was no treatment for secondaries, only what the leaflets euphemistically called 'management'.

Or it could be nothing, pleaded a lone voice inside. It could be nothing.

But Gina had been through this before: hope was more slippery to cling to, knowing what she knew now. 'Nothing' didn't need immediate tests.

The phone slipped from her hand, and somehow she managed to catch it before it bounced on the stairs and cracked onto the wooden floor below.

'Gina, what is it?' Nick grabbed her wrist. 'What's happened?'

'I've got to go in for tests.' She corrected herself. 'More tests. After my routine appointment.'

'When?'

489

'Tomorrow lunchtime.' Saying it made it real, and Gina felt the ground lurch sickeningly away from her.

'I'll take you,' said Nick at once, and something in his expression caught her, the instinctive way she'd caught her phone. She felt held. Safe with him. 'What time?'

She shook her head. 'I don't want you to take me.'

'Really. What time? It's fine. I've got nothing else I'd rather do. You can't go alone. I can make notes, if you want. If you need someone there to ask questions.' Nick reached for her but she pulled away. 'What? What did I say?'

'Nothing.' Gina covered her face and tried to pull her racing thoughts together. Nick wasn't Stuart, and she wasn't the person she'd been that time around. This wouldn't be exactly the same. It couldn't be. For one thing, she knew what would happen next, one way or another. This time, she could do it on her own. She was a different person.

She took her hands away from her face and gazed straight into Nick's eyes. 'I don't want you to feel sorry for me,' she said fiercely. 'I don't want you to organise me, and I don't want you to feel you have to be there because I'm sick.'

'Not this again,' said Nick. 'Let other people worry about how they feel about you. You just concentrate on what you feel. What *you* want. I want to help you. You don't have to let me, but I want to. What can *I* do to make the bit *you* have to do easier?'

Gina managed a watery smile, then it froze. 'Will you look after Buzz?'

'Tomorrow? Sure.'

'No, I mean if . . . if they find something and I can't

manage? I can't bear the thought of him going back into a rescue, wondering why I abandoned him. Just when he started to trust humans again.'

It was the mental picture of a miserable Buzz roaming the park searching for her after she'd gone, the eight years that George had said he had left of his better new life, that suddenly made it real for Gina. What if she didn't *have* eight years? The tears came from nowhere. Nick wrapped his arms round her and let her sob into his shoulder, stroking her head and murmuring into her hair.

'Why don't we meet you after your appointment, in the park?' he said. 'Me and Buzz. It's going to be a perfect June day. We'll have a picnic ready, and we'll wait there until you're finished – we're in no rush – and then we'll drink cider in the sunshine and eat cake and look up at the clouds, and just enjoy being in the sun together. Whatever happens.' He dropped a kiss on her head and Gina felt cocooned in a warmth that crept into all the cracks of fear in her heart. It didn't make the fear go away, but it strengthened her.

She breathed in the smell of the Magistrate's House: the old plaster, the fresh new wood, the dust and beeswax, the years of human love and fear, the dogs and children that had run through the parquet halls since it was built. It had weak spots and decay but it still stood.

'I know this isn't ideal,' Nick went on, 'but something about it feels really right. Like this house did, the first time I saw it. Sometimes people come into your life at strange times, and you don't know why, but then it turns out that they're the exact right person for that moment. Don't you think?'

Gina nodded into the soft linen of his clean shirt, then raised her head. I need to get into this picture, she thought. Not watch it, be in it. 'I wish this was a better moment,' she said. 'But this is what we've got. I don't want to waste it.'

'Me neither.'

There was a long pause, then Gina leaned forward and kissed Nick, urgently and hungrily. He kissed her back, hands reaching around her waist, her hip, stroking and exploring her curves, and then they broke off, breathing each other's hot, quick breath, their mouths only a hair's breadth apart.

'Here?' whispered Nick. He didn't need to explain; she knew what she wanted too.

Gina thought, then said, 'No. Not here. My flat.' She smiled, filled with a weird elation. 'There's nothing in my flat. No history. Just us.'

Nothing for the witch-ball to see.

Nick slipped her hand into his, and they half walked, half ran to Gina's car, Buzz loping happily alongside.

Chapter Twenty-four

ITEM: a silver Mini Cooper on a key-ring, with two keys and a photo of Gina and Terry standing by her green Mini with white stripes over the bonnet, tearing up her L-plates, taken at a slight slant by Janet on Terry's new SLR camera

Hartley, January, 1998

Gina's stepdad Terry is doing something to the engine of the Mini, while Gina sits in the corner of the garage, pretending to make notes on *Macbeth* but really finishing a four-page letter to Kit.

Minnie's nearly finished, she writes, already on page four. *Terry keeps trying to explain how it all works and I keep nodding but it's not really going in. I keep imagining me and you in it. It's just big enough for the road trip. Not sure we could get it on the plane but I reckon we could get as far as Brighton. We'd have to talk in American accents and pretend Little Chef was Dairy Queen but . . .*

She stops and looks at what she's written. They have nicknames for everything: they call Kit's car (nearly new Volvo, used to belong to his mum) the Beast, but Gina's car so far hasn't been named. Is Love Bug better than Minnie? Is Love Bug . . . too much?

Love still makes her stomach twist, sending silvery ripples through her whole body. Before Gina met Kit 'love' was just a word, empty and over-familiar like 'house' or 'brilliant', but now it's unexpectedly bursting with magic and flowers and darker pleasures. Gina barely uses the word to refer to things like bands or cake any more. Her whole vocabulary's been scaled down in its honour.

A surreptitious rustle of cake packaging means Terry's helping himself to the last Bakewell tart.

Gina glances over at her stepdad, ready to tease him gently about his overalls splitting. Since Terry offered to rebuild the car for her, out of the blue, they've spent much more time together. Not talking, just . . . being. They've even developed a few in-jokes of their own.

The Mini came from the garage of the old lady across the road who'd died just before Christmas. Gina had spotted it on the drive, being photographed for the small ads, and was struck by the Atherton-ish kudos of having an *old* old car instead of the third-hand Corsa Naomi's dad had got for her to learn in. This car is a bit of the 1970s, which is maybe why Terry likes it. It had only 6,043 miles on the clock, and homemade cotton covers stretched over the seats, pink cartoon Martini glasses protecting green leather-look plastic.

'It'll be good for you to know how a car works while you're learning,' had been his exact words, but Gina wonders if actually Terry was looking for an excuse to spend time in the garage, in peace. Since then the pair of them have enjoyed many companionable evenings with a packet of Bakewell tarts and the local radio filling in the gaps between Terry's occasional car-mechanics tutorials. Gina writes her long, emotional letters to Kit while pretending to revise, and Terry tinkers with head gaskets; the productive silence humming between them is so much nicer than the increasingly tense conversations her mum initiates about revision and university and why she's spending so much time 'with Naomi' these days when Naomi almost never comes round to their house any more.

Gina now associates the smell of oil and WD40 and instant coffee and artificial cherry flavouring with a deep sense of peace and, of course, Kit.

I've been looking at the gig guide for next month and we could—

'You'll be careful in this car, won't you, love?'

Gina glances up from her letter, and sees Terry gazing at her with an awkward expression twisting his sandy moustache. He looks like a teddy bear who's had his scarf nicked. She's seen Terry's worried face a lot lately. He's always worried about something, but never likes to overstep the mark, on account of him not being her dad. 'Course I will,' she says cheerfully. 'Anyway, the rate we're going I'm not likely to be driving it till I'm forty, am I?'

He smiles, and Gina goes back to her letter, pleased she's defused that one. She starts to sketch him – Kit's really encouraging of her drawing, and thinks she should go to art college – but when she glances up, Terry's still looking at her.

'Why'd you ask?' she carries on, determined to keep

things jokey. 'Are you scared I'll make you take me out driving?'

'No.' Terry wipes the engine head. 'I'm sure you'll be as good at driving as you are at everything else, love. It's just that I had a car like this when I wasn't that much older than you are now. It's bringing it all back.'

Gina says nothing, but gets the impression Terry's trying to share something important with her, in his tentative way. The garage seems to bring out these unexpected revelations, like the bits of old newspaper she sometimes finds in the car itself. Normally they're just nice little things about her mum, glimpses of a funnier, gentler woman than the one constantly on her case about teenage alcoholism, but this time Terry is looking at her, and she folds her book down, just in case he can see the letter.

'And you weren't very careful?' she prompts.

'No.'

'I don't believe that.' She tries a smile. This is strange new adult territory they're negotiating, very cautiously, over the Mini's friendly rounded roofline. But then she is an adult. She's seventeen.

Gina can tell this personal-advice business is killing Terry, but he's determined to get it out. 'Young men aren't always careful. Even nice young fellas. And I don't mean with cars, love. I mean with . . . people's feelings.'

There's a world of concern under those bushy grey eyebrows: concern and love and a hint that maybe Terry knows more about her secret relationship with Kit than he's letting on. It checks her more than a million lectures from

Janet, and a tiny grain of doubt creeps into the rosy glow that surrounds Kit.

'*I*'m careful, though, Terry,' she says, and they blush the same blush, as the other implication lands. He doesn't mean what *he* thinks *she* thinks he means – cringe – he means, in general. And Gina wants to tell him that Kit is careful with her heart, careful not to make promises he can't keep, although she's quite happy to promise him the rest of her life because, as far as she's concerned, she's met the one. Straight away. No precious time wasted.

But she can't tell Terry that. Because he'll tell her mum, and her mum will go insane.

'Don't tell Mum,' she says, without knowing why.

'You're very precious to your mother, Georgina,' says Terry. 'She might not tell you often enough, but it's true. You're precious to us both. Her, because you're her little girl and me . . .' He pauses. 'Me, because, well, you've let me have a go at being a dad. In a way. We're both so proud of you. You've got the whole world ahead of you.'

He looks mortified but proud as he says it, and Gina wants to hug him. The car, Terry, Kit, these winter revision nights . . . she has an instinct that this will feel warm one day, when she's looking back on it. It's all ahead of her, all ready to happen. Her car, Kit, her future.

But the Mini is in the way, blocking the small garage, and her English folder is on her knee. So she smiles, and says, 'I know, Terry.'

Terry gazes at her, and Gina thinks he looks tired.

It's on the tip of her tongue to add, *I love you*, but that's really not his thing, so she blows him a kiss instead, and

Terry pretends to catch it, just like he did when she was small enough not to be embarrassed.

Gina's appointment was midday, and at Nick's insistence, while he was getting breakfast croissants from the deli over the road, she called Naomi and told her.

'I want to come,' Naomi said at once, in her determined voice. 'No buts, Gee, I'm coming. I'll be there at the hospital at ten to, and I'll wait for you. It's like church weddings: they can't throw members of the public out.'

'Fine,' said Gina. She didn't have the heart to argue, and secretly she was relieved.

'Happy now?' she added to Nick, when she put the phone down.

'Almost.' He put the bag of pastries on the counter and flicked on the kettle. 'Did you phone your mum?'

Gina started to argue but, deep down, again, she knew he was right. This time – if there was going to be a 'this time' – it would be different. This time she was going to be honest about it all.

Janet sounded surprised to hear from Gina outside their usual calling times and happily agreed to a morning coffee, on the condition that Gina didn't mind leaving by eleven thirty, as she had a Gardeners' Club lunch in Chippenham Avenue.

'Now drink this,' said Nick, pushing a cup of coffee at her. 'And eat this. Or at least pretend to eat it, and feed it to the dog while I'm not looking.'

Buzz watched them anxiously from the basket. He hadn't touched his breakfast. Gina tried not to read his subdued body language as being any kind of Sign, and failed.

'Let me get my things ready first.' She checked she had her phone, purse, lipstick. Everything ready to put her face back together afterwards. She needed to keep moving, keep her hands busy so her brain wouldn't think. 'You just be there with the picnic this afternoon. I'll text you to let you know when I'm leaving.'

'I can take you to your mother's if you want.' He checked his watch. 'I don't have to be there for Lorcan, he knows what he's doing . . .'

Gina stopped packing. 'No. No, for that I really have to go on my own.'

'Fair enough.' He got up and kissed her on the forehead. 'I know you're in safe hands with Naomi. And we'll be waiting. There's no rush.'

Gina noticed all the flowers on the way to her mother's house. The poppy splashes in front gardens, the very late bluebells banking the roadside. The black-and-white house on Church Lane was ripe with pink fuchsias; the new owners had invested heavily in hanging baskets, something, Gina thought randomly, that would please her mother, although the fuchsias inside them wouldn't – they'd always been on the 'common' list, along with red-hot pokers and pampas grass.

Little shards of memories were whirling back to Gina all the time, as if she had to remember them before it was too late.

Janet had the kettle boiled ready when she walked in, and for once Gina was glad. There would never be enough time for this, but she knew she had to get away before her nerves went.

'It's lovely to have a surprise visit from you, love. Did you see the hanging baskets on number seven Church Lane on your way over?' Janet called over her shoulder, as she tiled the biscuits. 'What did you think? I'd have thought some nice white trailing sweet peas would have been more in keeping.'

She sounded so unusually jolly that Gina felt even worse about what she had to say. Do I have to tell her now? Can't it wait another half-day? In case it's nothing? Terry would tell her, she thought. Terry understood that things had to come out eventually.

'Mum,' she said, gently. 'There's something I need to talk to you about. I've been up to the hospital this week.'

Janet turned round, and her expression was hopeful. 'Is this about that egg business?'

'No.' Gina motioned to the kitchen table, where she was sitting with her cup of tea. 'I went for my annual check-up on Monday. They called me in again today to run some more tests.'

The moment stretched out into a silence. Janet's eyes didn't leave Gina's but they grew slowly more round.

'Mum,' she prompted. 'Come and sit down.'

Janet clutched the plate of biscuits and walked stiffly to the table. The ring of chocolate digestives sat between them like a sort of talisman. 'But that doesn't necessarily mean anything, does it?' she said. Not a question. A statement.

'They're always mucking things up. They had to do my blood-sugar tests three times before they got a proper reading. This'll be like that, won't it?'

'I don't know. They wouldn't call me in if they weren't worried about something. I'm not saying there is something but . . . I think it's better to be prepared. They've promised to get back to me as soon as they possibly can about the results. I should know after the weekend.'

Janet's mouth formed, 'Georgina,' but nothing came out.

Gina could hear a faint chattering sound: it was Janet's wedding ring jittering against the china mug as her hands shook. She seemed to have shrunk back in her chair, as if the cancer was there in the room with them.

'But you'll be fine, love, won't you?' Janet insisted, her voice brighter than her expression. 'They'll do what they did last time, pop you on that chemotherapy treatment and – and what-have-you.'

She really has no idea, thought Gina. The weight of it pressed down on her shoulders; now she had to tell her, with no Stuart here to help.

'It depends.' For a second, she thought about sugar-coating it but there was no point. This was going to happen at some stage. Better that they both got used to the idea now. 'It depends if the biopsy detects something, and it depends where it is. And whether it's a recurrence or something new. Fingers crossed it's nothing. Or at least something they can treat quickly.' Gina made the corners of her mouth pull up, even though the last thing she felt like doing was smiling. Be brave, she thought.

Janet's shoulders dropped. She smiled, a ghoulish puppet

sort of smile, then her face crumpled and she put her hands up to her face and sobbed.

'Mum?' Gina hesitated, then put her tea to one side, stood up and crouched by her mother's chair, half expecting to be batted away.

Janet did wave her away, then slumped back, and let Gina put her arms around her. They sat there, Gina perched to the side of Janet's chair, while her mother wept.

Oh my God, she knows, Gina realised. She knows much more than she's been letting on. Maybe she was being brave for me, not the other way around.

They weren't the quick, angry tears Naomi had cried the first time she'd told her; they were uncomfortable, heartbreaking sobs, like an animal keening, and Gina felt as if her own insides were being torn away. She'd never heard her mother cry like this. Janet had always prided herself on her self-control. But all Janet's mourning for Terry had happened while Gina was in hospital herself, recovering from the crash. By the time she'd been discharged, whatever grief Janet had suffered had been controlled, banked down into the low simmer of misery she had maintained ever since.

This sounded like grief. It sounded to Gina's ears as if she'd already died, and a tiny part of her felt irrationally angry.

'Come on, Mum,' she said. 'I'm still here.'

She stroked Janet's back through her cashmere cardigan, her best one for Gardeners' Club, and felt the bird-like sharpness of her bones. Gina didn't have much left to bolster Janet today; her own tears were rising to the surface again.

She made herself think of Nick, of the picnic waiting for her in the park after the tests. All she had to do was get through the next few hours. Break them down into minutes, she thought desperately. One at a time.

I've done this before, she told herself. I can do it again. Little bit by little bit.

'Please, Mum,' she said, rubbing her shoulder. 'It's just more tests. Let's try to think positive. I just wanted to tell you so you were . . . prepared this time.'

Janet gulped, and sat up. It took her a while to get her breathing under control, but Gina waited.

'You always were such a coper,' Janet said eventually, wiping her eyes with the side of her finger. 'Even when you were a little girl. I can remember when I came back from Huw's . . . from your dad's funeral. You'd made me some cakes with your Auntie Gloria. Your little face.' Her face crumpled. 'Your little face . . . wanting to make things better for me with your cakes.'

Gina was momentarily distracted from the absurdity of a three-year-old 'coping' by this new revelation. Janet had never mentioned Gina's dad's funeral before.

'That was Dad's funeral? I didn't know you'd been to a funeral,' she said. 'I thought you'd been away on holiday.'

'Well, what could we tell you? You were too young to understand.'

Gina looked at her mother, her eyes glazed as she replayed a moment in her mind that she was in but had no memory of. What else hadn't she told her? Surely it was time her mother shared some of those memories of her father. Gina thought of the memory box she'd already started making for Willow, with notes and photos and stories about her and Naomi and their adventures together, before and after Willow had come along. Real memories, not borrowed ones from aunts' albums.

'You were wearing your little yellow pinafore with the sunflower pocket,' Janet went on, staring into space. 'I kept it. It's still in the attic, in a box.'

'You kept it?'

'I kept all your baby things. I wanted to pass them on to your children.' Janet bit her lip, struggling. 'I always hoped . . . I know I haven't been the mother I wanted to be. We don't have the relationship I thought I'd have with a daughter, and that's not all your fault, Gina. I thought that maybe if you had children I'd have another chance to do it again. Better.'

'Or you could just try a bit harder with the daughter you've got?' It was out of Gina's mouth before she had time to realise she was speaking, not thinking. 'You never share things with me.' Her voice trembled. 'Why did you never tell me that story about me and the cakes until now? Why won't you share anything about your relationship with Dad? Like when I was born. It's part of *me*. You don't want to talk about anything difficult. But that's half my life! You can't just pretend it didn't happen, Mum. I'm *here*!'

Gina's randomly swinging moods were pummelling her again. The uncontainable rage that came and went had swept back in, and she knew she shouldn't be directing it at her mother, but it was as if she was possessed by something else. Something bigger and angrier than she was. It was the stress of the tests, she hoped. Maybe it was easier for them both to get angry about something else. She didn't have infinite time to hear these things about her dad. And if Janet didn't tell her them, then he would disappear.

Janet closed her eyes. 'Sometimes you're very like your father, Georgina.'

'Am I?' demanded Gina. 'How? And don't tell me because I'm brave. He was a soldier, he didn't have a choice. I don't have a choice either.'

'He wasn't brave. He was reckless. And he was cruel.'

'It was his job!'

'You didn't know him.' Janet bunched her hands into fists. 'I had to grow up listening to you wanting to turn him into a saint, and I let you, because I thought it was the very least I could do, making you grow up without a dad. But because of him I was *worried* about you, Georgina, all your life. I worried about him when he was on duty, I worried about him when he went off and couldn't tell me where. I worried because . . .'

'Because what?'

'Because sometimes I wondered who exactly I'd married.' Janet's eyes were strained with the effort of admitting something hard. 'And Huw died before I ever felt I knew him properly, and then I didn't know which parts of your father were going to come out in you. Like that drinking phase you went through, it worried me sick. And I'm sorry if you think I disapproved of you and Kit, but I didn't want you to make my mistakes.'

'What were your mistakes?' A cold feeling settled on Gina. 'Are you saying I was a mistake?'

Janet recoiled. 'What? No! You were the best thing in my

life. You *are* the best thing in my life. My girl. My beautiful girl.' She grabbed Gina's hands, and the ferocity in her eyes was shocking.

They stared at each other, and Janet seemed to be struggling with herself.

'What do you remember about your father?' she asked.

Gina was thrown by the change of tack. 'I remember him being tall,' she said. 'I remember him taking you to the races. With that swing tag you had for the enclosure that he gave me. I remember him smelling of tobacco and that big navy wool coat he had. But that's about it. I wish I remembered more.'

Janet took a couple of shuddering breaths, and Gina knew there was something she didn't know, that her mother was deliberating about whether to tell her. A darkness closed over her, sharpened with curiosity.

'Mum?' she said. 'Tell me. Whatever it is, I need to hear it. I'm not ten any more. Tell me about my dad.'

The irony of Janet keeping unpalatable truths from her while she'd hidden behind Stuart's version of her chemo didn't escape Gina.

Janet twisted her ring around her finger. 'Well, he was tall. Dark hair, like yours, lots of it. I was always having to cut it to keep it army-regulation length. He had a lovely laugh – very deep and Welsh. Your gran used to say he sounded just like Tom Jones. I met him in the local pub when he was stationed near where we lived. He was a bit older than me, nearly thirty. Swept me off my feet, quite literally. We were mad about each other. And he decided we had to get married, so we did.'

That much Gina had more or less guessed for herself. 'But that's all right . . . isn't it?'

'That was all fine. If he hadn't been in the army.' Janet stared at her ring. 'Not even just the army. Huw always wanted to be in the SAS. That was his ambition – he said it was the only way to get the proper experience of soldiering, even if it meant going into dangerous places. Being married didn't change that. We'd only been married four months when he finally passed the selection process, which was why we moved up to Leominster.'

She paused. 'And that was when I realised just how much your father could drink. He wasn't always violent, just . . . went into himself. My dad never drank so I'd never seen a man drunk before. But by that time I was on my own with him. I didn't know much about army life. I didn't know much about life at all – I was only twenty-one. Huw was a nice man, but he'd seen things I hadn't.'

Gina held her breath, stunned. It had never occurred to her that there might be reasons like this for the gaps in the story. Mum not *wanting* to remember. A very different Janet started to take shape in her imagination: not a mum, a young girl, scared, newly married. 'Mum, you don't have to . . .'

'You said you wanted to know about your father.' Janet's lips were set in a line.

Gina nodded unhappily.

'Anyway, you came along. I thought maybe having a baby might calm him down a bit, make him see there were more important things in life than going on SAS missions. He adored you. He really did – I'm not making that up. You were the apple of his eye. He used to carry your photo around everywhere, his lovely baby with his brown curly hair. Things were all right for a bit. He went to South Africa and trained troops, instead of getting posted to Northern Ireland – that was where all the dangerous business was going on, undercover with the IRA. And then I found out . . .' Janet stared out of the window. 'I found out just before your third birthday party that he'd volunteered to be sent out there. Actually volunteered.'

Janet's fingers tensed around Gina's hand.

'It's really bad that the army wouldn't tell you what happened, Mum,' she said, trying to meet her in the middle. 'Don't they owe you that, at least? Can't we find out now so many years have passed?'

Janet shook her head, and Gina couldn't read her expression. It was tight and angry and sad all at the same time. 'They wouldn't give us any information because they don't know themselves. Your father wasn't where he was supposed to be when he died. He'd . . . gone off somewhere, acting on his own initiative, they said. Which is fine and dandy when it works out, of course. When it's doesn't, they suddenly won't tell you a thing.'

Gina's whole body tensed, braced against what was coming next.

'I asked who I could – but they wouldn't tell me anything.' Janet looked haunted. 'Huw was always reckless, but drink made him think he was invincible. And they were all deep undercover, they had to be with the IRA. It took the unit a long time to find out where they'd taken him . . .' She covered her mouth with her hand, then said, 'There was no body to bury.'

The tension released and Gina felt herself fall like a stone inside. Her dad, the handsome, smiling man in the Ascot photograph, half her DNA, half her personality, dying alone, undercover somewhere in Belfast.

'He knew he was going into danger,' said Janet, bitterly. 'He knew there was a real danger he'd be killed, and he still went. We weren't enough. It was bad enough letting me down, but I'll never forgive him for leaving you.'

'Mum—'

'Don't even think about saying it was for the greater good. I was twenty-five, a widow with a little girl, and I had to go home to my parents – who hadn't wanted me to marry him in the first place, believe me – and start again. Huw had no family – they were all ex-regiment anyway, which was why he'd gone in himself. That was why we never talked about it. It was easier to forget. What could I tell you if you asked? Nothing. I didn't know anything, and I was heart-broken, and angry, Georgina.'

'But how could you just forget all about it when you had *me*?'

Janet flinched as if the words had physically slammed into her. 'Oh, Georgina, because *you* made it all worthwhile. You were my reason for getting up in the morning. Your little hands on my face, your smile when I took you out to the park.' Her mouth contorted as she struggled to smile and not cry. 'We were such good friends when you were little, you and me. Such good friends.'

A lump formed in Gina's throat at the yearning in her mother's voice.

'When you started school, and I couldn't be with you all

the time, that was when I started to worry about you. You were such a daredevil. Climbing things, jumping off things, no fear at all. I worried that you'd got your father's recklessness. I worried you'd got his temper too. I couldn't bear the thought of anything happening to you. It used to make me sick, worrying that you'd get a taste for drink at school. That you wouldn't know when to stop either. I probably worried far too much but I couldn't help it. I felt like I hadn't worried *enough* before and look what had happened.'

Gina felt ashamed of the hours she'd spent moaning to Naomi about her mother's paranoid questions and curfews. 'Didn't you talk to anyone about it?'

She snorted. 'Who'd I talk to? No, I just got on with it. Terry was good, though. He understood. He'd have made a good father, Terry.'

'He *was* a good father,' protested Gina. 'He was a lovely father to me.'

Janet looked up, as if Gina had said something unexpected. 'Was he?'

Gina nodded. 'Of course he was.'

They sat for a moment, letting the words sink in as fresh ghosts moved between them. Huw Pritchard, now fleshed out into three dimensions, headstrong and dangerous. Janet as a devastated young widow, left alone with a baby at the same age Gina had been drinking wine in central London bars. And baby Gina, reckless. Gina didn't remember being reckless. She'd always thought she'd been too rule-following, if anything.

There's so much I've never asked, thought Gina, and

suddenly she wanted to. She needed to know her mother better.

'I know I was hard on you growing up.' Janet's voice was sorrowful. 'But I couldn't stop myself. You were so young when you met Kit – all I could think of was how trusting I'd been at your age. I thought I knew everything. When you were in that accident, they could have taken any part of me to keep you alive. My heart, my liver, anything. I'd have had your cancer a hundred times over, if I could have had it instead of you.' She looked at Gina with red, anguished eyes. 'You know I'd have it now, if I could. My beautiful little girl.'

Gina gulped and flung her arms around her mother, unable to bear the pain in her voice. 'I'm sorry,' she sobbed, into Janet's hair. 'I'm sorry, Mum.'

'I don't know how to tell you how much I love you.' Janet was struggling to get the words out. 'I used to pray you'd have a baby so you'd be able to experience all the love I had for you, and maybe it would have brought us closer. I got it wrong. I didn't mean to hurt you about it. I didn't realise it would be painful for you.' She looked tortured. 'Oh, Georgina. When you were little it was so easy – we'd just cuddle and put everything right. Soon as you were growing up, I didn't know how to talk to you any more. We never seemed to hear what the other one was saying. But I still loved you. So much.'

'I should have told you more,' said Gina. Her mouth was wobbling; she could barely form the words. 'I shouldn't have kept things from you.'

'Georgina.' Janet rested her cheek on Gina's, as she used

to when Gina was a child, after the bedtime story. 'You'll always be a part of me.'

Gina squeezed her eyes shut. Then she opened them, because she didn't want to look at what was crowding her mind. 'Mum, they're only tests,' she said. 'You've got me for ages yet.'

'Not long enough,' said Janet. She gazed at Gina as if she was seeing her for the first time. She was, thought Gina. Like I am. 'There'll never be enough time for me to be with you.'

Gina buried her head in her mother's chest and let the tensions and fears of the past days out, and felt Janet's arms tighten around her, as if she could keep every bad thought away.

Chapter Twenty-five

Gina didn't know if it was her, or some strange weather effect, but as she walked through the wrought-iron gates into the park, the light seemed two shades too bright, like sunshine trapped under a dark raincloud a few minutes before a storm. All the colours around her felt so intense they hurt her eyes: the roses in the beds were a deep velvety red, the leaves a glossy emerald. The grass had been mown and the fresh green smell reminded her of banana sandwiches, of summer-afternoon sunbathing after games with Naomi, a smell you could almost taste.

The warmth of the afternoon had thickened the air. It hummed with bees making their way from one unfurling flower head to another, and now the sound of the offices turning out started to filter through as well. The park was filling with people, ready for the weekend in their rolled-up sleeves and bare legs. Gina smelled sun lotion and office sweat and perfume and the tangy smell of barbecue from the grill restaurant on the high street.

Her skin tingled as she felt herself opening up to take it all in. The soft heat pressing on her face, the distant barking of dogs in the wood mingling with the muffled sound of traffic nearly blocked out by the dense hedges, the crunch of the gravel underfoot. It was too loud, too bright, too hot, too detailed, but she wanted to let it flood into her and be part of her.

I need to be aware of every single moment, she thought fiercely. I need this to be part of me. I need to be here.

She had made herself focus on every moment at the hospital. Gina was determined not to detach as she had six years ago, letting Stuart ask the questions while she floated somewhere above herself. As she'd promised, Naomi had met her outside with a notebook and a checklist, insisting that she'd ask any questions Gina didn't feel up to, but this time Gina had been the one to stay calm in the room while Naomi sat stunned next to her. Gina knew what the answers would be now: it made the questions easier to ask when they couldn't tell her anything she didn't already know.

There were more tests, another biopsy, ultrasounds, a scan. A squeeze of the hand from Naomi, two coffees that went cold, undrunk, a dark snigger at the horoscopes in the glossy mags Naomi had brought to read while they waited. The nurses were kind and cheerful, and Gina kept her mind focused on the picnic waiting for her on the hill, in an hour, half an hour, ten minutes, until it was over, and they were walking through the white corridors, out into the sunshine.

Naomi hugged her by the directions board, rocking her from side to side. 'You're amazing,' she'd managed through the tears. Then they'd giggled about the awful pregnant-woman statue in Reception, that looked like a Moomin, then hugged and hugged again for several long minutes, saying nothing.

'It'll be fine,' said Gina, and Naomi wiped away her tears and nodded through a watery smile.

And now Gina was walking through the gates of the park it was as if everything was erupting around her, summer condensed into one intoxicating afternoon as if it, too, had to pack in as much as possible to one perfect day.

Gina could see them at the top of the hill: Nick sitting on a large tartan blanket with Buzz lying next to him. She wondered where he'd got it from, that blanket and the *Wizard of Oz* picnic basket.

It's like Kit said, she thought. I don't have to do it all at once. I just need to get through today, and today, and today, and make it the best I can.

Nick saw her – Gina knew she was easy to spot in her favourite red sundress, the one with polka dots and the gypsy neckline that made her feel like she was on holiday. She was wearing her lucky knickers too, her expensive perfume, her best lipstick, her favourite shoes. Enjoying them, not hoarding them for some imaginary day in the future.

He raised a hand and waved, and she waved back, and he had to grab Buzz's collar to stop him rushing down the hill to greet his mistress. Then he let go, and Gina watched Buzz bounding towards her with a soaring heart.

And maybe it'll be fine, Gina thought. Maybe it won't. But I know what I've got to do this time, and I did it once. I can do it again. And this time I've got some real happiness with me, true happiness, for however long.

She caught Buzz's collar, and stroked his ears in greeting but as she looked up the hill to where Nick was opening the cider, the unfairness nearly tripped her up. It *was* unfair.

Nick was the man she'd waited her whole life to meet, a man who made her want to do things, visit things, see things. Not show her, like Kit, or tell her, like Stuart. Someone who'd help her be her best self. And just as he'd reached out, the ground had shifted underneath them both.

But who knows how long anyone has anything for? she argued. I've got love, and a home, and a dog, and a job. Naomi, and Mum, and Willow, and myself.

Nick waved again. Her heart turned over and began to lift, like a balloon slipping out of a child's hand, up into the sky, a red dot against the clouds.

Gina set off up the hill, Buzz by her side, and as she made her way along the path, out of the warm bowl of the park, a soft breeze brushed her bare arms. It was a delicious, caressing sensation that made her aware of each hair.

She had the Polaroid camera in her pocket, and she took it out, ready to capture the moment but something stopped her.

Nick rose, ready to ask how she was, what had happened, but she put a finger on her lips. Slowly, deliberately, Gina walked into the picture, closing her eyes as she felt Nick's arms go around her, Buzz's cold black nose rest against her leg and the yellow sunshine warm the crushed grass around their blanket.

Gina clicked the shutter in her mind. Forget about what came before, or what's going to come. Focus on this exact moment, when you've got everything you need: this is living.

Now.

Now.

And *now*.

Acknowledgements

A Hundred Pieces of Me has been a very personal and sometimes hard story to write, and I'm grateful to my sensitive and skilful editor, Francesca Best, and my unfailingly brilliant agent, Lizzy Kremer, for their patience and encouragement over the past months, as well as the wonderful teams at both Hodder and David Higham Associates. I'm grateful too to Andrew Pugh and the renovation specialists who hacked plaster off the walls really quietly, made their own tea, and answered every dim question about render several times until I understood what they were on about. Any howling mistakes about old buildings are definitely not theirs.

Making my own Hundred Pieces of Me board has made me appreciate all the things that bring me happiness, big and small – Herdwick sheep, Herefordshire sunsets, coffees with my best friend, the new Routemaster buses, toast – but at the top of my list is my parents' windswept haven of peace on the Irish Sea; they taught me that you don't need things to remind you of love, when you have it in your heart all the time.

@lucy_dillon   LucyDillonBooks

Lucy Dillon

Lucy Dillon lives in a ramshackle Georgian farmhouse (less Pemberley, more Miss Marple) in a village just outside Hereford, where she writes novels in between meeting the daily requirements of her dogs, and keeping out of the way of the builders. After nearly a year of renovations, she's learned enough to know that it's best left to the experts. She can, however, tell you more than you need to know about lime plaster. And that Classic FM on headphones drowns out the sound of most building work, apart from drilling.

Lucy grew up in Cumbria and often goes back, particularly for the annual, highly competitive local agricultural show where her ginger biscuits are unbeaten. Her long-term ambition is to be placed in the rum butter class. At school, she wrote a play about Mary, Queen of Scots, which apparently only had two major historical inaccuracies, and edited the school magazine, all of which set her up for her first job after university, in publishing. Working for a fiction editor taught her some invaluable lessons about how books are written, then re-written, and then re-re-written, as well as how satisfying it is to watch a pile of pages magically turn into a novel you can hold in a bookshop and read in the bath.

A Hundred Pieces of Me is Lucy Dillon's fifth novel for Hodder & Stoughton. None of the characters are based on her family, or her builders, although the dogs might recognise themselves a bit.

If you were starting over with only your most treasured possessions, what would you keep?

Here are a just few of things *I'd* always hang on to . . .

My Herdwick sheep egg cups

My grandmother's engagement ring

The hippo my mum knitted for me

My big puppy dog

Head over to my Facebook page to see more 'pieces of me', and share yours on Facebook or Twitter with the hashtag **#100piecesofme** – I'd love to see them!

LUCY x

 LucyDillonBooks lucy_dillon

A Q&A with Lucy Dillon

What would be at the top of your list of a hundred things?

Top of my 100 things list would be my dogs, Violet and Bonham – they bring a lot of happiness into my life, not just with their lugubrious expressions and wrinkly feet that smell of biscuits, but because every time we go out for a walk, I notice something that I'd probably have missed otherwise – a pink-streaked sunset, or fat blackberries in the hedges, or the change in the air when spring's coming or summer's fading. They're good company, and are always pleased to see me, and they're beautiful to watch when they're tracking an invisible scent, ears flapping and tails up like question marks.

What is your earliest childhood memory?

Playing on the beach outside my parents' house in Seascale – the smell of salt, and sea rosehips, and Ambre Solaire SPF50 suncream, and hot sand, and the sound of the waves in the distance. I know it must have been 1976 because it never seemed to be that warm again for a long time.

Do you collect anything?

I collect old romance novels – I love those old-fashioned dust jackets with winsome nurses in clinches with handsome doctors. And Vivienne Westwood shoes (they're quite rare in a size 8), old postcards of the village I grew up in, costume jewellery, cookery books, especially American ones from the 50s and 60s ... I sympathise with Gina and her houseful of boxes.

When was the last time you wrote or received a handwritten letter?

I'm a bit old-fashioned about postcards: I have a box of them on my desk by my computer with some stamps, and I try to send them instead of thank you emails or texts. It's always nicer to get post than a text, and I keep postcards friends send me in the pages of cookery books, so I find one now and again and have a nice moment, thinking about them.

If you had the opportunity to live one year of your life over again, which year would you choose?

Any of my three years at university probably. But this time round I wouldn't worry as much about my Finals, I'd say no to the hairdresser who cut off my long hair aged 20, and I'd pluck up the courage to join Footlights instead of mooching about college, miserable that I'd never find anything original to say about Jane Austen. No one has anything original to say about Jane Austen. If Jane Austen came back now, even she'd struggle. Those three subtle changes would free me up to enjoy more of the things I didn't have time to enjoy. Having said that ... I do genuinely believe that the best year of your life could well be one that hasn't happened yet, so I might want to book in 2014, or 2020.

What three things would you take to a desert island?

A Nespresso machine, my guitar and the dogs to keep me warm at night.

When was the last time you did something for the first time? What was it?

I've just started running – actually, running is probably overstating it a bit. It's mainly stumbling, interspersed with jogging, at the moment, but I'm putting my faith in the 'Couch to 5k' regime to get me running eventually! I've always been envious of runners, with their long strides and serene expressions (and great legs), so I thought it was time I made a final concerted effort to join them while my knees are still up to it. I also learned to make choux pastry this summer. Hence the running.

What did you buy with your first pay cheque?

A Mac lipstick, in Russian Red. My first, very low paid, job out of university was as a press assistant in an office over the road from Selfridges on Oxford Street: I used to walk round the Beauty Hall and Food Hall in my lunchbreak in a state of consumer rapture, even though I couldn't afford to buy anything more expensive than the occasional sandwich. When I finally got paid, I splashed out what felt like an outrageous sum of money on a lipstick, after the make-up artist spent ages finding exactly the right shade for me. I wore it every single day, right down to the swivelly tube: it made me feel really glamorous and 'London', and I've only ever worn red lipstick since.

What's your favourite food?

Bread. I love bread, particularly something called a beacon loaf which I've only ever found in the village bakery in Gosforth. It's a delicious treacly, malty loaf and it's the crack cocaine of the bread world. When my sister and I were little, my mum used to have to buy three at a time, because we would scoff a whole one in the three-mile drive between the bakery and our house. It's the only recipe I don't actually want to have, because if I learned how to make them, I would turn into a gigantic beacon loaf, in the manner of Veruca Salt.

Tell us about a guilty pleasure.
Mascarpone mashed up with icing sugar. I urge you *not* to try it. The slippery slope to Hell is covered in mascarpone, with Irish Dairy Milk handrails.

What's your favourite karaoke song?
I do a mean 'If I Could Turn Back Time' by Cher. Especially the low honking parts.

What was the last song you listened to?
The last song I listened to was The Viking Literally Song from *Horrible Histories*. No day is complete without a bit of *HH*.

What's your secret special talent?
I can waltz, cha cha cha and foxtrot.

What can you always be found with?
A cup of coffee.

What's your idea of perfect happiness?
A huge sofa, a new hardback, a coal fire, dogs each side of me, and rain lashing down on the windows. Or a night of Scottish reeling that never ends, with a bar that never runs dry.

A note from Lucy Dillon

Cancer, especially breast cancer, is something that will, sadly, probably touch all our lives at some point; currently, in a lifetime breast cancer affects 1 in 8 women (and 1 in 868 men). I won't presume to go into detail about such a complicated and important topic here, but I found Macmillan Cancer Support (www.macmillan.org.uk) and Breast Cancer Care (www.breastcancercare.org.uk) straightforward and helpful sources of information and support while I was researching this book. The stories and everyday bravery of women just like Gina were inspiring, and I'm even more admiring than ever of the work the fundraisers, supporters and researchers do to help those facing breast cancer.

Ten tips for being a good client, gleaned from the builders working on my house, and my own 'slow learner' experience

1. **Decide what you want.** House renovators, as far as I've gathered, tend to fall into two groups. People who know what they want, and people who don't. People who know what they want may have stacks of mood boards, and irritatingly specific requirements about lighting that may not always be possible outside a showroom, but they're easier to work with than people who don't know what they want, and take three weeks to decide where to put light switches. Some things will only occur to you as you go along, but it saves everyone's time if you've at least *thought* about how many plug sockets you want in your sitting room before the electrician arrives. (Not surprisingly, when you're invoiced for two builders standing around for a whole day while you hem and haw about grout colours, your mind will be focused.)

a) **Decide what you want between you.** This is my builder's biggest bug-bear: doing a job to the exact specifications of one person, only for their other half to come back and decide it's completely wrong and needs re-doing. Re-painting a room is fair enough. Moving a whole oak floor is a nightmare for everyone. So is standing by as a couple come to blows about what kind of taps they really wanted.

2. **Put proposed works and costs in writing,** so there can be no confusion about what was included in the quote. Extras will inevitably crop up but it's important to communicate exactly what you want. It's much harder all round when the work's been done. Or not.

3. **Get a kettle, plenty of tea, coffee, milk and biscuits;** leave out for the builders. They can then make their own and not bother you. Popular biscuits: chocolate digestives, bourbons. Unpopular: Nice biscuits.

4. **Make lists** of what's vital, what's important and what can wait. Do not harass the builders about items on List 3 while they're in the middle of vital structural work, but do not be fobbed off about items on List 1. If you haven't employed a project manager to deal with the various tradesmen, establish who the foreman is, and have a regular 'end of the week' conversation, so you know where you are. Write things down.

5. **Pay your invoices on time.** You don't want the

plumber to be 'hard to get hold of' when everyone's waiting for him to put the water back on.

6. **Ask questions.** The thing about renovations, according to my brilliant electrician, is that you learn by doing them. The trouble is, not only is renovation work quite stressful (you only have to look at *Grand Designs* to work that out) but most people have done up one, maybe two houses before. Your builders, on the other hand, have hopefully done lots. So ask. Their last client's problem might be your solution.

7. **If you can't work out where to put lights or switches,** photocopy your fittings and stick them to the ceiling/walls with Blu-tack until they look right. Also, put a plug socket in a cupboard so you can charge all your chargeable stuff in one place.

8. **Hide your expensive hoover.** Someone will use it to hoover up the seventy tons of brick dust that'll be generated. There is always dust. Even if you're just having some shelves put in. Isolate the work if you can; cover up everything. Move out, if at all possible. If not possible, get noise-cancelling headphones and some gin.

9. **Take lots of photos** – it's good to have a record, and better to remind yourself just how horrible it all once was, and how much nicer it is now.

10. **Be professional but friendly** – compliment all the great work the builders have done, as well as

moan about the paint splatters on the new tiles. After all, renovation work can go on for ages. There will come a time when the house will seem strangely empty without three men in overalls, listening to Radio 2 and drilling . . . stuff.

a) **If your builders are following you on Twitter,** make sure you only ever tweet nice things about them. And don't follow them obsessively to see if they're complaining about the Nice biscuits again. Actually, best not to follow your builders at all.

Greyhounds: some reasons why they make the perfect pet

If you're thinking of getting a dog, then spare a thought for the thousands of retired greyhounds looking for a second life away from the track. Not only are they real pedigree dogs, with ancestry you can trace back through several generations, should you want to, but they've been specially bred to be easy-going and companionable. And nothing says love like a greyhound leaning silently against you with its full weight . . .

1. Contrary to what you might expect, **greyhounds don't need endless exercise.** They're sprinters, not joggers, so a couple of twenty-minute walks and the occasional mad dash around an enclosed field or park will do them fine. If you want to walk further, they're perfectly happy to join you – as long as you wrap them up in winter.

2. Their **laidback temperaments** make them ideal pets: calm, gentle and affectionate, a greyhound is basically an elegant love sponge with a quirky personality to match his aristocratic

looks. OK, so you might have to keep food well out of reach of that long nose but they don't yap, dig or shed hair as much as other breeds, making them great for owners with dog allergies, and they're used to a routine from their racing days, so will fit into yours quickly.

3. **You get what you see**: rehoming a fully grown dog means there are no surprises, unlike puppies, which can often grow into something you weren't expecting. Rescue centres rehabilitate ex-racers, and fosterers will assess their needs and personalities so you can be matched with the right dog for your specific circumstances. Not all of them are huge either – greys come in all shapes and sizes, from muscular racers to smaller and more delicate dogs, and in every colour.

4. **Some do like cats**. Like many dogs, greyhounds are prone to chasing cats (and other furry creatures) – the difference is that they're fast enough to catch them. But not all greys see moggies as a challenge. The rescue centre will test them with a (willing) cat volunteer to see if they're chilled out enough to share their home with a feline friend, and many pass with flying colours.

5. **They come with their own, ready-made social life**. You'll definitely make friends when you adopt a greyhound, not least because no passer-by can resist saying hello. Since greys spend most of their working lives in kennels,

rarely meeting other kinds of dogs, they socialise best with other hounds, so rehoming charities and owners' clubs organise regular 'greydates', fun days, and fund-raising walks.

6. **They're stunningly beautiful** to look at, even when they're sprawled upside down on your sofa. To own a greyhound is to have a little piece of history in your home: from Egypt to Elizabethan England, the soulful eyes of the greyhound gaze out of tapestries, portraits and photographs. Few dogs have lived such colourful and respected lives.

7. **There are thousands of them waiting in rescue** for a new home. After a short racing life, many dogs are abandoned or put down if they're injured, not quick enough or just too old. And yet as a long-living large breed, often reaching ages from twelve to fifteen, they still have many years of love to give – and make devoted friends to their forever owners.

Useful links:

Greyhound Rescue West of England: www.grwe.com
Retired Greyhound Trust: www.retiredgreyhounds.co.uk
Greyhound Gap: www.greyhoundgap.org.uk
Greyhound Rescue Wales: www.greyhoundrescuewales.co.uk
Scottish Greyhound Sanctuary: www.scottishgreyhoundsanctuary.com
Celia Cross Greyhound Trust: www.celiacross.org.uk

LUCY DILLON

The Secret of Happy Ever After

When **Anna** takes over Longhampton's bookshop, it's her dream come true. And not just because it gets her away from her rowdy stepchildren and their hyperactive Dalmatian.

As she unpacks boxes of childhood classics, Anna can't shake the feeling that maybe her own fairytale ending isn't all that she'd hoped for. But as the stories of love, adventure, secret gardens and giant peaches breathe new life into the neglected shop, Anna and her customers get swept up in the magic too.

Even Anna's best friend **Michelle** – who categorically doesn't believe in true love and handsome princes – isn't immune.

But when secrets from Michelle's own childhood come back to haunt her, and disaster threatens Anna's home, will the wisdom and charm of the stories in the bookshop help the two friends – and those they love – find their own happy ever after?

'Lucy Dillon's voice is gentle and kind throughout . . . perceptive and well handled. A heart-warming piece of escapism for long winter nights.' *Red*

HODDER

LUCY DILLON

Walking Back to Happiness

Juliet's been in hiding. From her family, from her life, but most of all from the fact that Ben's not around anymore.

Her mother **Diane** has run out of advice. But then she insists Juliet look after her elderly Labrador and it becomes apparent that **Coco** the dog might actually be the one who can rescue her daughter.

Especially when it leads to her walking dogs for a few other locals too, including a spaniel, **Damson**, who belongs to a very attractive man . . .

Before she knows it, Juliet realises she has somehow become the town's unofficial pet-sitter. A job which makes her privy to the lives and secrets of everyone whose animals she's caring for.

But as her first winter alone approaches, she finally begins to wonder if it's time to face up to her own secrets? To start rebuilding her own life? And maybe – just maybe – to fall in love again?

'Witty, heart-warming and a very real tale
of loss and redemption' *Stylist*

HODDER

LUCY DILLON

Lost Dogs and Lonely Hearts

Rachel has inherited a house in the country, along with a rescue kennels. She claims she's not a 'dog' person. But then she tries to match the abandoned pets with new owners, with some unexpected results . . .

Natalie and **Johnny's** marriage hasn't been easy since they started trying for a baby. But will adopting **Bertie**, a fridge-raiding, sofa-stealing Basset Hound make up for it?

Meanwhile **Zoe's** husband has given their kids a Labrador puppy, and left her to pick up the mess, literally. She's at the end of her tether, until her pup leads her to handsome doctor **Bill**, whose own perfect match isn't what he was expecting at all.

As the new owners' paths cross, and their lives become interwoven, they – along with their dogs – all find themselves learning important lessons about loyalty, second chances and truly unconditional love.

'Heart-warming, fun and romantic. *Marley and Me* fans will love it.' *Closer*

HODDER

LUCY DILLON

The Ballroom Class

When three couples join a new ballroom class, they're all looking for some magic in their lives.

Lauren and **Chris** are getting married, and Lauren's dreaming of a fairytale wedding with a first dance to make Cinderella proud.

Not wanting to be shown up on the dance floor, her parents **Bridget** and **Frank** have come along too. They normally never put a foot wrong, but Bridget's got a secret that could trip them up unexpectedly.

Meanwhile **Katie** and **Ross** are looking for a quick-fix solution to their failing marriage even though neither is quite sure who's leading who anymore.

As friendships form over the foxtrot, the rumba rocks relationships, and the tango leads to true love, all the students in the Ballroom Class are about to face the music and dance . . .

> '*Strictly Come Dancing* with added off-floor love,
> betrayal and glitz makes Lucy Dillon's dazzling
> debut a must for ballroom fans.' *Mirror*

HODDER

Love books?
Love giveaways?
Love fun?

Then you'll love

WISH LIST

Join our women's reading community on Facebook and sign up for our weekly email newsletter, and you'll never be stuck for something great to read again!

- Weekly reading recommendations from our fantastic range of women's fiction and non-fiction

- Giveaways

- Sneak previews of big new books

- Exclusive content such as short stories, author interviews and writing tips

- Quizzes & polls

- Competitions

- And lots of literary fun!

Join us at

/WishListBooks @WishListBooks
www.hodder.co.uk/wishlist

WISH LIST

The place to discover books you'll love.